Dial M for Milkmaid

By Julie Ann Carver

Published by

A division of d+2

Copyright 2013

Well, some of my close friends agreed to let me name a few of the characters after them. You know who you are! You've contributed to my life and this book in so many ways. Thank you for all your encouragement and support.

Inspector Beaumont and the Special Homicide Investigation Team are the literary inventions of Judith Ann Jance. If you like good detective novels (or Seattle for that matter), she's definitely worth checking out.

Barbie is copyright by Mattel Toys

Manufactured in the United States of America

Dial M for Milkmaid
Fiction, Mystery

ISBN 978-1-58884-008-0

Chapter 1

Helping Out an Old Friend

"This had better work," said Binky. The small dark man sat beside Harry in the old Volvo, a rust-red 1991 wagon that was dented and bent from being rolled. They were parked on a street facing down a steep hill, their eyes scanning a nearby house.

"It's a simple plan," said Harry. "We worked it all out on the way over here. You and I cover the front door, Red and Farnsworth the back door. Since there are only two ways your guy can leave the house, and there's a wall on either side, I would think we got everything covered."

Binky nodded. He offered Harry all the reassurance of a dead armadillo at a Texas barbeque.

"What are you worried about?" asked Harry. "You have a bullet proof jacket on. This is your party anyway. Tell me what's so important about this guy. What's his name again?"

"Manny Ballston. Let's just say he owes me something and I don't want him to skip town without settling accounts."

"Sounds like a familiar theme with you, Binky," said Harry.

"What?"

"The whole reason I'm here is because I owe you something. The irony of this situation hasn't escaped me. You're using one dubious favor to call in another," said Harry. He looked away, squinting as he scanned the house, the street, the rear view mirrors and the sidewalk, taking it all in like a rest stop garbage can eager to deal with the world's refuse. He was dead broke, strapped to the point where he'd do anything, even Binky's dirty work.

"Okay, okay. So I am. I'm just a little bit nervous," said Binky.

"Why? You used to enjoy this game. Playing detective was your favorite game when we were kids, wasn't it?" Harry leaned over and nodded, over and over and up in his face until Binky nodded too. "This is just like we were playing detective again," said Harry, that dead armadillo stare finally making him look away.

"Not quite," said Binky. "When we were kids, you used to dress up like a girl when we played. Called yourself Fu Chan."

"You called me Fu Chan," said Harry.

"That's another thing," said Binky. "We used toy guns when we were kids."

Harry chuckled, a hollow laugh. Binky was the one with the Kevlar vest and the custom fitted suit. Harry was sporting thrift store hand me downs, and he could barely afford those.

"Maybe I'd feel better if you were crossed dressed," said Binky.

"Maybe I'd feel better too," said Harry.

"We've been here ten minutes. When will this be over?"

"Soon," said Harry. He squinted, studying the house closely. No sign of movement. His mind started churning through possibilities.

"That's why you're here," said Binky. "This is still your game. You grew up to be a real detective."

"While you grew up to be a..." Harry stumbled for a minute. "What is it exactly you do, Binky?"

"A little of everything," he said proudly. "Investments, land development, personal services."

"Pimping, loan sharking, information trafficking," added Harry.

The dark man glared at Harry, then smiled. "Yes, but my real estate holdings should be your only concern. You forget that I am your landlord and the rent on your detective office is past due."

"How can I forget," said Harry. "You drop by every day to remind me. It's also why Red and I are here today to help you. You said something about taking this job off the rent."

"Yes, I did," said Binky. "But only if we are successful. If I get what I need out of Ballston, you'll get what you need. And just to be clear, it comes off the interest and fees from the rent past due."

Harry nodded and went back to studying the house again. Still no sign of movement. Ballston might not even be home and this could end up a blank trip.

Binky continued his nervous blabber. "Fact is, Fu Chan could probably handle this guy all by herself and we wouldn't need Big Red and Farnsworth."

"Binky, don't you think I can handle this? I'm an ex-Marine, ex-Seattle cop, and Fu Chan all rolled into one."

"You should start acting the part. Seems like it would be easier now that you have breasts."

Harry felt wounded. Binky knew the story behind Harry's breasts. Recent events had left him with free breast implants, a gift from a doctor and his ex-wife.

Binky continued. "It's stupid the way you try to hide them under that jacket. You're just setting yourself up for premature back pain by hunching over like that. I can see them plain as day. I thought you wanted breasts anyway. You always thought it would be fun to have them. Real ones, I mean."

"It's not as much fun as you think," said Harry. "I like to dress up in women's clothes but it's not like I can take these off when I'm done playing."

"Didn't you always want them?" asked Binky.

"Don't we always want what we can't have?"

Binky made a low grunt. "At least I'm satisfied when I get what I want."

"Yeah, but for how long?" said Harry. He looked down at his breasts, bulging 38C mounds of flesh that only made him feel self-conscious. "They're a permanent part of me for now, at least for a year or so until my chest heals and stabilizes. I have to hide them in the mean time. People take issue, Binky. A man with breasts is not in their everyday world."

"The everyday world is boring, Harry, or haven't you noticed?"

"Thanks for saying that. Now you sound like the Bill Binkley I know." Harry clapped him on the back like an old friend. He scanned the house again. "I think we're ready. Let's see where this latest adventure takes us."

There was a squawk and Harry picked up the flat plastic Barbie face lying on the dashboard. He pressed the pink button next to the fashion icon under her blazoned Barbie logo. "Go ahead, Rita."

"Farnsworth and I are in position. I see activity inside the house. You're clear to try the front door."

"Roger," he said. He pressed the pink button again. "Despite how they look, these things work pretty good."

"I just wish Lenny could have gotten us a real set of walkie-talkies," said Red.

"It's on his list," said Harry. "We'll get the equipment we need slowly but surely Rita. Stay focused. The client is anxious to get this job over with." He winked at Binky. They got out of the Volvo and Harry tucked Barbie in his jacket pocket. "It's simple, Binky. We walk up the front steps. Ballston takes one look at you, gets scared, and heads out the back door, right into Red and Farnsworth. Come on, let's make it happen."

They walked across the street and down the hill, then cut in, going up a few steps to the porch of the house. It was built in the style of the old Victorian houses that spilled out of downtown Seattle and into the hills of the surrounding neighborhoods. Harry waited by the steps while Binky went to the door and knocked. Harry saw some curtains part. He smiled and nodded to someone. Whoever it was didn't seem to notice Binky pressed close to the door.

It happened quick. The door flew open. Manny Ballston was slightly larger than Binky. Harry watched as his smile turned ugly when he realized it was Binky at his front door. Nothing new there, Binky had that effect on most people. Instead of slamming the door shut and running away Manny did the unexpected. He jumped up and chest butted Binky, knocking him backwards. Harry watched his friend hit the ground as Manny stepped on him and made a beeline for the street.

Harry acted like he was going to get out of the man's way. At the last minute he dropped down low and stuck his leg out. Ballston stumbled but didn't lose any momentum. Harry pulled Barbie out of his pocket and hit the pink button. "Rita, I could use a little help up here. The target took to the street and I'm in pursuit."

"Copy," she said. He stuck the walkie-talkie back in his pocket and concentrated on the footrace. Manny bolted into the street and headed uphill, Harry beginning to sprint as he narrowed the gap. Harry cornered him next to the Volvo where Ballston suddenly turned, a weighted sock in his right hand.

"Nice little homemade blackjack," said Harry. "What have you got in there? Quarters? Fishing weights?"

Manny smiled, baring a row of teeth that made him look like a ripe Halloween pumpkin. He let out a low chuckle and swung it over his head. Harry didn't wait, he saw his opening. He punched Ballston in the stomach. The man's hand went limp and he released the sock. It flew behind him and smashed into the front window of the Volvo. There was a hole, the weighted part resting on the dashboard, the end of the sock dripping out of the hole like a wad of snot from a little kid's nose. Harry let out a groan.

Manny fought back, throwing random punches at Harry. He easily avoided them. There is something to be said for the training you get in Marine combat infantry school. Harry took his right foot and pushed it into Ballston's instep as he twisted. The guy went down hard but he was quick. He rolled into the street and up into a standing position. Now Harry was cornered with his back to the Volvo. Manny started stabbing at the space around him with his fists. Harry ducked and blocked. He could see Rita rounding the side of the house and beginning to angle into the street. He inched downhill towards the front of the Volvo, his back flat against the passenger side of the car. He felt the low empty space of the hood of the car behind him and he didn't feel so trapped. Then he saw his chance he took it.

Ballston threw a high punch, moving at Harry in an attempt to bend him backwards over the front of the car. Harry twisted and ducked, turning his back into a ramp that lifted Ballston right onto the hood. The guy slid forward, falling off the front of the car. He slammed against the back of the pickup truck parked next in line. He got up and hit the Volvo hard, his fists coming down in unison on the hood of the car. It made a slight dent, barely noticeable in the sea of dents that already covered the hood. Ballston hit it again, throwing in a kick for good measure. Anger issues. The old Volvo groaned and began to shake. The emergency brake cable had been stretched and tightened to its limits and the brake barely functioned. Harry heard it slip. The car lurched forward, pulled downhill by gravity. The shift knob shook, snapping into neutral. Before his brain could process what was happening Manny Ballston was pinned between the Volvo and the pickup truck. He screamed, a quick sound, like a barnyard animal makes when the farmer snaps its neck, and it was over.

Harry didn't know if it was the look of surprise that made Manny's eyes bulge out or whether they had been squeezed out like some kid's toy bobo, but it was the oddest death mask he had ever seen. There was a rasp of air and his head fell forward, pulling his chest down as he bent at the waist and dropped onto the hood. The bulging eyes turned up toward Harry and a line of drool ran out of Manny's mouth and onto the car. The eyes went blank and stared at Harry, still bulging outward like a Saturday morning cartoon character.

And that was when Harry realized what had happened. A human life had been lost. His insides twisted like it was filled with snakes. He felt like throwing up.

Rita came up beside him but Harry didn't seem to notice. He stared down at the limp form lying across the hood.

"We just wanted to ask you some questions," he said. He waited for the bulging eyes to pardon him, but there was no forgiveness. Binky and Farnsworth joined them and everyone stood around as a crowd of people began to come out of their houses and assemble for the latest neighborhood street show.

Chapter 2

Canned Tuna

Carlos Pinal awoke in a panic. He heard noise and activity around him, the whirr of hydraulic motors and the sound of metal beating against metal. There were men shouting orders, moans and cries, and mumbling in several different languages. He tried to move but he couldn't. His hands were tied behind his back and he was trapped in a small cage.

There was a rumbling sound beside him and he saw a worker roll a flat cart holding small cages with other people locked inside them. He twisted his head, looking in the other direction where there were more carts filled with cages. They were in a big room with a high ceiling, wire framed lights dimly shedding a yellow hue over everything. There were exposed pipes in one corner, industrial size, and the walls were shiny, made of stainless steel. There was a big door at one end, thick and heavy, mounted on giant hinges. It looked like a door you'd see in a submarine only much larger.

Another cart full of cages came through the submarine door as a worker maneuvered it to one side. Carlos couldn't know how many carts there were in the room, but judging from the noise and moans around him he suspected there were a lot more than he could see. A forklift appeared at the door holding a larger cage angled back on its forks. There was a man standing inside of it, his arms strapped to the bars on either side, his head held in place with a collar that fastened to the bars behind him. The man was choking as the forklift jerked the cage about. It drove through the door and into the room. That's when Carlos realized how big the room really was.

The forks shifted straight and dropped to the ground, releasing the cage. The driver backed the forklift out the door and shut the motor off. Carlos recognized the man in the cage. They called him Chinatown Joe. He was the one his cousin introduced him to when he first got dragged into this mess.

It sounded like a great plan. Go to America and find jobs. Make lots of money. For men willing to do manual labor it is easy to find work in the land of opportunity. Americans don't like to get their hands dirty and as long as they are willing to pay for the privilege, he didn't mind taking the money. His cousin Luis had gone three times and managed to send enough money home to feed his family well and afford to do it again. He had been caught by authorities and sent back to Guatemala every time but it did not stop him from going again. "One time when I am in America, they will pass a law and make all the illegals a citizen. Then it will all be worth it. I will be an American and I can bring my wife and family there and finally lift them out of poverty."

Filled with such dreams, Carlos had followed his cousin into this venture. It took all the money he had, but he promised his wife he would send for her and the children as soon as he could. Chinatown Joe had been the man his cousin knew. He was the man he had given all his money to, the man he had trusted with his dream.

A middle aged Asian man walked into the room dressed impeccably in a fine suit with a silk tie, his skin yellowed to the point of jaundice. His shoes were black and shined, as dark as the waters that flowed through the rivers of hell. The heels clicked against the concrete floor, an expensive sound that made you stop and listen. Carlos looked at the man's face, staring into narrow eyes that contained only emptiness. He parted his lips and smiled, lips that could suck the life out of the world. The man spoke. "Call the meeting to order please," he said in a soft voice.

There was banging on the pipes in the corner with a hammer. Most of the murmur died but a caged man in the back shouted arrogantly. Carlos couldn't understand the language.

"Parliamentarian," said the soft spoken man in charge. A thick, heavy set thug sprang into action. He went right to the noise and removed something from his pocket. There was a zap, the sound of electricity discharging, and then silence.

"Thank you," said the man. He walked over to the cage containing Chinatown Joe. "Now that we are all here we can begin the meeting. We will skip introductions. I am sure most of you know this man, and it is not important that you know each other. As for me, you may call me Mr. Che."

His heels clicked as he walked across the floor, passing between the cages. "So, introductions complete, I move that we proceed directly to the main order of business, the reason for this meeting. Do I hear any seconds?"

There was no sound in the room except the clicking of his heels. "No one seconds my motion?" Something kept the caged people silent, respect, fear, maybe they couldn't understand English. It didn't matter. More clicks.

"Ah," said Mr. Che, as if suddenly understanding why there was silence. "Maybe you need more details on what led to this meeting." He drew a breath, the lips again sucking the life from everything around him. He began slowly, as if he were explaining it to a child. "Usually everything runs smoothly and we have no need of these after action meetings. You should all be at your destinations by now, well on your way to your new lives here in America. It's only when we have a problem…" He let the word trail off, the clicks of his heels coming to rest in front of the cage containing Chinatown Joe.

"There was some trouble at the docks tonight," said Mr. Che. "You were all there, hence your presence at this meeting. I need you to bear witness to the details. We must analyze what went wrong, learn from our mistakes, and do better next time. That is the purpose of this after action meeting to which you have all been invited." He paused for effect. "My rules are simple. I encourage you to be honest and speak freely. In return I will see to it that Joe here does not retaliate against you."

Silence prevailed. The clicks started again. "Let me tell you a little bit about our meeting room. You're at my private facility, headquarters for my operations. This is what we call the retort room. You see, this facility has changed hands many times. I only recently came into possession of it. In the past it was a boatyard, a cannery, a fuel stop and marina, even a trendy restaurant. One owner tried to make it into a brewery. When I acquired it, it had been a marine research laboratory. I often wondered why none of the owners decommissioned this room. The stainless steel alone would be worth the money in scrap weight."

The heels stopped at a wall and he ran his hand across it, feeling the smooth flatness of the metal. "Stainless steel, industrial grade. Cold, pure, resists bacteria and germs, incorruptible." He said it in a voice used to describe a lover, deep and sensual. "It resists heat as well, heat and pressure. A normal wall in this room wouldn't last ten minutes. No. Wood, plaster, even stone would crumble under the job done in this room." He started pacing again, his heels drawing their attention to the door. "Magnificent door, isn't it?" he said. "As thick as any bank vault. I thought of making it into one. All I would need to do is install a lock. Sadly, once I close that door nothing inside can get out, and anybody outside can get in, so, it's not a good place for storing valuables.

"Have you figured out yet what it was used for?" he asked.

Silence. The meeting participants were unusually quiet, an orderly group. But then, Mr. Che had the floor.

"Have you ever heard of a retort?" He began pacing between the cages, a pensive tiger examining his prey close and personal. He looked into each of their eyes as he walked and spoke.

"A little more history then. This room is a legacy from the cannery days. A retort is a kind of giant pressure cooker. They used to pack cans with fish and wheel them in here by the rack full. Then they'd close this pressure sealed door and turn on the steam. The temperature in this room can reach five hundred degrees and the pressure more than three atmospheres. It was enough to kill the bacteria and cook the fish in the cans. The lids would seal as the room was later cooled and the pressure released."

Carlos heard the heels walk next to his cage. A shiver came over him. The man looked into his eyes. Carlos wanted to look away but he couldn't. It was like being trapped in a cobra's gaze.

"The room is fully operational, you know. All I had to do was restore the boilers that produce the steam to operate the mechanics behind it. I guess you are all wondering which side of the door you will be on when this meeting is adjourned. That is to be seen." The heels stopped in front of Chinatown Joe. "In a moment I will open up the floor for you to speak." He looked at Joe, pumping his eyes full of venom, enough to immobilize any prey. "For now, Joe, you are the not allowed to talk. I will yield the floor to you later and give you time to add your comments. Meanwhile, pay attention and listen."

He turned to the caged people. "So you don't waste my time, here is what we do know. There were no less than fifty men representing ten different law enforcement agencies on the Seattle docks tonight. State, local, and Federal. We had the whole food chain on parade just for us. I realize you were all inside a shipping container. When the agents opened the container there was fighting and guns went off. Many of you ran, some of you escaped, only to be picked up by my men who are always there to watch every operation. Some of the people who traveled with you were captured by the authorities. We are compiling a list of names. They are likely being questioned at this very moment. They will probably be processed and deported home by the Federals."

A voice rang out from the back of the room. "At least they're not being questioned like this. At least they can sit in a chair and answer for their actions."

Mr. Che became agitated. "Who said that?" he asked. There were quick clicks of his heels as he traversed the room. "I say, who said that? You're out of order. I did not yield the floor yet."

There was no answer. "No matter." He sighed. "You make a point. Unlike your friends being questioned by the authorities, you will not be sent back home. If you cooperate I will have you moved to the other side of the door and you will remain in America. That is the best I can offer you at this time. Either way, I will have my after action report, and we will see which of you survives the test of truth and loyalty."

He moved back towards the door and stood beside Chinatown Joe. "I will yield the floor at this time. Rather than hear you all individually, I have directed my men to interview each of you. Anything you have to say to me can be said to them." He snapped his fingers and nodded.

The room was filled with commotion as a stream of people entered through the thick door. There was noise everywhere and talking in several languages. A man came up to Carlos and started saying something in Japanese. When he didn't answer the man moved on. Finally someone came to him who spoke Spanish. Carlos told him everything he knew. The man took a marking pen out of his pocket and wrote something on a placard on the top of the cage before moving on.

Carlos' neck ached and he yearned to stretch. If he could only scratch his nose he would be happy. Instead he tried to rub it against the bars of the cage. The bars were cold. It was hard to imagine what the man said, that this room could become a giant pressure cooker, heating these bars to a temperature that would make them impossible to touch. Maybe he didn't want to think about it.

The interviewers were bringing sheets of paper to Mr. Che who read each report. He made some notes on each page and handed them to a small man standing beside him who put the papers inside a leather folder. When all the interviews were complete and the papers read, Mr. Che nodded. "Some of you are dismissed at this time," he said. The interviewers left and workers came into the room. Some of the cages were offloaded from the carts. Carlos heard shouts. He recognized the sound of his cousin's voice.

The carts were wheeled out of the room with the remaining cages on them. Carlos could hear his cousin clearly shouting behind him as they wheeled him through the door. His cart contained his own cage and a woman's but a third cage had been offloaded and left inside the room. His cousin continued to shout behind him, calling out to him by name. Carlos cringed. He felt the hand of the reaper on his shoulder loosening its grasp. He tightened his lips and closed his eyes. The cart moved further outside and out of range of the noise coming from the retort room.

Chinatown Joe was still in the retort room. Shouts and noise echoed off the sides of the room. Mr. Che called for his thug again. "Parliamentarian, please restore order," he said quietly.

The Parliamentarian heard him and whipped out his electronic device, a supercharged piece of engineering that had been custom made for him by an old man from Taiwan. He pressed a button and it crackled. The noise began to fade, but he still stepped forward and thrust the device into one of the cages. There was a scream, then silence. Total silence.

"Thank you," said Mr. Che. "Let us hope we maintain order and have no need of your intervention again." Thug nodded and faded into the background. Mr. Che turned to the seven cages that remained in the room. "I know all of you speak English here, so you understand what I am asking. I also know you are anxious for us to come to a final determination for the after action report. Believe me, this meeting will be over shortly."

Mr. Che turned to Chinatown Joe. "And now I yield the floor to you," he said in a whisper. His voice echoed stainlessly off the walls and he was heard by everyone. "What do you have to add to our findings, Joe?"

Joe said nothing.

"How was it that there were over fifty Government men there tonight, hmmm? We must come to the conclusion that someone invited them, otherwise there would be no reason for them to be there. We know that you did not inform them directly, Joe, but instead delegated that task to one of the men currently in this room." He turned to the cages. "Now, who can that be?" he asked. "I yield the floor to any of you. Since Joe has nothing to say, this is your opportunity to speak."

There was silence.

"Last chance," he said, shouting to all who could hear him. "I know you are afraid, and rightly so. Your fate will be sealed, but if you speak I will spare the others. I give you this chance again to meet your fate knowing you acted honorably."

Silence.

Mr. Che looked about the room, then turned to Joe again. "And you as well? Nothing to say?"

"What can I say?" said Joe.

"You can at least admit your plot. Don't die trying to make a fool out of me. It can't be done." He sighed. "I know you had twice the number of people in that container as you turned over to accounting. The figures don't match, which is why you made sure the Government men got tipped off. In all the pandemonium, there was no way to get an accurate count of the contents, no way to verify the bill of lading. And you keep the extra money paid to you by the human cargo." He moved close to the bars. "Double dipping. How much was it, Joe? Was it worth it?"

As cold as it was in the room, Joe began to sweat.

"The least you can do is point out your cohorts in this room and spare the other poor souls your fate."

Joe was quiet.

"Still nothing to say?" He turned to the room. "None of you?"

"Please," came a whisper from a cage in the back. "Spare my life."

"You're out of order. That is not a relevant statement. If you have something to add, something to help finalize the after action report, then say it. Otherwise, remain silent."

"Please," came the whisper again.

"What does it matter?" said Joe. There was fire in his voice. "You're going to walk out of here and cook us alive anyway."

"So?" asked Che. "How is this relevant?"

"Just get out of here. I'm sick of you and your meetings and your business process. After action report? You take the fun out of skirting the law."

"It takes effort to run an organization like ours, Joe," said Che, his voice as chilly as a winter morning. "Vision, too. This is a six sigma company, the first of its kind in the crime world. An empire of evil based on the principles of Wall Street, run with the efficiency of a multi-national conglomerate. Not to mention the profitability. Wasn't your share enough?"

Joe looked away, avoiding the cobra's gaze. He knew the truth. Yes, it was enough money, but something was missing, something that had drawn him to crime when he was a youth. Excitement, the thrill of danger and a quick reward. The power. His betrayal of Che and the organization had nothing to do with money, it had to do with fulfilling some deeper need that kept nagging at his insides.

"I am curious, Joe," said Che. "Curious why you betrayed me."

Joe turned to stare at him, his eyes defiant to the last. "I have principles you can't understand, Che."

Che looked back, staring hard at him. Joe didn't change his expression. His lip was locked tight, his jawline firm and trembling.

Che turned his back to Joe and walked towards the exit, the sound of expensive heels echoing off the walls. Human beings were such a disappointment at times. He had come to expect that, but once again he had misjudged someone. Joe had been a trusted associate, a leader and one of his star managers. Where had he gone wrong? Where had the company gone wrong?

Joe squirmed. The heels clicked away the moments left in his life. In the periphery of his eye he saw something move, a blurry vision from another reality. Death, the greatest predator, parted the curtain to the next world and waited patiently in the wings for the last act of Joe's life to come to an end. Joe turned to his audience, the words welling up inside him like a Texas gusher.

"There's a flaw in your model, your vision. It's stupid. Wall Street steals more in a year than you can in a decade, and they do it legally. By all the rules of economics this organization shouldn't exist. If you had any brains you'd be running a real company instead of pretending you're the Emperor of Japan."

"So! That's what you think?" said Che. He moved back to the cage, cocked his head as he stared through the bars at Joe.

Joe was quiet again, the defiance gone. He shook his head from side to side. "Just get out of here. Leave me die in peace. Thank God it will be over quickly. When you shut that door and turn on the steam I'll suffocate before I feel the first blast of heat."

"I see," said Mr. Che, his hand going to his chin. "Did you think that I didn't consider that?" He nodded his head to the thug, who opened the cage. Joe saw the oxygen mask in his hand, the kind worn by firefighters that covered his whole head. Joe started to scream but his voice became muffled under the mask as the Parliamentarian slipped it over his head. He felt the straps tighten and the mask pull snug to his face. Thug locked the cage and nodded to the man.

"As I said, Joe. You can't make a fool out of me." said Mr. Che. "Meeting adjourned."

Chapter 3

Job Offer

Mr. Che walked out of the retort room followed closely by his short little aide Mr. Lo, who held the leather folder containing the text of the interviews. Outside was a larger room, another part of the old fish processing plant, industrial gymnasium size with concrete floors and a high ceiling, caged lights, suspended cables and things dangling overhead. The carts with their caged inhabitants sat off to the side, attended by workers. Mr. Che walked over to the carts, his heels clicking with every step. He came to a halt in front of them, pausing to look over each cage before addressing them.

"I would like to make you an offer," he said. "I need people like you to work for me, people with language skills, an international background, strong motivation, and a desire to progress in their job. I can offer you long hours, a sense of service and accomplishment, and the satisfaction that you are contributing to an organization that rewards hard work, loyalty, and integrity. I will provide you with sick benefits through our company doctor. Some of you may be offered housing based on your skills assessment and placement. Your job may require travel, sometimes at little or no notice. If you are prepared to accept these terms as well as a few others, I am prepared to offer you at this very moment, a job in my organization."

There was no applause or dancing.

"Now, who will be first to accept my generous offer?"

Carlos thought about it. Right now he'd agree to just about anything to get out of this cage. He had come to America to work and now on his first day here, he was being offered a job. Inside his head he heard his father's voice saying, "Don't ever say no to a job."

"I will," he said. "I will work for you."

"Splendid," said Mr. Che. He nodded to one of the workers who released the clamps that held the cage together. It fell apart in pieces and Carlos stood up. The worker cut the bonds that kept his hands tied behind him. Carlos immediately rubbed his neck.

"Do I have any other takers on my offer?"

Two other voices rang out and they were also freed from their cages.

"Fine," said Mr. Che. "I think we've got the cream of the crop here, Mr. Lo," he said. The short man nodded. "You all appear to be motivated individuals, men ready to do whatever it takes to reach our strategic goals. Am I right?"

They all nodded, grateful to be out of their cages.

"I want to work for you too," came a man's voice from a cage, a thick, middle eastern accent.

"Oh, I'm sorry," said Mr. Che. "We're all done hiring for the day. I only want enthusiastic people, those who want to be first in line. You know what I mean. Eager beavers. You should have spoken up sooner."

"Please," said the middle easterner.

"No begging," he said. "I hate that. No room for whiners in our organization, right men?" He turned to his workforce and they all smiled at him, board room nods of approval with yes men faces.

He turned to the cages. "Thank you for your time and consideration. As I said, we have our hiring quota for today." He turned to the new recruits. "You've made a wise decision for your future. Welcome to the organization. Mr. Lo, would you administer the loyalty oath?"

Lo took what looked like a small curling iron out of his pocket. He toggled the switch and monitored a small gauge built into the handle.

"We have all taken the oath," said Mr. Che. He bared his arm and held it out. There was an odd scar that looked like some kind of symbol. He nodded to his men and they all bared their arms, revealing similar scars. He turned to Mr. Lo who again checked the small gauge on the curling iron. "And now you must show us your arms," he said to the recruits.

Reluctantly, Carlos rolled up his sleeve, not knowing what to expect. The others followed suit. Workers grabbed them, holding each man's arm tightly in place. Mr. Lo stepped forward and placed the curling iron on their arms each in succession, then they were released. Carlos felt pain, deep searing pain that went to the core of his being. He had been badly burned in an accident when he was young but this was different. It was like someone had placed fire and ice on his arm at once. The agony went on long after Mr. Lo removed the device from his arm. One of the other men screamed and passed out, falling to the floor in a heap.

"Looks like we have someone who failed the test," said Mr. Che as he pulled his shirt sleeve back into place. "Put him on that cart please," he said to Carlos and the other man.

His arm hurt but Carlos helped lift the man and place him on the cart.

"Tomorrow I want you both to report to human resources, but for tonight I have a few small chores to ask of you. Please roll the carts back into the retort room for us."

Some of Che's men smiled. Some just stared off to the side, vague and disinterested. Carlos saw a man in the back of the crowd with a blow gun that he slowly raised to his lips. It was pointed straight at him.

Carlos hesitated, then remembered everything that had happened with crystal clarity. He knew he had no choice, even though he really did. Death was always a choice. Death is an honorable choice in some situations. If he did this vile thing, he may spend the rest of his life wishing he were dead. Many thoughts began to seethe in his head, but Carlos slowly took the handles of the cart and wheeled it towards the door.

The men in the cages started to protest. Carlos drowned it out. For him, each step became a journey closer to hell. He had killed livestock, chickens, pigs, and cows, and he had no problem with vermin like insects or nasty birds, but these were human beings. He entered the retort room. In the dim yellow light from above, he saw his cousin in the back of the room in a cage. Chinatown Joe looked alien and strange in his oxygen mask. His eyes filled the goggles of the mask, pleading with Carlos as he passed. Amazing what a man can say with his eyes, they really do communicate the soul.

His cousin began to shout his name. Carlos gripped the handle of the cart tighter. He stared at a spot on the floor ahead, an empty place that was just a stain on the concrete. The cart came to rest beside the cage that held his cousin. Carlos refused to make eye contact with him even though Luis was shouting his name. Despite that, his peripheral vision took in every detail, as if this moment became expanded and frozen in time, allowing him to see everything at once. The limp body of the man who fainted was lying on the cart. The stain lay dull on the floor. Carlos wondered how it was made. He heard his cousin shouting his name in disbelief as he slowly turned his back to him and began to exit the room. He stared into the pleading eyes of Chinatown Joe once again, the eyes of a condemned man.

Carlos drowned it all out, his head pounding like a pile driver inside his skull, the blood chilling in his veins. He moved past the door, past the other man wheeling his cart into the retort room. Carlos wondered if the other recruit had the same thoughts as he pushed his cart through the door, each step moving further into an inescapable nightmare. The deed is done, thought Carlos. I did what the man wanted. I am alive for now.

He started to move behind Mr. Che and join the other workers. Che stopped him. "What about the other cart?" he asked. The workers had consolidated the remaining cages on the last cart.

Carlos looked over at the cart. One of the cages contained a woman who could have been his mother's age. The men were shouting but she was praying. He could hear the words on her lips, soft and quiet as if she were talking to a priest in a confessional. She made the sign of the cross as Carlos slowly walked over and took the handles.

He pushed and the men in cages shouted louder. He drowned it out but he could not stop the sound of the woman's prayers from reaching his ears. They were not for her salvation. Instead she was asking God to spare the soul of the man who was pushing her cart.

"Forgive him Lord, for he does not know what he does," she whispered.

Carlos could feel the sin weighing heavy on his heart. Thou shalt not kill.

He closed his eyes, fighting something inside him that tried to rip free, something that wanted to rise out of his gut and choke him.

The woman continued to pray, the men to shout, and as he pushed the cart through the heavy door of the retort room he could feel the air around him grow thick, as if it had been hot and pressurized already. He stared ahead at the last cart he had put in the room. The man who had fainted looked as if he were beginning to stir. Carlos could see movement and flutter in the man's eyelids. The shouting became a cacophony of noise as Carlos released the handle of the cart and turned to leave. His cousin shouted at him, calling him names, crying, pleading, swearing. His words stabbed at the back of his brain as he exited the room.

Mr. Che was waiting for him outside. "Please close and seal the door," he said.

The giant door swung easily on its hinge, shutting out the noise and protests of the doomed souls inside the room.

Mr. Che turned to the other new recruit. "Help him," he said.

The second man obeyed, turning wheels that moved giant pressure locks into place, sealing in the steam and the heat that would cook anything left inside to the consistency of canned tuna.

Mr. Che walked over and stood next to Carlos, his heels clicking away like seconds on a clock. He looked into Carlos' eyes and smiled.

What do you do when the devil smiles at you?

"What is your name?" he asked softly.

"Carlos," he said. "Carlos Pinal." Carlos smiled, a lame and weak smile that showed no pleasure behind it. The devil widened his grin, baring teeth that looked like they could pick the soul off his bones like fresh barbeque.

"Good job Carlos. As a reward, you can operate the machine that will release the steam. Nothing like a little on the job training, eh? Now pay attention so you can get it right." He turned and singled out one of his men. "Mr. Morris. Would you please show the new guys how to operate the retort room?"

Morris stepped forward and indicated a small wheel attached to a pipe that had an arrow on it. The arrow pointed towards the room, the words "Caution, hot steam" written next to it. "Go ahead," said Mr. Che. "You've earned it. Please do the honors, Mr. Pinal."

Carlos looked across the room, eager faces all waiting to see what he would do next. One man even mouthed the words and more than a few gave him nods of encouragement.

Carlos turned the valve, slowly at first, but the men started a chant behind him. "More. More. More!"

Carlos opened the valve further. He could hear the hiss of steam as it roared through the pipe. "More. More. More!" It was like a sporting event, or the kind of encouragement you would hear at a drinking game.

The valve came to a stop. The steam continued to hiss through the pipe. Mr. Che started to applaud. The room joined in, thunderous applause as if he had brought down the house.

"Back the valve off a quarter turn," said Morris. "It keeps it from sticking."

Carlos obeyed.

"We have to monitor the pressure," said Morris. He led Carlos closer to the door where a large white gauge showed the pressure rising to one and a half atmospheres. "That looks good, but check the temperature too." He moved to a thermometer looking gauge that showed the temperature in the room to be about a hundred and ten degrees. "Always follow up with a visual inspection," said Morris. He led Carlos over to a spyhole, a round piece of glass that gave him a glimpse of the inside. Morris took a peep first, then offered it to Carlos.

The man who had fainted was running around. He alternated between pounding the walls and holding his hands over his ears. He could see Chinatown Joe flinching in the cage. Some of the cages were rocking and shaking. He looked away.

"All right," said Morris. "Now, you write all that down on this clipboard. Fill in this chart, see?" He indicated the form as he handed a pencil to Carlos. "Write your name at the top in that space that says operator, then fill in the date. It's the fifteenth," he said.

Carlos followed the instructions and filled in the form.

"And now, you wait ten minutes and take the readings again, writing it all down."

"Very good Mr. Morris," said Mr. Che. "I can see that out Train the Trainer program wasn't wasted on you. Bravo." He began to applaud and the team followed in like. Che raised his hand. "Well, looks like things are in good hands here. Mr. Morris, will you continue to instruct the new recruits? Let the other fellow run through the data collection, but please allow our new friend Carlos to continue the visual inspections." Mr. Che spoke to Carlos personally, his voice in a delicate whisper. "It takes about thirty minutes at three atmospheres to cook flesh. At that point, all the bacteria has been killed, all the meat has been cooked to the tenderness of a fresh roasted ham. Better than a Butterball on Thanksgiving Day, you'll see." He clapped him on the back. "Well, carry on. Let's go men." He drew his entourage around him and after a minute or two they shuffled away through a side door. A few remained behind.

There was silence for a while until Morris pointed to his watch and spoke. "Ten minutes," he said. "Time for another cycle." He grabbed Carlos by the hand. "Come on, let's go have another look," he said, maneuvering towards the spyhole. "There's a point where they all get still and turn white as statues. I'm curious to see how that one guy running around free turned out."

He pushed Carlos towards the wall, pressing his eye towards the peephole. The old lady was frozen in prayer and might have been a statue seen at the Vatican. The one who had fainted had fainted again, becoming a still life in motion, a pose worthy of the Discobolis of Myron, the Laocoön, or any other masterpiece of white marble from the ancient world. Inside the standing cage Chinatown Joe squirmed, twitching like an epileptic having a Grand Mal. Then there was his cousin, his mouth contorted in a way he had never seen, as if the right side of his face had suddenly grown limp and shriveled.

"All right," said Morris. "Don't hog the view." He pulled Carlos away and pressed his eye to the spyhole. "There's enough for everyone. Who's next?" he asked, trying to keep the eager ones from fighting like dogs to be the first in line to see.

Chapter 4

Turds

"I needed to see you, Harry, but not like this." Lieutenant Bernard was pacing. It helped him think. The mind doesn't just stop at the brain, it's hard wired into the body, controlling autonomic breathing, gastric sensations, reaching all the way to the toes with neurons that turn around and relay information right back to the brain. Matt Bernard knew that when his body was working, so was his mind.

"It was an accident," said Rita. "We got statements from all the witnesses. He threatened Harry with a homemade weapon. He fell across the car and hit the car in anger. That's when it slipped a gear and crushed him. That's what the coroner will say. Manny Ballston brought this upon himself."

Bernard shook his head. He was a detective and didn't get to be in charge of the criminal investigation department for the Seattle Police by being slow on the job. Little Rita Rockwell was becoming quite a detective, laying her facts and arguments out like a conga line of information, but she had a way to go. "You telling me I should write this one up as suicide by Volvo? You're overlooking some of the facts. What about the fight? Your witnesses also report that Ballston and Harry were fighting. Were they angry enough to want to kill one another? Isn't that enough motive for you to consider homicide?" He paced a minute, Harry and Red looking at the floor like wounded animals.

He turned his attention on Harry. "And you. Sitting there all quiet in the corner. Why were you after this guy? Did you want to kill him?"

"I told you, I was working for a client. We were just going to question him."

"Who was the client?"

Harry looked away. "Can't tell you that. Client privilege."

Bernard shook his head. "Don't give me that crap. Come on. Who's your client?"

"Lay off me Matt," said Harry, spitting the words out like poison. "Cut me some slack. I watched a man die an hour ago." He stared into

Bernard's eyes. "I can't wait to go home tonight, retreat to my hole in the wall apartment where I can tell myself what a good job I did today." He mimicked talking to himself. "How was work today, Harry? Oh, fine, kind of killed a man with a car. Oh, really? What was that like? "

Bernard looked away. He started pacing again. "Lots of people get killed with cars every day," he said softly. "They're called accidents."

Some of the madness seemed to fade from Harry's face.

"Okay," said Bernard. "I'll let you get by for now. Protect whoever it is you want to protect." He turned to Red. "Rita, your case is tight, your facts well presented. I'm convinced that Harry did not attack Manny Ballston with the intent to kill him. Eventually when all the evidence and facts are reviewed, I'm convinced Harry will be cleared." He took a deep breath. "I've just have one more problem left to solve." He fidgeted with his hands until he became self-conscious of it. He rubbed them together a bit, then settled them gently at his side. "Here's the deal, Harry. A death was involved. Until this case gets settled and you're cleared, I have to hold your private detective license and your gun permit."

"I don't carry a gun these days," said Harry. He didn't tell Bernard that he couldn't afford a gun let alone the ammunition to use it.

"Oh," said Bernard. He thought all detectives carried a piece. "Okay then. These are standard questions, standard procedure. You understand?"

"Sure," said Harry. "I promise not to leave town."

Bernard laughed and Harry smiled. "That's good. I may have to hold you to that." Bernard opened a folder on his desk and pushed some papers in front of Harry. "Sign these, then I'll sign them and we'll officially begin the process. I don't expect the investigation to take more than thirty days on the outside."

"Thirty days?" said Harry.

"Yeah, yeah. Thirty days," said Bernard. "At the most. Don't worry, I'll try to do all I can to push this through the system but as I said a man was killed. We have a process to go through." He signed the papers after Harry and tucked them back in the folder. Matt reached for the back of his neck and rubbed it. "This still doesn't solve my problem." He sat down at his desk opposite Rita and Harry. "Your company has a work on demand contract with the city. I have work for both of you under that contract."

Harry smiled. "Thanks, Matt. You haven't used the contract since Couture. Rita and I could use the money. What do you need done?"

Bernard breathed deep, in and out. "I've got witnesses I need to question, some I have to hold, some I have to release. Something went down the other night on the Seattle docks and I need to find out who was there and who did what to whom. I may never see any of these witnesses again, which makes it even more important that we do a thorough job."

"Great, Matt," said Harry. "I can question witnesses from now until midnight."

"No you can't," said Bernard. "You don't have a license to operate at the moment. Your contract states that you will perform your duties for the City of Seattle as a licensed detective. Right now you don't have a license."

For a brief second Harry had seen a way out of his mounting debt. Rita jumped up and started to say something but Bernard gave her the hand, putting a stop to her like a school yard crossing guard. His hand twisted until he was pointing at her as he looked at Harry. "You don't have a license but she does. That's why I'm structuring this job a little different. Rita's in charge of all the interrogations. She conducts all the interviews, writes up the statements, and signs all the final reports."

Rita began to slowly sink back down into her chair. It was like watching Miss America squat to receive her crown. Her eyes sparkled, her smile grew as wide as Texas, and for a moment the big redheaded lesbian knew what it felt like to have everything right in her world. Like... fist fighting and cunnilingus all at once.

Bernard wasn't finished. "You can't do any police work on behalf of the department, Harry. No questioning witnesses, no phone calls, no interviews, no line ups, nothing."

Rita thought about Harry, who needed the work, and her winning smile turned down at the edges. Bernard knew what she was thinking, but before he could voice it there was a knock at the door. He started to say 'come in' but the door opened and in stepped a man in a tailored suit, shined country club shoes, and a smile that ran across his face like a dusty mountain road. His hand flattened the hair on the back of his head with a lick of saliva. "Sorry," he said. "I was waiting outside but I haven't got all day. Mayor said to keep this thing moving."

"Van Dorn," said Bernard. "Don't you have any manners?"

"Hey, I knocked first. Manners are one thing but we have an investigation to conduct," said Van Dorn. He smiled at Rita and Harry. "I know we've met, but not since my promotion. My name is Franklin Van Dorn, Chief Inspector for the Mayor's Office and head of the Urban Research Department."

Bernard shook his head. Van Dorn had worked for him at one time, but he was a bad detective. Management rewarded him by giving him a promotion. Bernard was glad to be rid of him, glad he was somebody else's problem, but that didn't stop him from butting heads with him from time to time.

"Nice hair, Fu" said Van Dorn. "Long hair suits you. You should get it curled."

"The sight of you is enough to curl anyone's hair," said Rita.

"The Urban Research Department?" asked Harry. He and Van Dorn had both worked for Bernard. Like Bernard, he didn't have a high opinion of the man's skills as a detective. More than once Harry had saved an innocent man from going to jail by overturning Van Dorn's shoddy work.

"There's only one Urban Research Department," said Van Dorn.

"Then properly, it's *The* Urban Research Department," said Harry, pronouncing it 'Thee' and emphasizing the 'The'.

"And I'm the head of it," said Van Dorn licking his hand and pressing the hair down flat on the back of his head. He smiled. "The Mayor has appointed my office to lead this investigation. Bernard, have you briefed these two?"

"I was just finishing up," said Bernard. "You can have them in a minute."

"Them?" said Van Dorn. He nodded sadly towards Harry. "I heard only one of you will be working for me. Seems like the other one has a problem with their license. We can't have a murderer conducting our investigations, can we?"

"It was an accident, Van Dorn," said Bernard.

"Maybe it was," said Franklin.

"Maybe?" said Rita. "I was there. Did you check the facts?"

"I'll wait and read the report," said Van Dorn. "I'm a busy man these days."

Harry laughed. "So speaks the head of *The* Urban Research Department." He emphasized 'The' again.

"What's so funny?" asked Van Dorn.

"The Urban Research Department," said Harry. "T.U.R.D. Seems to fit you well."

Bernard sniggered and Rita fought to keep a deadpan face.

"It's okay," said Harry. "I knew an Inspector Beaumont who worked for the Special Homicide Investigation Team, the SHIT squad for short. But he was good. Anyone can deal with shit, but tell me about turds, Franklin. I hear they just stink up the place until somebody flushes them away."

"Enough," said Van Dorn. He looked at Rita. "Come with me. There's a briefing downstairs in fifteen minutes that I want you to attend, then we'll get started with the interviews."

Rita stood up slowly, waiting for a nod of reassurance from Bernard. When it came, he held up his hand and addressed Van Dorn. "I'll send Harry down there in a minute. I just have a few things to finish up with him."

"He's not working for me," said Van Dorn. "He doesn't have a license."

"You're right. He's not working for you. He's working for me, assigned to your team as a consultant to Rita. He doesn't need a license to consult. I'm soliciting his opinion. She's green and I want Harry to evaluate her technique and thoroughness. You know all detectives must undergo a peer review. We expect the same thing from our contractors. He will work with her until I have the assurance that she is competent enough to work independently."

Van Dorn tightened his lip. "It's okay," said Bernard. "You can go now, Chief Inspector Van Dorn of The Urban Research Department. I'll send Mr. Takanawa down in a minute so he can attend the briefing."

"Take your time, Fu," said Van Dorn. He looked as if he wanted to say more, then turned and left. Rita stopped to beam a smile at Bernard and Harry before she followed him.

When the door shut Bernard was the first to laugh. "TURD," he said. "It's perfect."

Harry joined in. "As good as the South Lake Union Trolley. What is it with the Mayor's office and these bad acronyms?"

"Hey, I liked riding the SLUT," said Bernard. "Had a t-shirt that said so."

The laughter died. "He'll do okay, though," said Harry. "It's Van Dorn. His momma knows the Mayor and she contributes heavily to his causes and especially to his campaign. He'll do okay."

"You know it. It's a shame that the good detectives have to struggle while some of the bad ones get all the breaks. Way of the world," said Bernard.

"Yep," said Harry. He didn't believe it though. The world was more complex than that. Bernard was giving him a big break by letting him work and collect a paycheck. Thank God for people like Matt.

"So, Harry. Let me fill you in on some details that you may not hear from Van Dorn. This bust at the docks the other night was big. Human trafficking. People packed up in shipping containers like cattle. What interested me even more was the assortment of characters that showed up. I think we had at least one from every agency and cop squad within a fifty mile radius. Wouldn't surprise me if the Campus Police from the Tacoma Community College were there, it was that crazy."

"What are you telling me, Matt?"

"Be careful. There are a lot of eyes on this one. It makes me wonder who put together the guest list for this party." He dug through a pile of papers in the corner of his desk. "Here's something else to look at." He passed a photograph of an arm over to Harry. There was a burn mark on it, oddly shaped, but it definitely looked like something. It wasn't an Asian character, or even a residual tattoo scar, but it was something. "What do you make of that?"

"I don't know," said Harry.

"You may see this mark on some of the people you interview. Just want you to be aware of it. We suspect it's some kind of new gang thing. We picked up a few perps who don't quite check out. They work for the shipping company that owned the containers. They acted offended when we suggested they had something to do with the contents. They showed us a bill of lading that said it was fishing supplies from South America. We're in the process of getting a court order to look at the records for International Freight Ltd."

"You really think looking at employee records and shipping documents will help?" asked Harry.

"No, but you know me. I track down every lead I can. I suspect they know something that they're not sharing with us. These were not your standard shipping company executives."

"No?" asked Harry.

"Definitely not," said Bernard. "These boys had guns and a small army to help them unload a shipment of fishing supplies. Sound like standard procedure to you?"

"Maybe for International Freight Limited it is," said Harry.

There was a buzz and Bernard picked up the phone, listened a minute, and then set it back in the cradle. "They're ready for the briefing. Van Dorn says they're waiting for you to get started."

"Guess I'll go see what it's like working with turds."

"Yeah," said Bernard. "It's easy. Just keep your mouth shut and your head above water."

Chapter 5

Career Placement

Carlos woke up early, showered, dressed and walked over to the building that housed the Human Resource Office. It was ten minutes to eight and he was told not to be late for his eight o'clock appointment. He had no trouble finding the office, there were signs everywhere pointing the way. When he found the door that read "Human Capital" it was locked, but there was a row of chairs outside the office. The man from last night, the other new recruit, was also waiting for the office to open. Carlos sat beside him. Neither made eye contact and the silence lay heavy like the events of the night before.

"Good morning, my name is Carlos Pinal," he finally said, extending a hand.

"And I am Ngu Then," said the other man.

"I'm from Guatemala. Where are you from?" asked Carlos.

"Micronesia. A place called Colonia."

"I didn't see you in the trailer at the docks last night."

"There were a lot of us in there. I was having trouble breathing, especially after people started using the toilet in there. One of the buckets tipped over near me. I was disgusted. It's all I could do to keep from throwing up. But I'm in America now and the long hard journey is over. I can put that behind me at last." He looked at the ground. "Along with everything else that has happened."

"Your English is pretty good," said Carlos. "Where'd you learn to speak?"

"My Dad was an American. He worked for some big corporation that sent him there for something, I don't really know what. He lived in one of those compounds they all like to hole up in, you know, the walled villas."

"What happened to him?"

"One day the job was over. He had been there on and off for ten years. I was seven at the time. He said he was coming back for me and my mother. He never did."

"Sorry," said Carlos.

"I came here to search for him." Ngu looked off, staring into an open window. "I hope he'll be glad to see me."

At eight o'clock sharp the door opened.

"Hello," said a woman. She was dressed in an impeccable black suit with a short skirt and a pair of western style boots. "My name is Kathy and I'll be handling your orientation and paperwork today. Please come in."

It was a simple office, the kind you'd expect to see in any small company, modestly decorated with corporate art, mahogany credenzas, and barrister bookcases. There were no file cabinets but there were two small cubicles each with a chair, a keyboard, and a computer screen. She directed them to sit handing them each a stack of paper. "I'll need you to fill out this information. It's standard stuff we need for payroll and there's also the emergency contact information, last place of residence, stuff like that. Don't worry about the social security number if you don't have one. Just leave it blank, we'll fill that in for you later."

It didn't end there. Kathy kept producing more papers for them to fill out. There were even two tests, one of them the Myers-Briggs Type Assessment, the other some kind of weird intelligence test. It had pictures and he had to circle what was wrong with each picture. Things like a reflection in the mirror that was backwards or a table with a missing leg. There was even a section where you had to figure out what three dimensional shape would be created when you folded up a flattened image.

Kathy collected the tests and began the personal interviews starting with Ngu. She escorted him through a door on the other side of the office. There was a gold embossed plate on the door that read "Director, Human Capital". Ngu was in her office over an hour and Carlos waited patiently outside for his turn. He looked at magazines on the table, an odd mixture of titles that ranged from the normal human resource publications to eclectic things like International Fishing Charter Quarterly, Cable and Line, and even Forbes. There was a plaque on the wall, an award presented to Kathy Daily for modernizing the human resource department. Mr. Che's name was engraved in gold beneath her name.

Ngu finally came out of the office, all smiles and teeth. "I'm going fishing," he said. "Got a job on one of the company boats."

"Great," said Carlos. "When do you start?"

"Tomorrow," he said. "They need me. The boat has been down a man ever since they lost someone in an accident last month."

"Sounds dangerous," said Carlos.

"Fishing is dangerous but I'm good at it. I worked on a trawler that fished out of Colonia. We got paid in shares just like this deal. If the boat did well and we caught a lot of fish, shares were big and everyone made money, otherwise we split the losses."

"Pretty risky if you ask me," said Carlos.

"I don't know, I made good money last time I worked on a boat. Also, this is a company sponsored boat so we won't be held liable for the losses."

The door opened and Kathy stepped out. "Mr. Pinal?" she asked. "Please come into my office." Carlos gave Ngu a smile and waved goodbye as Kathy motioned him in. "Would you like a bottle of water?"

"Yes," he said. "Please."

She gently pressed the door closed and took two bottled waters out of a small refrigerator next to her desk. She set the water down in front of a chair and told him to take a seat. She sat in her chair with the grace of the Queen of England. Carlos drank his water while she sorted through a thick pile of papers. She turned sideways in her chair and tapped on a keyboard, staring at her screen for a minute. She focused a small camera on him. "We record all our interviews. Do you have a problem with that?" she asked.

"No."

She tapped some more keys and turned to face him. She opened her water and took a sip, clearing her throat. "You have some skills, Mr. Pinal, and I see a note in your file from Mr. Morris who said you did an excellent job last night during your trial run. He recommends you highly. Very impressive."

Carlos sat quietly and listened. "We like your Meyers – Briggs results, too. You're an ENFJ, an extrovert and a natural leader of men."

He took a sip of water and cleared his throat. He had no idea what she was talking about. "I was a shift supervisor at a mill house," he said. "I was a good manager."

"Very impressive," she said, but her eyes betrayed her condescending attitude. "Most of our executive slots are filled at this location, but after you've been with us for a year you'll be eligible for transfer to one of our other branches." She smiled. "We'll notify you."

"Thank you," he said.

She shuffled through some papers and read a few notes she had made. "I see you grew up on a farm and have some agricultural experience. What kind of crops did you grow?"

"A small vegetable garden for ourselves, a field of hay, but we also grew corn and beans. We grew enough to trade with the neighbors for their crops and other things we needed. The rest we fed to our animals."

"So you're familiar with the care and feeding of livestock?"

"Of course," he said. "I was able to mix feeds to achieve different results depending on what the intention may be. By changing the feed you can encourage shiny coats in show animals, bulk muscle in livestock, or even prevent disease in chickens. I've cared for these and other animals. I had a prize horse for a long time, but I had to sell him during a bad year. I always regretted that. The horse and I had a bond, and I could tell he felt betrayed, but I had no choice. My family needed the money." He looked sadly off to her right as he thought about it. "I never got another horse after that."

"Did you also butcher animals and process meat?"

"Yes," said Carlos. "Mostly chickens and pigs, a cow during a good year. Every now and then a goat. It's all pretty much the same. We made a lot of sausage, a lot of ham. Steaks were a luxury."

"Have you ever milked a cow?" she asked.

"Cows and goats," he said. "My mother taught me how to make butter and also the secrets of making cheese."

"Your English is quite good. Where did you learn to speak, Mr. Pinal?"

"I went to school at the local mission," he said. "The priests taught us Spanish, English, and French." He paused. "I was born Spanish but I can read and write English. French, not so much. Also mathematics."

She looked up.

"The priests taught us mathematics," he said. "And religion, of course."

"What denomination were they?" she asked.

"A sect of Catholic," he said.

"Are you a Catholic?"

"I claimed to be Catholic at the time," he said. "My father told me that if I went there and told the priests that I was Catholic, I would get a good education. They also fed you a good lunch every day you attended school. I said I was Catholic."

"Do you claim any religious preference?" she asked.

"Preference? I prefer to talk to God on my own terms."

"Explain."

"He hasn't been very good to me in this life. I don't regret anything, each life holds special pleasures, but I do say my prayers at night and ask for His blessings. Still, nothing seems to come my way."

"Have you lost faith?"

"That's a good question," he said. He thought for a minute. "I don't know."

"Honest answer," she said. She scribbled something on the page of notes in front of her. There was a ding from a speaker attached to the computer. She turned and read the screen before facing him again. "I wish I had more time to talk to you but I have another appointment."

She gathered up his paperwork, singling out a few sheets where he had missed the required signature. She placed them in front of him and handed him a pen. "Please sign here," she said. When he was finished she looked it over and fed it into a machine next to her desk. The machine scanned and shredded each sheet, storing it in the Corporation's Human Resource files located in some offshore system. She tapped some keys and looked into her screen.

"Perfect," she said. "There's a vacancy in the dairy. As good a place as any to start."

Carlos smiled. The way she said it made him feel lucky, like he had just won a prize in a lottery.

"One last thing and then I need to run," she said. "I'm working with a recruitment team in Bellevue today."

Carlos nodded politely. He didn't hear her. He had a job.

She pointed the camera at him and said, "Now, look here while I take your picture for your access badge."

He posed and smiled.

"Oh, no, Mr. Pinal," she said. "Try to look sinister."

Chapter 6

Kidnapped

Trish stared at herself in the dressing room mirror. She enjoyed having lots of nice clothes and considered it a reward for her hard work. She was one of the best divorce lawyers in Bellevue and her legal practice depended on image. She had to project a tight, pulled together look that was the mainstay of any successful individual.

She liked the look but needed a second opinion. There was a salesgirl standing just outside. She parted the curtain and smiled, eyeing the woman carefully. "Those Jimmy Choo boots you're wearing tell me you have a lot of taste. What do you think of this outfit?" Trish struck a few model poses. She was a shapely woman and worked hard to keep herself fit. She once put on a plastic garbage bag to escape a downpour. She made it look so sexy that she caused a car accident when people turned to look at her.

"I like the pencil skirt, but it's all wrong with that top."

"Really?" asked Trish, surprised to hear that answer. She turned and looked in the mirror again. "I kind of like it."

"It's the dark purple pattern done in pintucking at the top, and it pooches out at your waist making you look fatter than you are."

Trish didn't like hearing that. "You're no help," she said smugly. "I should ask my ex-husband Harry. He's a drag queen and he's always right about my clothes."

"You have a drag queen for a husband?"

"Ex-husband," she said.

"Is he gay or something?" asked the saleslady.

Trish thought about it. "No. I don't think he ever had sex with a man." She stared off into space and smiled. "But he's pretty good with a woman."

"Then why does he dress up like a woman?"

"I dunno. I guess, like me, he likes the clothes." She spun and looked at herself again in the mirror. "He started doing it when he was a kid. Guess it stuck with him." She turned and struck another pose. She giggled. "He has breasts now," she said. "Just as big as mine." She didn't mention that hers were artificial as well.

The saleslady smirked. "No!"

Trish laughed. "Oh, yeah. I saw to that. I was the DPA for his medical decisions. Some madman abducted him and put breasts in him. After the police found him they asked me if they should take them out or replace them."

"Replace them?" said the salesgirl. "What was wrong with the ones he had?"

"Did I mention they were exploding breast implants?"

The salesgirl smiled. "Ingenious," she said, her head slowly nodding in admiration. "What's a DPA?"

"Oh," said Trish. "Durable Power of Attorney. Gives me the right to make all his medical decisions in case he's incapacitated, which, in this case, he was. The doctors told me they could remove the exploding implants but needed to put something in their place, otherwise his chest wouldn't heal right. Something about the way the nut case had cut him up." She circled, jutting her breasts out and taking a critical look at herself in the mirror again.

"Yeah," she continued. "When they asked me what I thought about it I told them, yeah, do it! Great idea. Replace 'em. Put bigger ones in. They had me sign some papers and said they'd do the best they could."

"Which was..." egged the saleslady.

Trish cupped her breasts, twisted again and admired her shape. "They replaced them with something of equal size, which made him a nice 38-C."

They both laughed.

"I'm Kathy, by the way," said the saleslady.

"Trish."

"I think I know you," said the saleslady. "You're Trish Takanawa, the divorce lawyer, aren't you?"

"That's me," she looked nervous. "The Bellevue bitch." She hated that nickname but it was well known. "I'm good, so if you ever need a divorce..."

"You don't remember me," said Kathy. "You handled my divorce five years ago. Bastard was cheating on me and you made him pay."

"At least Harry never cheated on me," she said. "What was your name again?"

"You also handled a divorce for another person I know. In this case I knew the plaintiff, a man named Jason L'Enfant."

"I remember that case. I represented Caroline L'Enfant. That was recent, a couple of months ago. Her husband was beating her. She tried divorcing him three times and he beat her for it. Each time it got worse until he finally broke her leg. Spit on her and dared her to try and run now. When she came to me I took the case pro bono. So, you know the plaintiff. How is he doing?"

"He's all torn up." She was going to say more but Trish piped in.

"Most guys are after a divorce. Tears them right up. I'm all torn up too. Pity he doesn't have her to kick around anymore."

"Pity," said Kathy. "You should see the man."

"No thanks," said Trish. "Seeing him in court was enough or me." She turned and faced the mirror again. "So, you don't like this?"

"Maybe you should check with your drag queen ex-husband."

Trish snorted. "At least he gives me an honest opinion."

"I gave you an honest opinion," said Kathy. "Those loose little pleated blouses are so last year. You need a solid color with an infinity scarf. Here, let me help you. You're what, a size nine?"

"Seven," said Trish, gritting her teeth.

"Okay," said the saleslady. "I'll be right back."

Trish looked in the mirror again, then reached into her purse and pulled out her cell phone. She took a picture of herself in the mirror and sent it to Harry. The salesgirl came back with a long, tunic thing and a circular scarf of some kind.

"Here, let me help you off with that top," said Kathy. She moved in close to Trish.

Trish pushed her away slightly and hit the speed dial on her phone for Harry. "I need a second opinion."

Kathy was again pulling up her top. Trish dropped the phone and it fell to the floor rolling behind the curtain. She started to protest but Kathy had her arms up as she draped the tunic thing half over her head. Before pulling it down she took the infinity scarf and wrapped it around Trish's neck. Trish started to scream but Kathy gently stepped behind her and placed her in a choke hold while clamping down over her mouth.

Trish went limp in her arms. Kathy pushed her through the curtains and dropped her into a laundry cart that was just outside the dressing room. She pulled some clothes over the top and hid her underneath, then she took out her cell phone and dialed.

"Morris. Meet me at the loading dock. I have some dirty laundry," she said.

"Be right there," he said.

She hung up the phone and dialed another number. "Mr. Chairman?" she said. "Good news. We managed to recruit the woman of interest. I'll have her at your office within an hour." She hung up the phone and put it away. She turned and noticed herself in the mirror. She pulled the sleeve of her blouse down, just enough to cover the odd shaped scar that was burned into her arm.

She pushed the cart through another curtain and into the hidden part of the store. Her expensive heels clicked on the concrete floor as she made her way across the warehouse. She felt empowered, all tough and cowgirl, successful in her job. She stopped on the loading dock. Morris was nowhere in sight. She looked at her shoes, turned her feet to study them. She snickered, then stared down at the cart as she sneered at Trish. "What do you know? They're Lucchese boots, you fashion imbecile,"

Chapter 7

F.A.Q.s

"So, you telling me you saw nothing?" asked Red.

The answer came back in a slew of non-English.

She paced behind the man, suddenly grabbing him and pushing his head into the table as she twisted his arm.

"Ow!" he yelled. "Let go of my arm!"

She released him. "So, you do know English," she said.

Harry sat alone in the next room watching her through the one way glass of the interrogation room. He couldn't help but notice the strange burn mark on the man's arm. It matched the one he had seen in Bernard's picture.

He heard his cell phone beep. He had forgotten he left it on. It was Trish. "What does she want now?" he said out loud. He switched the phone off instead of answering it. "She'll never leave me alone."

When he tried to think about how he felt about her he just got confused. He loved her but it was a difficult relationship. He wondered what the problem was and how he could fix it. He thought she was vain and a little conceited and self-absorbed, but then he had his faults too. They had been married only two years when she came home and caught him wearing her clothes. "I think she was more embarrassed that I was the same size as her," he chuckled. She had gained some weight since they got married and he had lost some. A bad balance for a marriage, he learned. After they separated, she showed him. Lost all that weight and some!

Separated.

Were they separated? They were still technically married, even though she told everyone she was his ex. What's up with that?

Maybe they just had bad luck. They tried twice to have a child but both times something went wrong. He had begun to think that they weren't meant for kids, so he focused on his career. He was a war veteran and a young and rising detective on the Seattle Police Force. She was working hard on her legal practice. Maybe they just needed some time before going down the kids and family path.

Truth be known, she felt cheated when she caught him in her clothes, as if he were with another woman. Instead she found, in some weird twisted way, he was the other woman. He confessed that he still loved her but it was hard for her to understand. In the end she wound up making fun of him to bolster her own pride. Harry had dealt with that before, but Trish got mean at one point. He wondered if it was her mean streak that led her to decide to finally straddle him with breasts. Sounds like something a vengeful lawyer would do.

He looked down at his breasts and cupped them in his hands. "No she didn't do this to me," he said out loud. "It was a madman named Couture." His eyes began to blur and he slipped into a dark place. His hands wrapped around his waist and he bent over, a curled fetus on a straight back chair. "He took my ribs," he said. His breaths became short, staccato yelps from a child that huddled deep inside him. He looked her in the eye, realizing at once that his inner child was female. "Fu Chan," he whispered. His hands ran down his sides, over the scars of the missing ribs. Harry definitely had more of a female shape these days than male. And he thought other people were confused.

The sounds from the next room crept into him like a thief in an unlit house. Once aware, he slowly began to focus on them. It pulled him back from the short walk through the jungle of his mind. Thank God. It was too easy to get lost in there.

Red was screaming at the small man, Chou Lin, as his name read in the file. This guy claimed he was not part of the human trafficking operation, but from a fishing boat that was docked nearby. That didn't make sense to Harry. The Seattle docks were a shipping and receiving port, mostly containers. There aren't any seafood plants anywhere in that area, let alone a place to tie up a fishing boat. He looked at his notes, jotting down a few new ones he thought of. There are a lot of questions he would have asked, a few lines he would have pursued more aggressively, but this was Red's show.

Red looked at Harry through the mirror and saw only herself and Chou. She needed help. Harry could make all the gestures he wanted but she couldn't see him through the one way glass. Chou Lin laughed, a cocky sneer that announced that she would never break him. Harry had seen that defiance in hundreds of perps. Chou Lin was a bona fide bad guy with no respect for the law. Harry had sat on the sidelines and watched long enough.

Time to see if he could get anywhere, but he had to be careful. Bernard was very specific. No witness interviews, no police business whatsoever.

He decided to try something. Chou Lin had never seen or met Harry so there was a chance this would work. There was an empty briefcase in the corner. Harry stuffed his notes in the case and went to the door of the interrogation room. Red slid the peephole cover aside and saw Harry. She started to say something but Harry shushed her. Red opened the door.

Harry went to the chair beside Chou Lin and set the briefcase down.

"Who the frig are you?" asked Chou.

Harry smiled wryly and nodded, then winked. He looked at the burn mark on Chou's arm and touched the sleeve of his own jacket in the same area. Chou nodded and smiled.

"What has Mr. Lin been charged with?" he asked Red.

Rita was caught aback. "I don't know."

Harry became angry. "Then why are you questioning him?"

"He's a suspect," she said.

"Suspected of what?" he said.

"I don't know exactly," she said. "Smuggling, importing without a license, human trafficking, loitering."

"Sounds like a pretty generic list," said Harry. "Standard police trick for holding someone twenty four hours. Has Mr. Lin been officially charged with any of these?"

"I don't know," she said.

"Go and find out then," he said sternly. "I'll wait here with Mr. Lin until you return. Go! Find out! My time is valuable."

Rita hesitated for a moment, then turned and left the room. Chou Lin was handcuffed to the chair but she alerted a guard on her way out to watch the door.

As soon as she was gone Harry spoke to Chou Lin. "What did you tell them?"

"Nothing," he said. "I swear." He was scared. "I wouldn't betray Mr. Che."

"Good," said Harry. "I would hate to give him a bad report."

"Will you be able to get me out of here?" he asked.

"Let's see what this bitch says you're charged with. If it's nothing, I could have you released in no time. There's a problem, though."

"Problem?"

"This seems to be the first stop in a long chain of questioning. When the Seattle police are done with you they plan on turning you over to the Feds."

"What could they want with me?"

"That's what I need to know," said Harry. "Anything they could possibly charge you with and make it stick?"

"I'm not sure," said Lin. "I was assigned to the IST."

"IST?" asked Harry.

"Incident Support Team. One of Che's new initiatives. Our job was to ferry people away quickly after they landed. Load them up on the boat and move them out of the area. The boat got away but I was in the forward cell on the dock and got caught in the raid."

"How many made it to the boat?"

"Thirty or forty I imagine, including the crew."

"Which boat did you use that night?"

"The old fishing trawler. *Dare Me*," he said. "But you should know that." A light seemed to come on in his head. "Who are you?"

Harry changed the subject. "Where is that lady with the list of charges?"

As if on cue, Red appeared at the door with a sheaf of papers and passed them to Harry. It was a packet from Van Dorn's briefing. Harry scanned it like he was reading it, then put it in his briefcase. He turned to Lin. "Based on what I know, you should take the Federal plea. If they offer you a reduced sentence, it's your best bet."

"What about my family?" said Lin. "Che promised."

"I'll pass the information on and we'll see how it lands. Good luck, Chou," he said. He turned to Rita. "I want to talk to you in private."

They started to leave but the door was blocked when they tried to push it open. They eased off and Van Dorn entered the room.

"What are you doing in here?" he demanded of Harry.

Harry tried to push past him but Van Dorn stopped him.

"Well?" he said.

"Observing," said Harry.

"Observing what?"

"Not in front of Chou," he said. "It's unprofessional. Let's take it outside."

Van Dorn thought about it, licked his fingers and pressed the hair flat in the back of his head. He stared at Chou who gave him the evil eye until he turned and followed the others into the corridor.

Chou was left alone in the room. Who was that guy? He acted like a lawyer but he never said he was one. Come to think of it, he never even said who he was.

Chapter 8

Winners and Their Trophies

"Nature has much to teach us," said Mr. Che. He sat behind his desk staring into his ant farm. "Insects, as opposed to Man, are so organized and efficient." He stared at a group of them right now as they worked to carry food to their queen. This society was all about fertility and continuity of the species. Well-organized, admirable to a fault. Perhaps this is what God meant when He said the meek would inherit the earth.

The ant farm was tremendous, the envy of any ten year old, consisting of thousands and thousands of ants. In place of a wall behind his desk he had installed thick plates of glass, some angled at odd intervals, as much a work of art as a working ant farm. Above, on the next floor above his office, the farm flattened out and opened into a room full of dirt. His glass ceiling was dotted with mazes of tunnels that were insect superhighways. Upstairs was a private room with a sand floor. He liked to go there and throw food on the sand and watch the ants carry it away. Sometimes, when he ached for a new distraction, he would secure a nemesis or an infiltrator to the shackles he had installed.

One of his victims was there now. Che stared into the ant farm watching a worker carry another piece of food to the queen, wondering if it was part of the man shackled nearby in the soundproof room.

A gruesome way to go, but so ingenious. First a few explorer ants find you, laying chemical paths back to the rest of the colony. Soon this ant superhighway becomes clogged with a force that would rival a Brazilian construction crew in the middle of the rain forest. They crawl into every orifice, every crease of the body, an itch that cannot be scratched. Hundreds and thousands come, he had witnessed it firsthand. Every part of the body becomes covered in ants. They sting with formic acid, chew with clenching mandibles, and break off little pieces that they carry away. They strip everything, the soft meat going first, the eyes, the skin, the contents of the skull, until nothing is left but the bones and sometimes even they disappear.

He smiled, thinking of the hours he had spent in that room, the confessions he had heard, the cries for mercy, the screams and the silence afterwards.

He swiveled in his chair, turning to the people beside him. There was a meeting going on in his office. The attendees said nothing while Mr. Che went on about ants and society in general. He was a great man, a visionary. Their thoughts were simple beside the Chairman. As minions they shared his vision (and his fortunes), their loyalty burned into their forearms by a small foreign device.

And the cries of his enemy went unheard just ten feet above them.

Che moved away from the wall, his heels clicking as he walked across the polished wood floor, coming to a halt in front of the bound and gagged woman. He pulled her head up by the back of her hair and looked into her face. "You're sure this is the one?" he asked again. Trish stared back, her eyes full of fear.

"Yes," said Kathy. "I'm sure."

Mr. Che turned to a man beside him, thick but muscular under the skin. The eyes were sharp as well, attentive to detail and alive with passion. "And what about you, Jason?" he asked. "Are you sure?"

"Yes," he said. "She's the one. That's Tricia Takanawa. I remember her from court. She's the one who broke up my family."

"Then we are sorry for your loss," said Mr. Che. "But please remember: the Corporation is also your family, and we support you in your time of loss and sadness." He clapped Jason L'Enfant on the shoulder. "Your ex-wife has already been attended to, and she is paying dearly for her disloyalty even as we speak."

"Thank you, Mr. Che," he said, bending at the waist in a sign of respect.

Che clapped him again on the shoulder, twice this time. "You're a good man, Jason. Loyal. You've proven it over and over. I'm always willing to use the Corporation's resources to help one of my best men."

L'Enfant bowed again. "Thank you, Mr. Chairman. Thank you for the compliment."

"You need to put this behind you," said Mr. Che. "Get it out of your mind, this whole unfortunate business. Once you do that, you'll be able to concentrate on your work again. Become more successful, more satisfied, more efficient."

"Yes, sir," he said.

Mr. Che studied Jason carefully, looking deeply into his sharp eyes. He studied people with the same intensity as he did his ants, although it was much harder with ants. They seem so interchangeable, yet they are each as unique as humans are. DNA is an incredible invention, whether by God or by accident.

"I give you this woman as a gift, Jason, so that you may find closure to these sad events and move on with your life. Revenge is a good thing. Like confession, it purges the soul." Mr. Che turned and walked away, his heels clicking as he made his way back to the chair behind his desk. He stood beside it, his back to Jason as he turned again to stare at the ants. "Do with her as you wish," he said.

Jason L'Enfant thought about it. There was silence in the room, so quiet you could almost hear the ants as they rumbled on with their lives behind the glass wall. Jason finally broke the silence.

"She bested me in court, even took Caroline away from me. Even your high priced lawyers couldn't fight her off."

Che became agitated. "Which is why I grant you this special boon, Jason." He turned away from the ants, his steps echoing off the floor as he crossed the path back to his most loyal man. "You rank high in the organization. You directly impact the bottom line through a number of projects. I appreciate and reward good performance and loyalty Jason." He paused before continuing, pointing to the gagged woman. "She was the one who betrayed you. Why would any woman want to leave you? You provided everything for your wife, yet Caroline tried to divorce you three times and failed." He turned away for a moment. "I apologize for the problem with my lawyers. They thought it was impossible, but this Takanawa woman succeeded in making it happen."

"Perhaps she should share the same fate as my ex-wife," said Jason.

"Excellent," said Mr. Che. He turned and clapped Jason on the shoulder. "A wise choice as well. Now they can both contribute to corporate profit, and perhaps then you can move beyond this." Mr. Che smiled, baring teeth that again held venom. He nodded to Kathy who walked to the door of Che's office to admit two burly men attended by Morris. They went right to Trish and pulled her to her feet. She grunted but was helpless in their grasp. They dragged her towards the door, Trish struggling like a fish trying to shake itself free of the fisherman. Kathy nodded respectfully to Jason and Mr. Che. She smiled, feeling successful herself. "I'll see that she is properly oriented to her new role." She turned as the men pulled their prize catch through the open doors.

Che turned to Jason and smiled. "Your wife was an outsider, wasn't she?" he asked.

"Yes."

Che breathed deep, his head nodding in agreement. "Have you met the new girl in accounting?" he asked. "She's a darling and eager to succeed. I daresay she would make a fine candidate for a new Mrs. L'Enfant, now that you're divorced. Would you like me to arrange an introduction?"

Before Kathy could close the doors there was an interruption. A thin man in a laboratory coat stormed into the room. He had a thick package with him, about the size of a large box of flowers, which he dropped on Che's desk with an audible thump. "About time you opened that door," he said.

"We were just on our way to see you, Doctor Mandelle," said Kathy.

He turned, his face full of anger for interrupting him. He saw the men holding Trish firmly in place. The fish was definitely losing its fight. Mandelle moved beside her, studying her like a prize heifer at an animal auction. "Then I'll see you later," he said to her, his voice low, a dark promise that came out in a whisper.

Che's eyes narrowed, his lips drew tight into a thin line. Nevertheless, he smiled. "Doctor Mandelle. Always a pleasure to see you."

"I have a complaint," said Mandelle.

Kathy smiled, about to close the doors before L'Enfant stood up. He chuckled before turning towards Che and bowing. "That you again, Mr. Chairman." He nodded to Kathy and the men. The room was suddenly cold and empty as they all left, leaving Mandelle alone to face Che.

The Chairman turned his back to Mandelle and stared into his ant farm. "What is your complaint this time, Klaus?"

Mandelle looked down at the floor and cleared his throat. "Well, not so much a complaint as a plea for efficiency. Your demand for flesh is frightening. I strive for efficiency in our dairy operations, but you disrupt my plans. I hardly have time for my research, for testing new protocols. I am working harder than ever."

"Good," said Che, turning to smile at Mandelle. "You have a new assistant. He has experience in animal husbandry."

"I've met him, but will he share the passion that I have for this work?"

"Mentor him," said Che. "He is trainable?"

"Yes, but…"

"Were you happy with last quarter's share?" asked Che.

"Yes, but…"

"At the top, as Chairman, I must prioritize resources and direct the future of our organization. The farm is more than a production center for milk, more than a living laboratory for your research. It serves many purposes. It is also a cadaver mill, a source of stem cells, and, at times, a bordello for the men."

"I know all this," said Mandelle. "I helped design the business model. What concerns me is your sudden need for more raw materials."

"The flesh you harvest is essential to the success of the Manila Project. I will not yield on this. You need to keep up the same level of production."

"And you need to be careful," said Mandelle. "These collections can easily draw attention to us."

Che stood up, his hands resting on his desk as he leaned towards Mandelle. "I know the risks."

"Then pay attention to them," said Mandelle. "Don't bring the police down on us."

"Don't worry about the police," said Che. "This operation can stand any scrutiny from the outside world. I am careful about that."

They stared at each other like wildcats defending their territory. Che finally softened. "Look," he said. "The Manila Project is close to completion. I expect to take delivery of the prototype by the end of the week. Once we reach that milestone I promise we will stop the collections."

Mandelle stared back at him. "That's not what I want. I need the collections for my research. I just want them to slow to a reasonable pace. As I said when I came in here, I'm overworked these days with your incessant demands."

"And I told you that I will stop these demands next week, but only after I am assured that the Manila Project has all the raw materials it needs."

"Have I ever failed to meet that need?"

Che smiled. "No, my friend. You've done exemplary work, and for that I am grateful. At the same time, I have given you fulfilling work and a medical research facility that would rival any major hospital. Where else could you continue your experiments in clandestine safety? Where else could you draw a salary that nets you twice than the national average of a fully certified MD? I pay you more than most hospital administrators, and you get to do work you love."

"True," said Mandelle. "True."

"However, since you have brought this to my attention I am going to go one better," said Che. He went to his computer and tapped the keyboard. "There," he said. "I have increased your Corporate share by ten percent, a small bonus for your hard work."

Mandelle looked anything but satisfied.

Che acknowledged the package the Doctor had laid on his desk. "This is the latest trophy?" he asked.

"What else," said Mandelle. "It will be a few weeks before I'm able to process Joe. The meat was cooked but the mark of loyalty is intact. I had an idea for making it into a lampshade, maybe designing a new line of Auschwitz table lamps."

Che ripped the paper away from the package. It contained a human arm, stuffed and mounted on a flat base. The hand open, reaching upward as if it sought some prize to grasp. Che picked it up, hefting it in his hands. "Not as heavy as I thought," he said. He squeezed it. "Such a lifelike feel."

"That's because it has been tanned, drained of blood, the muscle removed and the arm stuffed with inert material."

"I am glad your skills include taxidermy," said Che. He set it down on the desk and admired it like a soccer mom with a trophy from the latest game. "Excellent work, Klaus. You have more than earned your bonus."

Mandelle smiled. "If that is so, then perhaps you should consider increasing it a little more."

Che laughed, a cackle that sounded like he was choking on a piece of food.

Mandelle stopped smiling, his eyes becoming cold and narrow.

Che stopped laughing as his eyes mirrored Mandelle's. The two men looked at each other, a pregnant pause that begged to be filled. Without warning, they both broke out in laughter.

"Okay then," said Che. "I will add another five percent when you deliver me the loyalty oath of Chinatown Joe."

"Done," said Mandelle. The two shook hands. "Back to work then."

"Yes," said Che. "Back to work. Thank you my friend."

Mandelle turned to exit the room as Che began to type on the keyboard again. "One more thing," said the Doctor. "What do you do with these things after I deliver them?"

Che stopped typing and began laughing again as he turned to look at his ants for a moment. They were extremely busy. He focused on one that was carrying a huge piece of food through a tunnel that led to a storage chamber. He saw Mandelle reflected behind him in the glass, the evil doctor smiling as he waited patiently for his answer. If anyone would appreciate his madness, it would be Klaus. "Why not?" he said. "Come with me." He picked up the trophy and moved a few steps away to a small door beside a bookcase. "Hold this," he said, passing the trophy to Mandelle who accepted it eagerly. There was a scanner beside the door similar to the ones located everywhere in the facility. Che rolled up his sleeve and displayed the tattoo on his forearm to the scanner. There was a beep and the door popped open.

They went up a short flight of stairs and turned into a corridor. Mandelle's jaw dropped as he entered the room, the trophy nearly slipping from his hands.

Chapter 9

City Heat

"What was that all about in there?" asked Van Dorn.

"What?" asked Harry. He found if he played dumb with Van Dorn it usually worked.

"You know what," said Franklin.

"What?" asked Harry.

Red stood quietly nearby, wanting to disappear back into the room with Chou Lin. She knew better to come between Harry and Van Dorn. They were old adversaries. Maybe adversary wasn't quite the right word. It was more like competitors in a sporting event. The only difference was that Harry had game. Watching them spar was like seeing a fight between a battle ready soldier and a small whining child. It almost seemed like Harry was reigning in his ability, going easy on Franklin so he wouldn't get hurt.

"Okay," said Van Dorn. "If that's the way you want to play." He seethed for a moment, licked his hand and flattened the hair on the back of his head. "Bernard's office," he said firmly. "Now."

Harry smiled and moved down the hall. Red started to follow but Van Dorn stopped her. "You," he said. "Back to work."

She frowned and looked toward Harry. "It's okay Rita," he said. "You're doing fine. I'll give Bernard a report on your progress. Keep up the good work."

Van Dorn was livid by the time they got to Bernard's office. Once again, he didn't bother to knock but instead pushed the door open and announced his presence.

"I'm in the middle of something here, or haven't you noticed?" said the lieutenant. He saw Harry standing in the doorway behind Van Dorn, a wry grin on his face. He narrowed his eyes and Harry lost the grin. Just like old times, he thought.

"He was in the interrogation room," said Van Dorn.

Bernard turned to Harry. "What were you doing in there?" he asked.

"Observing. Just like you said."

"Big Red wasn't even in the room," said Van Dorn.

"She had to go to the bathroom," said Harry. "I was waiting until she got back."

"You're supposed to observe from behind the glass," said Bernard. "Or didn't I make myself clear about that?"

"I followed your orders," said Harry. "No police business."

"You're not a detective, Harry," he said.

"And I didn't represent myself as one either," said Harry. "I was in no way connected with the Seattle police or with anyone in this investigation."

"Did you talk to the perp?" asked Bernard.

"We exchanged words," said Harry. "He asked me what he was charged with. Rita didn't know. I wanted to tell her to never start in investigation without knowing the charges. You told me to help her improve."

"I didn't tell you to talk to suspects," said Bernard, his voice harsh now. Harry became silent. Van Dorn smiled. Bernard turned to him, irritated. "What are you so happy about?" he asked.

Van Dorn tried to look serious again. He licked his hand and sheepishly patted the hair on the back of his head.

"Get out of my office," said Bernard. They both turned to leave. "Not you," he said to Harry. "You're done for the day."

Van Dorn had his back to Bernard. The lieutenant didn't see the cynical smile of satisfaction he gave Harry. He turned to Bernard. "Glad you see this my way," he said.

"I told you to get out of my office," said Bernard. "And shut the door behind you. I don't like disciplining someone in front of other people."

Van Dorn obeyed but lingered outside. Bernard got up and closed the blinds to the window of his office, staring sternly at the head of The

Urban Research Department who quickly moved on. He drew a sharp breath, then sat down in the chair behind his desk. "What's this all about," he said, his voice softening.

"I followed your orders, Matt. I didn't represent myself as the police."

"Then tell me what you were doing in the interrogation room?"

"Like I said, Rita looked like she needed some help and some hands on guidance. She didn't know the charges."

"Don't give me that crap," said Bernard. "The door is shut, Van Dorn is gone. What really happened?"

Harry drew a deep breath. "I saw the mark on Chou Lin's arm, the gang marking, the one you told me about."

"Gang marking?" interrupted Bernard. "I didn't call it that."

"Just a hunch," said Harry.

"Okay, what next?"

"I went in for a closer look. I touched my sleeve in the same place and the perp thought I was his lawyer come to rescue him. Not the police. He mentioned a name. Mr. Che, and a boat, the *Dare Me*."

Bernard sat back in his chair. Harry had a way of getting things done. The lieutenant smiled, then looked down at the papers on his desk. He shuffled them around and pulled one out of the pile. "Got a report on that boat. It was tied up on the docks the other night."

"Where is it now?" asked Harry.

"Still there as far as I know."

"Maybe I should go check it out," said Harry.

"Maybe you should stay put," said Bernard. "Did you forget, you're not a detective. You have no license."

Harry frowned. "I know. No work either."

"Second that," said Bernard. "You're done for the day. Don't go back downstairs. Don't go near any suspects. Stay away from Van Dorn. That's an order."

"Yes, sir," said Harry.

"Come back tomorrow," he said softly. "We'll try again. Maybe Van Dorn will cool off by then." He smiled. "How's our girl doing, by the way?"

"Good," said Harry. "She's a natural." He thought about how she slammed Chou against the table. "She has a way of making people open up and talk." He smiled. "She's getting the hang of it."

"That's what I want to hear. Now get out of here, I got work to do. Go back to your office and write me a report so I can justify your time today. I want it first thing in the morning." He looked down at his desk into the pile of papers.

"Okay, Matt." Harry moved towards the door but hesitated.

"Something else?" said Bernard, looking up.

"Any way I can get my car back?"

"Sorry. It's in Impound for now. You need a ride somewhere?"

Harry paused, thinking.

Bernard nodded. "Well?"

"Like you said, I'm out of a job. I was thinking about looking for some work. You know I did some fishing once, and I heard about this boat that was short a few crewmen..."

He started to say more but Bernard raised his hand. "I don't want to know." He looked down at his paperwork. He heard the doorknob turn. "Metro 21 bus goes right past the docks on its way to West Seattle," he mumbled. "Stops a block away on Fourth Street."

Chapter 10

Fodder

Carlos followed the instructions written down on the piece of paper. It was a precise mixture for feed, standard work for someone raised on a farm. It brought back memories of his childhood. There was the exactness of the mixture and the fact that there were three different mixtures, all to be fed to animals on different growth cycles. American agriculture was so far advanced compared to his country. Or maybe it was the fact that he hadn't worked on a farm in a long time. There must have been many advances since his youth.

"Okay," said Carlotta. "Now add it to the oatmeal."

He followed her instructions, pausing to write it down on the piece of paper.

"I'll let you get away with that for now," she said. "But you better have it memorized by tomorrow."

"I think I have it down," he said. "One pound of blessed thistle to one and a half pounds of fenugreek seed."

"One point five six pounds of fenugreek," she corrected.

"One point five six of fenugreek," he repeated.

"Now, you want to mix that in a six to one ratio with the oatmeal, and then you're done with formula number two. Put it in the white bin on the cart."

Carlos followed the instructions. He noticed a pill dispenser mounted to the handle of the cart. "What are these for?" he asked.

"That's domperidone," she said. "They each get one tablet a half an hour before feeding," she said.

"What does it do?" he asked.

"I really don't know," said Carlotta. "Maybe it protects them from diseases."

That would make sense, thought Carlos.

When they were finished with the preparation work there were three different mixtures, one in a red container, one in white, and one in blue. "Fill up the juice jugs," she said. "We give them juice with their pills. By the time we visit all the stalls it is time to start over again, this time with feed. The stalls have a red, white, or blue tag which indicates the type of feed they get. Simple?"

Carlos nodded. He felt comfortable with farming. The work was satisfying and he had a knack for caring for things, plants or animals.

"Finish loading the cart," said Carlotta. "Keep your rubber gloves on and try not to handle the feed too much. When you do, use the measuring cup and pour a level amount of mixture into each bowl."

Carlos did as he was instructed. The cart was prepared and he stood behind the handle ready to push it. Carlotta had her own cart, a large rack on wheels that held empty sterile bottles. She smiled at his eagerness and she swept her hand forward indicating it was feeding time. He pushed the cart down a worn path and through a set of stainless steel double doors marked with a simple sign that read DAIRY.

It was the cleanest barn he had ever seen. It didn't smell like most of the ones he had been in where the air was heavy with the smell of animals, hay, and feces. There were hoses and electrical sockets hanging down from beams that criss-crossed the ceiling. The lighting was bright and cheery. He could feel warm air blowing out of the ducts that ran overhead. He angled the cart around a corner into the first row.

"Start with the juice and pills," said Carlotta. "One cup and one pill each. There are two, sometimes three per stall so get them ready all at once. Makes it go quicker."

Carlos thought it strange, but he filled two cups with juice and dispensed the pills out of the mounted container near the handle of the feeding cart. He turned and peered into the stall.

The floors were concrete, flat and cold, and he didn't see any hay scattered about to absorb droppings. There were bars with a large red tag in a placard mounted at eye level. Below the placard was a shelf with two full bottles of milk sitting in them. Carlotta took them and replaced them with empty ones, putting the full ones on the bottom shelf of the cart. She banged on the bars and something stirred in the dark corners of the stall. He stared at it for a long time before recognizing what he was seeing.

Carlos realized something horrible. It looked like a jail cell, and inside there were two women. The women were ragged and desperate looking, wearing smocks, cropped pants, and shower sandals. They each had a tag in their ear, just like the kind you would find on a dairy cow. He half expected to see a tattooed lip. One of the women came right to the bars, grabbed the juice and pill out of his hands and downed it in one gulp. She held her hand out for the second cup and pill.

"For Gabrielle," she said, indicating the second woman in the cell. She moved aside and Carlos saw the other woman in the corner. She was sitting down, a breast pump pressed to her chest, milk squirting from a tube into a bottle at the other end. She looked up at Carlotta.

"I'm finally producing," said Gabrielle, holding up a half full bottle.

"Good," said Carlotta. "We have to wait for other signs, though. I'll have the doctor come look and maybe he'll approve moving you to the dormitory."

"That would be wonderful," said Gabrielle. She took the pill and juice and did the same thing as her roommate, downing it in a single gulp. "How about food? Can I get something to eat now? I'm hungry."

"You know the rules," said Carlotta. "We'll be back in a half an hour with the feeding cart. Be patient." She motioned to Carlos that it was time to move on to the next stall. Carlos and his world of oatmeal formulas continued on, rolling down the aisle like the good humor man. His mind was reeling and again he felt the insides of his stomach twist. He looked down at the floor, trying to ignore the women in cages. At the next stop it was the same, except this time his hands shook and he had trouble pouring the juice. Carlotta exchanged the milk bottles then reached over and grabbed his arm to steady him.

"It's okay," she said. "The first time I saw this place I had one thought."

"What was that?"

"Thank God I'm on this side of the bars," she said. "For you, I'm afraid it's worse."

"How can it be, I'm a man and I'm already on this side of the bars."

"They told me you were raised a farmer," she said.

"True," said Carlos. "I like the work but this is disturbing."

"Then brace yourself," she said. "The day may come when you have to butcher the livestock."

Chapter 11

Double *Dare Me*

It was a short walk from the bus stop to where the F/V *Dare Me* was tied up. It was ninety six feet of rusting hulk and it smelled of rotting seafood and diesel fuel. Rope was skewed across the deck, spotted with oil, frayed and discolored. It looked like spaghetti that had been splattered with dark brown sauce. There was a stack of crab traps on the stern, spewed about like blocks that a kid had forgotten to put away when done playing. The deck was littered with debris, splinters of wood, and flakes of chipped paint. The sailors on this boat obviously had no pride in their vessel. Either that or the captain was lax on discipline. Harry remembered fishing boats and boats in general being a lot neater. There was a reason for this. A tumble of rope or patch of oil is an accident waiting to happen, especially on a rolling sea.

"Ahoy," he called. "Anybody aboard?" He didn't hear an answer right away so he walked down the short gangplank and stepped on board. The boat rocked under his weight.

Two crewman, every bit as tidy as the boat, stepped out of a passageway and onto the deck. One had a half open shirt covering a set of dirty thermals, the other a pair of greasy brown overalls, a flannel shirt with rolled sleeves and a pair of boots that looked like they were permanently decorated with dried scales and fish blood. They didn't look happy.

"Whatta ya want?" said the one in the boots.

"Is the Captain on board?" asked Harry.

"Who's asking?"

"I'm looking for work. I'm an experienced fisherman and I need a job."

"This boat already has a full crew," said the one in thermals. They started to turn but Harry took a step forward.

"That's far enough," said Boots. Harry glanced down at his arm. The gang symbol glared at him in the sunlight from the rolled up sleeve of the flannel shirt. He caught Harry staring at it and quickly rolled his sleeve down to cover it. The guy in thermals picked up a boathook, the kind used to grab lines or snare big fish so you can drag them on deck. The pole was about four foot long, the curved tip bright and shiny as if the steel tip of the hook had been freshly sharpened.

"Hey," said Harry. He took a step back but remained on the boat. "Just looking for work," he said.

"Then look elsewhere," said Boots. "Told you this boat had a full crew."

"Too bad," he said. "I'm a shrimp shoveling mother fucker." Harry glanced to his side and into the hold. The hatch was open and the inside looked clean, almost brand new, like there hadn't been a fish in it for weeks. It was the only part of the boat that looked clean.

"This ain't no shrimp boat," said the thermals. He took a step forward, his right hand grasping the pole as he tapped it in the palm of his left.

"That's okay," said Harry. "I've worked all kinds of boats, fished for just about everything. Looks like you're getting ready to convert over. I see the traps. Crab season's coming up soon."

"What about it?" asked Boots.

"I can mend traps and splice line." He looked around the deck. "I know how to use a wire brush and paint and varnish. Looks like you could use some help getting ready for season." He noticed that none of the buoys for the traps had any markings on them. Usually there was a number painted there or a tag that indicated the permit number for Fish and Game. It would have been useful information.

"We can handle it," said Thermals. "Now get out of here, you long haired shithead."

A voice called out from the pilot house above. "What's going on there?"

Boots turned. "Look what ya did," he said. "Went and woke the Captain."

A man came out of a door on the top deck wearing a denim shirt and jeans. Harry spotted the same gang symbol on his arm just before he pulled a pea coat over it. He glared at Harry. "What's all this ruckus? I gave you men orders to let me rest."

Boots turned to the Captain and spoke. "Just some swab looking for work."

"I told him we had a full crew," said Thermals.

"Then what's the problem," said the Captain, glaring at Harry.

"Thought you might need some other help," said Harry. "I can repair traps, mend nets, polish and varnish as good as anyone." Harry glanced around, drawing attention to the messy deck.

"That so?" said the Captain. "Got something to say about my boat?"

"No sir," said Harry. "Just thought you needed some help."

"Who sent you?" asked the Captain.

"Nobody," said Harry. "I've been wandering the docks looking for work. Lot of men out of work these days."

"So they say," said the Captain. "Well we ain't looking for any hired hands, so you can go look elsewhere." He turned to go back into the pilot house.

"Are you sure?" asked Harry. He moved around deck, looking into holds and eyeing the winches and machinery. "I could coil this rope for you, straighten out this tackle. Varnish the rub rails and fix these broken traps."

The Captain turned back and faced him. "We like this boat the way it is, don't we?"

The men nodded, growling as they bared their yellow teeth.

"So shove off, and don't come back here for nothing." As if to enforce the Captain's orders, Boots took a step towards Harry. Thermals shifted the boathook from hand to hand, ready to use it.

"Okay, okay," said Harry. "Sorry I asked. You don't know any other boats looking for able bodied men?"

"Let me see your hands," demanded the Captain.

"What?" asked Harry.

"Your hands! Hold them up so I can see them."

Harry held his hands up.

"They look like the hands of a landlubber. I don't see any calluses or cuts. You ain't no fisherman. Shove off!"

"It's been two seasons since I worked on a boat. I've been bagging groceries to get by. Please, if you'll only give me a chance."

"Get out of here before I have you thrown overboard," said the Captain. He turned his back on the whole affair and moved towards the pilot house.

"You heard the Captain," said Boots. "Scram."

"Wait," said Thermals. "What you got there under your coat?"

"Nothing," said Harry.

"Looks like he's got a gun under there," said Boots. He grabbed a hefty belaying pin from a nearby pin rail, holding it at his side like a baseball bat. He took a step towards Harry. "Open her up and let's see what you have there."

The Captain stopped and turned to listen. Thermals beat the hook in the palm of his hand as he stepped forward and stood beside Boots.

"You heard him. Open up your coat and let us have a look," said Thermals. The tip of the hook glistened in the sunlight as he tapped it in his hand.

Harry had seen all he came to see, all he was going to see. He backed away slowly from the scowling crewmen and moved towards the gangplank. "Sorry," he said. "Sorry for disturbing you."

Thermals raised the hook over his head. He was quick with it, and Harry felt a whoosh as he ducked to avoid the deadly tip. He turned sideways as the tip doubled back, this time slashing across his chest. There was a ripping sound as the hook caught his clothes. Harry twisted, the hook jerking him around like a speared mackerel. It ripped free and he stumbled, falling backwards across a pile of loose line scattered across the deck. He fell into a stack of crab traps.

Boots moved in ready to finish him. "Stop," yelled the Captain. "Let him go. I think he got the message. I'll not have some fool getting hurt on my boat."

"Get out of here before I make you really sorry," said Boots, the belaying pin shaking in his hand.

Harry got up and untangled himself from the pile of rope and traps. He held open his jacket, his ripped shirt hanging in fragments underneath. Peeking through the shreds was a bra sporting a well formed pair of 38c's.

Thermals was the first to laugh. The hook dropped to his side and his other hand pointed. Boots, being closer and just as sharp, added his own cackle. The Captain stared in disbelief. "I've seen sailors like you. I run a descent ship here, no place for the likes of you. Now shove off."

"Okay, okay," said Harry. He gathered himself up as dignified as he could, pulling his ripped jacket together to hide his breasts.

Boots leered at him. "Not so fast there." He moved in, blocking Harry's path to the gangplank. He stood defiantly, his hand grabbing his crotch like a gangsta rapper checking his goods. "I know you she-men pack meat, but I wouldn't mind visiting a few of your other love ports. How about you, John? You game for trans-sandwich?"

John nodded his agreement.

The Captain was about to say something. He had his mouth open anyway. Harry studied the deck like a last chance quarterback betting on a game play. The obstacles charted, he made his move. In true quarterback style he faked one direction then sprinted in the opposite. Boots flinched and before he could react Harry was past him. John swung the boathook up and sprang after him, but he tripped over a spaghetti coil of rope and stumbled. He caught himself, looking for a moment like he was going to recover, if it hadn't been for the pool of oil staining the deck. John slid like he was riding a skateboard. He hit the railing and bounced off, stumbling as he went down. The boathook flew from his hand like a loose baton in a twinkle twirler parade. It was all the time Harry needed. He was a jackrabbit running from a coyote, down the gangplank in three bounds and around the corner of the nearest building.

The Captain surveyed the human litter left behind, looking like rag dolls in a jumble of kids toys. "How many times I got to tell you idiots to keep the deck clear and tidy." He shook his head sadly and disappeared into the pilot house.

The two crewmen turned to each other and laughed. Thermals picked himself off the deck and found his boathook among the deck debris. "Too bad about the tranny," he said. "That could have been fun." He hung the hook on the bulkhead near the door to the passageway.

Boots snickered. "I don't know. Would have been fun for a while, but we probably would have caught a disease." He put belaying pin in the pin rail. "Come on," he said. "Let's get back to our game."

Chapter 12

Trophy Room

The door lock clicked in response to the scan of Che's arm tattoo. "Go on," he urged, his hand open as he indicated the way in. "Please."

Sensors lit the hallway as the door swung open. Mandelle gently pushed it and stepped inside, Che close behind him. There was a short flight of stairs. At the top it turned and opened into a hallway. On the walls were numerous trophies, mostly the arms he had harvested and prepared for Che, but there were many things he had not recognized. The arms stretched out from flush mounted boards that could have easily held the heads of elk or deer or other prize animals that had been hunted and killed. They reached upward, the tattoos on the turned forearms facing them, lined like trees along the main road that led to a mansion.

There was a large picture on one wall looking like corporate art. Mandelle studied it closely. It was a patchwork similar to a quilt made of squares of different colors. On close inspection they were pieces of skin, each engraved with a tattoo, sewn into a pattern that spread across the framed ten by five piece in a creepy mosaic. There was a long thin table under it. Che took his latest trophy from Mandelle. The arm of Chinatown Joe's second in command had been freshly made into a stuffed free standing object d' art. He placed it on one end of the table next to an arm that was under a rectangular glass case. He turned it, positioning it to his liking, reading the tiny inscribed plate at the bottom. "Those who follow blindly keep fate at arms length." He turned to Mandelle and laughed.

"I understand the inscription now," said the Doctor.

"These are the arms of the disloyal," said Che. "Those who have left the organization or retired before their time."

There was a doorway at the other end of the hallway. "What's in there?" asked Mandelle.

Che smiled and patted his friend on the back. "Some other time perhaps," he said. "For now, enjoy this."

"This is incredible," said Mandelle. He had wondered what fate his work had met. Chinatown Joe was not the first trophy the Chairman had ordered. Mandelle looked around but he did not see the embalmed and stuffed head he had done a few months ago. Maybe it wasn't for this room, leading him to speculate about what prizes may be behind door number two.

Che saw Mandelle look reverently at the door. "Someday, Klaus," he said. "I promise." He took the doctor by the arm and gently led him to the mysterious door. He held his arm tattoo next to the door lock scanner and it beeped. Che pressed a button down on the keypad controls and displayed his own. It beeped twice. "There," said Che. "I have granted you access to this and the room beyond. There is nothing interesting to see there now, but I promise there will come a day that I walk you through this door."

Mandelle was honored. He didn't know what he had been awarded but he knew it was special. He and Che shared a common sickness, a malady that festers in a soul lacking in humanity. "Thank you Mr. Che." He looked at a pair of eyeballs floating in fluid, resting in mounted spheres on a brightly polished piece of wood. "I was wondering if you would tell me the story behind this delightful item," he said, pointing to them.

Chapter 13

Night Life

Harry headed back to his office by way of the city bus. Bernard wanted a report and he was determined to give him one. The office was locked and empty and it was late. Sue Yen, their self-appointed office assistant, was probably at one of her college classes right now, which was a good thing since they shared a desk and a computer. Two hours later he had enough down on paper to call it a night. Well, it wasn't exactly on paper, that's just a phrase. It was more like having enough electronic bits to attach to an eMail and hit send. He filed his report, turned off the computer and the lights, and locked the office door.

It was dark outside and the ever predictable rain had settled in over the city. He was tired and as the events of the day ran through his head he became sullen. He felt the weight of it all. He wiped his eyes in a damp sleeve, choking back tears that tried to blur his vision. A man was dead. Harry could see his bulging eyes staring back at him, squeezed out by the weight of an old Volvo.

It cascaded in his mind from there. His car, his trusty horse, was gone, impounded by the Seattle PD as evidence. He had worked for them and knew what that meant. He could be on foot for a while. He had ridden the bus all over town and walked until his feet were as tender as expensive, rare cooked steaks. "Get used to it, Harry," he said to no one in particular. He pulled his jacket tighter around him. He told himself it was to fight off the misty rain that had come up suddenly, but it also hid the ripped clothes underneath.

There's a saying in Seattle: if you don't like the weather, wait an hour. Harry had lived through a number of Northwest days that included rain, hail, wind, blinding sunshine, and even snow, all within a matter of hours. There's no season for this phenomenon either, it could just as easily happen in July as in January. The common defense against this cornucopia of meteorology is the Columbia-type sports jacket, or some such similar outerwear. Seattleites rarely carry umbrellas, it's some kind of cultural thing to invite the weather, which is mostly rain, inside your space rather than fight it. Seems more natural. After a while you get used to it and ignore it, about as annoying as insects buzzing around you on a summer night. At least you're outside, and it doesn't do any good to complain about the weather because no one is listening.

Despite the damp night, the streets were full of happy people. Capitol Hill came to life after dark. Harry passed by coffee shops and bars packed tight with crowds of revelers. Conversation peppered with laughter floated outside where it dripped onto the sidewalk and mixed with the rain. He turned a corner and the wind whipped open his jacket. The torn shirt shook in the breeze like a set of Tibetan prayer flags and the air chilled his chest around the exposed bra. A couple waiting at the crosswalk caught a glance and gave him a curt smile. He replied with a sheepish look, feeling exposed, caught naked at the podium and it's not a dream. The ridicule aboard the *Dare Me* drove it home and made him feel freakish. He was glad he lived nearby.

He turned at the entrance of the Binkley Arms, his name for the old building that was owned by his landlord and friend, Binky, aka William Binkley. He walked up the steps of the decaying apartment building, his calves aching with the effort, his feet throbbing with every step. Six floors up he slipped the key into the lock and opened the door.

"Welcome home, Harry," he said to himself, pushing the door to his apartment closed behind him. He shook the wetness from his coat, stopping to squeeze part of the sleeve over the sink. "How was your day?" He spoke in a mock voice, a politeness usually reserved for such questions. He threw the keys on the kitchen counter and emptied his pockets.

"Oh, just wonderful, Harry," he said, answering himself. "I got to watch a man get squeezed to death today."

"What was that like?" he asked himself.

"Oh, only the most gruesome thing I've seen since the war." With the mention of those words a floodgate pressed against his inner walls, threatening to overtop them. He tended to forget about his war experiences. Memories of blown up body parts and bloody battlefields filled his mind.

"Interesting," he said out loud, trying to rub the vision from his eyes. He shook his head as if he could flick it off like the evening rain. "Come on Harry," he said. "Don't focus on the down side of the workday. Look at the plus side, our girl Red is doing a great job at questioning witnesses."

Harry laughed to himself. "She is," he said, his voice reverting back to normal. He went to the refrigerator and got a glass of water. "It's been a long day. Lots of questions." He took a drink of water and sniffed the air. "Home smells good. Something smells good." He turned and walked into the bedroom, startled by a girl lying on his bed.

"I thought you were in class," he said.

"Class was over hours ago," said Sue Yen. Her head angled as she looked at him with a curious eye. "Do you always talk to yourself?"

"Yeah," said Harry. "Doesn't everyone?"

"I don't," said Sue. "Have you considered getting a dog?"

"I like talking to myself," said Harry. "It's how I work things out. Helps me take something inside and make it tangible, put it in words I can sort of understand. Ever have a feeling you're trying to describe, something pulling at you deep inside? Try talking to yourself. Brings it out, makes it real."

Sue shook her head, her lips curling into a smile. "You're deep honey." She paused. "Deep. Deep. Deep. You know, you don't have to talk to yourself. You can talk to me."

"Why drag you down?" he said.

She eyed his shirt, the bra peeking out between the ragged tears from the hook. "From the looks of it you had a bad day." She got up and crossed the floor, putting her arms around him and giving him a slight squeeze. She gently removed his jacket. It was wet and heavy with rain and she hung it up in the bathroom. Then she came back for the shirt. She took it off slowly, as if she were diffusing a bomb, gentle and slow. "You won't be wearing this again," she said, tossing it towards the waste can in the corner. She missed and it landed beside in a heap. Instead of picking it up she ran her hands across his stomach, then moved to his back. She undid the bra and she heard him sigh. She kissed him gently on the shoulder while she ran her hands across the muscles in his arms.

He felt uneasy, nervous, like a nerd at the school dance.

She sensed something, let it go and gave him a peck on the cheek.

Harry stared at her. She was wearing a short dress, sleeveless and full of color, out of place in the black fashion world that held most of Seattle captive. She smelled like fresh air after a hard rain, clean and new and healthy. He couldn't help but breathe in every part of her. Something moved inside him, something he had no words for. He pulled her toward him and kissed her back. She invited it, an appetite that could not be sated. Her muscles relaxed and she felt weak. Her right foot came off the floor and she sagged in his arms. His scalp tingled. He was about to slip into numbing passion when something stopped him. Her foot dropped, a hammer against the anvil floor.

"We should be careful," he said, holding her close while pushing her away. "I hear office romance is bad for business."

"That would be true if I ever saw you around the office," she said, both feet on the ground again. "It's a pretty empty place these days." She pulled away from him, confused, but she had decided long ago to let this relationship go at its own pace.

"No clients busting the door down?"

"Bernard called, and Lenny of course. Nothing you don't already know about."

He gave her another kiss. "Thanks for helping me out," he said. "I never realized how helpful it would be to have someone at the office during office hours."

"That was Rita's idea. She's pretty good at business. It's nice how you let her do what she wants."

"She does a better job of managing the money than I ever did. We're all getting regular paychecks, enough to get by at least. And look at you! I'm so proud of you handling all those skip traces."

She beamed like a cocker spaniel. "Rita set up the direct connection on our computer and got me access to some of the law enforcement systems. I do ninety percent of the work from my desk and the rest over the phone." Her voice got somber. "It's about all we have going for us, Harry. Not a lot of business coming in the door or the internet." She stood before him, sad and ashamed. "I have plenty of time to study."

Harry touched her cheek. "Hey, don't worry. You just keep studying. Rita and I just got some temporary work with the city. Ought to help a lot, get us through this month at least."

She covered his hand with hers, smelling the scent of his skin. "Why are we talking about the office?"

"I don't know. Let's change the subject. I'd like to know what you're doing in my bed. And how did you get in here?"

"One question at a time, babe," she said. She rubbed her cheek against the back of his hand and let it go. "First, I got in here with a key."

"You have a key to my apartment?"

"Momma does," she said. "I could have gotten one from Binky, but Momma keeps one for emergencies. She gave it to me, sent me to check up on you. Her witch's sense told her you're in trouble. I see she was right."

Harry groaned. He had helped Mrs. Lee out many times and she repaid him in food, kindness, and free medical attention. Sue Yen, her daughter, always seemed to be part of that formula, but he suspected Mrs. Lee had other reasons for throwing them together.

"I do what Momma says," said Sue. "We've had this conversation before. Let's just skip to the part where I actually do what Momma says."

"And what did Momma say to do?" asked Harry.

She raised her voice, speaking with a heavy accent like her mother. "You bathe, clean body, check wounds. Two cups of tea. Change dressings." They both laughed. She moved closer. "Seems like you're okay. Your shirt is ripped but I don't feel any fresh scars." She turned him around and around, running her fingers across his skin, seeing if she could find them by memory. As her arms reached around him, her fingers glanced across his breast. He retreated. "Hey," she said. "Sorry."

He looked wounded. "It's okay. They're just sensitive."

"I keep forgetting that you have them," she said. "The oversized shirts hide them pretty well." She smiled, trying to make him feel comfortable again. "They're nice breasts," she said. "It's okay. I've seen them before. Nurse training, remember?"

She tried hard not to stare at his naked breasts, but something fascinated her about it. The whole idea was incredibly bizarre. In the end, she found that breasts or no breasts, he was still Harry Takanawa, the kid she knew from the neighborhood who always looked in on her mom and ran errands for them. He loved Mrs. Lee's cooking, especially her kway teow and he was always polite when he came for dinner. And then he grew up into this war hero, and then a decorated police veteran and now a private detective. One of his first cases was for her mom. Mrs. Lee lost touch with Sue and was worried, her old school witch's sense alerting her to trouble. It didn't take long for Harry to find her holed up in a Tacoma meth house with her brutal boyfriend. It took him even less time to rescue her.

She rubbed his shoulders deeper. "How did your meeting go today?" she asked.

Harry cringed. "I killed a man with the Volvo. Watched him die before my eyes."

"You ran him over?" she asked.

"We fought," said Harry. "I was parked on a hill. He got trapped when the Volvo slipped a gear and it rolled forward. It squeezed him to death against a parked truck." He sat down on the side of the bed and buried his face in his hands. "I can't get the image of his bulging eyes out of my mind."

Sue Yen pulled his hands away from his face. "It's just the PTSD, honey," she said. "The Post Traumatic Stress Disorder. It makes you feel distant and disassociated. It kills your self-esteem. You told me all about what you went through in the war. Now that you're home and out of the Marines, you go and become a detective, looking at dead bodies and seeing all the sick things people do. And if that isn't enough, you go and get kidnapped by some madman who tortures you, cuts you open, and sticks exploding breast implants in you." She ran her hands across his back and petted his hair gently. "You've had a rough year, sweetie."

"I have," he agreed.

"Give yourself a break about this Volvo thing. It sounds like an accident."

"It was," said Harry.

"Then take it at face value and move on," she said. "Meanwhile, finish getting undressed. I'm going to do what Momma sent me here to do." She went into the kitchen and put a tea kettle on the burner, took a large cup out of the cupboard and placed her mother's tea ball filled with herbs in it. Then she filled a large pot with hot water. She took a washcloth from a cabinet and swirled it in the pot with some soap and carried it back to the bedroom. It wasn't the first time Harry had benefited from her nurse's training. She was an expert at sponge baths.

"Nice breasts," she said.

"You said that before," he said.

"It's worth repeating. They're nice breasts. Mind if I touch them?"

He laughed at the question. "Go ahead. Why not?" he said. She dipped the washcloth in the warm soapy water and gently passed it over his skin. He began to feel the tension of the day finally fade. He let out a deep sigh. "I'm really confused these days."

"I'm not," she said. "As long as one of us isn't, I figure everything's okay."

"It's just that I feel uncomfortable with these breasts," he said.

"Do you think I feel comfortable with these?" she asked, thrusting her rack in his face. "There's not a woman I know that doesn't see something wrong with herself, and breasts are only the beginning."

"I'm getting used to the stares and the comments," he said. "People have a problem with gender blur. It's like they want me to decide if I want to be a man or a woman." He looked into her eyes. "They don't know that I've already decided I'm a man."

"Don't I know it," she said. She reached down, swabbing his crotch with warm, soapy water.

"It's just that I'm a man who likes to wear woman's clothes," he said.

"Why don't you just dress like a woman all the time then?" she said. "I know you like that. Seems like everyone would be happy then. No one at the office would have a problem with it, especially me. And you won't have to hide those beautiful breasts."

Harry took a deep breath. Uncomfortable. Time to change the subject again. "Why do you come around here, Sue? You know I'm married."

"You can't call what you have a marriage, especially when your wife continually corrects everyone. She makes no secret of letting everyone know that you're her ex."

He laughed. "She sure does, but inside I think she knows better."

"You are some kind of romantic, aren't you?"

"I try," he said. "So, answer my question. Why do you come around?"

"You saved me, Harry. Saved me from a life of drugs and beatings from a brutal boyfriend. I love you for that." She kissed him, holding his chin so he couldn't escape.

"Is that the only reason?"

"Isn't it reason enough? I know one day you'll come out of your funk and maybe take notice of me. I've been here your whole life."

"You're ten years younger than me, Sue."

"Seven," she said. "But who's counting. Look, I know your wife has issues with your cross dressing, but I don't care."

The tea kettle blew and she dropped the washcloth back into the pot of warm, soapy water. She went into the kitchen, poured the tea and brought it back into the bedroom, placing the cup on the nightstand next to the bed. "It's too hot to drink," she said. "Let it cool a minute." She picked up the soapy washcloth, squeezed the excess into the pot and began rubbing him again. "I think you should be Fu Chan all the time," she said. "What's the Fu Chan Detective Agency without a Fu Chan?"

Harry thought about it. "That would be fun," he said. She heard the false enthusiasm in his voice.

"It would," she said, her voice lilting upward, reassuring him that it would be fun. "What's it like being her?"

"Fu Chan?" The question caught him by surprise.

"Yeah," she said. "I imagine it's like having a secret identity. Like Clark Kent and Superman, Bruce Wayne and Batman, Peter Parker and Spiderman. Fu Chan is definitely a superhero."

Harry hadn't heard it that way. "She is, I guess. Except every one of those heroes ended in *man*."

"Excuse me," she said. "Maybe I should have said Linda Danvers and Supergirl, or Barbara Gordon and Batgirl." She stopped, noticing they all ended in *girl*. "Okay. How about Diana Prince and Wonder Woman or Selina Kyle and Catwoman?" She purred, her body arching like a kitten as she smiled at Harry.

He couldn't help but laugh. Sue Yen had a passion for life and it was catching. He reached out and hugged her, as if he could squeeze another helping of passion juice out of her.

"What's wrong with Fu Chan and Harry Takanawa?" she asked. "Seems like you'd want to be her all the time."

"Even though I'm a man?" he asked.

"A man can do anything he wants in this country, anything he works toward. Why not be Fu Chan? Other men work hard to become women. You're not the first. Ru Paul's made a fortune out of being a woman. And he did it by being true to himself."

Harry sighed and looked down at the floor. "I'd like to be Fu Chan," he admitted. "But I can't. Fu Chan is a fantasy life. I have a real life."

"There's nothing wrong with a little fantasizing," she said, wrapping her arms around him and planting another kiss on his lips.

"Fantasies can get dangerous, Sue," he said. "People can become jaded, even trapped in their fantasies."

"I'd love to see you trapped in my fantasy." She dipped the washcloth in the pot and squeezed it out. "Oh," she said, looking down at his crotch. "Seems I'm not the only one thinking about fantasies." She reached down and gently squeezed. "You asked me before what I was doing in your bed. I think it's time you found the answer to that question."

Chapter 14

But I Didn't Have Breakfast Yet

Bernard set the phone back in the cradle and got up from behind his desk. "Thank you both for coming in early today, and thanks for the report you eMailed me last night Harry. I read it over. Read your reports too Rita. Good work, both of you."

"Thanks," said Harry. Rita just beamed her usual smile, her eyes sparkling like gems turning in the bright sunlight.

"Got something else for you, Matt," said Harry. "I toured a fishing boat yesterday after I left your office."

"Not the *Dare Me*?"

Harry nodded.

Bernard frowned. "Harry, sometimes you ignore all the rules about police procedure."

"You told me yesterday, no police business, no detective work." Harry looked off to the side. "Besides, I have no license. I figured I was out of a job, so I went looking for a gig aboard a fishing boat. I used to be good at fishing."

Bernard's frown turned into a smile. "Did you catch anything?"

"There is something fishy about that boat," said Harry.

Bernard winced.

"Sorry," said Harry. He cleared his throat. "She has all the looks of a dilapidated fishing boat, but here are the facts. It was three in the afternoon and the Captain was asleep."

"So," said Bernard. "Lots of boats go night fishing."

"True, but I think he was resting up from the night before," said Harry. "What time did you say that raid went down on the docks?"

"About 3 A.M.," said Bernard.

"Okay," said Harry. "More facts. If she was out fishing, then why didn't I see any Fish and Game tags on the buoys? I also got a look at the hold where they dump the catch. It was clean. I don't just mean clean, there wasn't an inch of slime anywhere. It was the cleanest part of the boat."

"Maybe they just got through washing it down," said Rita.

"Okay, so they cleaned the hold but didn't bother to stack the traps, stow the line, or even sweep the deck." He shook his head. "Uh, huh. This crew didn't look like the sort to do much work. They were busy playing some kind of game when I came aboard."

"Okay," said Bernard. "Go on."

"I met the Captain and two of the crew. I saw that gang tattoo you're so interested in on both the Captain's arm and one of the crewmen," he said. "I'm betting the third man had the same tattoo. I didn't get a peek because he had on long sleeves. Also, once I got a glimpse of the tats, they both rolled their sleeves down and hid them."

Bernard nodded, taking it all in. "Anything else?"

Harry shook his head.

"If Van Dorn asks about yesterday, I chewed you out and gave you the afternoon off. Got it?" The both nodded. Bernard's phone rang. The lieutenant spoke a few words, then hung up the phone. "Now, before you go back to questioning witnesses I want you to take a little ride with me."

"Me too?" asked Red.

Bernard laughed. She was eager as ever. "Yeah. Me too." he said.

"I thought Van Dorn wanted to see Rita by nine thirty," Harry said.

"He will. This is a short ride and it won't take long."

The door read *Emergency* but Harry knew the minute they pulled into the parking garage at Harborview Medical Center that they were going to visit the medical examiner.

Quinton Warrington had seen better days. He didn't start out in life wanting to be a coroner; it was a career he sort of stumbled into. Bernard was glad he did, he was a good detective and an excellent evidence technician. The job was making him old before his time and he knew it. Quinton was 38 going on 50. After a curt handshake he retreated into his office and passed the show on to Leah Spoelman, the latest in a long line of assistants that he hoped would find the same passion in this job that he did.

At least Quinton had taste. Leah was just as beautiful as his last assistant. She had long auburn hair, captivating eyes, and a smile that had a touch of cynicism to it. It was the way it turned up at the end on one side giving her a wry kind of look. She was dressed professionally, a thin white top, short grey skirt with a perfect pair of legs that stretched down to her stiletto heels. She made a lab coat look sexy, but Harry thought she was the kind of woman who could make anything look good.

She had them don gloves and follow her. "These are the dead bodies your team sent over from the raid the other night," she said, opening four drawers and sliding out the meat racks. "You boys need to play nice together. I don't need all this business."

"Thanks for the commentary, Leah." Bernard looked them over quickly and singled one out. "Over here," he said.

Leah was sharp. She saw Bernard examining the tattoo on the forearm, honing right in to his main point of interest. Harry was just as observant. "So this is why we came on this little field trip. A chance to examine these tats up close and personal."

The Lieutenant gave him a look that said it all. This trip was all business. "What do you make of this?" he asked, pointing to the tattoo on the body.

"This guy over here has one too," said Rita, staring down at a lifeless arm. She pulled a pencil and a small notebook out of her pocket and began taking notes.

"That's definitely not ink," said Harry. "This is too perfect looking. Looks like it was all done at once."

Leah's smile curled a little more. "Go on," she said.

"Branding iron?" he asked.

"No," said Leah. "I checked that. No evidence of iron filings, no metal particulates. The scar tissue would have been different, more like a burn."

"It's so perfect, it looks like a machine made it," said Harry. He bent over to study it closer. "Just look at the design. It's precise and intricate." He looked up at Leah who was studying his rear and not the subject. He straightened up. "Ink is sloppy, it's drawn on like art, and it fades, especially when it's on the forearm like this one. This tat looks as fresh as the day it was made." He ran his fingers over the marking. "Wow," he said. "Feel this."

Red was the first one to reach across the table and give it a try. It felt different, like something familiar. She kept passing her fingers across it like a blind woman reading a Braille novel. "It's raised, almost like an embossed business card."

"How about a laser?" said Harry.

Leah nodded. "You're good," she said. "That's exactly the conclusion I came to."

"A laser?" said Bernard, his voice betraying his disbelief. "What makes you say that?"

"A design with this much detail could only be done by a laser," she said. "Two lasers, actually, simultaneously focused on a single point. A single laser would char the skin, and that skin is not charred."

"You're good, too," said Harry.

Leah beamed. "You're right about it being made all at once, like a branding iron. It also looks like the intensity was quite painful. The raised skin is actually scar tissue."

"Do you think the machine that did this was designed to do that? Be painful, I mean?" asked Harry.

"No doubt," said Leah.

"Do you have any pictures of it that I can have? I didn't bring my camera," said Harry.

"Honey, I'll cut it off and mount it in an embroidery hoop if you want."

"Hold on Harry. You're not allowed to collect evidence," said Bernard. "Remember? No police business." He turned to Leah. "And you're not allowed to destroy evidence." Then he murmured something under his breath. It came out like, "Mumble, mumble. Cut it off. Humph!"

"I was only joking," said Leah. "Why would I slice it off? That would change the look. The skin holds moisture. Once you cut the skin it dries out fast."

"Sorry." Bernard looked chastened. "I forget you have a highly developed sense of humor down here."

She continued, her voice all business. "I don't have a picture," she said. "But I have a plaster cast of it in the other room." She looked at Bernard. "It's the least intrusive and damaging procedure and it preserves evidence."

Leah stood up straight. The heels, the crisp lab coat, the long hair. It all added up to an impressive sight. She held their attention. "This man lived in the sun, worked hard, and ate a lot of seafood," she said. "Smoked cigarettes, chewed his inner lip, had a mild case of gout, and is missing two fingers recently. What else do you want to know?"

They were all quiet and she looked them over like a school marm getting ready to correct an unruly class. Finally she smiled, her wry smile that made everything good again. Rita went back to studying the other body. Bernard nodded his head in respect. He'd have to keep an eye on Leah Spoelman. He'd have to tell Quint that this one's a keeper.

"Okay, then," she said, moving to one of the open drawers. "You can stay as long as you want, look all you want. I'll be over here prepping this one for med school if you have any more questions."

"What do you mean?" asked Harry. "Prep him for med school?"

"Medical cadavers," she said. "We pass the John Does and the Organ Donors to the Medical College at U Dub, but they have to be processed and prepared first. Bodies can get mold, there can be no cross contamination. Organs have to be removed for disease and notes left for the students. Makes extra work on our part but saves the college hundreds of thousands of dollars."

"What do you mean?"

"Cadavers are expensive," said Leah. "They can cost upward of twenty thousand dollars apiece. And every med student needs one." She looked him in the eye. "Or don't you agree with the program?"

"Oh, I agree," he said. "Anything to bring down the skyrocketing cost of education. What's the name of your program?"

"It doesn't have a name, but I was thinking of 'Fresh Meat for Freshmen' or 'Doctor, Take My Body'. Why? You know a celebrity spokesperson looking for a cause?" Leah moved closer and sniffed Harry. "You've had sex recently," she said. "I can still smell her on you."

Bernard was inspecting another body. He overheard Leah and looked up, arching his eyebrows. Red stopped what she was doing. She leaned forward and sniffed her boss. Harry backed away.

"Don't be shy about it," said Leah. "It makes you more attractive to me when I smell another woman on you. Don't know why. I'm not the only women to feel that way."

"How about me?" asked Red. "How do I smell?"

"Back off babe," said Leah. "I only like men."

"Too bad. Thought we had something in common."

"I doubt it," said Leah.

"I work weekend nights at the Rose Hips as a bouncer. I thought I saw you there once or twice."

"That lesbian bar up on Capitol Hill?" asked Leah. "Yeah. Maybe once. Okay, maybe a few times. They have great Cosmopolitans there."

"Best les bar in Seattle," said Red.

"And you're the bouncer, you say?" asked Leah.

"I like fist fighting and cunnilingus," said Red. She gave Leah the once over. "If you ever change your mind."

"Yeah, yeah," said Leah. "I know where to find you. I'll bring my boxing gloves." She stared at Harry. "You have an interesting mind," she said. "What else do you have?" Her eyes scanned his front, settling on his crotch where it gave Harry an unsettling feeling.

He didn't know how to act. "I have tits," he blurted.

"Yeah, yeah. I noticed," she said. "So did my last boyfriend. Yours are nicer. Besides, I wasn't interested in your tits." She looked him up and down again. "Or do you like boys?"

"Women only," said Harry. "But I have to warn you, I'm married."

Leah sniffed. "So, it's your wife I smelled on you?"

Harry looked guilty, his eyes breaking contact with hers. Bernard looked over and arched another eyebrow. "I thought so," said Leah.

Red cleared her throat. "This one over here has the same tattoo," she said.

Leah continued to look at Harry while she spoke to Red. "Close, with a subtle difference. This is the sixth laser tat I've seen since I started work here."

"Do you have plaster casts of those?" asked Bernard.

"Something better," she said. "Cross stitch."

"Cross stitch," said Harry.

"Hey, everyone has a hobby," she said. "Mine is cross stitch. Except I don't like those American Sampler things you get at the craft store. I think cadaver tats are much more interesting."

"What other hobbies do you have?" asked Harry.

"Why don't you come to my hobby house and I'll show you," she said.

Sexiest lab coat he had ever seen.

"We don't need the plaster casts," said Rita. She had been busy. Using a piece of paper and a pencil, she had made a rubbing of each of the tattoos in her little notebook. She held them up, comparing them through the paper. They were so similar, yet each one was slightly different.

"The big redhead is right," said Leah. "There are subtle differences. They look alike at first glance, but each tat is different." She pointed to the design and a smaller, more intricate design inside it. "It's unique."

"Almost like an identity chip," said Harry. "I wonder if it can be read like a bar code."

"Whoa," said Leah. "That's creepy. Like the end of the world and the antichrist. Six six six." She stood there, perfect posture, a runway model with the fall cadaver line, what all the trendy coroners are wearing these days.

"This is something new," said Bernard. "This is some kind of new gang tat that we've never seen."

"This is nothing new, Lieutenant," said Leah. "That tat you saw wasn't fresh. My guess is it was at least five years old."

"Five years!" said Bernard. "How is that possible."

"Want to review my evidence? I got microscans, scar tissue progressions, chromatography, same analysis I ran on all the tattoos. I can tell you within a month the date these guys were burned."

"Five years?" said Bernard again, the disbelief heavy in his voice. "Why are we just now seeing this?"

"Maybe they just moved into this area," said Red.

Leah added. "Maybe the gang has some kind of funky body disposal rules, something that destroys the evidence along with the body. You haven't seen this because the gang makes sure the members are properly retired."

Harry spoke up. "My guess is they've been around a while, operating out of our sight. We happened to disrupt whatever they were doing on the dock the other night. Caught them by surprise. If we hadn't done that they could easily continue working without our knowledge."

"Okay," said Leah. "That would make sense. But there's one more body that came in with the mark. He wasn't part of this group from the docks." She closed two of the open drawers to get access to one below. Harry watched as she bent over and reached for the handle. She stopped, turning her head to catch his eye with a smile. She slowly slid the drawer open.

Bernard broke up the party. "Look, we don't have a lot of time. We need to get back to the station. Let's pack up and get out of here."

"I want to see what she has to show us," said Harry.

Bernard glanced at his watch. "Hurry it up then. I got a meeting in fifteen minutes and we need to leave."

Quinton came out of his office. "Well, how'd my new assistant do?" he asked.

Bernard smiled. "She's a keeper, Quint. Thanks, as always. Appreciate you giving me a call on this one."

Quinton nodded. "It always amazes me."

Bernard looked puzzled. "What do you mean?"

"You know. You talk to the living, the survivors, the suspects, the witnesses, but often it's the dead who have the most to tell us."

Bernard nodded as Red came up beside him.

There was an audible gasp from across the room, and a wincing sound, as if someone had just stepped on a small dog. Leah released the handle of the drawer and stood up, staring at Harry. His face was contorted, twisted with lines that etched his face with horror, pain, and surprise.

Staring up at him from the bottom drawer was Manny Ballston, his eyelids shut but unmistakably bulging. His arm laid bare, the burn mark of the gang tattoo glaring black and red against his mottled blue skin. His right finger was frozen, pointing at Harry as if to say, "You're the one. You're the one who put me here."

Chapter 15

Irritating Small Dogs

"Where have you been all morning?" barked Van Dorn. He had all the charm of a purse dog yapping at you. Add his spit stroking hair routine and it's almost the same thing.

"We were with Bernard checking out something at the coroner's office," said Harry. They were standing near a bank of desks outside Bernard's office. Harry set down a small stack of paperwork he was scanning. "We were just finishing up. Getting ready to file this."

Van Dorn scowled. "Did you finish your interviews this morning?" he asked Red.

"We haven't started yet," said Red.

"We're behind schedule," said Van Dorn.

"Not because of us," said Harry. "Rita conducted six interviews yesterday and submitted the last of the paperwork on them just a moment ago. How many did your guys do?"

"That is irrelevant. I'm only interested in what you are doing," he said. He began to launch into some dialog about it all but Harry wasn't listening. All he heard was "Yip, yip, yap," similar to the sound a Pekinese makes when it wants to be irritating. Bernard came out of his office and stood behind him and signaled Harry. He seemed to be hearing the same "Yip, yip, yap" that Harry was.

"What's your problem Van Dorn?" said Bernard, putting a stop to the barking menace.

"What's yours?" he fired back. "I'm trying to figure out why you diverted my resources from their assigned tasks this morning." He looked sure of himself as he licked his hand and pressed the hair flat against the back of his head.

"First of all, they are people, not resources," said Bernard. "Second, if you want to get technical, they are my resources under my contract on loan to you. That being said, they will follow my priorities when I direct them to. Unless you have a contract that says otherwise?"

Franklin didn't know what to say. "What was so important that you needed them?" he asked.

"You're office isn't the only one conducting investigations at this time. I have my own information and leads to track down. I needed Harry and Red to evaluate some evidence at the coroner's office. I took them there because it's safer than bringing the evidence here. Easier, too."

"I get that, Lieutenant," said Van Dorn.

"Good."

They both stood staring at each other, a yip dog versus a bulldog. It was obvious Van Dorn would be the first to back off.

"Can I have them back if you no longer need them?" he asked.

"Yes," said Bernard. "But you have to say pretty please first." He said it in the most serious, authoritative voice Harry had ever heard.

"What?"

Harry watched as Van Dorn's lip quivered. Bernard was tight lipped as he waited for a reply. Van Dorn said nothing and Bernard motioned for his people to come with him. "Wait!" said Van Dorn, mumbling something under his breath.

"What was that?" asked Bernard. "Louder, I don't think I heard you."

"Pretty please."

Bernard smiled. "See, now. That wasn't hard." He turned to Red. "Rita, would you please help the head of The Urban Research Department with whatever he has for you to do today. Report back to me when you're finished and I will see you get credit for the work time."

Van Dorn waited for him to say more. "What about Fu?" he asked.

"Mr. Takanawa has something else to do and I can't spare him at the moment," said Bernard. "Besides, yesterday you complained about him, so I have temporarily suspended him from working with you."

"Will I get him back?" asked Van Dorn.

"Not without the magic word," snorted Bernard.

Van Dorn started to say something. Before he could spit it out, Bernard interrupted him. "Sorry. Not today. Try again tomorrow."

Van Dorn looked at Rita. "Is she clear to work alone?"

"Yes," he said.

"She doesn't need to be watched anymore?" asked Van Dorn.

Bernard stared back at him. "Not unless you want to watch her, which might not be a bad idea considering the report Mr. Takanawa filed." He squinted at Van Dorn, angling his head to the side. "Have you read her reports? You might learn something from her."

Van Dorn fidgeted for a moment, then motioned to Rita. "Come on," he said. "We're wasting time."

Rita turned to Harry. "Will I see you later?"

Harry looked at Bernard. "Maybe," he said. "I'll check in with you either way. Good luck. You'll do fine."

She had her famous million dollar smile on her face again. Rita was simple, she just needed encouragement and guidance. On the other hand, Van Dorn did not respond to encouragement the same way, let alone guidance. It takes all types, thought Bernard.

When they were alone, Harry asked him, "What do you need me for, Matt?"

"Don't know exactly, but I got an emergency call for you on my phone."

"What's it about?"

"Sue is trying to track you down. Says it's important and you should call your office. Also turn your phone on."

Harry checked his pocket. Sure enough, his phone was off. When he hit the 'on' key it flashed and went dead again. "Out of power. Got a phone I can use, Matt?"

"Sure," said the Lieutenant. "Use my office if you want privacy."

"I'm okay out here," he said. He went to a desk and dialed his office.

"Fu Chan Detective Agency," said the voice on the other end.

"It's Harry. What's up Sue?"

"Did Jan Filbert get a hold of you?" she asked.

"Jan Filbert?" he asked, surprised. "You mean my wife's secretary?"

"Ex-wife," corrected Sue.

"Yeah, yeah. What does Jan want?" he asked.

"Trish didn't show up for court this morning. Jan's trying to track her down."

"I haven't seen Trish in a while. She calls every now and then. I think I've seen her once or twice since my surgery."

"Good," said Sue. "And you don't need to see her either, Harry. She's bad for you."

"I agree, but we're still married," said Harry. He thought about how everyone always corrected him by adding –ex, most often Trish. "At least in the eyes of the State we're married."

"Why didn't you get a divorce?" asked Sue. "She's the best divorce lawyer in Bellevue. She could make it happen in a heartbeat."

"I never signed the papers," he said. "I think she quit trying to chase me down."

"You don't have to sign the papers in this state. That's old fashioned."

"Don't I know it," said Harry. "She could've had that divorce any time she wanted."

Sue was quiet for a moment, deciding what to say. "I don't think it's just you, Harry. I've talked to Trish. She's having a hard time letting go."

"What's there to let go of? I'm a sick transvestite that makes her feel like less of a woman than she is. I deserve to be divorced and stuck with a pair of oversized tits for the rest of his life."

A detective looked up from a nearby desk, glanced curiously at Harry, then looked back down at his work.

"My, we're being hard on ourselves this morning," said Sue.

"Just calling it like it is, Sue."

"That's all good, but from what I'm hearing, you're the one with the problem. Besides, I would have thought I raised your self esteem last night. Or was I wrong about that?" She paused, thinking about sex with Harry. "From my perspective, I raised more than that last night."

Harry laughed nervously. "I don't know how to handle you, Sue."

"You knew what to do last night," she said.

"Let's not talk about that right now," he said.

"You sure know how to make a girl feel special," she said. The down turn in her voice was obvious.

"Come on, Sue. I didn't mean it like that. You know what I meant."

"No I didn't, Harry. The least you can do is be sensitive of my feelings."

"I'm sorry, Sue. Like I said last night, I'm just confused. Bear with me while I work through some of this junk. I do appreciate you helping me. I appreciate it a lot."

"It's nice to be appreciated," she said, obviously disappointed.

"I wish I could say more than that," he said. "I know how you feel about me, Sue. You make it perfectly clear." There was an awkward silence. "Did Jan leave her number?" asked Harry.

"Don't you have it on your phone?" she asked.

"My phone's dead," he said.

"So that explains why you didn't call me this morning, all thankful and glowing." Harry was silent. "Or why I keep calling and you don't answer. Okay, let me look up Trish's office on the internet for you." He heard the clicking of keys in the background.

Harry decided to say something. "Thank you, Sue."

The clicking stopped. "For what?"

"For helping me, for being with me," he said. "For talking to me. For validating me as a person. For understanding that I still have Post Traumatic Stress Disorder, for..."

She interrupted him. "Okay, Tiger, that's enough. You had me on 'thanks for being with me'." The charm was back in her voice. She read him the number to Trish's office off her computer screen.

"Is Trish's cell phone number listed on the web?" he asked.

"No," she said. "But wait a minute. I've seen it written down on the blotter on your desk. It's inside a doodled heart that's the dot at the bottom of a big question mark." She set the phone down, moved her keyboard, and got the number for him.

"That's it," he said. "Thanks."

"Call me later with your plans," she said. She wanted to add 'see you tonight?' but something stopped her. She heard the phone disconnect and she slowly dropped hers back in the cradle. She looked over at her microbiology book, scanned the empty office, and slowly cracked the book open.

Harry dialed Jan who picked up on the third ring. "Harry, thank God you called," she said. "Have you seen Trish?"

"I haven't seen her in months," said Harry.

"Heard from her? Maybe she left you a message on your cell phone?"

"My cell phone's dead," said Harry. "When did you see her last?"

"Yesterday," said Jan. "She had a clear schedule for once. Said she was going shopping for some clothes. I called on the off chance that you might have gone with her."

"I see," he said. "Shopping with her drag queen husband?"

Jan apologized. "I didn't mean it like that," she said. "I'm just trying to track her down. It's not like Trish to miss a court date."

"No, it's not," said Harry. "I'll check the police reports."

"I did that already," said Jan. "Also checked her apartment and called the hospitals. No luck."

The wheels began to turn in Harry's head. Feed his head a mystery and watch it work. "Did she say what store she was going to?"

"No," said Jan. "But I saw some ads on her desk from Macy's and Nordstrom's."

Harry laughed. "Trish shops there but more often she buys at the bargain stores. She really loves to stretch that clothing dollar."

"I know," said Jan laughing. "She told me how she introduced you to Cross Dress for Less."

Harry took it like a punch. "You mean Ross?"

Jan had used the name Trish called it. "Yes," she said meekly. "Look, Harry. You're a detective. Can you help me find her?"

"I'm working on a case right now, Jan. I can't drop everything because Trish missed a court date. Have you tried her other boyfriends?"

"She doesn't have any boyfriends," she said. "As far as I know, you were the last person she slept with."

That was far from the image Harry had in his head. "No boyfriends?"

"Come on," said Jan. "She's the Bellevue bitch, the most dangerous shark in the divorce aquarium. Men hate her."

Harry felt like he had been punched in the heart. Old feelings began to stir. "Okay, Jan," he said. "I'll help you track her down her."

When he hung up the phone Bernard was standing over him. "You look like you were just hit with a baseball bat," he said.

"Worse, Matt. Lovestruck."

"Not that cutie minding your office?" he asked.

"Wish it was," said Harry. "Trish is missing."

"What do you mean missing?"

"She missed a court date," said Harry.

"That doesn't mean she's missing," said Matt. "Maybe she had a flat tire or a problem with the plumbing and had to stay home."

"She would have called in. She's missing," said Harry. He touched his heart. "I feel it."

Matt had seen this obsession before, the look in Harry's eye, the earnestness in his voice. Harry got on a track sometimes and it was hard to derail him. He'd think of nothing else until he solved this puzzle about Trish. Matt suspected something deeper, that Trish held the keys to Harry's self-esteem. This was a chance for Harry to find something more than his missing ex-wife.

"Okay," said Bernard. "If you need some time to look for Trish, go ahead. Just remember, you're not a detective. You have no license. You're just a husband out looking for his wife."

Harry was relieved. "Thanks, Matt." He began to scoop up papers and notes.

"And don't forget. Put some thought into this tattoo thing. I still expect you to read Rita's reports and help me with this mess. I got lawyers and Feds breathing down my neck to release some of these guys. I need thorough work. Call me if you think of something. You're still on my payroll."

"Okay," said Harry. "Thanks."

Harry turned to leave but Matt put his arm on his shoulder. "Where you going to start?"

"Last thing Jan said was she went shopping. Also, she might have left a message on my cell phone. I won't know until I go home and recharge my phone."

"Be careful," said Bernard.

"What's there to worry about? Trish was never the type to attract trouble."

"I'm not worried about you getting hurt physically," said Matt. He patted Harry's shoulder, then his heart. "I've seen Trish maul you worse than any thug you went up against."

Harry had to agree. "Okay, Matt. Thanks. I'm just going to stop off at home, make a few cell phone calls, check out a few stores. If I don't call you by the end of the day it means everything's okay and I'll see you tomorrow morning."

Bernard had that old sinking feeling. "Right," he said.

Chapter 16

Shark Cage

Trish looked through the bars again. There was nothing to see but a blank wall. She had visited clients in jail but she had never been in prison herself. So this is what it feels like.

"No, it isn't" she said. "I'm innocent."

Her lips turned down. How many times had she heard that from somebody? For that matter, was she innocent? How many times had she destroyed somebody's happiness in the name of winning a case? Every divorce was settled from the debris a broken marriage. She knew it was a dangerous profession, more than once an irate husband or damaged child had found her, spewing angry words at her like a scatter gun. It was a dirty business.

Then again, her clients came to her. It wasn't like she was an ambulance chaser scouring the hospitals for the next case. Couples brought the debris and misery on themselves. She only got involved when they needed legal help out of the mess they created. All she did was hang out a shingle and wait for people to show up at her doorstep. How easy was that?

Too easy! Did she think she could escape the collateral damage? If you handle explosives long enough you're bound to get hurt. Like a kid playing with firecrackers, it was the law of odds. Now she had pissed off some crime lord who wanted revenge, all because she had done what someone else wanted her to do.

But she had done what was right! Jason L'Enfant was a bastard. He beat Caroline until he broke her leg. She wasn't a wife to him, just an obsession. Something to put in his house like another trophy on the shelf, or an extra case of beer in the refrigerator, there for him to admire or use at his whim. He deserved what he got.

Her mind continued to teeter back and forth, playing both prosecuting attorney and defendant in the landscape of her inner life.

Maybe it was just karma. After all, she had ruined her own marriage. Loving someone meant accepting them, all of them. Maybe she hadn't given Harry a fair shake. Like Caroline, he had been reduced to some kind of toy for her to play with when she wanted. When he didn't live up to the image of the husband that she had in mind...

She alternately bolstered and beat herself, and she was good at playing both parts.

There was a jingling sound, a key turning in a lock. The bars swung open. Two men entered and pushed her into the only chair in the room. They stood on either side of her, hands firmly gripping her shoulders, pressing her into the chair. Another man stood outside smiling and gripping a small satchel. "Good afternoon," he said.

Fear swept over her like a wave crashing against a rock. She was suddenly wet with perspiration.

"Don't worry," said the man. "My name is Doctor Mandelle."

The perspiration didn't stop. "Did you say Mengele?" she asked.

He laughed, entering the cell and placing his satchel on a nearby table. "You flatter me, Ms. Takanawa." There was something sinister in that laugh. "I have actually studied the good doctor's work, kind of a hobby with me."

"There's nothing good about the butcher of Auschwitz," she said.

He opened the satchel and reached inside. "Still, Doctor Mengele eluded all attempts to capture him. He died a natural death in Argentina, long after the Nuremburg trials ended and all his companions were tried and sentenced."

She cringed as his hand emerged clasping some kind of weird instrument. She felt the grips on her shoulders tighten as the men held her in place.

"Relax," said the Doctor. "I'm just here to examine you," he said. A hand turned her head sideways and she felt a sting in her ear. He recorded something in a notebook and put the instrument back into the satchel.

Her ear hurt. She wanted to reach up but her hands were quickly seized. The men wrestled her into some kind of restraint that kept her hands behind her back. They fastened it to the chair and she couldn't move at all.

"Let's start with some questions before we get too far along." Mandelle relaxed. "Have you ever been vaccinated for smallpox? Diphtheria? When was your last tetanus shot?" He looked up from the small notebook. "You don't have to answer me all at once." He leaned close to her ear, pulling on something attached to it as he whispered into it. "Then again, don't try me. I haven't got all day. I have many other patients under my care that I need to see."

He noticed the perspiration, took a small cloth out of the bag and gently wiped her.

"Believe me when I say that I want you to live, and I want you to be healthy. I am a doctor, despite what you think. I took an oath." He gently clasped his forearm and the men behind her laughed. "Now, answer my questions."

She thought about it, considered her options. The words came slow. "I don't know," she said.

"You don't know about what?"

"My last tetanus shot," she said. "I had a full immunization spectrum a few years back, after my divorce, when I went travelling overseas."

"I see," said Mandelle, making notes. "You appear to be in good health. Do you exercise regularly?"

"Yes," she said.

"What kind of exercise?"

"Yoga. Pilates. I run sometimes."

"You are not into the zumba craze?"

"Tried it," she said. "Not for me."

"Yes," he said, nodding his head slowly. "Do you or your family have a history of heart disease?"

"No."

"Any mental disorders?"

She hesitated. He looked up from his notebook. "No," she said. "Not that I would admit." She paused. "To you, anyway."

"Come, come," he said. "I am your doctor. You must trust me. I have your best interests at heart."

"I find that hard to believe."

"Nonetheless, you must believe it."

"Then why am I restrained like this?" she asked. "No doctor ever examined me under duress."

"It is for your own safety," he said. He put the pen and notebook down. He took out a pair of scissors and snipped them in front of her. She cringed, pulling away. He lowered the scissors and began cutting her blouse from the bottom up. One of the men ripped the shreds away and threw them on the table. Then he cut off her bra and exposed her breasts. She shut her eyes.

"Lovely," he said, staring at them. He put the scissors down and reached up, beginning to knead them, groping her like she was a cheap hooker.

"Stop that!" she said.

He stopped, picked up the notebook and jotted something in it. "I see you have breast implants," he said. "Have they ever caused you any discomfort?"

"No," she said.

"Ever have children?"

She hesitated. It was painful question. Harry had wanted children but she refused. She loved her body and couldn't bear what childbirth would do to her.

"Just answer the question," he said, picking up the scissors and lowering them towards her pants. "If you don't answer me you will force me to examine your cervix."

"No," she said quickly. "Never."

"Even adopted?" he asked.

"No. I had a niece. It was enough to see what my sister went through. I didn't want kids."

"I see," he said. He set the scissors down well out of her reach and picked up the notebook. He wrote a few more notes. "Have you ever been a wet nurse?"

"What kind of question is that?" she asked.

He grew stern. "Just answer it," he said. "It would be much easier if you cooperate. I have other ways of getting my answers." He reached into the satchel again.

God, he even sounds like a Nazi, she thought. Then she considered the alternatives. "No. I've never been a wet nurse."

His hand came out of the satchel holding a stethoscope. He placed it on her chest, listening carefully as he moved it around. "Breathe deep, please," he said. He listened a while longer then put it away. He took out a sphygmomanometer and took her blood pressure, recording it in the notebook. He put it all away and removed a hypodermic, filling it with liquid from a small vial.

"What's that?" she asked, her voice quavering.

"Just some vitamins. As I said, I want you in perfect health." He nodded to one of the men who reached down and held her arm steady. He swabbed her upper arm with an alcohol wipe and slipped the needle in gently, pushing the plunger until it was empty. She started to cry.

"Don't worry," he said. "It's nothing bad. Really. Just some vitamins and hormones. I want you on the accelerated plan," he said.

"What's that mean?"

He packed everything away in his satchel and closed it. "I'll be back tomorrow to visit you again."

"That doesn't sound good."

"I told you, I'm your doctor now. I get a bonus for keeping you healthy."

She laughed. "As if I believe that."

"It doesn't matter if you do or you don't," he said. He stood up and nodded to the men.

"What about my blouse? My bra?"

"Yes," he said, patiently, slowly. He stepped out into the hall. "Carlotta?" he called.

A woman entered with a small suitcase. "All done?" she said.

Mandelle nodded and left. Carlotta spoke to the men. "That will be enough," she said. "I can take it from here. Release her and wait outside." The men obeyed, locking the two of them in the cell together. "How do you feel?" she asked Trish.

"Okay, I guess." Her hand went to her ear, feeling something plastic stuck in it. She tugged at it.

"Don't do that" said Carlotta. "You'll only make it hurt more." She set the suitcase down on the table and opened it, taking out a plastic bag. She gathered up the remains of the blouse and the bra and stuffed them in the bag. She reached into the suitcase and took out a tape measure. Trish could see that the case was filled with shirts and bras. "What size are you dear?" asked Carlotta. "Do you know?"

"34 C.

"Are you sure?" she asked. "Do you mind if I measure you?"

"I'm a size seven," she said.

Carlotta laughed. "You should be an eight," she said. "You don't really wear junior miss, do you?"

Trish gritted her teeth.

"Let's see." Carlotta went to work, diligently taking measurements and referring to a chart. She dug in the suitcase and took out two bras and two shirts. "Here," she said handing one set to Trish. She neatly folded the other set and placed them on the table, then closed the suitcase.

Trish held them up and stared at them. The shirt had a fold that opened and the bra had flaps that clasped at the strap. "This is a nursing bra," said Trish.

"Yes," said Carlotta. "Go ahead and put them on. It's okay. Better than standing there half naked."

"But I'm not nursing," she said.

"No," said Carlotta. "Not yet."

Chapter 17

Fu to You

Harry opened the door to his apartment around lunchtime and threw his keys on the table. "Don't know why I bother locking it," he said. "Everyone else has a key." He went to the kitchen counter where he permanently had his telephone charger plugged in. He took the phone out of his pocket and jammed the connection into the hole. The phone lit up and beeped. He went to the fridge and got a glass of water. There was a plate with a sandwich on it next to the water jug with a note on it from Sue. "Had a great time. Call me," it said. He took a bite of the sandwich and moved it to the counter, leaning over to focus on the phone.

It didn't take him long to find the message Trish had left him. There was a picture of her taken in a dressing room mirror wearing a mis-matched outfit. Harry saw the problem immediately, the skirt she was wearing screamed for a solid top, not that pleated tent she was wearing. He looked away and thought about his initial reaction. Here he was again, dressing her like she was his personal living doll. Truth was, he knew her body type, knew what looked good on her. She realized he had an eye for it, and maybe that scared her more than anything. Her manly ex marine police husband should not know the secrets of women's clothing. All she needed from him was a simple, "You look hot."

He checked the time the photo was sent: 10:35 AM yesterday. He punched a few more buttons and found a voice message that was recorded a minute later. It started with Trish talking excitedly about clothes, then something was obviously wrong. A sales girl was trying to help, he could hear her in the background. There was a clunk, then muffled sounds, maybe choking. Harry listened carefully but the tiny cell phone speaker distorted the sound. There was a thud and the rustle of fabric. The message went on in silence for a while, then he heard voices that he didn't recognize, then the message exceeded the time and cut out.

He dialed her number. No answer. It went straight to voice message.

He went back to the picture she sent of herself in the dressing room mirror. He took a few more bites of the sandwich and listened to the voice message again.

His phone rang and it startled him. "Hello?" he said.

"So, you're finally answering your phone. It was Sue. "Did you solve the Case of the Missing Trish yet?"

"Not yet," he said. "Oh, and thanks for the sandwich."

"You're home," she said. "What are you doing there?"

"Charging up my phone," he said. "Jan was right. Trish left a message on my phone. I have an idea where to start looking for her."

"Need my help?" she asked.

"Maybe," he said. "I might have to make a tour of women's dressing rooms. I have a picture of the last one she was in."

"Silly, you don't need me for that," she said. He said nothing. "You haven't been in the bedroom yet, have you?"

Harry set the phone down on the counter and went into the only other room in his apartment. She had laid an outfit on the bed, skirt, boots, tights, a top and a jacket. There was another note, this one to Fu Chan. "I think you'd look hot in this. Later –SY." Harry shook his head and laughed as he set the note down. He went back to the phone.

"Very funny," he said. "Now you going to come and help me?"

"What? Help you get dressed? Go out and look for her?" she asked. "You don't need me, Harry. You know what to do. Now do it. I'm going to class in an hour." She hung up the phone.

Harry stared at the outfit she had chosen. It was one of his favorites. The boots were the ones he had worn in the battle against his last nemesis, Carol Huntington, also known as Dr. Couture. The heels had caused him to lose his balance and he broke one off when it got stuck between the planks of a dock as he was chasing Couture. He threw them out but Sue Yen had retrieved them from the trash and had them repaired. They were all shiny and brand new looking. He picked them up and studied them.

"High heel boots," he said. "Most superheroes have better mementos of their adventures than high heel boots." He set them back down on the bed.

He took a deep breath. Cross dressing was the furthest thing from his mind these days. He wondered why. He had always enjoyed it but now there was something ugly about it. Couture had forced Harry to wear an outfit, even dance for him on demand. The mental and physical torture had finally put pressure on his inner psyche and forced the emergence of Fu Chan, the name he gave to his feminine side. It was Fu Chan who killed Couture, using the same high heels that Couture had meant as torture. Harry had been little more than a whipped puppy during all this. He had to admit that his feminine side was his stronger side.

He corrected himself, a habit his therapist had gotten him into. His feminine side was not his strongest. It was equal in strength to his masculine side. They just had different strengths, different abilities. Perhaps Sue was right. Put together with her secret identity, Fu Chan was a superhero.

Harry realized he had been wading in the tidal marsh of his mind. He went back into the kitchen, checked the clock and called Jan, Trish's secretary. "Any word?" he asked.

"She still hasn't reported in."

"Have you tried her phone recently?"

"Yes," said Jan. "Still no answer."

"My guess is it's out of power and rolling right to voice mail," said Harry. "What time did she leave the office yesterday?"

"A little after ten."

"She called me at 10:35," said Harry. "I have a picture and a voice message she sent around that time. If she left the office she couldn't have gone far. Did she walk or is her car still in the parking lot?"

"Car's still here," she said. "I thought she came in early, parked and walked to court this morning."

"The point is she walked. She couldn't have gone very far to shop," he said. "I suspect she'll be easy to find. I'll start by checking all the stores within a fifteen minute walk of your office. Any ideas where I should start?"

"That's easy," said Jan. "She loves Jenny's Boutique over near the Glam-o-rama."

"You been there?" asked Harry.

"Of course," she said. "It's a big store with a lot of consignment and boutique clothes."

"Been in the dressing rooms?" he asked.

"Yes," she said. "Small. Like getting dressed in a closet."

"Curtains or walls?"

"They're high walled cubicles made up like dressing rooms."

"Know anyplace that's nearby and uses curtains?"

She rattled off a short list. Harry jotted them down.

"I think the Bargain Depot would be the best bet," she said. "I heard her mention the name more than a few times."

"Okay," he said. "I'm off to find her. I'll be in touch."

His phone needed more time to charge. He took a five minute shower. When he got out of the shower he stood and stared at the outfit while he dried. He looked in the closet at his ill-fitting sport coats and his boring shirts and pants. In the end there was no debate. He reasoned there would be a lot less questions if Fu Chan wanted to look in a woman's dressing room than Harry Takanawa. He dressed quickly before his logical mind told him not to. In less than a half an hour he was ready to penetrate the most private woman's dressing room in the city.

He studied the picture on the phone one more time, then listened to the voice message she had left him. He had an idea of where the dressing room might be. The pale beige curtains narrowed it down. Most dressing rooms had doors and walls and were carpeted. The curtains reeked of a smaller store and the tile on the floor was not in the best shape. It screamed cheap, bargain warehouse. He went through a mental inventory of stores that he had frequented in his heydays of shopping for clothes with Trish.

He looked up, staring out the kitchen window at the brick wall a few feet across the alley. His eyes unfocused, looking in the distance like he was manning the crow's nest of the Titanic. The wall blurred into memories. "Trish made me confront myself," he said out loud. "I owe her a lot. I may not be in love with her, but I love her. I have to find her."

He checked the contents of his purse, unplugged the cell phone and threw it in the bag. He slung it over his shoulder and hurried out the door.

Chapter 18

Monthly Meeting

Mr. Che ran through the Power Point presentation as if he were addressing stockholders, but in essence, that is how his organization worked. Each man took a portion of the profits, participating directly in the success or failure of the company. These monthly meetings were about transparency and trust, the essential teambuilding that made an organization cohesive. The principles of Wall Street, when properly applied, worked just as well in his organization as any other. It's all in the company's strategic plan that he and his executive team authored, if you care to read it.

"So you can see that, thanks to your management team, the losses from the fiasco at the Seattle docks a few nights ago have been recouped. Our efficiency analysts have managed to turn waste into profits again. The culprits that betrayed us have paid for their deed, and we even managed to recoup some funds when, mixed with a generous amount of offal from our fishing venture, we sold their remains to the cat food plant in Everett."

There were chuckles around the room.

"I can add that the company we used as a front for the operation has already changed hands three times, the profit has been laundered through our subsidiaries and associates, and we no longer have anything to do with International Freight Ltd." He looked at Mr. Lo. "I understand that it will soon be liquidated somewhere in Africa and the paperwork buried forever. To replace that we have set up a new company, BTF Inc., so please make a note to use them when planning your next international shipment."

A man raised his hand.

"Yes?" asked Mr. Che. A moderator made his way over, passing him a wireless microphone.

"Just curiosity, Mr. Che, but does BTF have any meaning? Is it short for something?" He passed the microphone back.

"Actually, it just sounded good, but if you want to turn it into some kind of acronym, by all means do. It makes it easier to remember."

"How about Beat The Fed?" someone shouted.

Mr. Che smiled, but then became stern. "Please refrain from shouting out of order. Raise your hand if you have a question or something to contribute." He scanned the room. Order had been restored. "Now, on to our regular business. To whoever put the severed middle finger in the suggestion box this month, we get the joke, but please use a pencil and paper next time as it made it quite difficult to read the other suggestions."

There was a murmur. Che frowned and the sounds quickly subsided.

"Of the ideas we could read, some of them were excellent recommendations. You are really taking our efficiency efforts to heart. The one we particularly liked this month was to actually have our fishing fleet engage in fishing while transporting contraband. Our management analysts have calculated that acting on this idea will add as much as twelve percent to the revenue stream from this operation. So, thank you for coming up with that one, and all of us will see a little more in our shares when this idea is put into play."

There was mild applause.

Another idea we liked was "Bring Your Child to Work Day." Great idea, builds family values and supports our core principles. We are in the process of appointing a committee to help guide that. The question has arisen about what exactly we should show our children, should we have department tours, and should they be allowed to accompany parents on operations, handle weapons, etc. I know you're all excited about having parent-child activities like this, but we must explore the issues before we act. There will be more on this at next month's all hands meeting when the committee gives us a follow up report.

"Speaking of family activities, the family pot luck picnic was a great success. I think everyone that attended had a good time. The results of the shooting contest are posted on the Company SharePoint, along with the winner of the raffle for a weekend in sunny L.A, donated by one of our generous partners in the hotel and entertainment business. Thank you all for attending, and we'll see you again at next year's picnic."

He took a deep breath and smiled. "The corporate logo contest is still on. It's been almost two years since we took ownership of this facility and we have yet to brand it with our own identity. We're looking for something beside that old knife through the skull that conquered the world kind of thing, something more modern and upbeat. So, for you artists out there: get your pens, paints, favorite photo editor, whatever you prefer, and get busy.

"Check the training calendar this month. In addition to usual martial arts and weaponry classes I would like you all to attend the ethics training. It's mandatory, just like the valuing diversity class. Both are scheduled next month. Have you met your yearly training requirement on your individual development plan? Check with your supervisor if you are unsure.

"An update on our pursuit of six sigma certification. Six Sigma, as you recall, is achieved only in organizations that use continuous improvement to increase process and profitability. It involves the identification and removal of defects and a commitment to quality. You know that this is more than a simple goal to me, it is an imperative. We will become the most efficient organization ever designed, with all the benefits Wall Street has to offer, and a focus on underworld markets. These markets are as unregulated as most American industries, but they offer us the benefits of world wide profits, of which each of you share.

"Which brings me to the reason you are all here today, to hear the quarterly share. Each share this quarter is worth roughly one thousand, sixty six point eight six seven dollars American which, based upon your election of currency and the number of shares you own, will be deposited directly in the account you have registered in your profile on our secure website." He drew out the tension, building the excitement as if they were getting ready to draw lottery balls. "Which will happen as soon as our comptroller Mr. Otto Kreps hits the button." He pointed to a small bald man seated close by at the head table.

Otto's hand hovered above the laptop. Music filled the room from the tinny corporate speakers hidden in the ceiling. Mr. Che nodded and Otto hit the return key with a flourish. The audience began to clap. Otto stood and raised his hand to Mr. Che. The applause grew.

"No, no," said Mr. Che, extending his hands to the audience. "You are to be applauded." He began to clap. "It is you who have achieved these efficiencies. It is your hard work that has made this corporation what it is today. Remember that you can also choose to reinvest your shares, or a portion of them, back into the Company pool, giving you the opportunity to increase your number of shares and therefore, your profits next quarter. Just update the preferences in your profile. Thank you all for attending today."

Che walked over to Otto as the crowd dissipated. "How much was our capital reinvestment this quarter? Roughly?"

"About eighteen million," said Otto.

"Does that include funding the Manila Project?"

"Yes, sir. The research for that project is also being supplemented with internal resources from our dairy farm. In addition to being profitable, the dairy also provides a source of raw materials for the Project. The research demands a large amount of stem cell material."

Mr. Che laughed. "Yes. Who would have thought mother's milk would be so profitable. They buy it by the case in L.A., the truckload in New York. They put it in their trendy drinks. Latte de la Madres and Breast Milk Shooters. Some actually buy it to feed their babies. I have a leading sports figure who swears that consuming the milk actually improves his game. But I never dreamed it would be a ready source of stem cells, spinal fluid, and organs. A beautiful concept, Mr. Kreps."

Kreps bowed humbly. "My contribution to efficiency, Mr. Che."

"I will need to travel later in the week," he said. "Jason L'Enfant will be in charge during my absence, but I want you to alert me if there are any changes to the budgets."

Chapter 19

Pretty Woman

Harry left the apartment, his heels clicking down the steps. He felt comfortable in the skirt. The short jacket was cut for his figure. He didn't have to hide his breasts. He stood up straight and didn't hunch over like he was trying to smuggle something. It was the first time he felt good about himself in a long time.

"Why?" he asked himself, talking out loud. "Why?" he said again, correcting it an octave, adding a slight Oriental twang that somehow made it easier for him to imitate a female voice. As if he were an actor playing a part, but he was no actor. It was the voice of Fu Chan.

At the bottom of the stairs the feeling went away. Binky and Farnsworth were entering the building. Farnsworth saw a beautiful woman, exotic yet familiar. He did the gentlemanly thing and held open the door. Harry tilted his head and smiled as he stepped through the door, confident that his illusion was working.

Then there was Binky.

"Caught you playing dress up again, didn't I Fu?" he said.

Harry dropped the falsetto. Binky had the presence and the aura of an empty casket. You didn't want to get too close. You might just fall in. "What do you want Binky?"

"Almost didn't recognize you, Fu," said Binky. "It's been a while since I've seen you."

"That was a long time ago, Binky. Back when we were kids."

"You seem to be enjoying it," said Binky. His eyes scanned up and down, taking in a big gulp of Fu. "It reminds me of when we were kids. Remember how we used to play detective? You found those old clothes in your basement and put them on. Then I caught you playing dress up and made you go outside and play. I named you Fu Chan. Do you remember?"

"I remember," said Harry. "Fu Chan. Daughter of Charlie Chan. Number One and Number Two son couldn't solve their way out of a paper bag. I'm the smart one of the family."

"It was fun until your mother found out what we were doing," he said.

"Yeah," said Harry. "Wonder what she would say about me now."

Binky thought it, but he never said it. Turning in her grave.

Harry's inner eye looked away. Thoughts of his mother brought conflicting feelings to the surface. He tried to swim away from them but they caught up with him, forming a whirlpool around him that threatened to pull him under. He looked away from Binky, staring at a crack in the tile in the corner.

Farnsworth grunted, as if he had finally understood a joke. He laughed in his irritating guttural way and said to Harry, "Want to play?"

"Watch it," said Harry, his eye filled with madness. "I killed the last person who asked me that."

Binky chimed in. "You wouldn't kill my man Farnsworth here?" he asked.

"Harry wouldn't," he replied. "But I can't vouch for Fu Chan. Now get out of my way." They were pushing him towards the edge. Trish was more important than this crap. Farnsworth put an arm on Harry's shoulder. It was instinct. He twisted and grabbed Farnsworth's arm, bending the thumb outward. Farnsworth cringed, his body off balance. All Harry had to do was sweep his foot across the ankle and Farnsworth would be on the ground. Instead he pushed him away and moved past Binky.

"I was on my way to see you," said Binky. "Hoping you had a minute for your old friend. Where are you off to in such a hurry anyway?"

Harry stopped. "Trish is missing," he said. "Instead of being a pain in the ass, why don't you help me for a change?"

Binky could tell Harry was all business. "Okay," he said. "Can I give you a lift somewhere?"

"It's the least you can do," said Harry. "Because of your stupid thing with Manny Ballston, my car was impounded and my detective license suspended."

Binky didn't know what changed him. Maybe it was because Harry looked like a helpless woman. Maybe it was friendship, or something like it. But the Grinch's heart grew a little. Not much, just a little. It's Binky after all.

"Farnsworth!" he said.

By some kind of mental telepathy Farnsworth knew what Binky wanted. Well, maybe it was more like a trained collie reacting to the way his master voiced a command. He led them down the front steps and onto the sidewalk towards the car, rubbing his arm along the way. He held the door open for Fu and Binky motioned for her to get in. "Where we going?" he asked.

"Bellevue. Near Trish's office."

Farnsworth got in the driver's seat and headed out of Capitol Hill towards the floating bridge that ran across Lake Washington to Bellevue. Harry was surprised. It used to be free, but now it was a toll road. It wasn't like Binky to spend money.

Binky broke the silence first. "Sorry your license is suspended," he said. Silence. "What did you tell the cops?"

Harry was belligerent. "I didn't rat you out, if that's what you're worried about."

Binky was tactful. Years of street smarts. "You still love her, don't you?"

"She's my wife, for God's sake."

"Ex-wife," corrected Binky.

"Wife," said Harry. "She's always been there for me. She was there during my recovery from that bout with Couture."

"Oh, yeah," said Binky. "You gave her medical power of attorney and look what she did. Fixed you up with a nice pair of tits."

"She's missing," said Harry flatly.

"How long?" said Binky.

"Officially? Since yesterday morning."

"Don't you think you're overreacting?" asked Binky.

"Jan, her secretary, called. She missed a court date."

"She may be sick, maybe injured," said Binky. "Have you tried the hospitals?"

"Jan did," said Harry. "No luck."

"What makes you think she's missing?"

Harry took out his phone and cued up the message. "Listen to this," he said.

Binky listened twice before saying anything. "What do you make of that?"

"I'm not sure," said Binky. "Sounds like a struggle."

"That's what I thought," said Harry. He brought up the picture of her before the mirror. "I'm on my way to find the dressing room in this picture. It's her last known location."

"Who's that behind her?" asked Binky.

Harry stared at the picture. "What do you mean?"

"Right there," said Binky. Harry stared. Binky finally took the phone away from him and forwarded the picture to his own cell. "You really need to get a better phone. They have all kinds of advantages."

"Like a bigger bill?"

"You get what you pay for, Fu" said Binky. "All you have there is a phone." He held his up, the latest gadget infested superphone you could buy. Harry cringed to think what he was paying in charges every month. The phone let out a beep and Binky opened his email and called up the picture. He was able to enlarge the photo and zoom in to what looked like a shadow on Harry's tiny phone. There was an arm holding up a hanger with some clothes, an eye and part of a head popping out behind it.

"Must be the salesgirl in the voice message," said Harry. "How could you see that on my phone?"

Binky zoomed in and moved the image around. "All I can see is her eye." He enlarged it. "Looks like they're blue."

"Wait, what's that?" asked Harry. He pointed to a blur on her arm.

"I don't know," said Binky. He zoomed in further but couldn't make out anything in the distortion.

"We're in Bellevue," said Farnsworth.

"There's a place in an old mall by sixth," said Harry. "It's a relatively new place called Fashion Bargain Depot. I'm going on the assumption that she's been everywhere else." Farnsworth drove on. Harry turned to Binky. "So, what's the truth about Manny Ballston? What were you really after yesterday?"

Binky was quiet. He looked away.

"You might as well tell me," said Harry. "Look, I didn't tell Bernard anything, but he'll find out eventually. I've always found it better to level with him. You may not trust him, but I do."

Binky remained silent.

"Think about it," said Harry. "And don't leave me hanging for long. We're old friends, as you say. Anything you tell me about Ballston will be kept confidential. You know that."

Binky looked as if he was going to say something, then stopped.

"Okay, then. Old friend." He spit the words out like poison. "I expected more from you than just a free ride." There was a pause of silence. "Just remember I lost my license over you." More silence. "Look, if you won't help me with your case, our case, then maybe you can help me with another. You have a lot of contacts. Ever hear of someone called Mr. Che?"

Farnsworth grunted and the car swerved.

"You know something?" asked Binky. "Spit it out!" he said.

"I don't know nothing Boss," he said. "Last person I know who made inquiries about Mr. Che has no tongue anymore."

"So you've heard of him?" asked Harry.

"One of his men tried to recruit me once," said Farnsworth.

"Recently?" asked Binky.

"It was a long time ago, maybe a year or so. Same dude who has no tongue now."

"Why didn't you join?" asked Binky.

"I liked your retirement program better, Boss. Once you sign on with Che, you can't quit."

"What do you know about Che?" asked Harry.

"Not much, just what I was told. Che is a Dragon Lord, Tong Empire. Modern day Chairman Mao with his own multi national organization. He has a philosophy. My advice is to stay away from Che. Everyone that mentions his name seems to disappear."

"There's Trish's office," said Binky, pointing it out.

"Yeah," said Harry. "Make a right at the next street," he told Farnsworth. It's down the block on the right. Looks like a home improvement store."

"That explains the name," said Farnsworth. "I think it was something like a Home Depot at one time, one of the smaller stores."

"Some other kind of depot, I think," said Harry. Farnsworth pulled into the lot. "Would you wait for me? I'll only be about ten or fifteen minutes."

Binky nodded.

"Time for Fu Chan to go to work." Harry smiled and winked at Binky as he got out of the car.

The store had the feel of home improvement, but the clothes were cheap and plentiful. It had obviously been named to recycle the old signage. The old 'Depot' part of the sign had been topped with 'Fashion Bargain.' He remembered it being a place that sold expensive granite countertops and bathrooms with spigots on every wall. It was doing much better as a discount fashion outlet.

He went right to the junior miss department and grabbed a few things off the racks. Then he headed for the dressing rooms.

He made it past the Hun that was guarding the door. She counted the number of garments and said, "Aren't you a little too old for this line of clothes? Have you tried the women's wear?"

Fu Chan made a petite hmmmff as she walked past her.

He saw curtains, the right color and texture. He started searching, getting down on the floor on all fours and scanning behind the folds. He took out his own phone and dialed her number. He heard a faint sound. He couldn't hear it standing up but down close to the floor it was audible. He crawled around, checking empty stalls while he dialed again. It didn't take him long to find it. It was on vibrate, hidden under the fabric. He grabbed it and headed out the door.

"That was quick," said the Hun.

"You were right," said Fu. She hung the clothes on the restock rack. "Not my style." She started to head for the front door.

"Woman's department is over there," said Hunny, pointing to the right. Fu veered towards it, not wanting to arouse her suspicion by looking like she was rushing out of the store like a thief. Once she was out of sight though she made a dog leg and went right to the car.

"That was fast," said Binky.

Harry held up the phone and smiled.

Binky just shook his head. "Nice work, Fu. Maybe you are the smartest of the Chans." He nodded to Farnsworth who knew what to do.

Chapter 20

Charge!

Farnsworth guided the car back across the floating bridge that spanned Lake Washington. Bellevue disappeared behind them. The traffic had become lighter since the road had added tolls and diverted the traffic jam towards Interstate 90, the only other way into Seattle across the lake. Seated comfortably in the back, Harry called Trish's secretary Jan to give her an update while Binky fidgeted with some new app he had downloaded to his superphone.

"You really need to get one of these," said Binky, punching tiny buttons, his finger vibrating like an old time telegraph operator.

Harry looked at his own unit and smiled. Simple layout, simple payment plan, just the way he liked it. He heard Jan pick up the phone.

"Have you heard from Trish?" asked Harry.

"No," said Jan. He could hear the inflection in her voice, the sound of worry.

"I found her phone," he said. "I thought I'd let you know. It was on the floor of the dressing room at Fashion Bargain Depot. It was on vibrate, hard to hear, which is why nobody answered it when you or I called."

"Great," said Jan. "That's a start."

"It's a big step," said Harry. "I'm going to hold on to it, take it to my office and analyze it for clues. Her phone is a little more modern than mine. Should be easy to hook it up to a computer and scan it. There was a partial picture of a saleswoman at the store that I'm interested in. I want to see if I can identify her, maybe download the photo."

"Sure," said Jan. "Keep it as long as you need."

"That's the problem, Jan. It's running out of power. Does she have a charger in the office?"

"No," said Jan. "It's her personal phone. The charger's probably at her house. Do you have a key?"

Harry laughed. "Even if I did I'm sure she changed the locks." They were on the bridge and headed back to Seattle. It would be a hassle now to turn around and go back to Bellevue.

"Maybe you can buy a charger at the mall," suggested Jan.

"Maybe," said Harry. "I just called to let you know I was on her trail. I'll check in with you if I find out anything new."

"What about your other work? I heard you say you were busy yesterday," she said.

"I shifted everything to my partner and staff so I could work on this. Trish is more important to me than anything else."

"Thanks, Harry. That's so sweet." He could hear the relief in her voice. "I don't know why she gave you up."

Harry looked at his reflection in the window of Binky's car. Fu Chan frowned back at him and he knew the answer to Jan's question. There was a beep signaling low power. "Thanks, Jan. My phone's about to go dead so I gotta hang up. I'll be in touch soon. I'll bring you her phone when I'm done with it."

"Keep it," she said. Her next words came out like a prayer. "Give it back to her when you find her."

Harry was quiet. The prayer demanded an answer. Don't all prayers?

"I'll do that." He thumbed a button and disconnected. He stared at his reflection in the window for a while, seeing it and the blur of the scenery behind it. It was soothing on his brain, until he couldn't ignore Binky any longer. His landlord was pounding on the screen of his small superphone like it was a piano.

"You don't happen to have a charger for this type of phone?" he asked Binky, holding out Trish's phone. It was similar to Binky's, a fully loaded superphone that could do all sorts of things.

Binky sighed. "Let me see it," he said. Harry passed the phone over to him and watched him examine it. "No luck, Fu. But I have an idea. Why not try your old pal Lenny?"

Fu smiled. "Good idea. You know, you'd make a fine detective if you ever tried."

"Yeah," said Binky. "You're such a raving success. You make me want to give all this up for your job." He leaned forward. "Farnsworth, you heard the lady. Stop by Lenny's on our way to..." he turned to Fu. "Where do you want us to drop you off?"

"Lenny's would be fine. I can walk to the office from there."

Binky laughed. "In broad daylight?"

"It's Capitol Hill," said Harry. "Even if I get 'read' nobody gives a crap. Besides, I just passed myself well enough to walk into a woman's dressing room, no questions asked." Fu took the phone from Binky and dropped it in her purse.

"Just don't talk to anyone," said Binky. "The voice is a dead giveaway. You need to work on it."

Farnsworth grunted. "They'll be looking at your tits anyway." Harry looked hurt, then laughed. Let them have their fun. If you can't take the truth from your friends, then what's it all worth?

He might have enjoyed having the breasts at one time, but they were scars that reminded him of what Dr. Couture had done to him. He should be grateful that they were no longer exploding implants. The thought of what would have happened, a detonation that close to his heart, it sent a shiver of fear across him like a wave of electricity.

Binky sensed it. "Are you cold?" he asked. "Farnsworth. Turn the heat up."

"I'm okay," said Harry.

Binky proved he was not immune to his surroundings or oblivious to the suffering of others. He put his arm on Harry's shoulder. "Sorry for my outbursts," he said. "Sorry if I said anything to hurt you. I play this role every day. Binky the landlord, the loan shark, the hustler. I get too used to it, so much so that I have trouble separating the real Bill Binkley from that made up one. I worry about you, old friend, so much so that I criticize you like your mother, God rest her soul."

Harry winced. Binky wasn't used to being human, that much was plain.

At least he caught his mistake. "Sorry. Unlike your mother, I approve of your cross dressing. Seeing you like this takes me back to the old neighborhood. When you dressed up like Fu, you were something different. You were no longer this bullied little boy, picked on by bigger kids looking for ways to let out their aggression. Do you remember?"

"I do," said Harry laughing. "As Harry, they terrorized me, but nothing was more terrifying than that first time you caught me wearing girl's clothes. We were, what, twelve? Thirteen? Instead of making me feel like a jerk, you made me go outside and play detective, just like nothing was different. It felt weird but it was exciting and kind of fun."

"Remember what you did to Billy Bad when he and his cronies showed up and made fun of you?" asked Binky. "I was scared, but I wasn't going to let you face them alone. They started in on you, making fun of Fu Chan. I didn't know what they had in mind but it didn't sound good." He suddenly became animated, coming to the good part of the story. "It was eight to two."

"Wait a minute," said Harry. It was more like five to two." He shook his head. "This story gets more spin every time you tell it."

Binky became serious. "It's part of the legend. The history of Fu Chan. You must admit, there is still some truth to the story."

"Keep talking," said Harry. "I can't wait to hear this part."

"It was eight to two," he said, emphasis on the eight. "You didn't need me. You moved so quick. Did a cartwheel and kicked one in the face. That split the pack up. Two of them moved away but you came up out of that spin with a rock in your hand. Slapped the nearest one right on face with it. Instant blood. I don't want to embellish, but I swear there were broken teeth."

"There were broken teeth," said Harry. "That much is true."

"Okay. Then I remember you took that same rock and threw it straight at Billy, fast, like it came out of a cannon." He illustrated with his hands, balling one into a rock and hitting the other until it opened with a splat. "Billy didn't look so Bad after that. Blood came out of his nose but he wasn't done. He reared back and took a swing at you. He didn't notice that you had a second rock in the other hand. You held that rock up perfect, raised it right in front of you like a shield, and he hit it just perfect. And there were broken bones."

"There were broken bones," said Harry. "But you did your part too. One of them bent down to pick up a stick. He would have whacked me good if you hadn't stepped on his arm when it was down. You must have jumped three feet in the air before coming down on it with all that force. There was a snapping sound and it wasn't the stick. At least, we never found out. The whole lot of them took off running."

They both laughed.

"Yeah," said Harry. He smiled. "That got me off their hit list. They never bothered me again, either as Harry or Fu Chan."

"We never got in trouble for that, did we?"

"I think they were afraid to tell their parents the truth."

"We were some bad assed detectives."

The laughter died down. The car rolled down a busy city street, stopping in front of a well kept shop, the words "Capitol Hill Pawn" painted neatly on the window. Fu stepped out of the car, very ladylike, placing one heel on the pavement at a time, then sliding gracefully out of the car to a full standing position. She shouldered the bag and said in her best voice. "Thanks for the help, Binky. You too Farnsworth." Farnsworth wasn't looking. He was staring at her tits.

Fu sneered at him. "I wish you'd put as much effort telling me about Che," she said.

Farnsworth cringed. His head spun around to see if anyone was listening, his eyes bulging as he shook his head in a fervent NO. He stuck his tongue out, his fingers making a pair of mock scissors as if to cut it off.

She looked away. "Now Binky," she said, all ladylike. "If you think of anything you want to tell me about Manny Ballston, you'll call me, won't you?"

"I'll call you."

"I'm serious," said Fu, her lip pouting, her eyes stern. "Don't make me pick up a rock and use it on you."

Binky started to smile, then saw she meant business. She held the gaze just long enough before it burst into a smile.

Binky chuckled. "You make me wish we were kids again."

"You are a child. All men are children, or didn't you know that?" She turned and went into the pawn shop.

A little bell rang as the door opened and closed. The shop smelled of cooking: onions, exotic spices and frying meat. Lenny parted a curtain as he came out of the back room.

Fu took the phone out of her purse. "Do you have a charger for a cell phone like this?" she said.

"Bring it here and let me see," said Lenny. He ducked behind the counter and produced a box that he placed on the counter. Fu set the phone down gently beside it, noticing that the box was full of chargers of all types. Lenny picked up the phone and studied it, then started rummaging through the box. "This one will do," he said. "It's an exact match, has the original name of the phone right on the charger." He moved the box to the side and placed the charger on the counter next to the phone.

"Does it work?" asked Fu. "Is there a place we can plug it in and try?"

"Of course," said Lenny. There was a power strip mounted near the cash register. He plugged it in and set it up. The phone lit up like a game show buzzer. He glanced at the phone and then stared at Fu for a moment. "Do I know you?" he asked. "You seem awfully familiar."

"It's me," said Harry, lowering his voice back to normal. "I'm on a case. Binky said I couldn't pass for a woman. I had to find out."

Lenny laughed. "It's not hard to make a liar out of Binky." He lit up. "Harry! How the hell are you? You look... Hot." Lenny knew all about Harry's cross dressing. The story was legendary among his friends, how Harry had been a top detective for the Seattle Police for years until he was exposed as a cross dresser. The reaction was mixed, but in the end Harry had resigned. It didn't matter to Lenny. He was still his friend, no matter what he looked like or how peculiar his tastes were. Besides, Harry was a good detective and Lenny was one of his best customers.

Harry laughed. "How much for the charger?" he asked.

"On the house," said Lenny. "Besides, I owe you for the last few skip traces you've done for me."

"I haven't been keeping up with it," he said.

"But I have. Really appreciate the quick turn around."

"It's all Sue these days," said Harry.

"She's good," said Lenny. He rang up a no sale on the cash register and took out a wad of bills, counted out two hundred dollars and handed them over.

"What's this for?" asked Harry.

"Payment," he said. "Just give it to Rita. She'll know what to do with it."

"Fine, fine," said Harry, surprised to have some cash. He reached inside the purse and opened a zippered compartment and stuffed the bills inside. "Business must be good."

"Great," said Lenny. "I've been watching that reality show, Pawn Masters. Modeling my business after those guys. People really like to barter these days. Running a pawn shop is finally the 'in' thing to do."

"About time," said Harry. "Good to hear that. Got something else to ask you." He dug around in the purse and found a pencil scratch of the tattoo that Red made at the coroner's office. "Ever seen a tat like this?"

Lenny stared at it for a minute. "Yeah. Some of the customers come in here with tats like this. Hell, I see a lot of tats. This is Capitol Hill." Lenny looked at it again. "It's certainly a unique design."

"Any idea where they're getting inked?"

"I can ask," said Lenny. "Is it important?"

"Maybe," said Harry. "Just be careful. Farnsworth just told me about someone who lost a tongue by asking too many questions. No direct inquiries, definitely not anyone with tat." He sniffed the air, impossible to ignore the scents coming from the back room. "Smells good in here. What'cha got cooking?"

"Philly cheese steak sandwiches," he said. "You want one?"

Harry sniffed again. "Sure smells good. Wish I could but I gotta run."

"Are you sure? I buy real prime rib and slice it thin. It's the secret to a great steak sandwich."

Harry sniffed again. "Sure is tempting, but some other time, Lenny. I really gotta run. Trish is missing and I have to track her down. This is her phone. Don't let me hold you back from your meal any longer."

"She'll turn up I'm sure," said Lenny. "Before you go, I got one more thing for you." He dug around in the box and pulled out a cable. He picked up the phone and studied it, then started digging in the box again. "This is it," he said, holding up another connection cable.

"What?" asked Harry. "What is it?"

He showed Harry the other end of the cable. It looked like a three headed hydra, but it was just different shaped plugs designed to connect to a variety of things. "This will let you download the stuff on the phone to your computer, or show it on your TV." He laid the serpent on the counter and picked up Trish's cell phone. "With this kind of phone you can take movies, photos, messages, all kinds of stuff." Lenny thumbed through the phone, showing Harry the goodies. "Look, she liked to browse the internet. Let's check her favorite sites." Harry watched in fascination. He really didn't know much about these modern phones. "Look. She liked the clothing stores and shoe sites. GPS maps. You could probably tell where she's been. They got an app for that."

"Lenny, I'm surprised. You know so much about this."

"Come in the back and we'll talk some more. I don't want my sandwich to get cold. And I got the fixings for one more on the stove, so don't say no."

Fu set the purse down on the counter, throttled the three headed hydra and wrestled it into the knockoff Dolce and Gabbana. She felt the weight of walking around in the high heeled boots and shifted. It would be good to get off her feet for a while. She took the jacket off and caught Lenny staring at her breasts, felt embarrassed. *They're a part of you now, Harry. I'm a part of you now. Fu Chan Detective Agency is on the case.*

Lenny looked away, caught in the act. He turned and walked through the curtains, staring down at the phone in his hands as his fingers tapped against the tiny screen.

Fu Chan picked up the purse and jacket. Binky may be a liar, but he was right about one thing. Harry needed to act the part. It wasn't so much acting, it was more like giving in to his desire to be Fu Chan. Maybe it was his nature to be feminine. That thought always scared Harry.

There are times when we are all repulsed by our inner nature, afraid to face our disowned self.

"This is going to be easy," said Lenny, continuing to hammer the phone with his fingers. "I can hook this to my computer and download the whole phone to a CD by the time we're finish eating." He smiled. "You know the best part about this?"

"What's that?" asked Fu.

Lenny heard the falsetto, caught himself glancing at her breasts again. She was all woman as far as he could see. If Harry was buried inside her somewhere, Lenny couldn't see it. He stood aside, parting the curtains as he invited Fu Chan to sniff the exotic perfumes of homemade Philly cheese steaks.

"You know," said Lenny, holding up the phone. "None of this shit is password protected."

Chapter 21

Coastal Watch

Bernard read through another one of Rita's reports. They were all very detailed and thorough. Like Harry, she managed to extract a lot of information from her interviews and more importantly she wrote it all down.

For her, it was the old conga line of facts dancing through her brain. She had to write it down so she could understand it all, it was part of her process. She did the same thing with jigsaw puzzles when she was a kid, taking every piece out of the box and laying them on the table first.

She did the same thing with facts. Once everything was out where she could see it the fun started. It was a mad combination of fill in the blank, Clue, and pin the tale on the suspect.

Harry had told him once that Rita was good at Clue. He had seen detectives like her before, a natural at their job. He read Harry's report, when? Early this morning? His old employee had said the same things. She had good analytical skills, a fair amount of intuition, and a penchant for danger, all good qualities of a gumshoe. Rita was ready to work on her own.

Bernard stood up and started pacing, his own conga line dancing in his head. His neck ached, his whole body ached. He stretched as he stared out the window. It was a nice day, the Olympic Mountains looked every bit of purple majesty, and Puget Sound sparkled where the sun broke through the thick clouds. He twisted, staring down at the people as they moved in packs on the street below. His mind drifted.

Interviews are never conducted alone. They're done in teams, even if one of the team members is hidden behind a mirror. He wondered how Rita managed to get anything done with Van Dorn in the room, wondered what she could do with a different partner. He had to get Harry back on the job soon.

The phone rang. Matt reached down and hit the speaker phone. "Bernard."

"Petty Officer Tom Walgamott," said a crisp voice on the other end. "Returning your call."

Bernard smiled. "US Coast Guard. I knew I could count on you." He sat down in his chair, picked up the handset and took him off speaker phone.

Tom laughed. "You still cruising around in that paddle boat of yours trying to catch a salmon?"

"Hey, it's not a paddle boat, it's a thirty eight foot deep vee Nor'wester. Enough diesel power to take me wherever I need to go."

"So when we going?"

"As soon I hear what I want to know. What 'cha got for me?"

"We checked out that boat you inquired about, the *Dare Me*. Your man was right, it pretty much looks like what he said, a rust bucket. He was sharp to say something about the traps and buoys and the lack of fishing tags or numbers on them. They're permit is in process, and it looks like they'll get it. The *Dare Me* is poised to become a reputable part of our fishing fleet."

"Poised to become?" asked Bernard.

"That's the odd thing," said Tom. "They were all rigged out for fishing but the hold was clean. We checked with the port services and they spent a lot of money on fuel. We asked them where they went and they said they were looking for fish and didn't find any."

"That's strange," said Bernard. "Are they poachers?"

"Don't know what they're up to, but here's another odd thing: The boat did this six times in the last two months."

"Six times!"

"And that ain't all," said Tom. "It changed hands three times during those months. I just met the new owners."

"What the? Do you have a list of the companies it went through?"

"Right here," said Tom.

"Was one of them International Freight Limited?"

"Yeah. They owned it at the time of the raid. It got sold to some African company two days ago. We're trying to find out who. That's why they're lollygagging around in port, just waiting for the new owners to show up and tell them what to do."

Bernard blew air. Tom continued. "I knew you'd like this puzzle, Bernard. You know, I'm a bit of a detective, too."

"Isn't everyone these days?"

"I checked with Fish and Game. Like I said, their permit for crabbing is in process, and they're likely to get one. Then I talked with my friend Bill Farbis over there. Briefed him on what's going on."

"I know Farbis," said Bernard. "Dedicated man."

"He's going to expedite and approve their permit, which will give Fish and Game the right to put a GPS tag on the boat. They have to report their movements and where they get their catch. The State biologists like to keep records of where the traps are set and how much they catch. Part of their natural resource renewal formulas."

Bernard was stunned. "That's good work, Tom. Guess you are a bit of a detective."

"Okay, a deal's a deal. Did I tell you what you wanted to hear?"

"It's a start."

"Good," said Tom. Then I got two questions for you. Your boat still docked in Gig Harbor and what do I need to bring?"

Bernard checked his watch. It was early, two o'clock He had more than three dozen suspects to process and was not even halfway through them. The State, the Feds, the Mayor, they were all after him to get this done. Get these people out of our jail so we can prepare for the next crime wave to hit Seattle. Transfer them to Federal as quick as possible. Not our problem anymore.

Bernard looked down at Rita's report on his desk. He had good people working on the case. Now that Sommers and Baily were also on it, they were making progress.

The Feds had their own agenda. Interviewed the same people as the Seattle Police but unlike Bernard, they weren't sharing information. They had their own angle, part of their classified investigation. All his inquiries were met with polite refusal. Thank you, Mister Bernard. We'll tell you what you need to know when you need to know it.

Tom interrupted. "What about it, Matt? It's a beautiful day out."

The sun refected off the computer screen, the glare hiding the words. It passed, the light from behind the words glowing as the sun retreated behind another cloud. No rain today. Cloudy but no rain. He stared at another report, this one filed by the head of The Urban Research Department. He'd already read two of Van Dorn's reports and figured this one was pretty much the same. What do you get when you pop open a turd?

He thought about Rita, about giving Harry a call, reading more reports, making more phone calls. He had a cell phone. If they found something out they could call him and tell him what he needed to know. The line was quiet. Tom was waiting for an answer. "It'll take me an hour to get there," said Bernard. "We'll probably have about three or four hours to paddle around. If you beat me there, pull it over to the fuel dock and top her off. You know where I hide the key."

"You don't sound too sure. Promise me you'll be there in an hour. You stood me up last time."

He looked at the computer screen, open windows splattered across it to show reports by Franklin Van Dorn and another by Rita Rockwell. He laughed. "I got the best minds working on this," he said. "I'm going to check myself out of the office to follow up on a lead. I heard you say you had more information to discuss, but didn't want to do it over the phone."

"Meet you in an hour," said Walgamott.

"Give Bill a call. If he's available, ask him if he wants to join us."

"Will do," said Tom. "See you soon."

Bernard took a deep breath and started to clean up his mess. Then he decided to leave it alone. He shut the computer off and culled through the pile of papers on the desk, pulling out a few. Sensitive information needed to be kept under lock and key. Things seemed to be shaping up. Information was coming in and being processed. Clues were being uncovered. He decided to get back to basics. Maybe there was a way to get Van Dorn out of the interview room and speed things up a bit. He closed the desk drawer and turned the key.

"Yeah," he said. "I know how to speed this investigation up. We've done enough urban research. Rita Rockwell, tomorrow you get a new partner."

Chapter 22

Beauty School Dropout

It was midafternoon on a weekday and Capitol Hill was bursting with activity. The collection runs the gamut, as Seattle is a melting pot, or as people like to say, a fusion. Streets and sidewalks were crowded with everything including students, tourists, nurses from nearby hospitals, businessmen, and of course coffee aficionados jockeying for tables at places like Stumptown and Café Vita. There were delivery trucks with all that go with them, shoppers, artists, homeless, and even an occasional street musician near the park. Now add to that drag queen, transvestite detective Harry Takanawa, decked out in his secret identity of Fu Chan.

It's been a while since I've been dressed like this in public, thought Harry. *In broad daylight, no less. Why did I tell Binky I would walk?*

His eyes met strangers and then darted away, refusing to stay focused long enough to read their reaction. Everyone is staring, secretly making fun of the man in women's clothes. He tried to silence his inner voice, feeding him heaping portions of guilt and shame. He recognized it as his mother's guilt, a gift she had given him when she discovered him cross dressing as a child.

Inside, he may be hiding but outside he felt exposed. There was some inner awareness that he was a man dressed as a woman, but outside all seemed right with the world. People hardly noticed him, as long as he kept swaying his hips, bobbing his head, and shyly smiling, gestures that made him undeniably a woman. Inside him there was conflict, layers of emotion that competed for attention: excitement, fear of being exposed, self-defamation, and shame that he shouldn't enjoy this, especially when, like the cherry on the top of a sundae, he felt this overall sense of completeness and contentment. Add to that the sensations, the breeze on his legs, the sway of the skirt, the gentle fabric of the blouse against his skin, and the constant reminder of the heels on the arches of his feet. Femininity was all about illusion. The world itself was full of things that were not always what they seemed. It was an odd symphony of emotions and sensations. He clutched the purse tighter and stared at the sidewalk ahead.

Why did he enjoy this guilty pleasure? When he asked himself he had no answer. His therapist and his support group had given him little more. There is not a lot known about cross dressing. It's on the books, but the shrinks haven't quite figured it out yet. Some societies accept it, some don't. Gender roles are sensitive in some cultures. Sometimes it comes down to individuals who take a moral stance on the issue, weighing in without really understanding the subject matter. Other times people have their mind made up for them by some pundit who says it's bad. They convince the public that they have something to fear from transvestites, like they will band together and turn on straight society, forcing men to return to the days of togas and kilts. It's the moral decay of Western civilization.

The office of the Fu Chan Detective Agency was not in a fancy building or a high rise office tower. It was in a simple, brown three story building just off Pine Street in Capitol Hill. The main door to the street was open. Harry crossed the threshold, glad to be out of the public eye. There was noise from the first floor office, a nondescript door with no lettering. He had no idea what went on there but it always seemed to be occupied during business hours.

The elevator was permanently out of order. It was no good complaining to the landlord, unless you wanted a rent hike to pay for the repairs. Binky put as little as possible into his properties. The heels clicked on the stairs. Harry's calves ached, he would have to get used to heels again. He was glad to reach the third floor and turn the knob to the office door.

The door swung open. "Can I help you?" said Sue.

Harry stood there, knee bent, toe down, his hip thrust out. These feminine ways were starting to become natural again. He remembered a time when he became so immersed in the act that it didn't stop when he put his pants back on. They say clothes make the man, but maybe that's not entirely true.

Sue's hand went to her mouth. She got up from behind the desk. "Oh my God!" she screamed. "Harry, it's you!"

He smiled. Being discovered by Sue was not the same as being caught in a police raid.

"Let me have a look at you," she said. "Turn around now."

He obeyed. She was impressed at how graceful he was. She almost expected a curtsey at the end, but there were flaws, obvious ones to her. She ran her fingers through his hair. No body, and that unflattering clipped back ponytail had to go. Certainly we can do more with that chest, he still seemed to be hunching over.

"I need to use the computer," he said.

"Uh huh," she said. "You're going to have to work on that voice, too. It's a dead giveaway."

He elevated it a bit, softening the gruff sound that had been the mainstay of the cop, the marine, and the detective in him. "Can I sit at your desk?"

"It's your desk," she said. "I just sit at it when you're not here." Sue cleared her books from the front of the computer. Harry smiled at her, happy she was working towards a better future. He plopped down behind the desk.

"You're going to have to do better than that," said Sue.

"What?" asked Harry.

"Stand right back up, missy, and sit down proper. Don't just plop there."

"What?" asked Harry again. "It's just you and me here."

"You heard me. If you're going to dress like that, you better start acting the part full time."

"But I have been," he said.

"Well, what makes you think you can park it at the door when you come in here? This is the Fu Chan Detective Agency. You're Fu Chan, and Fu Chan does not plop down in chairs."

Harry stood up and gave it a second try.

"Much better," she said.

It wasn't much of a desk, a dented refugee from a government surplus sale that came with a scribbled blotter covering a peeling Formica top. The computer wasn't much better. Sue had done what she could with the rest of the office but there are limits to what was possible. Still, she worked hard to make the place bearable. The tiny office barely had enough space to contain the two desks and few chairs that were shared by everyone. Harry had graciously given up his desk for Sue. The first thing she did was ditch the ratty blotter that hid the aging gunmetal surface of the old metal desk, replacing it with a fresh, new one. She had Harry take a hammer to the drawer, beating it carefully and greasing the skids until it could slide open and closed. When she cleaned it out there were papers from the former owner, a computer startup that must have been in business when the first microchip was invented. It had long since closed its doors. She hoped the Fu Chan Detective Agency would be more successful than that, and with it, Harry.

The office was quiet these days and she seldom saw her bosses. Red was busy downtown and Harry, well, he had been off on a wild goose chase looking for his ex-wife. It would be fine with Sue if he never found her. Sue had a natural enmity for Trish, even though they had never formally met, just opinions formulated by second hand information. Trish had some kind of hold on Harry, she didn't know what, but it was obvious they were not done with one another. Still, Sue was patient and Harry was a prize she deemed worth waiting for.

Let's leave it at that.

He fumbled in the purse for the CD of information that Lenny had downloaded off of Trish's phone.

"Uhh, uhh," said Sue. "Quit digging! Be graceful, gentle, like you have all day to find what you're after in that purse."

Harry looked up. "Okay," he said. "Right. Fu Chan doesn't fumble." He stopped groping and gently pulled the CD out and loaded it on the computer. It was actually quicker than fumbling. Sue moved in behind him and tussled his hair. She pulled the bottom drawer of the desk out and removed a makeup kit and a bag of hairstyling supplies.

"What's that for?" asked Harry.

"I think you know." She pushed his head backward and tilted it up towards the light, dabbing mascara under his eyes. She took out a sponge and began applying makeup. The computer continued to hum, the old unit reading the disk at a speed that would delight any TRS 80 fan.

"I was a beauty school dropout," said Harry.

"It shows, but fortunate for you, I wasn't."

Harry was surprised. "I didn't know you went to beauty school," he said.

"Went right after high school," she said. "Paul Mitchell Academy over by Northgate. I was top in the class."

"Why the career change? You could be a successful operator by now."

"I was on my way." She stopped and looked away from his eyes and down towards the floor. "You remember my boyfriend?"

"The asshole that beat you?"

"It's hard to keep a job in a glamour profession when you look beat up all the time. Not to mention being high on whatever it was he was feeding me. I got fired, blacklisted. Stories like mine travel fast on the wet hair wireless."

The computer stopped humming and Sue went back to fixing hair. It felt good to have his hair brushed. He usually ran a brush through it every morning, enough to pull it back and tie it up for the day. He relaxed as he began browsing the disk. Lenny had arranged everything in neat little folders. They had listened to the messages and viewed some of the texts but it was the pictures that interested him most. They started coming up one at a time on the screen: pictures of her and her little dog – a surrogate child in his mind. She gave more love to that animal than she ever did to Harry. There were pictures of her mother, a scowl on her face. Come to think of it, her mother never smiled much. There was a picture of Trish in Europe, her dream shot in front of the Eiffel Tower. They were supposed to go there on their honeymoon. Harry couldn't remember why the trip was cancelled.

"She doesn't look very happy," said Sue. "If someone took me to Paris I'd be ecstatic."

Harry let the slide show continue. A picture of her on the couch with her cat. The cat didn't look happy. Trish in front of her new car, the envy of anyone suffering from a mid-life crisis. Still not happy. Harry paused the slide show and pulled open the second drawer on the right hand side of the desk. He dug around until he found a manila envelope which he opened. Wedding pictures, pictures of he and Trish on their honeymoon. Instead of Paris, he had taken her to Westport, Washington for the weekend.

"You both look happy in those pictures."

Sue was right. No denying it. And the happiness was genuine. How did it all go wrong?

"What attracted you to her?" asked Sue as she continued to work the makeup into his face.

Harry sighed. "I liked her the moment I met her. There was something that welled up in me, a feeling that reached up from the pit of my stomach and grabbed me by the throat. I was speechless." He laid the pictures on the desk and looked out the window into a past that survived somewhere inside the paper walls of his heart.

"How did you meet?" asked Sue.

"Our mothers arranged it. I was back from the war and moping around the house. My mother thought I needed a wife. It was obvious after a few dates that we were a good fit. She was fresh out of law school, I was a Seattle beat cop. We had a plan, I was going to arrest them and she would put them away." He smiled. "She was fun back then. She liked to dance, go out to shows, and dine at the best places around Seattle – not the most expensive, mind you, but the best. She taught me to appreciate the symphony and the jazz clubs. I didn't feel like living much after the war. Trish changed all that."

He went back to browsing pictures on the computer while Sue worked on his hair with a pair of scissors and a comb. "What happened?" she asked.

"We were married three years. The same amount of time it took me to make detective. It was after that big gun fight with the meth gang. I got winged with a bullet but she was the one who went ballistic. Urged me to get out of danger, get a desk job. She was right, besides I'd had enough of the street. I wouldn't have applied for the job as detective without her urging me to." The alley outside his window became a blur as he stared into his past. "Three years," he repeated, the words coming out like a gasp. He stared deeper into his past, the brick wall across the alley a blur of colored rectangles.

Harry remembered his mother's words. "Three years," she had said. "How come you don't have kids after three years. How come you won't do me proud and make me a grandparent?" Once again, disappointment. It wasn't the only time he had disappointed his mother, definitely not the last.

He looked away from the window and back at the computer screen. He started up the slide show again. The modern phone held a lot of high quality pictures. He scanned through some photos of her in new outfits. She looked happy in those pictures, but he knew it was the clothes that made her smile and not him.

"Why did you separate?" asked Sue.

Harry let a few more pictures pass before answering. "Having a wife was good for me. The moms were right, we were a good fit. There's just this one thing." Harry picked up a mirror lying next to the hairbrush. Fu Chan stared back at him.

He was surprised at what he saw. Sue had been busy proving she was not a beauty school dropout.

She smiled. "You like what you see?"

"Wow. Can you show me how to do this?"

"I'm not done yet," she said. She went back to work while the slideshow continued. Something on the screen caught his attention. It was the dressing room picture he had been looking for. Trish looked terrified. The picture had been a self-portrait, taken at arms-length with no flash. There was a partial face behind her, a blue eye looking coldly out from under a crop of blond hair. There was an arm across her face, an exposed tattoo that ran out of the frame of the picture. He had seen the design like that recently on a body in the morgue. He stopped the slideshow.

It was definitely taken in the dressing room where he had found the phone. The curtains in the background were an exact match. He checked the time and date stamp on the file and it matched. She went missing at 10:34:42 AM. A little over thirty hours ago and the trail was still hot.

He advanced to the next picture, this one a blurred shot of feet, like the camera had gone off by accident as it hit the ground. The style was unmistakable, a prize boot worth more money than Harry could earn in a month.

"Cute," said Sue. "Gotta love those Lucchesi boots."

Chapter 23

Ngu Man on the Job

The thrum of the giant diesel engines was a comfort to Ngu, as was the roll of the deck and the smell of the open sea. He had fished for all kinds of things in Micronesia including shark, squid, and crab. He had even been diving to harvest urchins, a luxury that brought a high price in Japan and had sustained his family when every other fishery was out of season. He had spent his lifetime making a living off the sea. This work was comforting to him and he was good at it.

Ngu opened the bait cage on the side of the crab trap and put a can of frozen fish parts inside. The can had holes punched in it allowing the crabs to smell the bait without being able to eat it. Lucky John helped him maneuver the last trap onto the release plank. He clipped the long line onto the grommet that attached to the trap and he and Ngu pushed it overboard.

"Party time," said John.

"Huh?" Ngu didn't understand.

"That was the last trap," he said. "Now we just wait for them to fill up."

"What do we do in the mean time?"

"Anything we want," said John. "Do you like to gamble?"

"Not really," said Ngu. "Besides, I don't have any money."

Another one of the crew overheard them talking and chimed in. "You don't want to gamble with him anyway," he said. "Unless you want to continue to have no money."

"Shut up, Brett," said John.

"There's a reason they call him Lucky John," said Brett.

John focused on Ngu. "Since you don't have any money, I'll stake you for your share."

"What do you mean?" asked Ngu.

"Your share in the boat. We each get a percentage of the profit the boat brings in. They told you that, didn't they?"

"Yes," said Ngu. "But no thanks. I'd rather hang on to my money. I only recently arrived and I have to save everything I can."

"Why?" asked Brett.

"I want to go to Kansas City Missouri to look up my father," he said.

"Your father lives in America?" said John. "I thought you said you were from Indonesia or somewhere."

"Micronesia," corrected Ngu. "My Dad was an American living there. He met my mother and that's when I came along. Mom always wanted to go to America and find him but she died before we could save enough money."

"How do you know where he lives?"

"I found letters he had written to her from an address in Kansas City. That was when I decided to make the journey to America, even though it was her dream to find him."

A crew member stuck his head out from below deck. "You coming, Lucky?" he asked. "We're about to deal the first hand."

"Sure you don't want to play?" asked John.

"No thanks," said Ngu. "I think I'm going to rest." He went below with John, moving past the table where chips and cards appeared as quickly as birds and scarves from the sleeve of a magician. He went forward to his bunk, closing the door behind him to settle into the solitude. He laid in the fo'castle but the noise from the game filled the ship. There were cheers and shuts of anger, harsh words and nervous laughter. It ebbed and flowed with the sound of the waves against the hull of the ship and the constant thrum of the diesel. Ngu had a restless sleep, barely moving into the REM state before the Captain woke him and told him it was time to work again.

Out on deck the crew was agitated. John was gloating about his luck in cards and bragging about what he was going to do with all the money he won. It wasn't sitting well with Ralston, one of the crew who had lost heavily. Ngu felt uneasy working next to them as they handled traps that weighed hundreds of pounds. He turned the trap upside down, balancing it on the cable that held it over the open hold. Crabs spilled out and he rapped the cage, loosing the last of the last stubborn critters from the sides of the trap.

"Quit your bragging," said Ralston, glaring at Lucky John. He slammed the trap door shut and pushed it out of the way. It swung on the boom, over the side and down into the deep. The next trap on the line came up. Ngu looked inside. He had never seen a square, white crab before.

"Empty that one in the forward hold," yelled the Captain. "Quickly, lads."

They were square white packages, small bricks about the size of a cinder block. They weren't that heavy, and Brett appeared on deck to help get them stowed away. There were no crabs in the trap, the door had a piece of mesh stretched over it.

"Get that mesh out before we toss it back in the sea," said Ralston. Ngu pulled the bungee cords off and removed the cover that made the trap useless for catching sea life. The can of bait was still in the bait cage and they pushed the empty trap back in the sea.

This happened three more times. Ngu counted maybe fifty or sixty packages, all of equal size, weight, and color. "There's one stuck inside the trap," said Ralston.

Ngu made a move to get it but Ralston stopped him. "Let John get it. You've been doing all the hard work. It's his turn."

John shook his head and looked at Ngu. "It's okay. I'll get it." He turned the trap around and pushed against the white brick from the outside. It was stuck and wouldn't budge, caught on something. He flipped the trap over and reached inside. He was close and he stretched, wiggling through the open door as he extended his hand. Ngu moved outside the trap to help him, poking at the object with a billy club.

John wrapped his hands around the package and pulled. It came loose and he fell backwards into the trap. Gnu steadied the trap and John rolled to his feet inside the trap. He pushed the package through the door and Ngu scooped it up.

It happened quickly. Ngu went forward and put the package in the hold with the others. When he came back, John was inside the trap, Ralston holding the door shut as he spoke to him.

"I want to know if you were cheating. John. You were awfully lucky today."

"I don't cheat," said John. "Lucky John, you know me."

"Yeah," said Ralston. "Lucky John." He pushed against the door with his shoulder, a rubber bungee dangling in his hand.

John stuttered. "Hey, no hard feelings, Rawls. We were playing for fun. I'll give you your money back."

"Will you?" said Ralston. He held his hand out.

"Yeah, let me out and I'll go get it," said John. "It's in my other pants."

"Other pants," said Ralston. "Thanks for that information." He slipped the bungee in place, detaching the marker buoy as he kicked the trap overboard. Ngu saw the surprise on John's face as the trap crashed into the sea. The foam surged around him like an exploding washing machine, then the whole framework disappeared slowly, like the fading silhouette of a tree in the morning fog.

"What did you just do?" asked Ngu.

"Got bigger shares for us all."

Ngu ran to the bridge. "Captain, you have to turn the boat around," he said. "There's been an accident. A man may be drowned."

Ralston stood behind him. "Happened a few minutes ago, Cap'n," he said. "He got caught in a trap going after one of those packages. It was stuck in the cage and he went inside. We tried to help him, Ngu harder than I did. Then the boat lurched and the trap went over. Sank right out of sight, but I figure he was dead when he hit the water, cold as it is."

The Captain nodded. "Did we get the package?" he asked.

"Yes," said Ngu. "It's in the hold."

"I see." He looked off in the distance, then at his watch. "I don't see any reason to alter our schedule. I'll enter it in the log that he died in the line of duty." Ngu started to say something. "It's okay," said the Captain. "I'll make a note in the log that you tried to save him, too. You did your best, I'm sure. We'll put you in for a piece of his share. John didn't have any kin as far as I know. Good job, Ngu."

"Yes," said Ralston. "Good job." He clapped Ngu on the shoulder, smiling in a way that told Ngu he better go along with the story, or he may become crab bait.

"Okay, men. Back to work then," said the Captain. He nodded his head. "Bigger shares for everyone this trip."

"Aye, Captain," said Ralston. "Bigger shares for us all."

Ngu heard the cheers as the news spread through the ship. He tried to stay focused on his work, but an uneasy feeling crept over him. As he emptied another trap into the hold he saw a lone crab fall on the deck. He made a move to get it but the crab was quick, the claws raised in defiance as it scuttled sideways until it fell over the side and back into the sea.

Ngu thought about his predicament. Working on a boat depended on trust and understanding between the crew and the Captain. He felt neither, and as he stared at the space where the crab fell, he thought of how easy it would be to fall overboard and end this before it got started.

He had to keep his dream alive to see his father. Like the crab, he was free for now. He thought for a while, peering into the sea where the waves and the foam concealed everything from his eye. Yes, he was free. At least until he was drawn again by his own hungers into another trap.

Perhaps, like the crab, thought Ngu, my fate is also inescapable.

Chapter 24

A Whole New Day

The Chief Inspector and Head of The Urban Research Department was having a bad day. First, the cook was late and he had to make his own toast, even pour his own orange juice. At breakfast he had to listen to his mother go on about what he needed to do today, including what woman he should date this evening and what clothes he should wear and what to tell the Mayor when he saw him. Then he found out the Beemer was still in the shop and conveniently mother couldn't find the keys to the Mercedes SLS, the AMG being his second choice. That left the HumVee, the Miata, the rebuilt '69 Dodge Dart, or the Lexus IXC, all of which sucked in one way or another. He could always take the Ducati but motorcycles were risky with the unpredictable weather in Seattle. It got worse from there. He got on the toll road going over the floating bridge, only to be slowed to one lane for construction. What was the point of having a pay as you go speedway when it was like this?

He pulled into his parking space at the cop shop and locked the Lexus, plodding towards his office. An hour late, maybe more, but who was counting. He hoped the big redheaded bitch was on the job and not waiting for him to get started.

There was a pretty blonde on the elevator. He licked his hand and stroked the back of his head, giving her the famous Van Dorn eye. She looked away. Shy thing, he thought. He got off on the 10th floor and went to his office to have a cup of coffee and check the paper for news clips.

About mid-morning he strolled downstairs towards the interrogation rooms. The schedule said Rita Rockwell was working in room 3-B. He moved down the corridor only to find it blocked by Harry Takanawa talking to some cute brunette. He laughed. *Wonder if she knows he's a tranny*, he thought. He glanced down at her bump, an obvious bun in the oven that was well baked. Van Dorn licked his hand and flattened the hair on the back of his head.

"Excuse me," he said.

The brunette turned, and he had to gasp. Jen Meyer was stunning. She had a glow that was there long before she was pregnant. Men naturally gravitated towards her, and Franklin Van Dorn was no exception. Harry on the other hand was, well, Harry. He had undone everything Sue had worked towards and again pulled his hair back into an unimpressive ponytail. His clothes looked like he had slept in them, his pants wrinkled like a mountain range against his legs. His shirt had a slight stain on the front from a morning coffee accident.

Van Dorn suddenly recognized her. "You're that girl from the picture," he said. "The one of you and him..."

She cut him off. "Excuse me," she said rather gruffly. "We were talking here."

"I see that," said Van Dorn. "The conversation didn't sound very interesting from what I heard." He looked her right in the face and licked his hand.

It was all she could do to keep from throwing up, and she was sure it wasn't morning sickness.

"I came to rescue you from this weirdo," said Van Dorn, poking his chin towards Harry. "I'm sorry, we haven't been properly introduced." He extended his hairball paw.

She looked at it as if it were a used condom. "I'm Jen Meyer," she said.

"Chief Investigator Franklin Van Dorn of The Urban Research Department."

Harry started to open his mouth but Van Dorn shot him an evil glance. Harry just smiled.

"I've heard of you," said Jen. "You're that TURD?"

Van Dorn looked at the wall, then at Harry. Harry opened the door to the observation room adjacent to interrogation room 3-B. He held the door open and bowed like the doorman at the Grand Palace Hotel. Van Dorn shot him a derisive glance and stepped through. Harry smiled and closed the door behind him, remaining in the hall.

"Sorry about that," said Harry, turning his attention back to Jen.

She laughed. "Van Dorn is a piece of work, but you gotta admire him." She laughed again, unable to stop, trying to catch her breath. Harry had to laugh too. "Turd," she blurted between giggles.

"Seriously, though," said Harry. "I can't thank you enough for saving my life. If you hadn't removed those exploding breast implants that madman had put in me..."

"Look, Harry," she said, all serious and business like. "I responded that night, knowing I would put my own life at risk, but when I thought about it, when I imagined what it must have been like to have a bomb so close to your heart with some madman at the controls, by God I cried for you. I had to come help." A tear glistened in her eye. "You'd do the same for me," she said. "Probably even for Van Dorn or someone like him. Hell, you'd do it for anyone."

Harry smiled, the kind of smile that came with a tear too. "Thank you, Jen," he reached out and hugged her, a close embrace, a thank you that made words seem like shadow play across a dark paper screen.

Jen sniffled. "So," she said, pushing back from his grip. "How's it feel to have real breasts?"

Harry looked down and did a quick shoulder shimmy, shaking the bobbing flesh. "So. How's it feel to be pregnant?" he asked.

She laughed. "I got married last year, a nice boy who works for FEMA. I'm still using Meyer around here but I have a new last name. We got married up on the San Juan Islands. I sent you an invitation. He's the one I wanted to have babies with. A nice guy from Texas, a gentle man who treats me like a lady."

"You deserve nothing less, Jen," said Harry. "How is the little sidewinder?" he asked, looking at her belly.

"Doing good," she said, patting it for good luck. "Best thing that could have happened to me. They worried about me doing field work so they gave me a desk job in the tower. I got kicked upstairs."

"Speaking of kicking, is the baby active?"

"Every day," she said. "Wish I could have kept the field job, though."

"Come on, Jen," said Harry. A pregnant woman on the bomb squad? It's enough to put one life at risk and it seems politically incorrect to me."

"Me, too," she said. "I just miss the action, but being pregnant isn't bad. I still run, and the motion rocks the baby to sleep. It's only when I sit at a desk that he starts kicking. Maybe that's the problem."

Harry looked away for a moment, his face showing something she couldn't quite read.

"What is it?" she asked.

"Van Dorn," he said. "That nastiness he brought up. I'm sorry about all those pictures that got circulated about us. You know the ones with you leaning over me and holding my breasts just after you removed the exploding implants."

"I have the framed article from the Capitol Hill paper, the headlines reading 'Bomb Squad Bombshell Breast in the Business'." She laughed again. "Good publicity." She clapped Harry on the shoulder. "Look. I work in a male dominated world. It's like trying to play pro football. I find that even though I'm pregnant, I'm first string tough. If I'm not, if I don't play the game, I fall into the role of the woman on the team. I'm no longer an equal, but something else. If they're going to label me, I'd at least like to select the label. Besides, Harry, no matter what they say or do, I'm going to run this place one day. And believe me, no matter where the turds come from, I'll get rid of them with my trusty doggie scoop."

"Doggie scoop?" said Harry.

"You know what I mean. Don't you start giving me crap."

Harry hugged her again. "Oh God, I love you. Thanks again, Jen."

She patted him on the back, aware of the bump pressing against his belly.

"I better get in there," said Harry. "We planned a little surprise for Van Dorn and I really didn't want to miss it."

As if in response, the door to observation room 3-B flung open and Van Dorn steamed out of the room.

Jen released Harry. "Gotta run," she said, turning to retreat down the hall.

Van Dorn headed right for the door to the interrogation room. Harry stopped him, his hand snapping on Van Dorn's wrist like a boa constrictor squeezing a rat. The wrist went limp and Harry took off some of the pressure. "You know the new rules, Van Dorn. We can observe but not intervene. Now let's go back into the observation room next door." Harry squeezed just a little bit, his hand making maximum use of the pressure points of pain. He calmly stepped left, still gripping Van Dorn's hand as he pulled it away from the doorknob. His hand naturally twisted, pointing down, rotating Van Dorn's arm into an incredibly uncomfortable place. Gotta love that Marine Corps training. Semper fi.

With his free hand Harry opened the door to the observation room and led Van Dorn to a seat. Franklin rubbed his wrist and leered at Harry.

On the other side of the glass they saw Bernard staring at some belligerent thug. Rita was pacing, leading the interrogation, Bernard passive and observant.

"Okay, help me get your story straight, Purvis," said Rita. "You just happened to be strolling on the docs at 2:00 am, getting your exercise. Do you have sleep problems?"

"I usually work the night shift. Two A.M. is like lunch time to me."

"Lunch, huh?" She gripped his right arm, high and at the top of the sleeve. She ripped it down, exposing a tattoo, a burned symbol of misplaced loyalty. Bernard gasped at the sudden move but quickly recovered his composure.

Purvis began to sweat.

"Sorry," said Red. "Cheap fabric. I'll get you a sewing kit. It will give you something to do for the next 20 years while you're locked up."

"You got nothing on me."

Rita lunged, gripping his upper arm, pressing her thumb into the tattoo. It began to hurt, not as bad as when it was created, but close. The thumb pressed harder, pushing flesh to the very bone. She leaned in close. "Nothing, huh? Tell me now. Talk and I will make sure Che never finds out. Unless, you want to go back there?"

Purvis was thinking.

Bernard spoke up. "Look," he said. "We know you were involved with the whole human trafficking thing that went down the other night. We know Che is behind it. That whole empire is about to come crumbing down. Feds got their eyes on this now, and they've pulled in every resource on the west coast to make this happen. I got three squads of SWAT ready to hit anything within a hundred miles of here. The smart thing for you is to come clean. When we release you, it will be to witness protection. Otherwise…"

"Otherwise what?" said the thug.

"Well, you go up the food chain. Maybe the Feds will offer you something better. Right now you belong to Seattle PD and this is my offer. It's your call."

Red looked down at Purvis. "We netted a lot of you scum the other night. You're in stir with all your buddies. So many I'll be interviewing them for days. Law of odds is in my favor, one of them will talk and take the deal."

"Good luck with that," said Purvis. "That deal is a death sentence."

Red squeezed his arm tighter, imagining she was making a fist. She could see red spots appear on his skin around her grip. She rubbed her thumb hard across the tattoo, feeling the bumps. He looked up at her, gritting his teeth. "You think you're so tough."

She squeezed tighter, staring down into his eyes. His body didn't move but staring into his soul she saw him wince. Then his eyelids shut her out. When he recovered he said, "I'd like to go three rounds in the ring with you."

She breathed deep, moving closer. "I'd like that too," she rasped.

"Okay. That's enough," said Bernard. He nodded towards the one way glass and Harry picked up the phone and called for prisoner transport at 3-B. Rita loosened her grip and pushed Purvis away. She picked up the sleeve and threw it at him. He stood up, defiant, reached over and ripped the other sleeve off and threw both of them at her.

Bernard was next to him before he had a chance to move again. There was a blur, and suddenly Harry saw Purvis pushed up against the glass, his face flattened like a piece of bubble gum on the sidewalk. He looked like a flounder, his eye all googley in a pasty field of flesh.

The door opened behind him and two guards entered. "We'll take it from here, lieutenant" said one of them.

Purvis glared at them both. "Nobody will talk," said Purvis. "It's a death sentence."

"Witness protection will give you a new life," said Bernard. "Better than the one you have now." He glared back. "Think about it. You got twenty four hours before I release you to the Feds." He nodded to the guards who took him away. Bernard picked up his notes and followed Red next door to the observation room.

The door to the room hardly cracked open before Van Dorn was up and postured, leaning forward like a schoolyard heckler. "You've overstepped yourself this time, Bernard."

Red was first in the door. She clenched her fists but caught sight of Harry behind him, shaking his head and mouthing 'no' as he smiled. He motioned to the seat beside him.

Bernard sauntered in the room and calmly turned up the lights.

"You've overstepped yourself this time, Bernard," said Van Dorn again, as if it were his line in a well-practiced play.

"No I haven't," he replied. "And where were you all morning? It's after eleven. You're lucky I was here to fill in. You should be thanking me. We're on our sixth interview today."

Van Dorn licked his hand and flattened the hair on the back of his head. "Thank you!" he snorted. "Now that I'm here, I'll take over. You can go back to your office and push paper."

Bernard laughed, then frowned and leaned in real close. "Look, you little turd. You can't dismiss me like one of your house servants. Besides, this change is permanent. You are no longer working with my resources. I am."

"On what authority?"

"Didn't you hear?" said Bernard. "*My* resources. Now, if you want to make a case of this, let me show you some statistics. In the past two days, working as a team with Miss Rockwell, you managed to process eight witnesses."

Van Dorn smiled.

"We did five already this morning," said Bernard. "And it looks like we'll hit ten or more by the end of the day. And we're just beginning."

Van Dorn frowned, took a deep breath. "I'm going to the Mayor on this."

"I got a better idea," said Harry, giving them both an honorable out. "We're about to review the facts and debrief on the morning's work. Why not stay with us and brainstorm, Franklin. Help us piece this thing together."

Van Dorn snorted. "I'm still going to the Mayor." He turned and stormed out the door.

"Will you get in trouble?" asked Red.

"I can't wait to see how this turns out," said Bernard, smiling.

"If it's like the Sooka Case, he'll probably get another promotion," said Harry.

"You're right. Turds always float to the top." They all had a good laugh, then it was down to business. Bernard shuffled through his notes.

Harry started it off. "Well, we know one thing. Che and that tattoo symbol are definitely related. Every time we mention his name, a perp with a tat talks. The ones without the tat don't recognize the name."

Bernard looked at his notes. "That's not entirely true. There was one this morning. Kern was his name. He said something about butting up against Che's operations recently. Then he mentioned being approached by a recruitment team with an offer to join Che's organization."

"Yeah," said Red. "He said he refused."

"Did you see he was missing a middle finger?" asked Harry. "Looked pretty fresh to me. He kept rubbing it while he was talking. Wasn't long after that he stopped talking."

"What are you trying to say?" asked Bernard.

"Yesterday I asked around about Che," said Harry. "I heard tales about people losing their tongues. He uses scare tactics and creates legends like the old time warlords. No wonder nobody talks."

"They seemed nonchalant about going to jail, too," said Red.

"Yeah," said Bernard. "Did you catch that one guy this morning? He said something about still getting his share, even if he was in jail."

"Yeah," said Red. "Like he was some kind of corporate stockholder."

"Wait a minute," said Harry. He dug through yesterday's notes, pulling out a sheaf and reading. "Look, this guy here." He pointed, making the paper snap under his finger. "Armando Lorant. He made a reference to the Corporation. Used it like a proper noun. He even called Che 'The Chairman'."

"Yes. The Chairman," said Red, recalling the interview. "Chairman Che."

"It rolls off your tongue," said Bernard. "Like the man has a philosophy."

"Corporate philosophy," said Harry. "The most dangerous kind. I think he has Trish too."

"What?" asked Bernard.

Harry took a few minutes to catch them up. The abduction, the phone pictures, the arm with the tattoo.

"What does Che want with Trish?" asked Red.

"I haven't figured that out yet," said Harry.

"Couple of possibilities," said Bernard. "First question for you. Do you think the abduction was intentional or accidental?"

"Not sure," said Harry. "Considering her job, a lawyer, she might have some criminal enemies. Think she somehow messed with Che?"

"Or one of his men," said Bernard. "So let's follow that line. If she was targeted and abducted, why?"

"They sure picked a good spot. They must have been stalking her," said Harry. "What do you figure, Rita. You're good at Clue."

"If Che wanted her, it would have to be for something very specific," she said. "I'd start reviewing her clients. Look for one with a tattoo."

Something clicked in Harry's brain. Any discussion about the morning's interviews suddenly got pushed aside. "I gotta go, Matt," said Harry. "Time isn't on my side."

Bernard could see it. "You're clear. I know you want to find Trish. You can take the afternoon off if you want. Thanks for coming in this morning."

"What's the status of my Volvo? Can I pick it up?"

"Still in impound," said Bernard. "The Mayor's Office put a hold on the release. Said they want more time to review the evidence."

"So you're telling me…"

"You need Van Dorn's signature to get it out," said Bernard. He watched the wind fall out of Harry's sail. Time to puff them up a bit. "So what's your plan?"

"Plan?" asked Harry.

"Come on," said Bernard. "Don't pretend like you don't have one and you're not going to tell me. I saw your eyes light up a minute ago."

Harry twisted inside. Bernard watched his shoulders slump, his eyes lose focus and drop to the floor. He started to laugh. "It's really insane," he said, shaking his head from side to side. "I'm insane."

"We all know that," said Red. "Now tell us the plan."

"I'm going to put on a dress and chase her down."

It took Bernard a few seconds. Just about as much time as it took Red. They both burst into laughter.

"Yeah, yeah. Laugh it up," said Harry. "How do you think I got her phone?"

Bernard stopped laughing. "You mean you had to get dressed up to find her phone?"

"Like I told you, she was abducted in a women's dressing room. I figured it would be easier to look around in a women's dressing room if I was dressed like a woman. It's a… skill I have with disguise."

"Makes sense to me," said Rita. "I would have done it for you, if you asked me. I am a real woman, you know."

Harry smiled. "You're busy. Besides, looking for Trish isn't paying the bills."

Red touched him on the arm. "But it's just as important. You know that."

"Rita's right," said Bernard. "You need to go after Trish. Stay on payroll a few hours this afternoon, write up your last report, and I'll sign you out." He crossed the room and picked up the phone, dialed and started talking.

Red squeezed Harry's arm. "You're doing the right thing. I can stay here while you work the case of the missing Trish."

Harry laughed. "Missing Trish?"

"Sue already opened up a file on it under that name."

He moved his hand to cover Red's, patted it a few times. With a few short words, she and Bernard had lifted the responsibility he had on his shoulders and given him back his passion.

"These cases are related, Rita. The tattoo is a common thread, you're right about that. I'm going to take your advice, go to her office and look over her client list." He remembered what she had written on her job application. She really was good at Clue. "You going to be okay?" asked Harry.

"Don't worry about me. Everything's looking good for me. I managed to go from a turd to the undeterred. Working with Bernard is so much better than Van Dorn. And he's teaching me things, how to handle people, how to play games and bluff. I'm loving it."

"Then stay at it," said Harry. "Got any other ideas Nancy Drew?"

"Oh, no," said Red. "I think following her trail is a good plan. It's always worked for me. It's how I found you when you were missing."

Harry shuddered, remembering a nightmarish hell at the hands of a madman. Rita risked her life to find him.

Bernard heard Rita's last words. He put the phone down and faced Harry. "She's right. Follow her trail. See where it leads you. Just let me know what you're doing. Check in when you can, maybe we'll have something to share with you from our investigation. Meanwhile, go downstairs to documents. They're going to set you up with some fake id to support your cover."

"Thought I wasn't doing any police work," said Harry.

"You're not. You're just an ex-husband searching for his ex-wife," said Bernard.

"Just in a very strange way," added Red.

Bernard snorted. "Yeah. Either way, it wouldn't hurt to have some credentials. You can't go flashing your Harry Takanawa driver's license."

"But they'll need a picture of me as a woman," said Harry.

"Oh, don't worry. They got pictures of you in drag. And those guys are Photoshop wizards," said Bernard. "I just called. They're expecting you. If you don't like what they do, just have 'em lift your face off the poster of you and Jen on the wall down there."

Chapter 25

Butcher Shop

Carlos mixed the afternoon feed, readying himself for another round of tending the livestock, except they weren't really livestock. His mind knew that, but he had to keep thinking of them as livestock. It was a little trick he used to keep himself from going mad. The problem was, it wasn't working anymore and he was beginning to see behind the trick. Truth can be a terrible thing to face, but even more terrible to put off. Ask anyone who has lived a lie and faced it every day.

He loaded the cart, wishing he didn't have to do this again. To walk by the hopeless faces of women as they pass jars of milk through the bars. They take their feed gladly, some gratefully. Some look at him as if he could do something for them, most of them look away.

I'm little more than a dairyman, he thought.

He confirmed it, pushing the cart towards the large stainless steel doors leading to the room of stalls, the sign "DAIRY" printed in block letters over the entrance. There is a scent to these women, a strange odor that makes it easy for him to think of them as livestock. He hadn't noticed it the first day. It is a human smell, and it is not. It is the smell of sour milk and feces, musk and tears, and the overarching smell of disinfectant everywhere.

As he bumped against the doors Carlotta stopped him. A man was beside her. "Carlos, I want you to meet Doctor Mandelle."

"We've met," said Carlos.

"Good," she continued. "You're going to work with him today. He's going to train you on more of your farm duties."

The Doctor extended his hand. He was a lean man, aged and jaded. His face did not hold the compassion that a Doctor should have. Carlos took his hand nonetheless, and it felt like the soft part of a fish when it falls limply into your palm. He could almost feel the slime, and he resisted the urge to wipe his hand on his pants.

"You can call me Klaus," he said to Carlos. "It's my first name. Since we'll be working closely together we might as well be on a first name basis. Right, Carlos?"

Carlos nodded. He looked at Carlotta.

"It's okay," she said. "I got you covered." She grabbed the handles of the cart, smiled and pushed it through the door. The odor swept back and Carlos was thankful his wish had come true. A day away from the dairy. Carlotta seemed happy to tend the livestock, even enjoyed it.

Be careful what you wish for.

Klaus smiled. "This way please." He led Carlos out the back and down a long corridor lined with doors on either side. He had never been this way. They turned at the end and continued down another long hall. Every now and then he would pass an open door and see an office or a doctor's examination room or an occasional meeting room. Mandelle made light conversation with Carlos as they walked.

"We have a lot in common," he said. "I understand you did all manner of farm work in your time."

"Yes," said Carlos.

"And how are you finding our little dairy?" he asked.

"It's..." Carlos searched for a word. "Interesting."

"Yes," agreed Mendelle. "Yes. Interesting. You've raised cows before?"

"For a short time."

"Dairy or meat?"

"A little of both," said Carlos.

"Interesting, yes," said Mendelle. "Did you butcher also?"

"Yes," said Carlos.

"And what did you butcher?"

"Pretty much everything. Birds, chickens, pigs, goats, cows. Even wild game."

"Ahh," said Mendelle. "Wild game. Yes."

"Yes, Doctor Mendelle," said Carlos. "Wild game. Deer, tapir. I once watched some men butcher a cougar."

"And you ate the meat?"

"And the tripe," said Carlos. "It made a good soup."

"Tripe. Yes," said Mendelle. "Please call me Klaus, though. What else did you eat, Carlos?"

"Monkey, too. Lots of monkey."

"Of course. Monkey!" Mendelle was delighted, like a child looking forward to playing with a new friend. "The whole monkey?"

"Depends on the type of monkey. The mean ones are stringy, but the brains are sweet. The best ones are protected by law, but every now and then a few are killed as nuisances."

"Monkey meat. Yes," said Mendelle. "It's sweet, especially when properly prepared. It takes time, though. Time."

He stopped in front of one of the doors, staring through a small window at something inside. Carlos couldn't get a good look at what he was seeing. There was movement, thumps against the walls, muffled screams and cries. Mandelle smiled. "Monkey meat. Very sweet," he said. "But then, any flesh tastes sweet on an open fire." He moved away, continuing down the corridor, Carlos following close behind.

"Dog? I assume you've eaten dog?"

Carlos stopped. Mandelle took a few more steps, then stopped and turned. "Have you?"

"Have you ever been hungry, Klaus? Have you ever been so hungry you would eat almost anything?"

Mendelle stared back at him, his eyes hollow, as grey as storm clouds. "Yes," he said, his breath coming out heavy. "I have been that hungry, Carlos, my friend. Dog, squirrel, rat, snake. I've eaten out of trash cans. The ones behind restaurants are the best. And have you forgotten about bugs? Nutritious, they explode in your mouth like nothing else does. Crunchy, with a hint of goo. Yes. Have you been that hungry?"

Carlos stared into his eyes "Yes," he said calmly. "I have been that hungry. I have gladly eaten bugs. Quite recently I might add."

Mandelle's grey eyes launched twin probes deep into Carlos, deep into his soul. "Human flesh?" he asked, his voice sounding like the wind through a scarecrow. Like a gale, it whistled through the holes in his humanity deafening Carlos to all but the sound of the blood pounding in his brain.

"Was it curiosity, or was it hunger?" asked Mandelle. "I just want to know."

Carlos did not answer.

Mandelle waited patiently, Carlos feeling his insides burn under gaze of the Doctor's microscope.

"Yes," said Mandelle. "We have a lot in common, don't we?"

At the end of the corridor was a double door that opened to a small area. There was a sink where Klaus instructed Carlos to thoroughly wash his hands as he did the same. When they were finished he put on a pair of rubber gloves, offering a set to Carlos. Then he led him through another double door that opened into a large room. It was tiled like a bathroom, the tiles running a third of the way up the walls where stainless steel took over. Along the back wall there were rows of small square stainless steel doors, latched and lined up like a parade of refrigerator doors in an expensive kitchen. There were two identical stainless steel tables in the center of the room, tilted and indented ever so slightly, the sides rimmed, channeling everything towards a small hole at the long end.

Carlos looked underneath. There was a stainless steel bucket positioned directly under the hole. There was a heavy duty drain underneath each table and a spigot with a hose attached, making the room easy to clean up. Very fancy place to butcher farm animals.

Klaus walked over to the refrigerator doors. He pointed to a gurney near the far wall, instructing Carlos. "Bring that over here," he said. He turned and opened one of the doors. He reached low, pulling out a shelf. There was a body in it, draped in a fine white cloth, but definitely a human shape. Before Carlos could react, Mandelle ordered, "Help me move it to the gurney. They struggled, wrestling the body from the shelf and onto the cart. "Over here," said Klaus, helping Carlos guide the cart to the nearest stainless steel table. Carlos understood. He helped Mendelle gently move the body to the table. "Head faces down towards the small hole," he said.

Mendelle unwrapped the shroud, a thin veneer of cloth that barely hid the body. Carlos recognized the woman. She was one who had rushed towards him, reaching at him through the bars. He thought it was because she wanted to grab him, and maybe that was part of it. But there was something more, something she never managed to communicate to him. Carlotta had acted fast, swatting at her with a device that crackled with electricity like a cattle prod. He noticed that she was gone the next time they did rounds. The girl had fallen backwards and they had simply moved on to the next stall. And here she was now, still and quiet, her face not quite peaceful, as if death were unwelcome and sudden.

"How did she die?" he asked.

Mandelle stared at him. "That is not important, but we may soon see. Have you ever performed an autopsy before?' he asked.

"No," said Carlos.

"Then pay attention while I go to work." Mandelle opened a drawer that rested under the table. It was full of odd looking instruments. He took a big knife out of the drawer and reached down, gently cradling the girl's neck in his gloved hand. He turned the head sideways and slit the neck. Blood began to pour out, running in a thick stream towards the hole before dripping into the catch bucket under the table. "Always bleed from the head. It will drain in less time, and the blood is valuable, so you will get the most this way. Now, while this one is draining help me get another one out."

They struggled with the second body, a woman Carlos did not recognize. When she was positioned on the other table, Mandelle held the knife out for Carlos. "This one is all yours," he said. "Make the cut to bleed it, then we'll get started on the other and I'll show you what to do."

Carlos held the knife in his hand. He looked at the blade, judged the sharpness of the tool, then stared down at the face of the woman on the table. He gently turned the head sideways so she looked away from him, then he pressed the knife against her neck.

"What are you waiting for?" asked Mandelle.

Carlos let the knife slip along the neck, opening the inner and outer carotid and the jugular in one swoop. Mandelle breathed a sigh and Carlos let his hand fall to his side, the knife still clutched tightly in his grip. The blood flowed like a freshwater spring, marring the smooth stainless surface with a dark river that slowly edged towards the hole.

"Good. Good," said Mandelle. "This blood saves lives," he said. "Now, over here where you can watch me." He went to the other table and stood over the woman. Skillfully he slid the knife along her abdomen. Her insides burst like a ripe piñata. Mandelle reached inside and gently moved the organs out of the way. "Before we dispose of the body, there are several things we want to harvest. Do you know what stem cells are?"

"I've heard of them," said Carlos.

"They're found in ovaries. Also in the brain stem and in embryos seven to ten days old. They're very valuable and the Company uses them for advanced scientific research. It's our job to keep the supply fresh."

Carlos watched his hands move deftly through the body cavity. "Ah, what luck," he said. "This woman was pregnant. Come over here and take a look." He moved the organs out of the way and stood aside, allowing Carlos a clear view of the insides. "Reach in here and feel," he said. "See if you can locate it." Carlos hesitated but did as he was instructed. Mandelle nodded, satisfied, then he pushed Carlos aside, his hands moving down into the slit in the body. He opened his hands, grabbing what he could, then squeezed them, continuing to flex them in and out as if the her guts were some kind of fitness club hand exerciser.

He looked up and saw Carlos staring at him. "Ah, yes," he said. He stopped what he was doing and groped his way to her uterus, his hands deftly doing what he had done so many times before. The knife went in and soon he was holding a tiny placenta and fetus. "You can't even see that it's human yet, it's only one and a half inches long. When you find one of these, they are very valuable. Remove it entirely and place it one of these bio bags. Cut here, and here, like this, see?"

Carlos stared, trying to take it all in.

"Grab one of those plastic bags from the drawer," said Mandelle. Carlos took a biohazard bag from the drawer. Klaus passed him the fetus and went back to work. He tugged at another mass of tissue, gripped tightly in his hand as the body tugged back. He reached over with the scalpel and made some quick cuts. "It's not brain surgery," he said. "Just get the job done. Remove the tissue and go on to the next item. "While you're here, grab the ovaries." He made more crude cuts, occasionally stopping to let Carlos look over his shoulder and see what he was doing. "Okay, open the bio bag and let me drop this in." Carlos obeyed. "Now we move on to the brain."

Carlos watched with both fright and fascination. Klaus Mandelle had equally the hands of a master surgeon and a butcher. He seemed to oscillate between the two, like some kind of mad split personality, his demeanor would change with every swipe of the scalpel. There would be precision, master cuts of the knife followed by brutal tugging and wrenching of organs and innards.

When he was finished they sealed the bio bags and Klaus wrote some notes with a marker on the outside. He took it over to a table against the wall and placed it in a small Styrofoam cooler marked with a prominent biohazard emblem. He went to a nearby ice machine and poured a scoop of ice over the bags. "Now, we fill out the report," he said. On the table was a piece of paper, a rough diagram of the body. The top was printed with a number and the words MEDICAL CADAVER. Klaus made some notes, explaining to Carlos. "You make a little 'x' wherever you removed something. In the notes section beside you write the name of the tissue or organ. The reason for removal is always 'Cancer'. Then you sign here at the bottom." He did so with a flourish, the stroke firm, so important looking that it was unreadable "Take this and a packet of information from this drawer and seal it in a flat bio bag." He demonstrated, then returned to the table, inserting the package inside the open body cavity. Then he sewed the incisions closed with all the attention of a sweat shop seamstress.

"Now, we check the drainage." He went to the head and looked under the table, satisfied that the bucket contained all it could. "Move the bucket aside while I get ready for the next phase." He wheeled a machine next to the table while Carlos walked the bucket across the room. "Before using it, always check to see that this machine is full of fluid." He indicated a gauge on the side. "Bring me one of those jugs over there."

Carlos crossed the room, picked up a gallon jug labeled "Anatomical Embalming Fluid" and brought it back. Mandelle had already prepped the machine by opening the cap and inserting the funnel. The machine had a hose coming from it. He reached under the table and tilted the table flat, then jammed the hose into the hole where he had slit the artery. He adjusted some kind of collar that sealed it and pressed a button. The machine began to hum, pumping formaldehyde and phenols and preservatives into the circulatory system. It delivered the fluid at just the right pressure, adjusting to resistance as it slowly permeated the body until it bloated like an overripe peach.

"I'm sorry I got carried away," said Klaus. "I know you want to learn." He smiled. "Don't worry. You'll get plenty of practice. Besides." He patted the body on the other table, the sound flat and thick like pounding on a sandbag. "You're up next, and you got this one all to yourself. Cut her open and see if there's a prize inside."

"Can I ask something?" said Carlos.

"Sure. Whatever you'd like."

"What are we doing here?"

"Efficiency, my boy. Six Sigma. Maximize resources, minimize waste. It's all about process efficiency. And it keeps improving! These girls, they're the lucky ones. Wait until I show you the rendering pond."

Carlos had no idea what he said. He waited for more but there was none. He turned and faced the body on the table, moving quickly past her face, beyond the river of blood and towards the abdomen. Out of the periphery of his eye he caught movement. Above he hadn't noticed that the room had a high ceiling. Through the amphitheater windows above he saw lights behind the mirror, but they quickly went away. The loyalty oath on his arm began to burn. It irritated him a lot these days. He looked down at the body again, knowing that with every thrust of his hand he would be ripping his own insides out, too. He raised the knife above the abdomen, pointing the sharp edge at an angle, his thumb ready to press against the back side to guide the blade.

There was a beep and the machine on the next table stopped humming. The bloated corpse of the woman who begged with her eyes for help lay grey and silent.

Klaus motioned for Carlos to bring the gurney. He laid out a body bag and together they wrestled her into the bag and sealed it shut. They wheeled her back to the refrigerator and slipped her in, all the time Carlos wondering what the shelf life of the body would be in this state. Probably just like meat. Keep it at the right temperature, treat with preservatives. There were questions he didn't want to voice. Why are we preserving these bodies? Why did Mandelle consider these women lucky?

Carlos turned to go back towards the table. "In a hurry, aren't we?" asked Mandelle. "You'll get your turn. Be patient, my friend." He slid the shelf back into the wall, then rolled the gurney to another refrigerator and opened the door. On the shelf lay another woman Carlos recognized. Carlotta had mentioned that she had recently stopped producing milk. When she had disappeared, Carlos asked about her. Carlotta simply told him that she had been moved to the breeding grounds. Sometimes when the livestock is mated, she explained, the breasts start producing again. She assured Carlos that he would see her again.

"Give me a hand," said Klaus. "You know the drill."

Onto the gurney and over to the table, head towards the hole and one deep slit.

It went on.

Later, Mendelle showed Carlos how to do the paperwork. The body count was five today, which meant five available spaces in the dairy. Klaus picked up the phone and dialed. "Recruitment? Yes, I'd like to place an order. Five today. For the dairy. Can we expect replacements by the morning? We have a production schedule to keep."

Chapter 26

A Kiss Goodbye

"Yes, it's important, Jan." Harry had stayed behind in the relative quiet of the observation room to catch up on some phone calls. Jan was last on his list. "I need you to think about all of Trish's recent cases. Go back maybe a year. Search through the files if you need to. How many criminal cases did she handle?"

"That's easy," said Jan. "None. They're all divorce. Well, one name change, a living will and a business filing for a friend, and, oh, your power of attorney medical case. She spent hours on that, had me do lots of research. She was determined to get you those breasts."

"I see," said Harry. "Just stick to the facts, Jan. I need you to focus."

"She was disappointed when the doctors wouldn't upsize them. She laughed about it a lot. Wanted to make sure you got what you deserved."

Awkward silence. Harry stared down at his breasts.

"Then, again, she had her regrets. Used to say a lot of things like, why doesn't he love me like a man loves me." Jan reflected. "She used to say you made her feel like less than a woman."

"I did," said Harry. "Thanks for that information, Jan." Waves of emotion began to stir, too deep to want to remember. He began to regret making this call. It was as if Jan had no control over what came out of her mouth. "Can we get back on track?"

"I always wondered, was it your problem, or hers?"

Silence as Harry stared into his inner pool of reflection.

"She loves you."

The pool got deeper.

Jan, all nervous, said, "Do you think you'll find her? I've put all her clients on hold, rescheduled her appointments. I've been using illness as a cover, but how long will that last?"

More silence as Harry slowly came up from the depths. He cleared his throat. "I'm going out to look for her tonight. I want to go back to the dressing room where I found her phone, hopefully pick up her trail from there. How late will you be in the office?"

"Until five."

He checked the time. "Wait until I get there. It should be close to five. I have to change clothes and stop by my office, then I'll head your way."

"I'll wait for you to get here," she said.

Harry pulled a photo out from a file he had been reviewing. "After I hang up I'm going to send you a picture of a tattoo. See if you can remember anyone, client or otherwise, who had a tattoo similar to this."

He hung up, took a picture of the tattoo and sent it to Jan. He was getting spoiled using Trish's phone. He had used the phone for all kinds of things, the least of which was an x-ray into her life. He checked the time again. The reports were done and Bernard had released him, now he could focus on Trish. He stepped out into the hall, right into Van Dorn.

"Going somewhere?" asked Franklin.

"Leaving," said Harry.

"Have a nice walk." Van Dorn smiled and pushed his way past Harry.

Harry muttered something under his breath.

"Yeah," said a voice beside him. "Everyone who works with him has the same thing to say."

"Detective Baily," said Harry. "How you doing?"

"Okay," said the detective. "I got your old job now that you and Van Dorn left the department."

"Bernard couldn't have given it to a better person."

"You on foot? Walking?"

"Yeah," said Harry. "My car's in impound."

"Parking tickets again?" asked Baily.

"No," said Harry. "I killed someone with it. I'm under investigation. Seems like the Mayor's office wants to hold onto it for evidence."

"You need a ride somewhere?" asked Baily. "I'm on my way out."

"Going anywhere near Capitol Hill?"

The unmnarked cop car trundled up the street and into the heart of Capitol Hill. Harry called Sue and told her to meet him at his apartment and bring her bag of beauty supplies. Before he could explain he got a call from Jan and had to drop her.

"I remembered something," said Jan. "There was this character, Jason L'Enfant."

"Jason L'Enfant," repeated Harry. "One of Trish's clients?"

"The husband of one of her clients. Trish took the case pro bono, but wound up getting a big court ordered settlement when it was over. She seemed to have a vendetta against this guy. Told me he was scum and beat his wife." She paused. "Trish said you never beat her. You were always nice to her, Harry."

Harry put her back on task. "What was the wife's name?"

"Caroline."

"Caroline L'Enfant," he said. "You have pictures of either of them?"

"Got a wedding picture on file," said Jan.

"Good work. I want to see that picture. We're still on for five? Good! See you then."

Harry barely had time to disconnect the call before Baily was on the police computer. He entered L'Enfant and got a few hits. "Nothing on Jason, but the wife is listed." He punched a few more buttons. "She was reported missing about a week ago."

"Missing?" asked Harry. "Any details?"

"No, just that she's missing. A neighbor reported it. "

"Who filed the report?" asked Harry.

"It doesn't say," said Baily. The car pulled up in front of Harry's apartment building. He thanked Bailey and climbed the six flights of stairs to his apartment. Sue was ready for him when he opened the door.

"What's this all about?" she asked.

"I think you know," he said.

She answered nervously, her voice timid. "You going after her?"

"Tonight," he said. "Gotta work it while the trail is hot."

She threw her arms around him. "Promise you'll come back to me," she said.

"As soon as I find her."

"Promise!" she demanded. "She doesn't love you the way I do," she said.

Harry pulled her close. "I know that," he said. "Nobody loves me like you do."

She made a smug sound. "Just remember that. And promise me! I know how a girl feels when you come running to her rescue. She gets all gushy and grateful. Don't you fall for that act."

"So this is an act?" he asked.

"I'm the exception. Besides, I liked you long before you came to my rescue. I don't know why your mother didn't talk to my mother in the first place."

Harry laughed, then got serious. "Look, Sue. You got this backwards. You rescued me. After what that madman did to me, I needed a nurse, and you were all that and more." He smelled her perfume, dug his nose into her neck and inhaled deeply. He closed his eyes, and heaven was as close as he ever thought it would get for him. But then she kissed him, and lights lit up inside his brain, his eyelids fluttered, and his legs turned into oatmeal.

They broke apart, Harry unsure of how much time had gone by.

Sue smiled. "Okay," she said slowly. "You said you had a five o'clock appointment. Better sit down and let me get to work on you."

Chapter 27

Life on the Farm

"They took Babs away while you were asleep," said Trish.

Caroline had awakened from a restless sleep again. She was swollen and needed to be milked. She gathered up the equipment and prepared for it.

"She was just starting to produce," said Caroline. "I think they take them away to another barn."

"How soon before they come for us?" continued Trish.

"I try not to think about it," said Caroline. "I'm sorry."

"Sorry?" asked Trish. "For what?"

"For dragging you into this," she said. "If it wasn't for Jason…"

"I knew the risk," said Trish. "I don't hold it against you, Caroline. If anything, I hold it against Jason."

There was noise outside the cell. Carlos appeared with the afternoon cart. Trish scuttled across the cell to the other side where she took three small bottles of milk out of the mini fridge and put them on the collection shelf. Carlotta scooped them up and placed them in the cool storage side of the cart while Carlos handed her two bowls of oatmeal.

"Where did you take Babs last night?" she said.

"Out on a date," sneered Carlos. "She decided to sleep over."

"So she'll be coming back soon?" asked Caroline.

Carlos grunted, something between a smug laugh and a clever nod.

"I pray for you," said Caroline.

"It's true," said Trish. "I hear her. Every night and every day."

"I don't need your prayers," said Carlos.

"It won't stop me from saying them," said Caroline.

Carlos narrowed his eyes into dark little slits. "I killed the last lady who prayed for me. I pushed her to her death while she said them, calling to God every step of the way for my salvation."

"She had as much faith in you as in God," said Caroline.

"That's what I thought at the time," said Carlos. "I've had other thoughts since discussing it with my friends."

"You mean your peers and co-workers," said Trish. "Good people to discuss ethics and humanity with. I'd love to join the conversation one night."

"Say what you want," said Carlos. "The fact is, most people pray for themselves. That woman prayed that I would be saved just so I would release her from her prison. She was seeking a bargain with God for her precious life."

"I don't think so," said Caroline. "She didn't give up on you and neither will I."

Carlos moved closer to the bars, speaking in a low voice. "Don't waste your time. I gave up on me long ago. The things I did to save my life." He looked down and rubbed the tattoo, feeling the sting of a burn that never seemed to go away.

Caroline whispered back. "There's still time. Ever hear of redemption?"

"My father spoke about it a lot," he said.

Carlotta approached the cart with a handful of bottles. She had been busy making collections ahead of Carlos. "Okay," she barked. "What's keeping you? I've got half this row cleared already. Step it up!"

Carlos backed away and gripped the handles of the cart. Carlotta put the bottles on the cart and he pushed it to the next cell.

Chapter 28

To Hell in a Laundry Cart

Per Harry's instructions, Jan pulled her car into a lot a block away from the Fashion Bargain Depot. "Sure you don't want me to go with you?" she asked. "I'm not a lesbian but I could still be your cool partner just like Rita."

Harry laughed. "No one can replace Rita."

"Do you and her have relations?" asked Jan.

Harry looked as if he were hit with a mallet. "What do you mean?"

Jan looked chastened. "Sorry," she said. "I can be blunt at times. I was just curious. You know, she's a lesbian and you're a..." She was stuck on the word.

"A what?" said Harry. "Transvestite? Cross dresser? Drag queen?"

"Sorry I asked. I didn't mean to pry," she said. "I just thought, well, with Trish gone, you were free to live your life any way you wanted. I know you like women, she told me that much. I guess I figured lesbians would want to sleep with you. Maybe some of them anyway." Her hands fluttered in front of Harry. "I really don't understand why you do all this."

"Neither do I," said Harry.

She scanned him like she would any woman, comparing makeup, hair, accessories, style, her critical eye observing the details with the intensity of a body scanner at airport security. "Trish is right about one thing. You sure have a sense of style. I like that outfit." She smiled. "Let me go shopping with you. I can help you out."

"This is not a shopping spree, it's a missing person case. Red's just busy with other work, the kind that will pay the office bills."

"Precisely why you need me. I can watch your back."

"You've already done a lot," said Harry. "I appreciate you getting Trish's files together for me to review. The way you laid them out on the conference room table was really organized. I was able to get through all of them. It helps me get background on the person I'm looking for."

"For God's sake, Harry," said Jan. "She's your wife. Quit referring to her as the person."

"I know that," he said. "I'm trying to stay analytical, approach it like a case. If I bring my emotions into play I'll get off center. Spend time mooning about what was and what is and dwelling on my faults. That doesn't solve the case."

Jan started to say something but Harry interrupted. "That's enough. I don't want to talk about it." His hand lifted the door handle and it clicked open. "Thanks for staying late and for dropping me off here."

"You have the keys to her apartment, right?"

"Yes, thanks," he said. "It will make it easier to work the case if I stay in this part of town."

"It makes sense," she said. "I'll leave the files on her kitchen table for you to study." Her voice got wavy. "Just find her, will you?" She lunged forward to hug him, but stopped and laughed. "Sorry, I don't want to mess up your makeup. You really look good. And your boobs are fantastic. Showing some cleavage there."

Harry blushed. "Thanks. Guess I'm ready then. Wish me luck."

"Okay, call me if you find something out. It's almost closing time. You'd better hurry," she said. "Sure you don't want me to come with you?"

"Thanks, but no." Harry opened the door and smiled back at Jan.

Before he could shut it Jan pulled a pair of sunglasses from the visor and tossed them at him. "Take these. I thought all detectives wore sunglasses."

Harry looked at them, feminine designer frames with big, dark lenses that hid his eye movements. He slipped them on.

"They go with the outfit," she said.

He shut the door and moved on. She watched him walk away for a few minutes marveling at how he became more ladylike and feminine with every step. She laughed, then sighed, then shook her head before pulling the car onto the street and turning away from the Fashion Bargain Depot.

Harry adjusted the handbag, tugged at the bra, then straightened his top. It felt good to walk in the heels and hear them clicking on the pavement. It helped him get into character. Fu Chan was locked deep inside these days, confined to a cubicle Harry had built around her. Activities like this, ones that involved cross dressing, naturally lowered the walls. Now she was out, but Harry was still in control. He used her name but not her talents.

He considered all the things Sue had told him about Fu Chan, a larger than life person that she would like to meet. Is that why she encouraged this masquerade? Yet, he felt good in the outfit, relaxed. There was something nervous and exciting about it, like carrying a secret.

He thought about the consequences, the many times he had been discovered. He would probably still be a police detective if he hadn't gotten caught in a raid. He was in drag, and when word got around at the station, well, let's just say the work environment changed. He had certainly made Jan feel uncomfortable, if not curious.

There were a few light shoppers at the Fashion Bargain Depot tonight. Expected, it was close to closing time. Harry found a rack in his size and flipped through the hangers pretending to shop. Under the dark sunglasses his eyes scanned every direction. He easily spotted the cameras, but there was also a mirrored observation room that was high up on the back wall above the entrance to the dressing rooms. He moved to another rack with a different angle, sizing up the customers, wondering which of them, if any, were store security.

He flipped a hanger and a dress caught his eye. Something clicked in his brain and he pulled it out and moved to a nearby mirror where he held it against his body. Looking in the mirror, he laughed, realizing what he had been doing. Fu Chan was definitely out of the box.

He kept the dress, figuring he needed it as a passport to the dressing room. He flipped a few more hangers and completed his scans while selecting a few more things to try on. At the dressing room door the Hun was on guard again. She counted the items and gave him a stare. He gave her a petite smile and filed past her. As he rounded the corner he looked back to make sure he wasn't followed.

He checked out every stall. There was no one else in the dressing room. He entered the last one, irritated that there were no hooks. When he looked up he could see the high industrial ceiling, corrugated roof over metal beams. The curtains were suspended by a series of wires and brackets. You think they would have provided clothes hooks. He laid his clothes across a chair in the center of the room and closed the curtains behind him. Turning the opposite way, he lifted the curtains from the bottom of the other side and passed underneath.

It looked like any warehouse, boxed goods stacked as high as you could see, dim lights overhead that barely lit the floor. There were rows of racks on wheels, some with clothes on them, some empty. There were laundry bin carts full of clothes and goods. He passed an open box full of purses beside another full of bracelets and jewelry.

There was a noise behind him. He slipped behind a rack and between some hanging clothes. It was the sound of heels against the concrete floor. He heard a voice. "Is someone there?"

He stayed perfectly still.

"Hello?"

There was a moment of silence and then the heels moved away. Harry came out of hiding and headed back towards the dressing rooms. He heard his own heels clicking on the floor, thinking how stupid this had been. What had he expected to find? Now that he had seen what was behind the curtain, what next? He tried to think. He still couldn't make the connection between Che and Trish. There was nothing in the files that fit despite his effort to scan them all. And if Che did abduct Trish, where would he take her?

L'Enfant came to mind. His wife, Caroline, was also missing. Was there a connection there?

He looked up. There was a row of windowed offices along a wall, a wooden staircase that led to a second series above them. The place was huge, and maybe Trish was still here, secured or locked away in some hidden room. We wanted to look around more but not dressed like this. He should have worn casual clothes with shoes that did not click with every step.

He made his way back to the dressing room and lifted the curtains, preparing to duck under.

There was a soft meaty thud, the sound of something heavy coming down on the back of his head. His vision blurred, his feet grew numb, falling out from under him. He closed his eyes, bracing for impact as the concrete floor rose up to meet him.

Chapter 29

While You Were Asleep

The Hun finished examining the wallet and put it back in the purse. "Cheap D&G knockoff," she said, fingering the lining inside. She zipped it closed and tossed it on top of the limp figure at the bottom of the laundry cart. "Well, Miss Chan, they say curiosity killed the cat. Let's hope you have nine lives." She threw some things from the dressing room return rack into the cart, hiding her under a pile of clothes. "Call Mr. Morris. Tell him we have a pick up."

A man nodded to the Hun and walked off.

A plainclothes store security guard stood nearby. A strange tattoo peeked out from under his rolled sleeve. "Stupid girl," he said. "We may be a Bargain Warehouse but we can certainly afford security cameras. Especially in the warehouse."

"She's perfect," said the Hun. "No family pictures, no employment badge, a state issued ID. Nobody's going to miss her."

"Still, I wonder what she was doing in the warehouse?"

"Don't worry about it," said the Hun. "It's the design of our dressing room. She's not the first girl to get lost behind the curtains. Just be grateful that we met our quota. This is the last one. The accountants will be here tomorrow. We'll be selling this operation soon. "

Chapter 30

The Manila Project

"Inform air operations that I will a passenger on the delivery plane to Indonesia."

"Yes, Mr. Che."

"While I am gone tomorrow, you will be in charge, Jason. Don't do anything creative. I want business as usual. Status quo."

"Yes, sir."

"If you have any suggestions or improvements, write up a proposal and submit it with a budget. Two pages maximum. I will review your ideas when I return and we'll discuss them before taking action. You know how I hate shooting from the hip."

The shoes clicked across the polished floor of his office. Che stood before the ant farm and stared into it.

"I'll notify air ops. Should I also inform Indonesia that you are coming?" asked L'Enfant.

"If you wish. It does not matter."

"Any specific reason you're going?"

"Yes," said Che. "We have reached milestone B and are finished with the LRIP."

Jason looked befuddled.

"Sorry, I despise acronyms but it is hard not to use them," said Che. "They become part of a common language that binds us." He paused for a moment and looked sternly at L'Enfant. "It is obvious that you do not speak that language. I'm sorry, Jason. It means you must go back to school. Visit human resources while I am gone and have Kathy set you up with some training. She has a course we pirated from the Defense Department that will explain the acquisitions process. Their school is the best in the world. We use a modified version of their engineering process for all our projects."

Jason looked down at the floor. Che walked over to him, the sound of expensive heels clicking on the floor. "Now, now, Jason. I know you don't have a college education, but you have risen to a position of power in the organization. I expect you to follow the guidelines I established for you in your Individual Development Plan. We discussed all this at last quarter's review, didn't we?"

"Yes," said Jason, sounding more like a small boy than a powerful executive.

The Chairman turned his back on Jason and continued, the clicking sound moving away. "LRIP is Low Rate Initial Production," he said. "Meaning a small batch has been made to see if it meets the design specifications. In short, the Manila Project is ready for testing. I am going to Indonesia to pick up the prototype kit. I intend to quickly advance the project through the testing and quality assurance phase. I want to see if our investment was worth it."

"If it does what it promised, then it is worth ten times our investment, perhaps a hundred."

"Yes, I agree." The sound of the expensive heels stopped. Che was back behind his desk staring deep into the ant colony now, wondering about their individuality, wondering about their group mind. Do they have a word for betrayal in their language? Dissatisfaction? Stupidity? Angst? Are there any lazy ants? Are there ants that play hooky and call in sick?

L'Enfant moved closer. He didn't see the same things. They were just ants, Mr. Che's ingenious way of disposing of his enemies. Jason knew about the room but he had never seen it. He didn't want to either. It was well known that the room had many visitors, but none of them lived to tell about it.

Jason continued to laud Mr. Che about the genius of the Manila Project. "The perfect assassin," he said. "Undetectable, certain, like unleashing a lethal hit man. Once the target is chosen there is no hope of recall, no stopping it. You can kill anyone in the world, anyone you choose, from anywhere, even the comfort of this office." He cleared his throat. "Did you have someone in mind for the test? Someone in the world you wish dead?"

Che smiled. "I have a list of candidates. Difficult to choose. You know the criteria. They must be a public figure, their death easily verifiable by the media, and, preferably someone in conflict with our interests. I do not wish to topple a government, not yet anyway. We often need the constructs of government to help achieve our purposes, and it is the differences in governments that we exploit for our profit." He narrowed his eyes. "Yes. The choice is very difficult," he said. "I want to select five, maybe ten, a reasonable amount of test subjects. I will forward you the list I have, perhaps you can review them with your recommendations. There are over a hundred names and we need to narrow it down."

"I would be honored, Mr. Chairman," said L'Enfant.

Che stared deep into the ant farm, his mind still considering what their world was like. Jason stood nearby and Che wondered how long he would stay there, obediently waiting for the command to leave. The room was silent as Che watched two ants meet in a tunnel, their antennae waving a semaphore message to each other. Was it a greeting, or were they orders from the queen, or was it casual water cooler talk in the middle of their busy workday.

Either way, it was poetry, efficient as only nature can design.

Chapter 31

There's a Reason I Hate Doctors

Harry awoke with a headache. His back hurt, his right ear spiked with pain, and his face was swollen. He tried to move his hands but found they were restrained.

Doctor Mandelle hovered over him, smiling as he held a syringe with a long needle. "You're starting to wake up," he said. "I wasn't quite finished with my work." He held the syringe over Harry's left breast and inserted it up from the bottom for a shallow injection below the nipple. He pushed the plunger and Harry felt like he was being injected with cement. He started to scream but remembered that his voice would come out deep and masculine. He bit down on his cheek for a moment and told himself the pain will pass.

He knew what pain was. Harry could deal with physical pain. He had been wounded in the war, laid on the field of battle, been patched up by a field medic waiting for evac. No drugs except a couple of aspirins. After a while the pain becomes constant background noise and something happens to your mind. Fighting it makes you tired and you thankfully pass out, a short break until you wake up and start over again.

It was the emotional pain that challenged Harry. That was something elusive. How do you put a bandage on something that you feel? Yes there are metaphors, attempts to explain the healing process in terms we can understand, but the truth is we know less about the landscape of human emotions than we know about the human body.

The door behind Mandelle opened and Carlotta came in, holding a nursing bra and a top. "You finished with this bitch?" she asked.

Mandelle turned and looked at her like she had just told him playtime was over. "I haven't done a cervical exam yet, let alone conduct the oral interview," he said.

"It will have to wait. Mr. Che is accompanying the shipment tonight. I got Carlos putting another load on the plane right now, but I could sure use your help. There are a few things that need to be tagged and boxed next door, organs on ice that you said you would take care of."

"That was before you dropped this midnight addition on me," he said. "You think it's easy prepping the livestock? A quota of five?"

"I've done it before," she said.

"Right," he said, his voice betraying disbelief.

"Well, all but your part," she said. "You never taught me what you're doing now."

"And I won't," he said. "Not until I have it down. It's still in the research phase."

She cackled, then snorted. "I'd say your research was pretty successful. We got a full blown farm here operating at peak efficiency. Room for seventy five head, a hundred if we pack them four to a cage. The real genius is how you get them to lactate so quickly. I've used the oatmeal mixture, the fenugreek seed and the blessed thistle, and even with the domperidone protocol, but it takes weeks to bring the milk out. How do you do it in a matter of hours?"

"Research," he said. "Hard scientific research."

Harry moaned.

"Ah, I forgot you were awake," said Mandelle.

"Here," said Carlotta, setting the clothes down on a table. "I'll get the wheelchair and we'll move her to her cell. I hate to keep Mr. Che waiting."

Che! Harry was conscious enough to recognize the name. Above the pain he struggled to focus his mind. He could see Mandelle's forearm, the gang tattoo conspicuously exposed. The women with him had the same markings.

"Get the hood and the hobbles as well," said Mandelle. "She's ready, but semi conscious." He nodded to Carlotta and she left the room. He set the syringe down, exchanging it for a smaller one setting beside it. He filled it from a vial and waved it in front of Harry.

"You're a fighter, I can see," he said. "You like challenges." He chuckled, a laugh that sounded like an old man's last breath. He gripped Harry's chin, twisting it and looking her over. "Good stock. Prize cattle. You'll make lots of milk and in the end produce good meat. You will also contribute to my research, my process engineering. I have a requirement to produce mother's milk, metrics to measure, production quotas. I have defined all those parameters and focused my research to produce the most efficient farming operation of its kind. State of the art."

Carlotta came in, carrying the things he demanded. Mandelle set the loaded syringe down on the table. She helped him dress the livestock, locking the transport hood in place. Now Harry was blind as well.

"One more thing," said Mandelle. "Get me the iron maidenform."

Carlotta cringed. "Are you serious?" she asked. "What has she done to deserve that?"

"Don't question my orders," said Mandelle. "Get it. Now!"

She left the room. Mandelle looked down at the loaded syringe. It was set to go, and it would certainly take the fight out of her. Then he looked at her exposed breast, deciding to try something new. He got a new syringe from a drawer and filled it with his special mixture. He gave her a second subdermal injection, carefully aimed just below the right nipple. He patted it and the figure beneath the hood stirred.

He looked at the left breast and set the empty syringe down. "Perfect," he said. "One test subject, one control," He squeezed the right and left breast alternately as he rasped an old man's dying breath again. He jotted some notes on a piece of paper.

He picked up the loaded syringe. "Might as well," he said. "I prepared it for you. It would be a shame to waste it."

He waved it in front of her, dying breath falling on her like the wind across a row of pit toilets.

"Forget what you've heard here. For your own good," he said. He looked at the syringe in his hands. The figure beneath the hood moaned again. He pushed the needle gently into the arm. "And, oh," he said, driving the plunger down, "Pleasant dreams."

He had a second thought, patting the breasts like they were a drum. "On the other hand, not-so-pleasant dreams."

Chapter 32

Cow Down

Trish lowered the flap on her blouse and snapped open the nursing bra. The pads were damp and uncomfortable, just like they always were. She covered her nipple with the breast pump and turned the machine on. Soon the hum and vibration of the pump began to empty her mind of everything but the obvious.

"I'm a cow," she whispered, the sound leaving her mouth like a dead breeze on a still day.

The pump droned on. Carolyn was asleep on her bunk and she was alone with her thoughts.

She had voiced the truth and she repeated it again as she watched breast milk begin to trickle into the bottle. "I'm a cow," she said sadly. The livestock tag in her ear pinched and she moved it around. If only she had some salve or petroleum jelly to lubricate it, maybe it wouldn't hurt so much.

The machine droned on. The bottle on the table beside her slowly began to fill.

I have no idea where I am, she thought. *They drugged me, took me to that office and then to see that butcher Mandelle.*

A wave of fear passed over her.

They butcher cows.

She shuddered and the pump changed its key until she settled down and reseated the seal, but the fear was still there. She was an intelligent woman, blessed with an imagination. Now those traits turned against her, serving the fear up in heaping portions that would gag a fat man. It would wet the devil's appetite, a plateful of terror all wrapped up with lawyer logic and syllogisms.

They butcher cows. Mandelle is a Butcher. I am a cow. Mandelle will butcher me one day.

Strange how the human mind can architect defeat just as well as it can victory. In this case, it conspired with the emotions and the environment to paint a picture. The mind seeks to apply logic and sense to anything. This was the answer it was offering Trish.

"I am a cow," she whispered again, aloud.

Caroline had been quiet and awake. She heard Trish and got off the bed, moving in front of her. Trish had empty eyes, her hand cupping her breast and holding the seal. "Are you okay, honey?" she asked.

"What did they give us?" she asked. "Date rape drug?"

"What?" asked Caroline.

"How did you come to be here?" asked Trish.

Caroline looked away, staring at a wall. "He came for me in the middle of the night."

Trish knew who she meant but said it anyway. "Jason?"

"He took the boys first, sent them away with my mother and a couple of his men." She looked at Trish in horror. "He had my mother. I could tell she was afraid. She did everything he asked without question, without hesitation. I wonder what he held over her, what lies he told her to accept his control."

"Jason is a fiend," said Trish.

"Yes," said Caroline. "I still remember the beatings. I walked on eggshells around him, afraid that anything I did was the wrong thing. He had me convinced that everything was my fault, including his being part of this grotesque Company that he can never quit."

"I met the Chairman," said Trish. "Mr. Che."

"I've met him too. Had him over the house for dinner a few times. He was full of helpful hints of how I could flavor the dinner better, serve the food more efficiently, and improve my living conditions. Very helpful." She looked at the wall. "I got a good beating that night. Afterwards Jason played fire and ice, a game he enjoys." Caroline was silent.

"I don't understand," said Trish.

"He said if I didn't play with him he would play with one of the boys." Her eyes began to water. "That is what he held over me. I wondered if he would do it, if he had any love for any of his boys. I never called his bluff." She sniffed. "I knew if he did, he would do it to Mikey." Tears fell like dew from her cheeks. "Just because Mikey was my favorite." She looked at the bottle. It had stopped filling, and she wiped the tears on her sleeve and smiled. "Oh, look, you're on empty. Bet that feels better. Time to switch breasts."

Trish opened the flap and exposed her other breast, moving the seal in place over the nipple. Caroline went to the sink, wetting a washcloth. She moved back to Trish to wipe away the stickiness left behind from the milk. Her smile suddenly cracked and she snapped like a tree in a windstorm. The tears fell, a rain of emotion that burst from the clouds in her mind.

Trish reached out to her but Caroline steadied her hand.

The pump hummed, filling the silence.

"Think anyone's looking for us?" asked Trish.

"I don't have anyone," said Caroline.

"Neither do I," said Trish.

There was movement at the door. Carlotta slid into view, a cougar crawling out from behind a bush. "Ah, so sad," she said. "I hear so many sad tales from you girls."

"What's your story?" asked Trish.

The cougar straightened up, walking on two legs and pretending to be human. "It's none of your business."

"Something had to make you this mean. People don't come by it naturally," said Trish.

"Some do," said Carlotta. "Meanwhile, here's a new roommate for you to question. Someone to interrogate besides me."

Carlos came into view. He had a girl in a wheelchair with him. She was hobbled, a set of chains on her ankles. She had a bag over her head, something between a bridle, horse blinders, and some strange S&M mask. She had on a new, white nursing top, black skirt, shower sandals. The official school uniform at Mr. Che's Academy for Missing Girls.

Another animal. Another cow for the milk farm.

"Now don't you girls cause any trouble," she said as she brandished a cattle prod. Carlotta opened the door and Caroline moved to the far corner. "And you. Just stay put in that chair and keep filling your bottle."

Carlos wrangled the livestock inside, pushing the hooded girl into Bab's old bunk. She curled into a fetal position. Carlos removed the gag and the hood, then the leg irons.

Through all this, the pump hummed. Trish watched the bottle fill while Caroline stared at a blank wall, her face away from Carlos and Carlotta.

Carlos stood back, gathered up the equipment and left the room.

The pump continued to him, a second bottle to slowly fill with milk.

Carlotta closed and locked the door.

"I'll keep praying for you both," said Caroline.

Carlos sneered.

"Don't waste your breath," said Carlotta.

"Do you remember your childhood?" asked Caroline. "Was it happy?"

Carlotta squeezed the handle and discharged the cattle prod against the bars. Trish flinched and Caroline jumped back. There was an arc and a snap of electricity, then the smell of something burning in the air.

"Shut up," she said. "Don't make me open this door and come back in there."

Chapter 33

Reflections of the Past

Jason L'Enfant sat in Mr. Che's desk and stared through the thick glass at the ants. Che was gone and he was in charge, occupying the honored seat at the Chairman's desk. Che may be weird, but he paid good money. Still, he didn't see what Mr. Che saw. They were just bugs, a nuisance that needed to be exterminated.

Like his wife, Caroline. A nuisance. She had caused him great pain, tried to leave him and take the children.

Just like his mother did to his father. She tried, but dad made sure that she was never successful.

Staring into the ant farm he saw his past. There wasn't a lot of love in his house, his dad saw to that. A stern father who believed in discipline, he enforced it with a steady hand and a razor strap. By the time he was ten he had experienced everything his mother had been going through ever since their marriage. At first he was angry, but then when he saw her terror he redirected the anger toward his father. That didn't last, and after some father son sessions with dear old dad, he turned back against his mother. Then, after a short time and after witnessing a few more beatings, he went back the other way, siding again with his mother.

Such was Jason's early life, oscillating between his two parents, a pawn in some game they seemed to be playing with each other. In the end he wound up hating them both, but the damage had already been done. He stored all this information in his young mind where he unknowingly imprinted the idea that this was what marriage was supposed to be like and that beating someone is how you express love and caring.

He was a good student up until high school when he joined a gang where he learned he was not alone in his hatred of his parents. The gang became like a new family, teaching him skills that provided him with an income as well as respect. His dad recognized it and began picking on his younger brother instead. His mother just cried. It wasn't long before he left home.

He managed to avoid trouble with the law for years. The smart schoolboy also became street smart, eventually moving out of gang life by accepting an offer to join the Organization. One of Mr. Che's lawyers approached him, promising him more money, a brighter future, and protection from gang retribution. He took the offer. By thirty he had been around the globe twice and had gained legitimacy by achieving a GED and beginning a college education with a major in business. He married Caroline, mostly because of pressure. She was pregnant and refused to get an abortion like his other candidates for spouse. Nonetheless, when his first son was born he felt the same pride that any father would.

He rose to the top of the Organization, running various operations throughout the world. Che admired his cruelty which wasn't restricted to his family. He learned Spanish and traveled extensively in South and Central America. He had less time for college and his interest waned in education. Caroline never knew exactly what he did for a living. After a few beatings, she also learned not to ask questions.

The beatings.

They didn't start right away. He was loving and attentive at first, had his own ideas of what marriage should be like, but the old programming was strong. Using his father's image of what a man should be, strong, powerful, and in total control of his family, Jason slowly transformed into the monster that drove Caroline to leave him.

In the end she had bested him. She broke his family. He may have won his sons in the court settlement, but they did not give him the love and respect that he thought he deserved. He was working on a plan to correct that. With Caroline gone, he was giving them the full attention that he had given her, including the behavior modification techniques that could only come from a good beating.

Anger welled up in him as he stared into the ant farm.

It was all her fault.

All her fault.

He turned back toward the computer to continue his work, but remained distracted.

It was all her fault. I was a good husband and provided her everything. She wore the finest clothes, drove a nice car, lived in a fine home and had access to accounts with plenty of money. She lacked for nothing.

He stared at the monitor, his thoughts simmering in a pool of anger.

All her fault.

He slammed his fist against the desk. Objects on the desk moved, a tall one falling over. The top of it broke off.

"Dammit, Caroline," he yelled. "Look what you made me do!'

All her fault.

Time to put an end to his misery. Time for Caroline to pay the bill.

Emotions rose in him like the dead on All Hollow's Eve. He got up from the desk and headed out the door.

Chapter 34

Manila Envelope

The sound of expensive shoes clicking against the waxed floor of the laboratory caught Doctor Pershing's attention. He turned, his heart leaping to his throat, choking the words of greeting off before he could say them.

"Good afternoon, Doctor Pershing," said Mr. Che.

Pershing took a deep breath before answering. "Mr. Che. Good to see you."

"Is it?"

"Always a pleasure, sir." He bowed reverently.

Che smiled, but it did not make Pershing feel at ease. "I understand you have completed the testing. I have come to see your results and hopefully to take a prototype with me when I leave. I wish to advance our project to the user acceptance phase."

"Yes, sir," said Pershing. "I have prepared a kit for you. Ten tests, as requested."

"I thought I asked for twenty," said Che flatly.

Pershing started to back paddle. "I prepared only ten," he said meekly. "I can start tonight and have the other ten within a month."

"Ten will be adequate for now," said Che. "I will scale back the size of my test group." He cleared his throat. "I understand you have perfected the virus since last year's unfortunate results."

"A tragedy, sir," said Pershing. "We released the first virus without adequately specifying the unique DNA. The message was too broad. As a result, an entire family, four generations, were wiped out, leaving no one to inherit the fortunes we planned on reaping."

"Yes," said Che. "But it was a good test. It showed us the potential of the Manila Project. I only hope that you could reproduce that level again if required. It is useful to know that we possess the technology to obliterate an entire family tree if we so desire."

Pershing looked at him with the reticence of an atomic scientist, thinking about the vast implications of his discoveries for all mankind.

"You have the kit?" asked Che, his voice as crisp as a December peanut.

Pershing instinctively snapped to attention and bowed again. "This way, please."

He led Che to the other side of his laboratory and through a sealed door. They donned special equipment, safety gear and pressurized suits to maintain the purity of the clean room. Pershing opened a second door, a seal hissing as the flow of air rushed past them and into filtered ducts above.

The clean room was jammed with tables full of equipment. There were flasks filled with colored liquids that wobbled on platforms and circled like small tornados. There were incubators, banks of round, flat petri dishes visible through the glass doors. There were centrifuges and gas chromatographs, spectrophotometers and chromatography columns. There were shelves along the wall with vats and jars of reagents and chemicals. There was glassware, Bunsen burners, and racks of test tubes spewed about. There were animals in cages, some agitated, some lethargic, but all hapless victims of Dr. Pershing's protocols and experiments.

Pershing went to a fume hood across the lab, pulling up the window. He flipped on a light switch, illuminating the clean white surface and only thing inside, a small case about the size of a shoebox. He opened the case. Neat rows of vials were held in place with clips. Pershing reached inside and the top layer came out in a tray.

Che smiled as if it were a box of chocolates, as if the second layer of delight held more of the same. Pershing lifted out the second tray and set it beside the first. At the very bottom there were compartments containing small tools, rubber gloves, and empty vials with blank labels. There was a small booklet containing written instructions in several languages. He stood aside proudly, watching with satisfaction as Che's smile grew the more he explored the case.

"This is what you seek, Mr. Che," he said.

Che looked at it as if it were perfection personified. A virus, smaller than an ant. Efficient. Programmable. Armed with the DNA of an enemy, you release the virus into the general population. It eventually finds its target, the one it hungers for. And when it finds that person, finding the DNA a perfect match, it fulfills its destiny. It moves in, begins to flourish, and like salmon it reproduces as it never has before.

Che was aglow, like a ravenous shark in a feeding frenzy. "We all know death follows, but how does it happen, Doctor?"

Pershing pushed his finger inside his collar. "I have films of the early tests," he said.

"I don't want to see films, just explain it to me," said Che.

Pershing's collar began to itch. He rubbed his finger back and forth under it. "The virus is based on the common cold, so it spreads through the population quickly. Most people experience a mild flu, all except the intended victim. Once it finds the programmed match, the virus invades the host cells where it reproduces in the cytoplasm, the semi-liquid area between the outside of the cell and the nucleus. It is here, you may recall, where the ribosomes reside. These cellular structures are the assembly line workers of the cell, tirelessly moving along strands of RNA that are produced in the nucleus of the cell and based on the design of the DNA. This is how instructions are sent from the DNA telling the ribosomes what proteins to assemble."

"It's okay, Pershing," said Che. "You can dispense with the high school science lesson. I understand cellular biology and how DNA creates RNA which translates into protein."

Pershing bowed. "Sorry, Mr. Che. I sometimes forget that you hold several degrees from the best schools in the world."

"No matter," said Che. "Continue."

"As the virus grows, it injects its own messenger RNA into the cell where the ribosomes read it as just another set of instructions, a blueprint for a new protein. This new protein is a kind of reverse transcriptase, a compound that can penetrate the protective coating of the nucleus. Once inside the nucleus the compound locks itself around the DNA in a deadly embrace. It has found its mate, the reason for its existence. The DNA is permanently modified by the reverse transcriptase, blocking it from sending any new instructions outside the nucleus. It effectively stops all new cell growth. What happens next is subject to environmental factors."

"What do you mean?" asked Che.

"The virus stops the body from producing any new cells, no matter what they are. Any new cells." He paused, but it was obvious Che wanted him to spell it out.

Che was enjoying it, something about making men confront the horrors they would do.

"It depends." Pershing rubbed his collar again, uncomfortable with the Chairman's questions. Nonetheless, he continued. "Say, for instance, the target is infected by another virus, a cold perhaps. With the body's inability to make any new cells, there would be no antibodies, no defense against the attack of the new virus."

There was silence. "Go on," said Che. "Another example."

"Say they were to get burned or cut," said Pershing. "There would be no new cells, no healing. The wound would remain open until the reserves of the body were depleted. Depending on the severity, any wound could be fatal."

Silence.

"And?"

"With the DNA locked, no new blood cells are produced. The brain is slowly deprived as there become fewer and fewer corpuscles to transport oxygen. Muscles would similarly become affected, immobilizing the victim, adding to a slow and painful death as they rot away."

"Rot?"

"Decay is more accurate," said Pershing, his voice momentarily cracking. "Skin, as you know, replaces itself every 7 days. If the victim were to live that long, the skin would slowly peel away, exposing what was underneath. Can you imagine that?"

Che looked him coldly in the eyes. "I can," he said. "Can you?"

Silence.

The devil was on holiday again.

Che packed up the chocolates, sweets to nourish his appetite. He turned to Pershing and patted him on the arm. "You've done well, Doctor Pershing. You're an excellent bio-engineer. I don't know anyone else who could have done this. You're as genius, Doctor, a true genius."

Pershing was thinking of other things. Che had started the line of questions and he was still pondering all the things that could cause death once the victim were infected with the Manila virus. What it was like to stop growing on the cellular level? Some of it he had seen. He had mercifully murdered his test subjects once the data was collected and the results recorded. He had thought of all these things before, but laboratory tests were definitely different than field tests.

Che reassembled the case and tucked it under his arm. "I'm going to rest a day and take tomorrow's flight back to America." He clapped Pershing on the arm. "I'll let you know when to enter into full production. I read your reports. A hundred and eighty days to incubate the venom."

"Correct, Mr. Che."

The chairman patted the box under his arm. "I'll let you know. Meanwhile, take a vacation, a much deserved break. You earned it, Doctor Pershing. Tomorrow will be the last shipment of raw materials for a while. No need to proceed until the tests are complete. Please inform the corporate jet they will have a passenger returning with them tomorrow."

"Yes, Mr. Che," said Peshing. He turned off the light and lowered the window to the hood, following his boss through the sealed door, into the outside and into a world full of unknowns.

Che turned one last time. "Thank you, Doctor Pershing. You have earned your bonus this quarter. I will conduct the milestone review and inform you of the outcome."

"Yes, sir."

"Pershing, if they gave a Nobel Prize for death, you would be the winner. This year and every year as we celebrate your accomplishments for a long time to come."

Chapter 35

Family Reunion

"Hello Caroline."

The sound of Jason's voice brought back nightmare visions. She shuddered, the memories stirring in her mind like some mad hurricane of horror. The debris of her life swirled around her in a whirlwind. She saw herself being chased through the house screaming, locking herself in the bathroom, comforting the kids afterward as they recovered from another of Daddy's episodes.

She called the cops once, a mistake he made her pay dearly for.

"I've had my eye on you," said L'Enfant. His voice was chill, full of confidence. He was in full control now and there was nothing she could do about it.

"Leave her alone," yelled Trish.

"You're next, Missy," he said, as cool and as frosty as dry ice. He nodded to Carlos, who unlocked the cage for him. He leered at them both, his girth spreading across the entrance to the small prison. Trish started to say something. He turned to her, his icy stare making her cringe and scuttle to the corner of the cell next to the stainless steel toilet. She pressed herself backwards behind the paper dispenser into the tight space along the wall. The other girl in the cell was still passed out on the bunk. L'Enfant nodded again to Carlos. "You're the animal handler. You know what to do."

Carlos stared at him for a moment. The comment caught him by surprise and he felt a twinge that stirred some humanity deep inside. Jason stood aside, his eyes widening as he nodded, surprised that his orders were not being carried out. Carlos looked him in the eye then entered the cell, sweeping the dust of his humanity under a dark rug where it was out of sight. He went in and brought Caroline to Jason as faithful as any loyal

Labrador retriever. L'Enfant grabbed her by the arms and Carlos turned and locked the door. There was a leather harness hanging on the wall outside the cage. Carlos quickly worked it around Caroline, tightening the straps around her arms and leaving her as helpless and hobbled as any farm animal.

"You can keep my hands apart but I'll still pray for you," she said.

He yanked on the leather leash and she let out a squeal. L'Enfant laughed, a chuckle that would rival any cheap movie villain.

They moved out of sight and Trish uncurled herself from the corner. She sat on top of the toilet and started to sob. She could hear Caroline in the distance as they pulled her along. The sounds became faint echoes until she heard the big doors shut with the finality of a coffin lid. She closed her eyes and buried her face in her hands, embracing silence and darkness.

There was a moan. The shape on the bunk stirred.

Trish stared at the dark shape, then got off the toilet. She went to the bars, looking left and right for any signs of activity outside the cell. The girl on the bunk continued to moan. She moved across the room and sat on the floor next to the bunk staring at the girl's back. She remembered what it was like when they first brought her here. She was dazed and drugged but she still had some fight in her. That had quickly disappeared. The shark of Bellevue had no more teeth. She was as scared and as docile as any domesticated farm animal. She fingered the agricultural tag that hung like a plastic sign from her ear.

She felt something sticky on her chest and looked down. A milk stain spread out from her right breast. She quickly went for the breast pump and sat in the chair next to the small table against the wall. What choice did she have? The vibration and the hum of the machine lulled her as she continued to berate herself. She did not blame Caroline. She did the right thing defending her and getting her a divorce, but how could she underestimate a monster like L'Enfant? She should have looked deeper into his background.

The bottle beside her slowly filled and she switched breasts. When she was finished she sealed it and put it in the cooler. She cleaned herself with a wet washcloth, dried and put everything back in place.

She wondered if she would see Caroline again.

"Will it be my turn next?" she said, whispering to herself.

There was a moan from the bed. Maybe it was the act of milking, but she felt maternal. She rinsed the washcloth and squeezed out the water and sat on the floor beside the bunk. The girl moaned again. She saw the tag in her ear, remembered how it hurt, how the one in her ear still hurt now. She placed the damp washcloth over the girl's head, dabbing it on her neck.

The girl groaned. Trish went to the sink and filled a glass with water and moved back beside her.

"You'll be okay," said Trish. "The dizziness will pass. Here, take a drink of this." She brought the glass beside her, accidently hitting the tag on her ear.

The girl let out a scream, deep and resonant like a man in pain.

"Sorry," said Trish. "That's going to hurt for a while."

"What is it?" asked the girl, her voice low and raspy.

"A plastic tag. The kind they put in a cow's ear."

Her hand felt the tag gingerly. It was big and obnoxious, designed for a heavier animal with a thicker ear. The hole was much larger than a simple piercing.

Trish moved her hand behind the girl's head, cradling it so she could get a drink.

"Thank you," said the girl.

Trish flinched. There it was again, the voice sounding deep and masculine. She turned the girl's head gently towards her, watching as the rest of her body twisted to accommodate her.

The girl took a deep drink, her eyes cast downward in the cup. "Thank you," she said again as she slowly looked up.

"Oh my God," said Trish, her voice as shrill as a fire alarm. "Oh my God!"

Harry looked up into her eyes. "Trish?" he said.

She fainted.

Chapter 36

Federal Case

Bernard walked into the situation room at Seattle P.D., Rita close behind him. It was like being in the trading pit at the stock exchange ten seconds after the bell rings. There was so much talking it sounded like background noise from the middle of a beehive. The walls were a splay of maps and displays, photos and charts taped everywhere. One full wall was dedicated to white board, every piece of it filled with words and scribbles, looking like downtown graffiti. Three wall mounted monitors blared news feeds and weather channels. Mounted high on the wall, the digital clock labeled Seattle read 13:31 PST. Nine other clocks, all labeled and ticking, displaying other time zones, London included, just in case you needed it.

He and Rita worked their way through the maze of open cubicles and tables. Computer screens blared light down on desks cluttered with piles of paper, books and newspapers. They rounded an elbow in the room and reached the center of the beehive. There was a small theatre area, chairs arranged for the show. Franklin Van Dorn was seated in the front row next to a Government suit and a few skirts. Bernard chuckled as he saw the woman he was talking to look away and wince as he licked his hand and stroked the hair on the back of his head.

A good segment of the crowd was uniformed, so much variety he thought he was at a fashion show. Brown, grey, navy blue, all decorated with badges, name tags, and guns. He motioned to Rita and they took a seat near the back. One of the suits in the front row stepped up to the podium and tapped on the microphone. The noise slowly dimmed.

"Thank you for taking the time to come to this situation awareness and review meeting. I know it's the weekend and many of you have been working hard on this all week, whether in the command center or on the intelligence gathering teams. Our purpose today is to share information and discuss theories."

Bernard leaned close to Red and whispered. "That means they're clueless."

"First, we're going to start with a briefing from local Homeland Security Liaison Gary Torrence."

Torrence took the podium and the lights dimmed like it was the main feature. Overhead a light came on, projecting an image onto a white screen beside him. Rita leaned forward and smiled, wishing she had brought popcorn. "Thank you Agent Whitkowsky." He turned to the image beside him. "This is an aerial of the docks shortly after we arrived on the scene last weekend. It took some time to process the imagery, but from what you can see, there is no way anyone could have slipped through our nets. Pretty much we rounded up all the refugees as well as the people responsible for this abomination against humanity."

There was a murmur as the image cut to a slide that listed the seized assets. A couple of trailers, two cars, transport containers, and a semi truck. "We went over everything, got whatever fingerprints we could, documented evidence. The containers were disgusting. There were piles of human feces and they smelled of urine and the sweat of human cargo. There was garbage on the floor, empty food containers, dirty napkins, even a used tampon and a couple of bloody sanitary napkins. From our intelligence, they were in there eight days, no sight of daylight, no idea where they were, just the promise that when someone opened the doors again, they'd be in America." He paused for a moment. "We turned over the bodies of the three that didn't make it to their respective embassies. In one case, the family was with them and we still have them interned. We're trying to sort it out and we have a public affairs specialist working on it now."

There were images of the dirty containers flashing on the screen. Some of the people in the room remembered it that night. Eight days crowded in darkness, living off whatever food and water you carried in with you. In the worst overflowing pit toilet, in the smelliest garbage dump, in the most disgusting slaughterhouse, it wouldn't even come close. Hard to forget something like that.

Another flash and there was a bill of laden from International Freight Limited with an Indonesian address. "Has anybody tracked them down?" someone yelled angrily.

Torrence raised his hands. "Please hold all questions and comments for the end. Some of them may be answered along the way. But, yes, we did track them down. Their records are tied up in court. International was acquired by a shipping firm in South Africa and the company is in the process of transferring their records to the new owners. We got a request in through the court, but it may be six months before we see any movement on it."

The image flashed away, replaced by a jumpy live action movie. "This was taken from one of our choppers the night of the event." There was a crowd on the ground, a procession leading out of a container and into a prisoner transport bus. The camera panned the area. There was a flash and the screen became a negative image of ghostly silhouettes against a dark background. Like superman with x-ray vision, you could see through walls where heat revealed the presence of moving human bodies. "This is night vision mode with infrared boost. We used a GFG brand night sensor with Apex Capitol post processing to examine the footage for any sign of people. We mapped every image you see on the screen to someone who either works for the port, was in our operation, or was apprehended that night. All hands accounted for."

Bernard saw the imagery flash over a fishing boat. He wondered if Harry was right about the *Dare Me*. He had a thought but held it to himself. He took out his notebook and jotted down a few reminders. A call to his buddy at the Coast Guard could clear a lot of things up.

The shaky footage ended, thank God. Like a kid on a roller coaster, it was fun but it got a little nauseating after a while. The presentation switched to mug shots, person after person. Rita recognized some of them, people she had interviewed. She saw the parade of tats, the burned micro abrasions that marked the ones who knew secrets they weren't sharing. As crafty as she and Bernard had been, it was Harry who had cracked the eggshell when he duped Chou Lin into thinking he was Che's representative. She wished he was here working with them now. It had been days since she checked in with him. She wondered how much more he could have done if he was still working this case instead of out looking for Trish. He would have loved this briefing. Bernard was certainly enjoying himself, jotting notes and snickering.

She had thoughts of her own as the parade of evidence passed before her eyes. She looked at a flip chart to the left of the presentation, becoming overwhelmed with information. Someone had organized the suspects into categories. There were lists of names under different headings: Immigrants had several sub headings: Asians, South American, Native, and Unknown, which had the longest list of names under it. She recognized several of the names, found under all categories, tat holders that she had interviewed.

"They're hiding among the victims," she said.

People in front of her turned and glared. Torrence continued to drone on despite the interruption.

Bernard offered her his notebook, whispering, "Write it down for later." She snatched it out of his hands and started to scribble, her brain lit up like an amusement park midway. Her eyes tilted up towards the presentation, looking at once into the screen and beyond it, staring like a crystal gazer. She scribbled some more.

Something stood out to her. She whispered to Bernard. "Why no mention of Mr. Che?"

"Shh, said Bernard. Later. The show isn't over, and it's the Fed's show. Sometimes they don't want us to have all the facts, sometimes they save the best stuff for the climax of the show. Let's watch and see."

Torrence was wrapping up the presentation. "So we're asking for complete cooperation. Help us by assimilating your facts and giving us your summary. You can make a valuable contribution to this case." He folded his hands in front of him like a Sunday preacher. "I'm going to open up the floor now."

Red started to raise her hand but Bernard stopped her. He smiled and she nodded her head.

Van Dorn was the first to stand up. "Thank you Homeland Security Liaison Gary Torrence." He licked his hand and patted his hair down flat on the back of his neck. "Let me assure you the Urban Research Department is totally at your disposal."

Bernard heard someone in the crowd whisper, "Turd." He chuckled.

"The Mayor's Office has a theory. After questioning over fifteen witnesses..."

"We did thirty-five," Bernard whispered to Rita.

"...we found a pattern emerging," continued Van Dorn. "The Federal gang theory is correct. Organized crime is behind this whole thing."

"Duh," whispered Bernard.

"A South African mob, one we haven't seen operating this far north. They have shipping resources, shell companies, and enough manpower to run an international operation. They tried to surprise us by expanding into new territory, but with our interagency response, we surprised them."

There were nods of assurance as Van Dorn smiled like a game show host, licking his hand and wetting the back of his hair. And thank God we've never seen Bob Barker do that.

"This South African mob tried to smuggle a band of immigrants into our fair port, but with our combined effort we detected the crime, reacted with force, and upheld the mission of defending the homeland."

Despite the repetition and bull crap there were more nods of assurance from the herd.

"Enough of this," said Red, jumping to her feet as she dropped the notebook on her seat.

Bernard shrunk into his chair like he was sitting next to a drunk wedding guest getting ready to make an embarrassing toast. Red stood alone.

"You think this is some kind of plot to Lethal Weapon 2? Where are the bad guys? Where are the kruggerands? What about this Mr. Che? What about the tats?"

"What are you talking about?" said Torrence.

"I'm sorry," said Van Dorn, his voice coming over like a bullhorn. "This is Rita Rockwell, a contractor for the Seattle P.D. working under Lieutenant Bernard, who has yet to submit a report of his investigations to this office."

Bernard stood up. "We just like to be complete," he said.

"But sometimes the timeliness of information outweighs the completeness. Do you have something to share?"

Bernard sat back down

"You got this divided up all wrong," said Red. "It should be tats and non-tats, not ethnic or country of origin. Have you looked at this?"

"What are you talking about?" asked Torrence. "Tat? Non-tat?"

"You still haven't answered my question about Che," said Rita. "What about him?"

"Che?" said Van Dorn. He went to the board and wrote it down, spelling it different. "Chay? Any first name beside Mister? Did you happen to get an address?"

"Did you?" Red demanded. "Did his name come up at all in your fifteen interviews?" Van Dorn looked belligerent. "Are we sharing information here or not?"

"What have you got to share?" asked Torrence.

"*Dare Me*" said Red.

"Okay. I dare you'" said Torrence.

"No," said Red. "The boat, *Dare Me*."

There were murmurs but Van Dorn's bullhorn overcame them. "We questioned fifteen detainees. Not one of them mentioned this man Chay or any boat named *Dare Me*."

"It came up in one of our interrogations," said Red.

"All this based on one interrogation?" questioned Torrence. "And a decrepit fishing boat named *Dare Me*?"

Bernard stood up. "I sent a detective to investigate the boat. Coast Guard, Fish and Wildlife are tracking it.

"It was the transport for the illegals, not the semi-trucks," blurted Red.

Torrence fiddled with some control. He backed the presentation up to the roller coaster footage, stopping on the infrared image of the fishing boat. "We in the Federal service have access to assets beyond your ken, Miss Rockwell. As you can see here the images of the *Dare Me* show only the crew, four of them asleep in their bunks and one on watch but asleep in the wheelhouse. Hell, we woke them all up and questioned them all. They didn't see anything. Like I said, and as this image shows, they were in between fishing trips and asleep at the time of the raid."

Bernard picked the pad up from Rita's chair and began to scribble.

Van Dorn spoke up. "I don't know about this boat, but we interviewed the semi-truck driver who was there that night. He's just a contract driver from an agency. He had no idea what his cargo was. We checked him out. His story was legit."

Agent Whitkowsky stood up. "Our swat teams had a net around the whole perimeter," he said. "There was nothing and no one inside that perimeter that we didn't know about."

The room started to fill with noise. A din of theories circled like buzzards over dead carrion. Van Dorn was shouting something to a lady beside him. Torrence tried to call order and Red slowly sat back down in her chair. A woman in a blue suit bent down and shouted in her ear over the noise, trying to start up a conversation about her theories. Torrence raised his voice but nobody was listening. The slide show went blank, the screen fading to black as the noise and the discussions continued to dominate the room.

Through it all, Bernard continued to scribble in his pad, blocking it all out like he had a magic mute button. The noise continued to rise and suddenly it was like being in the trading pit again, except for Bernard, who continued to write inside a quiet bubble of solitude in the center of the crowd.

Chapter 37

Here We Go Again

Harry propped Trish up and wiped her down with the same washcloth she had used on him. She swooned, her vision blurred like she was looking up from the bottom of a swimming pool. She blinked her eyes as Harry continued to pat her softly with the washcloth. She breathed deep, emerging from the depths of the swimming pool towards the surface of her world. He wiped her forehead, gently supporting the back of her head with his other hand. She took a deep breath and smiled. "Harry, is that you?"

"Shhh," said Harry. "Call me Fu."

"As long as you speak in a woman's voice," said Trish. "You sound too much like my husband."

"Ex," said Harry.

"*Ex!*" emphasized Trish. "How did you get here?"

"Probably the same way you did." He stroked the lump on the back of her head and said, "I came looking for you."

Trish hugged him, an impulse born out of the emotion of the moment. She started crying. She held him so tight that he began to hurt. "It's going to be okay," he said. He patted her back gently. "It's going to be okay."

She suddenly broke free of him. "No it's not." she said, her voice elevated.

"Be quiet," he said. "This place is open. Someone may hear us. Talk in a whisper."

"Don't tell me what to do," she said angrily. "You always try to take control." She pushed him away. "I do what I want."

Harry felt the old triggers going off. He'd expected a better welcome than this.

"Look at you," she said. She began to laugh at him. "What can you do?"

"Have some faith," he said. "I found you, didn't I?"

She backed down, tears beginning to supplant her anger. Why did he always have this effect on her? She felt confused. He reached out for her but she backed away. "It's just the hormones," she said. She stared at the floor. "Why did you come here?" she whispered.

"You needed help," he said.

"I didn't ask to be rescued," she said.

"Jan called me and told me you missed a court date," said Harry. "She was worried about you. She checked all the usual places and tried to find you on her own. She called and asked if I would help."

"Good old Jan," she said. "But that still doesn't explain why you're here."

"Come on. Divorced or not, Trish, I'm here for you," said Harry. "I think of you a lot. We spent three years of our lives together, four if you include the dating. We were, no are, friends as much as lovers. If you were dying and needed me I'd be at your side."

She let that sink in. "Why did we fall in love in the first place?" she asked.

"It was arranged by our parents," he said.

She looked up from the floor and into his eyes. He had an honest approach to things that she couldn't resist. He cared for her, otherwise he wouldn't be here. "It may have been arranged, but I was attracted to you from the start," she said. "Who wouldn't be? You were quite a man, a war hero, handsome and ripped with muscles." She almost smiled, but her anger returned. "Before you got into…This!" She waved her hand at him, her eyes moving up and down his body, her face nodding in disgust.

"This?" he asked, looking down at the way he was dressed. His foot was arched at a feminine angle, his hands resting on his hips. He was certainly in character. "I'm dressed just like you are."

She let out a chuckle.

"What's so funny?" he asked.

"This is as absurd as it gets, Harry. Normally I'd cringe if I was in a room with another woman dressed the same as me."

Harry laughed and took a step towards her. She pulled back and he stopped.

"Stop calling me Harry," he said. "I told you, call me Fu."

"Okay, Foo!" She spit the words out like she had just swallowed poison. "As long as you keep talking in your high feminine voice so I won't forget."

Harry winced but he made every effort to correct it. She was right, after all. "Look, I know you have issues with my cross dressing."

"Issues?" she said. "Now why would you think that?"

Her tone of voice told him different. "I used this as a disguise. Truth is, I haven't dressed in woman's clothes since my encounter with Dr. Couture."

Trish was quiet. "It's been a while then, hasn't it?"

"Yes," he whispered, working to keep his voice feminine and elevated. "You disappeared in a lady's dressing room. Sue thought it would be the easiest way to penetrate the barrier and check it out."

"Sue?" she asked coldly.

Harry faltered. "My office assistant," he said. "Sue."

"Oh, yes," she said. The words hung in the air like an icicle dripping off a frozen roof.

"Anyway, I'm here," said Harry.

"Okay, hero. What now? How are we going to get out of here?"

Harry looked around, exploring the prison.

"We'll figure something out," he said. He tested the bars, examined the lock. If it wasn't electronic, he would have tried picking it. His brain took in every object in the room, observing and calculating. He started thinking of other plans. The element of surprise could be in his favor. His captors thought he was a helpless woman. At the right moment he could turn on them and release his inner Marine.

Trish watched him work it. She was thinking too, trying not to disturb him, calculating and processing data along with her own observations. The lawyer in her began to accept the facts. In the end she was glad he was here. He at least gave her hope.

"Maybe we could use our people skills to talk our way out of this," he said.

"Caroline and I tried that already," she said.

He stopped. New data. "Caroline L'Enfant?" he asked.

She caught him up on recent events, right up until they came for her. She drew closer, but Harry maintained his distance. He didn't back away but he stayed still as a statue in a public park.

"I was attracted to you, too," he said.

"Do you still find me attractive?" she asked.

Harry looked away. "I don't know how I feel about you. I'm confused about love."

Trish folded her arms in front of her. She looked him up and down. "That's not all you're confused about."

Harry looked down at the floor. "Yes. There's that too."

"I never really understood you Harry."

"Nobody really understands somebody else. Even the best of couples have trouble with communication."

"I see failed marriages every day," said Trish, nodding in agreement. "I make my living helping them unravel the mess. Good people with good intentions, and they wind up hating each other."

"I don't hate you Trish," said Harry. "Look, I'm here for you. I came to rescue you, doesn't that mean anything? I was your champion once. For you, I would be a clown."

She laughed, an odd thing for him to say. "Why did we fail at marriage?" she asked.

"I don't know, Trish." He looked into the past for a moment, but the present overwhelmed him. "It's complicated," he said. "Let's think about something easier. Let's see if we can figure a way out of this place."

She again watched him study the prison cell, examining the contents, testing the limits, looking for the weak spots. He was jittery and it reminded her of what he was like after the war. "Do you still have PTSD?" she asked.

"Post Traumatic Stress Disorder?" he said. "Yeah. It crops up from time to time."

"Howso?"

"Bad dreams, mostly," he said. "Sometimes anger, or other strange emotions. I cry for no reason."

"Like your early months back from the war?" she asked.

Harry sighed. It was easy to recall those days. PTSD laid a veneer across the mind, with all the strength of the lid of a pressure cooker and the fragility of a wet paper bag. Sometimes his head was locked down tight, other times as sensitive as an open wound. And all of it operating on a delicate hair trigger.

"I remember that feeling," he said. The veneer was peeling back and Trish was sorry for bringing it up. "It took me months before I could walk through the mall without scanning like I was on patrol, on edge and expecting trouble at any moment."

"You freaked me out sometimes," she said. "You still do."

"Some of the symptoms have never gone away," he said. "They just go into hiding." He bent down and grabbed the bars of their cage, trying to rattle them. "Well, we can forget about cutting through these bars with a file. And chipping away at the floor is out of the question. Maybe I can pick the lock." He stood up and examined the door, but there was no hole for a key. New electronic type. He'd have to pay closer attention the next time his keepers opened it.

"This is going to be harder than I thought," said Harry.

Chapter 38

It Depends

Bernard and Rita left the briefing, the noise becoming a faint din behind them as they got further away from the situation room.

Why didn't you present the intelligence we gathered?" asked Rita.

"They have that already," said Bernard. "Why be redundant? It's supposed to be brief."

"But you heard Agent Torrance," she said. "We're part of a task force and we need to share our information."

"We already did," said Bernard. "All our reports have been filed. The Feds already have all our information. They have every comment you submitted, every speculation, every observation."

"But Van Dorn said you hadn't filed any reports."

"He's right," said Bernard. "I filed my reports with the Feds, the command group that heads this task force, not the Mayor's office. Van Dorn has the same access to the task force resources as I do."

"Why are you keeping him out of the loop?" asked Rita.

"I'm not leaving him out of the loop," said Bernard. "Like you just said, we're all part of this giant task force."

"Then that means..."

Bernard could hear the gears turning in that giant redheaded brain. He nodded, waiting for the payoff like a slot machine player with empty hands. "Well?" he asked, as if it were the magic word. "What do you conclude, Detective Rockwell?"

She answered it like a question, straining for the reply like a schoolgirl in a classroom. "The Feds aren't sharing information with Van Dorn?"

Bernard smiled like it was Christmas.

"And you wanted to find out if they were?" she added.

"Go on," he said.

She stalled.

"What did you think about the information they presented?" he asked.

"Pretty incredible," she said. "I liked the helicopter footage."

"Did they present anything new? Anything that would help crack the case?" he asked.

"Not really," said Rita. "Lots of pretty pictures. An impressive summary of information." She looked up at the ceiling for a moment. "Then why bring us all in for a movie show? And on a Saturday?"

"Overtime," said Bernard. "Billing time is one way to show you're working hard on a case. Someone up high wants to push this. Either that, or they have budget money they want to burn."

"You're right," she said. "That room was filled with folks working this case, but I didn't hear anything new."

"It did stimulate my mind, though," said Bernard. "Which is another reason for these Hollywood productions. Everyone in that room had a chance to step back from the small part they were playing and see the big picture again." He took his notebook out of his pocket and thumbed it open to the page he had been scribbling on during the briefing. They stopped in front of the elevator and he pushed the up button.

Red leaned towards him and scanned his notes. "Whatcha got?"

"More questions," he said. "The big one I noted was the conclusion about the *Dare Me*," he said.

The elevator arrived and they got on. Bernard pushed the button for the floor that held his office.

"You heard the briefing," she said. "The crew was asleep when the whole thing went down. They aren't even considering the *Dare Me* was part of this. We wouldn't have considered it if Harry hadn't found a clever way to pull the name out of a suspect I was questioning."

"One thing I have written down that's odd," he said. "What's a fishing boat doing all the way in Seattle? They may have come this far for repairs, but if you fish in the ocean, seems like you'd want your home dock to be closer to the Pacific, maybe in Sekiu or Neah Bay."

"They must burn a lot of fuel when they go fishing," said Rita. "Doesn't sound too profitable."

"Another thing that doesn't make sense," said Bernard. "If the *Dare Me* was the ferryboat for the human cargo, then why were they all asleep?"

The elevator opened. "Maybe they were pretending," said Rita. "The scanner picked up people lying in their bunks. The assumption was that they were asleep."

Bernard nodded. She was good. He hadn't even considered that.

Rita followed Lieutenant Bernard to his office where he logged on to his computer. "See this?" he pointed out. "All the current information on the case filed in one place, everyone's reports, maps, the current sitrep, and pictures, available to anyone who has access to it." He pulled up a report by a Federal Agent named Bettermen and read through it, throwing things out loud to Rita. "They went fishing the next morning, actually left three hours after the raid started. We were still processing evidence at the time."

"Who cleared the boat?"

"The Port Authority," said Bernard. "Agents said it was okay."

"Makes sense," said Rita. "Infrared showed no one on board but the crew. Did anyone search the boat?"

He read some more. "Doesn't say." He studied his notes. "That's where I had a problem, and a question. The boat's equipped with a freezer unit. I wonder what a scan would look like if you packed it full of people. Would it be cold enough to hide the presence of bodies from an infrared scanner?"

"We could test that out," said Rita.

"Yeah," said Bernard. "If only we had a Zircon 95 Government approved super sensor with post processing imagery, or whatever the heck they said they used." His face lit up. "Excuse me," he said. "Let me make a quick call."

The phone rang twice before Tom Walgamot picked up. "Matt Bernard," he said, recognizing the number from the caller ID. "I was wondering when you were going to call me back."

"Got a question for you," said Matt. "Do you use infrared technology?"

"Doesn't everyone?" he asked.

"I don't."

"Well you should," said Tom. "It's pretty reliable and comparatively cheap. There are a bunch of companies putting out inexpensive models, everything from hand-helds to sophisticated base units with computers that do real time post image processing."

"That would be great if I knew what all that meant," said Bernard. "But since you're such an expert, let me ask you a technical question. If you had a bunch of people stuffed into a freezer, would I be able to see them with your high powered infra-red post processing imagery detector?"

"Depends."

Bernard laughed. "Just the kind of answer I'd expect from an expert."

"Well, it does," said Tom.

"Depends on what?"

"How sensitive is the thermal detector? What model is it? Has it been calibrated? Are the bodies in the freezer dead or alive? Do they have heavy coats on? How long have they been in the freezer?" he said. "Enough variables for you?"

"Okay, say I stick someone in the freezer. How soon before they become undetectable with the sensor?"

"Depends. Are they wearing winter clothes? Is the freezer well insulated?"

Matt interrupted him. "Okay, okay. Take aside all the assumptions. Is it in the realm of possibilities?"

There was silence for a moment. "It's possible, but I don't know. I'd have to know all the variables including the model number of the detector. Given the state of that technology, I would say it was a small possibility, but still a possibility. I'd have to do some tests to be sure." Something suddenly occurred to Tom. "Hey, it's Saturday. What are you asking me all these questions for? Here I thought you were calling me to go fishing. Kind of late today but tomorrow's Sunday. I don't have anything planned, do you?"

Bernard thought about it. "Did you ever plot the movements of the *Dare Me*?"

"Been almost a week since you asked me to do that. Man, you are all business today," said Tom. "What do you want me to do? Call my buddy over at Fish and Game? On a Saturday no less?"

"Not a bad idea," said Bernard. "Give him a call."

"Oh, so that's what this was about all along," said Tom. "You're at work, just fishing for information."

"Don't be like that, Tom," said Bernard. "You know me. I get a puzzle and I stay on it until it's solved."

"Not getting much sleep these days, are you?"

"Getting plenty of sleep," he said. "In case you haven't heard, we have a slew of people working on this. Feds right down to flatfoots. It's important to me."

Tom heaved a sigh. "In that case, I'll make the call. But it'll cost you. Weather's too nice not to go fishing, and it sounds like you need a break too. What time do you want me to meet you tomorrow?"

"Unlike you I've been working all week. I wanted to sleep in a little tomorrow. What say we shoot for ten?"

"Ten?"

"Eleven?"

"Eleven! This isn't the Matt Bernard I know. He liked to leave early, fish all day and come home late."

"That Matt Bernard was ten years younger."

"Then he's the one I want to go fishing with," said Tom.

Silence.

"Okay," said Bernard. "Ten."

"Any idea where you want to fish?" asked Tom. "What are we going for? Halibut?"

"Thought we'd try some crabbing," said Bernard. "I hear the salmon fishing is good, too."

"Can I bring a buddy?"

"Say what?" said Bernard.

"Look, now," said Tom. "If you're going to have me call my buddy on Saturday to ask him about work, I gotta have something more. You know there's a cost."

"Okay," said Bernard. "Invite him to go fishing with us. Those Fish and Game guys know all the sweet spots."

"It's not like there isn't enough room on that oversized tub of yours."

"All right then, Tom," said Matt, laughing. "He can bring a friend. See you tomorrow." He hung up the phone.

"What did he say?" asked Red.

Bernard blew a hiss of air out of his mouth, then smiled, thinking about his day off. "You doing anything tomorrow?" he asked.

"Not really. I thought we were working."

"It's Sunday," said Bernard. "I don't know about you, but it looks like we're going fishing."

"We?" she said.

"You're invited too," he said. "You coming?"

"Sure," said Rita. "But from the look on your face I can tell this isn't going to be an ordinary fishing trip."

"Rita, in case you haven't figured it out, there's nothing ordinary about me." Bernard said. "This will be like playing golf, except my boat can hold a lot more than four. The fishing will take my mind off things, and I'm sure the conversations will eventually turn to this case. Whether we learn something new or not doesn't matter. It will satisfy my curiosity either way. Besides, I'm betting this case gets solved by next Friday."

"Really?" she said, suspecting he was privy to some inside information. "How do you know?" she asked in a whisper.

He whispered back. "Feds never like to stay out more than two weeks." He switched tact. "You hear anything from Harry? How's he coming on his case?"

"Been so busy here I haven't had time to look him up. Gave him a few calls but Sue picked up at the office. She said he was using Trish's phone. She tried him a few times but it rolled over to the answering service."

"When was the last time you spoke with him?"

"Two, maybe three days ago," she said. "He was at Trish's office in Bellevue going through her files looking for suspects. I was thinking of looking him up. I'm not working at the Rose Hips tonight."

"Let me know what you find out," said Bernard. "He's welcome to go with us tomorrow, too. Always room for one more on my boat."

Bernard went to the door but found it was blocked.

"Inspector Bernard? Miss Rockwell?" The shined shoes, the dark suit, the polished look, right down to the perfectly level clipped identification badge; you didn't have to be a detective to know who you were talking to. Why don't the Feds just get uniforms? Mr. Shinyshoes didn't wait for an answer. "I'm Agent Wiggins. You can call me Gary."

"What can I do for you Gary?" asked Bernard. "I was just about to leave."

"I won't keep you long." Rita started to push past him. "You too, Detective Rockwell. I'd like to talk to you both for a minute."

"What's this about?" asked Rita.

Gary smiled towards Bernard. "Can we sit in your office?"

"Like I said, I was about to leave," said Matt. "And it is Saturday."

"It's about your theories," he said. "I'm curious about how you drew your conclusions."

"You heard our statements," said Rita. "You read the reports."

"Yes, I did," said Agent Wiggins. "But there are things that don't make sense. The boat for instance. We checked it out. It was clean."

"The *Dare Me*?" said Bernard.

"I'm sorry, I was outside your door and I overheard you talking. As I said, I'm curious and I'd like to discuss your theories."

"Nothing to discuss," said Bernard. "You guys seem to have everything under control. You got tons of data and plenty of facts to analyze from what I saw today."

He chuckled. "Yes, we do. And lots of people to sift through them. Problem is, after a week of sifting, everything seems to be falling through the strainer."

"Maybe your facts aren't stuck together right," said Rita.

"What do you mean?" he asked.

"Well, for one thing, your suspect list is organized all wrong," she said. "Instead of sorting it by nationality or race, try tats versus non-tats."

"What?" he asked. "I don't understand."

"Separate them into people with the tattoos versus non-tatoos. I think you'll find that there are wolves among the sheep."

Bernard interrupted them both. "Look, I'd love to discuss this with you all day but I have places to be and things to do," he said. "I don't know about you but I have tomorrow off and I plan to use it."

"I do too," said Wiggins. "Maybe we can discuss this in a more relaxed environment. Do you have any plans?"

"Going fishing," said Bernard.

"Fishing," said Wiggins, his voice in disbelief as if it were a lie.

"*Fishing*," said Bernard firmly, emphasizing the word. "Maybe crabbing. Dungeness are in season and they are one sweet crab."

"*Fishing*," said Wiggins. He stood there like a guest at a party who was wondering what to say to the host next. "*Fishing*," he repeated.

"*Fishing*," said Bernard.

Wiggins smiled, a Federal smile that showed perfect white teeth from an expensive dental plan. There was an awkward pause. "I heard you say there was always room for one more on your boat. Mind if I tag along?"

Rita rolled her eyes. Wiggins was like the kid who showed up late for the game and now wanted to talk is way onto the team.

Bernard thought about it. "You willing to chip in for gas?"

"Sure," said Wiggins. "I'll even bring some beer. What's your favorite brand?"

"Anything will do," he said.

"What about gear? Bait?"

"I got plenty of gear and you can buy some bait at the tackle shop at the marina in the morning. We're heading out around ten." Bernard told him the name and location of the boat. "Don't be late or we'll shove off without you."

"Thanks," he said. "Can we talk about your theories then?"

"Yeah, maybe," said Bernard. "I wasn't planning on making this a business trip. Ask me tomorrow after you get a few beers in me and we'll see."

"Great," he said, showing those perfect teeth again. Rita wondered if he practiced that smile in the mirror. There was something unnatural about it. "Mind if I bring a friend? We've all been working hard this week. We could use the recreation."

Bernard accepted the inevitable. His party had been crashed. "Yeah, bring a friend, bring two, three. Just keep it down to a small crowd. I don't have enough life preservers to go around. Now if you'll excuse me..."

The perfect smile nodded its head. "See you tomorrow then."

Chapter 39

Wet Dream

Harry had a restless sleep. He figured it had something to do with the drugs they had given him. In reality he had lots of restless nights full of bad dreams from all the flotsam that floated in his subconscious.

There were his experiences during the war, memories of men being turned onto meat without warning. Car bombs, snipers, suicide bombers, he saw comrades fall beside him, wondering all the time, why them and not me. There were his countless experiences on the Seattle police force which included shootouts with meth gangs, responses to emergencies like earthquakes and riots, and brutal accidents that made drivers education films look like romantic comedies. Then there was his recent encounter with a mad killer, a self-made butcher who called himself Doctor Couture. Harry was working a case when the killer captured him and tortured him until he lost all sense of self.

There were deeper issues, the stuff that happened to him in childhood, the loss of his father who, like him, went off to war for his country. His father's body was stolen by the enemy, or so the report goes. They never found it and he was listed as missing in action presumed dead. There was the anger his mother reaped on him when she found out he was cross dressing. There was the torment he received from an endless stream of bullies who seemed to appear again and again in his life. Sometimes it was racial, sometimes it was the way he dressed, but always because they found something different in him, something they would try to destroy as they tried to beat him into an image of their own making.

Life can be cruel.

One gang had even locked him in an animal cage when he was fourteen. They peed on him and threw dog food into the cage, tormenting him until they tired of that and abandoned him. Binky was the one who found him and let him out of the cage. He still had nightmares that made him claustrophobic at times. This was one of those times. The walls of this prison were beginning to push against his inner walls.

What separates the sane from the insane is the ability to keep the insanity bottled up safely inside. This was also the realm belonging to Fu Chan, the secret part of Harry's disowned self. With forces this strong it's only a matter of time before something breaks.

Trish heard him tossing and turning. "Are you awake?"

"Yeah," said Harry, wiping the sweat off his brow. He lifted himself out of the bed to find he was lying in a pool of sweat. "What the?"

"What is it?" asked Trish.

"I must have been having bad dreams. My bed is full of sweat."

"That's not sweat," said Trish.

"What do you mean?"

"Is it sticky?" she asked. "Does it taste like sweat?"

He began to realize what it was. "Oh, no," said Harry.

"Oh, yes," said Trish. "Are your breasts tender? Do they hurt?"

"Yes," said Harry.

"Better get up." She said. "I'll show you what to do."

It was awkward, but she showed him how to use the equipment and relieve the pressure.

It was more awkward than she imagined. For Harry, it was the most embarrassing thing he had ever done. As he sat there watching the pump slowly extract his bodily fluids and fill a small jar, it was an insane experience. Inside he was screaming as fears began to surface at every turn of his psyche.

First, breasts, and now this? What has Mandelle done to me? How is this possible to begin with? How long will I have to do this? Will it ever stop?

Fear. Pressure. Forces so strong they push up against the barriers.

Not to mention hormones.

Is this to be my fate? Stuck on some bizarre dairy farm until, like old livestock, I get put out to pasture?

There was a noise at the door. He and Trish looked up. Carlos was starting at them.

Trish was angry. "What happened to Caroline?" she asked.

"I don't know," said Carlos. His reply was belligerent, like a teenager being asked how the car got dented or why there's broken glass on the kitchen floor.

"I don't know why you lie," said Harry. "You're not very good at it."

"Shut up," said Carlos.

"What are you going to do?" asked Trish. "How long before you come for me? Or H-" she corrected herself. "Fu, here."

"Sooner than later if you don't shut up," he said.

"Livestock," she said. "Is that all we are to you?"

"Basically," he said.

"What if it were your mother in here?" she asked. "Your sister?"

"It wouldn't matter," he said. "I killed my own cousin not long ago. Is that close enough for you?"

Harry's mouth turned down. "Sorry," he said, using his best Fu voice. He slipped into character, his skills with people coming to the forefront.

"Don't be," said Carlos. "I did it to save my own life."

"And what's that worth now?" asked Fu.

Carlos lashed out like a snake, pounding the bars with his fists.

Fu jumped back, startled. The seal came loose and the pump whined until she settled it back in place over her nipple. "I have a friend who also has issues," she said. "Let me give her a call. She could help you."

"I don't need any help," said Carlos. "I'm beyond help."

Trish stepped forward. "No you're not," she said. "You're not beyond help. Nobody is beyond help. God loves you."

"God has no place here," he said.

"God is everywhere," said Fu. "I was an alcoholic. Prayer and acceptance of a higher power brought me back from the brink of self-destruction. I know what it's like to lose control of your life."

Carlos hit the bars again and she jumped back. He stared at her for a minute, a mean, glaring look that had all the warmth of an icicle stuck in your eye. His lip quivered and he hit the bars again, turning suddenly to disappear somewhere else in the barn.

"That didn't go well," said Fu. "Should we try Carlotta?"

"We should try everything," she said.

"Now I know what it means," said Fu.

"What?" asked Trish.

"Poor Carlos. I know what's it's like to make bad choices, but I also know what it's like to correct them. It takes strength and character. Resolution and, of course, accepting help, whether from friends or from a higher power."

"That's AA talking," said Trish.

"That's not Alcoholics Anonymous," said Fu. "That's not what I meant, Trish. What I meant was Christ. I know what he meant. I finally understand forgiveness."

"Fine time for philosophy," snorted Trish.

"This is life, Trish. Open your heart for a minute."

"I still don't get your meaning," she said.

"Just think about it. Christ's last words. 'Forgive them Lord, for they know not what they do.' Caroline was right to pray for Carlos. Wish I had met her," said Fu. "She sounds like a good woman."

Trish flinched at the thought. "You will meet her," she said. "She left just before you got here. She'll be back."

"Let's hope so," said Fu. "Let's pray. I think it's what she'd want us to do."

"I'm not much for religion," said Trish, "But I know how to pray. Anyway, it would take a miracle to get out of here. Definitely God's department."

"God helps those who help themselves," said Fu, once again studying the bars, the walls, the limits of the prison.

Chapter 40

Girl Talk

Red sat alone working on the payroll for the small detective office. It was part of her job but she had been busy all week with police business, and even though it was Saturday night, if she didn't do it, it would never get done. Also, she wanted to contribute to the fishing trip tomorrow and needed money in the worse way. She made out the checks to herself and Sue, making an entry in the ledger that the company owed Harry yet another payday. *Always pay the help first*, he said. It was his rule and she knew there would be money coming in soon, but there was something unfair about it.

If he were here she would argue with him. Again, for all the good it would do.

She looked over at his desk and saw his cell phone. No wonder he didn't answer it when she called. As if on cue, it rang, calling out for attention. She slid her chair over and picked it up. It was from Binky.

"What the hell does he want?" she said out loud. She was about to put the phone back on the desk when she had a thought. Maybe he'd heard from Harry.

"Hello?"

The voice was unmistakable, like chalk against the blackboard. "Sounding a little off today, aren't we Fu?"

"It's me, Binky," she said. "Rita."

"And where is your partner? I need to speak with him."

"I was hoping you could tell me," said Rita.

"I haven't seen him for a few days" he said. "He asked me to look into something for him. I did and I have some information he might find useful."

"When was the last time you saw him?" she asked.

"I gave him a ride over to Bellevue a few days ago, to his ex-wife's office," he said. "Last time I saw him he was all dolled up and going shopping for clothes."

"You're funny," she said.

"No, it's true. Farnsworth and I took him to some woman's clothing store over by Trish's office," he said. "Then we took him to Lenny's. He walked home from there."

"Walked?"

"I know. Lucky it's Capitol Hill. There are some places in this country where they'd beat him up for sashaying around like that."

"For his friend you sure don't act like it much," said Rita. "If you see him tell him I need to talk to him."

"Same here," said Binky. "I need to talk to him too."

"About what?" asked Rita. "The rent is paid."

Binky sounded insulted. "It's about a case he's working. He asked me to look into something for him, background on a man named Che."

Rita froze at the mention of his name. "I'm on the same case. What do you have?"

Binky hesitated. "This is all confidential."

"Everything in this business is. He's my partner. Now what do you have?"

"Tell him I met a one armed man who up until recently worked for this fellow," said Binky. "The man escaped from some compound that Che has on an island around here."

"Where is it?" she asked. "What island?"

"I'm not sure, and neither was the man," said Binky. "He was very nervous about the whole thing, but I convinced him to talk."

"Where'd you meet this man?"

"Confidential," said Binky. He hesitated. "Okay. He's was a friend of Manny Ballston. I was following up on some personal business and ran into him."

"Did he say where this island is?" asked Rita.

"Like I said, he didn't know," said Binky. "He worked on one of Che's boats. He escaped by jumping overboard. He swam to safety before he managed to die from hypothermia. Doctor said it was a miracle. His body temperature had dropped ten degrees when a group of native fishermen found him."

"It is a miracle," said Rita. "Especially that he did it with one arm."

"He had two at the time," said Binky. "He told me he cut it off himself."

"What?"

"That's what he said. There was something on his arm, something that he needed to get rid of. I thought he meant gangrene, or maybe frostbite from his swim."

Rita made a small noise of disbelief, a puff of air that came out in a hiss between her teeth. "Or maybe a tattoo."

"Right," said Binky.

"So, you believe this guy?" asked Rita

"True as words," said Binky. "I believed him. Evidently this fellow Che is dangerous. He covers his tracks well. Anyone who knew him or knew anything about him is dead. I feel weird just telling you this over the phone."

"It's okay," said Rita. "I'll be careful."

Anyway, I just wanted to warn Harry."

"Can I talk to this guy?" asked Rita. "The one armed man?"

"He's gone," said Binky. "Left town in a hurry, but he did settle Manny Ballston's account for me."

Rita snorted. She had been wondering what was in it for Binky. She softened. "Thanks, Bill," she said, using his given name. "Call me if you run into Harry. You have my phone number?"

"Of course," said Binky. "I got your number." The way he said it implied something different than a telephone, but Rita let it slide. Binky had at least been helpful. She hung up, her mind beginning to sift through the information. She had another idea. Jan's number was probably on his phone. She should give her a call and check in on Harry.

The phone rang until she heard a click. She remembered it was Saturday. It was probably the number of her office. She expected voice mail but Jan answered right away. "Harry?" she yelled.

"No, Jan, It's Rita."

"Oh," said Jan, disappointed.

"Have you seen Harry?"

"Not in the last four days," she said.

"Four days!" said Rita, her voice elevated.

"Calm down," said Jan. "He's been staying over at Trish's place while he searches for her. I was planning on checking in with him today. Where are you now?"

"At the detective office. Capitol Hill."

"Oh, good," said Jan. "I'm nearby at Pike's Market. I'm just getting ready to head back to Bellevue. Go downstairs and I'll pick you up in about ten minutes."

Red put Sue's check in an envelope, labeled it and set it on the desk. She tucked her's inside her wallet, shut the lights off and scanned the office. It was just as empty as her heart. She locked the door and went downstairs.

Jan was waiting when she got there. She slid into the car and they headed across Lake Washington towards Bellevue.

Trish's apartment was quiet and uninhabited when they got there. Jan went to the fridge to grab a few bottles of water.

"That's odd," she said. She held the refrigerator door open, staring into it. "He hasn't touched a thing." She reached in and took out a bottle of water and handed it to Rita.

"What do you mean?" asked Red.

"I brought him all this food, even a bottle of wine, but it's all still here in the fridge unopened."

"Harry doesn't drink," said Red.

"That's not what Trish says. Harry is an alcoholic, you know."

"Yeah. I know," she said. "I've taken him to meetings. He carries a chip in his pocket."

"Oh," said Jan. "He's that kind of alcoholic."

"Yeah," said Red.

"But Trish told me they used to drink a lot together. Wine every night, mixed drinks on weekends."

"Maybe they did," said Red. "But Harry doesn't drink anymore."

Jan was wandering around the apartment. "The bed hasn't been slept in. And look at this." She picked up a folder off the table. "The file he told me to drop off hasn't even been opened."

"When did you last see him?" asked Red.

"I dropped him off at the Fashion Bargain Depot a few nights ago. Then I went to the grocery store and came here. I brought him some food and the L'Enfant file he wanted to read."

"L'Enfant?"

"One of Trish's clients," said Jan. "Husband of one of her clients, I should say. Trish handled her divorce."

"Why was Harry interested in the file?"

"He was looking for motive," she said. "He was checking her client list for people who might have had a reason to kidnap her. L'Enfant was his prime suspect."

"What was L'Enfant's connection?" Red picked up the file and scanned it.

"Jason is a creep," said Jan. "The first time I met Caroline she had a black eye and two broken fingers. He used to beat her, which is why she wanted the divorce. She's a nice lady, good soul. Religious, but don't give that lady a drink, she'll go on. Told me all kinds of horrible things about her life."

"Why did she stay with him so long?" asked Red.

"She said it was her penance and a test," said Jan. "Something about how she strayed into wickedness with him, how he took her virtue and then some. At first he was charming, but then, after they got married, he became brutal and demanding."

Red could tell. The file had more medical records than anything else, all in the same name. You might conclude that Caroline L'Enfant was accident prone, but this sure beat the odds. It seemed like every extremity had been broken at one time or another in her ten year marriage to L'Enfant, not to mention the bruises and internal damage. There were mental health records, professional opinions that these accidents were anything but accidents, but what disturbed Red most were the reports that bore the names of his own children. What kind of beast hurts his own children?

"What did L'Enfant do for a living?"

"It's in the file. Sales executive for an import-export firm," said Jan. She watched Red turn the pages. Jan had read them many times preparing for the case. Then there were her personal conversations with Caroline. The conclusion was always the same. L'Enfant was a bastard. "One time Caroline told me about laundry day. She cleaned blood out of his clothes on more than one occasion, dutiful wife that she was."

"Blood?" asked Red.

"He said it was from fishing. He went on these business fishing trips to entertain clients. She said she also found lipstick stains on his clothes. He took too much pleasure in his work, and too much pleasure in demeaning her, if you ask me."

Red closed the file. "I get the picture on this creep. So what happened next?" asked Red.

"The beatings got worse. She got curious, asked him about the dirty laundry. It only got her more beatings. She learned to stop asking. Instead she prayed to get away from him. She tried a number of lawyers but they all failed or backed off the case for some reason. She prayed some more, until God led her to Trish."

"Really?"

"She became a project for Trish," continued Jan. "It was good for Trish. When you focus on someone else you forget your own problems and shortcomings. Trish needed that after Harry. She's a very controlling person, you know, always trying to make the world over in her own perfect image."

"Poor Harry. He didn't fit that perfect image very well," said Red. "They must have made quite a couple." Red opened the file and looked into it again. "Sorry. Back to L'Enfant."

"The way he spoke to Caroline in court, it was disgusting," said Jan. "Trish too. He would grunt and make quick movements, watch Caroline flinch and then laugh at it. It was obvious to the judge, but in the end he got the kids and she was out. Destitute, but free."

Red studied the picture of L'Enfant. He was smiling, but it didn't disguise the feral look that sparkled in his eyes. "Did L'Enfant have any tattoos? Any distinguishing marks?"

"Yeah, he had a tattoo. I only saw part of it. It was weird and when he caught me staring at it he pulled his sleeve down so I couldn't see it."

Red wished she had a picture or one of Leah's rubbings. "What did it look like?"

It only took a few words for Red to realize she didn't need the photo. Jan described it perfectly.

"Okay," said Red. "No Harry here, but at least he left me a clue. We have to find this creep L'Enfant. I have a few questions of my own for him."

"Where do we start?" asked Jan.

"There's an address in this file and it's not far from here," said Red. "Let's drive over there and check it out. Then I want to see this Fashion Bargain Depot where you took Harry."

"Oh, Goody," said Jan. "We're going shopping for clothes."

Chapter 41

Reflections

Carlos retreated around the corner, stopping to listen for a moment. He heard the words, "Forgive them Lord, for they know not what they do." The new girl had uttered them, just as he had heard Caroline say them. The old lady had also said them just last week as he pushed her to her death inside a giant pressure cooker. He heard his father's voice inside him, uttering some superstition about things that come in threes.

Something snapped, a shift in perspective that suddenly brought things into focus. He saw the barn as a prison. He heard the sighs of the confined women. The smell of oppression was heavy in the air. He was having trouble thinking of the girls as livestock. He remembered he had a sister, a grandmother, as well as daughters of his own. He was far from home, yet he knew what his wife would say, what any woman would say to the man she loves if she found him in such a situation. He turned and ran, slamming into the doors to the barn. They flung open, then banged against the brightly polished stainless steel on the walls behind them. There was a thud of finality as the doors shut behind him.

He hurried down the corridor that led to the outside world. As he began to push the door open, he saw himself in the glass and stopped to stare at his reflection. It was distorted, like a fun house mirror, an imperfect version of himself. He reached up and touched his cheeks, his hands moving with disbelief across the face of a monster. There were scars that were not there before, marks from knife fights with the other men, part of the entertainment package in this sick Corporate culture. His hair was mottled and clumped, as disheveled as his humanity.

It was the eyes that held his focus. He could not stop staring at them. There were circles, black wrinkle lines that shaped the sockets like the funnels of two black holes. In the middle were two dark centers that floated in a sea of red spider webs. Among the webs were spots in the sclera, stains that spread as if trying to hide the last bit of color. What caught his attention were the bottomless pits of darkness where his eyes should be.

Inside those pits he saw something he could not define. Haunted, hardened, void, perhaps these words come close but they did not describe what stared back at him from the depths. He stared until his eyes lost focus, blurred by tears he could not control. He wiped at them, his hands dirty and smelling of blood.

He pulled his hands away, looking at them, hands that had helped him birth his first child, hands that had until recently held his wife close beside him, hands that had gently stroked his mother's hair as she died. Hands that had prayed for her and begged God to admit her to heaven. What would she say about him now?

Hands that had killed his cousin. Hands of a butcher. Hands that now did the devil's bidding.

"What have I done?" he whispered.

Mandelle spotted him from down the hall. "Oh good. You're up," he said.

"Are you always up at night?" asked Carlos.

"I do my best work at night," he said proudly. "Come with me. I need your help."

They walked down the corridor to the other end, past examination rooms, past holding cells, past the injection room to the room at the opposite end of the barn to the place Mandelle called the butcher shop.

The room of no return.

Caroline was on the table, strapped own, bleeding slowly into a bucket centered under a hole near her head.

The woman who prayed for me. Gutted like the catch of the day.

"She was an organ donor, in good health and worth a lot of money," said Mandelle. "I've been busy all night. Help me with these containers. The plane from Indonesia is due back and I need to finish preparing this shipment."

Carlos stood still, unable to move. Mandelle picked up a pointer, a long stick, and whacked him with it. "Are you deaf? Give me a hand."

"A hand?" he asked, staring down at his palms.

"Have you gone deaf? Yes! Give me a hand."

Carlos looked at the meat on the slab. The face was exposed, the eyelids had been closed, the muscles twisted in an expression he could not fathom. How had she faced death? With fear, or with prayer?"

"Who will pray for me now?" he whispered.

Mandelle only heard the word pray. "Yes, you better pray. Pray that Mr. Che returns from Indonesia in a good mood."

"Don't tell me what to pray for!"

Mandelle was taken aback. "I don't understand this attitude. What's wrong with you?"

"Me?" he said. "I know what's wrong with me. What's wrong with you?"

"Nothing is wrong with me," said Mandelle. "I don't tell you who or what to pray for, but I do tell you what to do. Now take these containers to the refrigerator in the hanger."

Carlos stood defiant for a moment.

"Well," said Mandelle, anxious to get back to hacking at the body on the table. He waved an instrument in his hand, threatening Carlos with the sharp, odd shaped blade. "Don't make me call security."

Carlos grunted, his face hardened, but he picked up the containers. The sealed buckets were heavy and the handles bit into the palms of his hands as he held them. Mandelle stared hard, watching him as he slowly exited the room.

Outside the night air was cool and crisp. He took the path beside the water, the sound of waves lapping against the shore soothing his emotions. There was a slight dampness in the air, humidity left over from afternoon rains. He felt empty and the weather seemed to seep inside him as it tried to fill some void there. The weight of the buckets pulled at his arms and he stopped for a moment to rest.

He heard footsteps behind him and a voice cried out. "Carlos!"

He turned to see the man he had met only recently, the man he had been recruited with. "Ngu?"

"How you doing?" asked Ngu. "Thought that was you." He saw the sad expression and the lines on his friend's face. "Not so good from what I can see."

Carlos looked away hiding his eyes, afraid that Ngu had seen the same darkness that he himself had seen earlier. He covered his face with his hands.

Ngu reached up and gently pulled them away from his face. "No need to hide from me."

Carlos looked into Ngu's eyes. There was the same darkness, but something different too. The light from a nearby streetlamp reflected off them. There was an odd sense of peace coming from the depths of this man. Carlos suddenly felt tired and he sat down on one of the buckets.

"You okay?" said Ngu, bending over him to have a look.

Carlos stared out at the water, dark and foreboding in the middle of the night. Ngu pulled the other bucket aside and sat down beside him. He took out a pack of cigarettes and offered one to Carlos. "Smoke?"

Carlos shook his head. "I don't," he said, but he took the cigarette anyway.

Ngu had a lighter. He lit it, took one out for himself and did the same before putting everything back in his pockets. "How's work going?"

Carlos looked sideways at him, his head still facing the water.

Ngu took a drag of the cigarette. "I know what you mean," he said. "What have we gotten ourselves into?"

Carlos looked at him, wondering how fishing could be as gruesome as what he was doing. He took a drag of his own cigarette and coughed, then took another pull, this one deeper and fuller.

Ngu stared at the water now. "I watched them kill a man the other day," he said. He took another drag of the cigarette and blew it out, but it didn't bring him any satisfaction or release, not like smoking should. "I've seen accidents at sea before, but not like this. They shoved a man in a crab trap and pushed it overboard. It was deliberate and vindictive, done with such malice and glee that it caught me by surprise. These are my shipmates, men I'm supposed to trust and depend on."

"So you're not fitting in with the crew?" he asked.

Ngu shook his head. "I don't know," he said. "I'm trying to fit in but I keep thinking I may be next."

"Why did they kill him?"

"They were gambling," said Ngu. "I think he was ahead and I think this was a way to even out the winnings."

"How'd you feel about that?"

"I wasn't all that happy," he said. "The crew could tell. I tried to pretend but they could tell. They said it was a good thing, that Lucky John... that was his name... Lucky John's luck had finally run out."

"How is that a good thing?" asked Carlos.

"We all got bigger shares. One less person to split the catch."

"I see," said Carlos, taking it all in.

"I keep on pretending I'm happy but I'm not. I don't want the crew to feel I'm different but it's hard to fit in. This is not my style, not what I expected. Like I said, I think I may be next. What can I do, though, what can we do? We're both stuck in jobs we can't quit."

Carlos took a drag of the cigarette. He heard these things cause cancer. He took another drag and nodded his head. "Yeah," he said. "I'm not too crazy about the Corporation's retirement plan. Like you, I'm not so sure that this is the right line of work for me."

"You told me you got a job farming, right? Like you did back home in South America."

Carlos laughed, a cynical cackle that made Ngu feel uneasy. He took another pull of the cigarette, deep and unsatisfying, full of carcinogens and other nasties. "Let me tell you exactly what I do around here."

Chapter 42

Closed for Remodeling

Rita and Jan had a disappointing shopping trip. Fashion Bargain Depot was closed, the sign on the door simply saying, "Closed for Remodeling." Looking through the window it was obvious. There was no one inside and the place was as empty as an abandoned store in a dead strip mall.

The next stop was the L'Enfant's house but the result was the same. The lights were on but nobody was home.

Jan drove Rita back to Seattle in silence, each of them stewing in thoughts about their missing bosses. When she got to Capitol Hill, Rita offered to buy her a drink or a cup of coffee but Jan excused herself and drove off.

Outside the car, the Seattle rain fell like a shroud over her as Rita slowly walked. She decided to stop by the Rose Hips where she could cash her check. The big redhead's thoughts continued to swirl in her head but all she could think about was Jason L'Enfant.

Wife beaters were the worse. She had lived next door to one when she was a kid, a big man called Buck who constantly trashed his poor wife Candice. Her dad told her not to interfere, that it was their business, but there was more than one occasion when Rita wanted to smash the ever loving out of him. She would watch through the window as Buck pummeled his wife. She heard the trumped up charges, the claims that dinner was cold or his drink was not on the table or that she had failed at some other simple task. Then the fists came out, fully justified tools for behavior modification that made their marriage work.

For him at least.

Rita was just as disgusted with Candice for allowing herself to become Buck's punching bag. It was the price she paid for sacrificing her dignity and self-identity, something she had long ago given up when she first said "I do." Buck loved her then, and she swore that he still did, in his own special way, at least that's what she told Rita. Rita felt sorry for her and wondered why she never went to the police. She had all the evidence, the black and blue marks on her body, the doctor's reports, the vague explanations that left people wondering. It was the emotional scars that worried Rita, the ones that trapped her in the lie that became her marriage and her life.

Buck and Candice finally moved away, but the images of her stayed in Rita's head forever. She swore she wouldn't let any man, any person, treat her like that. Not Big Red. Not ever. It wasn't long after that when she asked her Dad to teach her to fight. The old man was delighted at the request and took great satisfaction in training her. As a former amateur prize fighter, street brawler, and drunk, he was more than qualified, and he taught her the right and the wrong ways to fight. He showed her how to unleash the brutal part of herself while keeping the mind in control. He showed her what human savagery can be.

Red touched that part of herself, the animal inside that can easily lose control. She struggled with it her whole life. People always seemed to recommend that she take classes in anger management. It wouldn't have mattered. She was quick to raise her fists. Not that she went looking for trouble, but she seldom backed down from a good fight.

Fist fighting and cunnilingus, my two favorite things.

Boxing was only the beginning of her training. After she discovered martial arts she really came into her own. Judo, Aikido, Thai Boxing, Samurai sword fighting, she tried it all. She wanted to start her own Fight Club but nobody could take her and nobody wanted to try. She earned the name "Big Red", given to her for her sheer size and the fact that once she saw red, it was over for you.

At home, Rita was glad she didn't go out for a drink. It would have been trouble. Anger grew in her with every passing moment. She set her alarm and went to sleep thinking about Caroline's medical records. She had a smile on her face as she imagined all the things she would do to Jason L'Enfant if she ever ran into him. In her dreams she hit him over and over, watching as his face changed from Jason L'Enfant to Buck, to all the despicable wife beaters she had ever met. She had ignored it long enough, and it was finally time to do what she could for cause she felt strongly about.

Looking over at her, asleep like that, her hand jerking like a dog's leg when it dreams of running, you'd think she was restless, but the smile on her face said otherwise.

Chapter 43

Forced Marriage Counseling

"You sure are passing a lot of milk," said Trish. She laughed and Harry winced.

Harry, or Fu, as he kept reminding himself, was filling another bottle. This was not the rescue mission he imagined either. This was disgusting, embarrassing, and above all humiliating. He knew it was possible for a man to let down milk, but it was rare. He had seen it during the war in POWs. Starving men sometimes exhibit something called *galaetorrhea*, a fancy word for male lactation. It had to occur more than a few times for doctors and scientists to give it a name.

But they never saw anything like this! The bottles kept filling and his breasts kept aching. It was flowing evenly out of both breasts with no sign of letting up, twice as much milk as Trish.

"Some rescue," said Trish. "Here you are, just a cow like me." She thumped the tag in his ear.

"Ouch," he yelled. "No need to get nasty."

"Maybe it's time to get nasty, Harry," she said.

"Fu. I told you to call me Fu," he said.

"I'll call you whatever I want," she said.

"Calm down," he said. "Don't draw attention to us. You want someone to come and investigate?"

"No," she said. "I just want to get out of here. For a brief moment, when I first saw you, I had some hope. But seeing you there pumping milk, well, it's not my image of a hero."

Harry looked away.

"Oh, don't be so hurt." She laughed. "You just go on with your milkmaid act and maybe I'll figure a way out of here."

"We're in a cage," he said, his voice as hollow as dry bamboo. As if he all of a sudden realized it. Shadows of childhood bullies taunted him from behind the jersey barricades that kept his sanity between the white lines. "It's not the first time I've been imprisoned."

"You were arrested once," she said. "Spent a night in jail. Remember being caught in that raid? You were in drag then, too."

"I was," he said, empty and factual.

"I got the call in the middle of the night," she said.

"You bailed me out the next morning," he said. "You got the charges dropped, the case dismissed, the whole thing settled without me lifting a finger."

"I kept us out of trouble," she said.

"Us?" There was life in his voice for an instant. "Then, why did you serve me divorce papers a month later? We swore a vow to each other. Why would you help me and then slap m down?"

Like a zoo caged baboon, he had just thrown his best shit at her. It seeped into open wounds and Trish seethed. "How does it feel having tits and a penis?" she asked.

"Again, thanks to you," he said. He grabbed them and turned as if to flaunt them, forgetting they were swollen udders and then paying the price. Strange new sensations assaulted his sanity these days.

"It's the hormones," said Trish, wiping a tear from the corner of her eye. "It's making us feel and say things we normally wouldn't." She put a hand on Harry's cheek. "Welcome to the world of womanhood."

Harry composed himself. He felt like a floodwall holding back a tidal surge of emotions. He was like concrete, trying to stay in place, knowing the storm would be over soon. Hard to use the brain under these conditions but he had to try.

"We've checked everything," he said. "The locks are electronic. This place is airtight and there's only one way in or out. The only time that door opens is when they come to take someone away."

"Or bring someone new," she said.

"That's it then," he said. "The next time they come, we need to be ready."

"We have no weapons," she said. "Everything in this room is fastened down or bolted to the floor or walls. Besides, they mostly come in the middle of the night while we sleep. They must drug our evening meal."

"Then we have to skip the evening meal and stay awake," he said. "How often do they replace us?"

"I don't know," she said. "I think it has to do with milk production. Babs was here three weeks. She was here with Caroline when I first got here but they came and took her shortly after that. I think Caroline's been here a week or two, I'm not really sure. I don't know why they came for her."

"It was obvious," said Harry. "L'Enfant wanted her."

"Wanted her dead?" asked Trish.

"I'm not sure," said Harry.

"Maybe to talk to her privately," she said. "Or worse, abuse her. He's probably off somewhere having his way with her."

"And that's better than dead?" asked Harry.

Trish was silent. Her lawyer mind was in overdrive, reviewing Caroline's medical details from the L'Enfant file, wondering what you could add to that impressive list of fractures and bruises. The soft hum of the breast pump filled the empty space.

"How long before they come for us?" she said in a whisper.

"We'll be out of here by then," said Harry.

"Right," said Trish.

"We will," he said.

"Keep telling me that, milkmaid," she said. "As usual, Harry, you're not being realistic."

"No, I'm being optimistic," he said. "And call me Fu."

"Fu," she laughed. "And where is this super woman I keep hearing about? The one that defeated a killer and rescued Rita from certain death?"

"Somewhere up here," said Harry, pointing to his head.

"Maybe that's the problem," said Trish. "We need her out here in the real world." She thumped him on the head. "You have a thick head from what I remember. How do we get her out of there?"

"I don't know," he said.

"Then we're lost," she said.

"Maybe we don't need her," he said. "I'm an ex-cop and Marine. This is just a disguise, Trish. Something I wore to track you down."

"Is it?" she said. "Is it really a disguise? Or is it the real you? Look at your hair, styled and curled all pretty. Oh, look. Your nail polish is beginning to chip."

"It's a disguise," he said flatly, his voice coming out like Harry and not Fu.

"So you painted your toes? Is that part of the disguise?" Her eyes demanded honesty. They were truth rays illuminating his insides with vampire killing sunlight. They left him no place to hide from her. "It's my disowned self, the part of me I try to ignore," he said.

"Was it your disowned self that got into my closet and tried on my clothes?" she asked.

"Look, I'm sorry about that," he said.

"Sorry I got home early that day," she said. She looked away from him. "It's not just that you had my clothes on, it's… well, that you had my clothes on. I'd be pissed at anyone who rummaged through my stuff like it was their own."

"I'm sorry about that Trish," he said.

"It's too late for sorry," she said. "Your little one man costume party cost you our marriage."

"I tried to ignore it," he said. "My disowned self, I mean. I purged all my woman's clothes before we got married. I don't know what got into me that day. Sometimes my disowned self is stronger than I can control."

"For God's sake, Harry," she said.

"Quit calling me that," he said.

"Okay, Fu. It's just hard to think of you as Fu when you talk and think like my ex-husband."

"We're still married," he said. "I'm not an ex."

"We're married in name only," she said.

"Why didn't you ever sign the papers?" he asked.

"Why didn't you?" she asked.

"I don't know. Maybe because I didn't want our marriage to fail. Maybe because I didn't want to admit it was over. How about you? You're the best divorce lawyer in Bellevue. You could've made it happen any time. Without my signature, or so people tell me."

She turned, refusing to look at him, refusing to show him her face. "Can't you figure that out?"

"I'm a detective," said Harry flatly. "Of course I tried to figure it out. When I think about it I come up with lots of angles, but I don't think I have enough evidence to conclude anything." He stared into her eyes, looking for something elusive, thinking there was something there, something that was no longer. "Why didn't you ever change your last name?" he asked, drawing closer to her.

"I don't know," she said. "I guess I got used to it. It's a powerful name. Better than Kwan. Trish Takanawa sounds a lot better than Patricia Kwan." She flinched away from him, aware of his gaze. She turned again to face him. "Why do you keep staring at me like that?"

"I'm waiting for you to tell me why you never finalized the divorce," he said. "Maybe you can skip all the guess work and level with me. Save me the trouble of wrong conclusions. Why didn't you ever get the divorce?"

She looked beyond him, off to the side where she didn't have to make eye contact. "Because I felt sorry for you," she said. "Your little cross dressing didn't just cost you our marriage, it cost you your job on the Seattle police force too. You were out on the street with no job, no money, no health insurance." She touched his cheek. "Believe it or not, I loved you. I had your best interest at heart."

"If you had my best interest at heart, then why did you kick me out of the house?"

"I had to do that," she said. "What would it look like? Me living with some pervert. What do you think my mother said when she found out?"

"Cross dressing is not perverted," he said.

She laughed. "Then what is it? Normal?"

He had no answer.

"I married a man," said Trish. "At least that was what the certificate said."

"And you don't think I was man enough for you?"

"Not in that striped dress I found you in that day," she said. "In full makeup, no less! How many times did you do that without me knowing?"

"I told you, that was the first time since we'd been married," he said.

"Right." She spit the word out of her mouth in disbelief.

"Look, I said I'm sorry," he said. "Do you think I would have done that if I knew how much it would hurt you?"

"I know you never wanted to hurt me." She thought about it before touching his cheek. "But wasn't I enough woman for you?"

"This had nothing to do with you," he said. "Cross dressing is entirely my issue."

"That's for sure," she said. "One in a long line of issues."

"I know. I have lots of issues. Shell shock, or PTSD, or whatever name you want to call the wounds of war. I was barely over that before I became a policeman. You think being a cop is a glamor job? Seeing people at their best? Name me someone who likes getting stopped by the cops. The only time you want to see a policeman is when you need one."

"So you had a few bad jobs," she said.

"Then there's my alcoholism," he said. "Something you encouraged."

"Me?" she said. "How can you blame me for your drinking?"

"You're right," he said. "I can't blame you for that. You never forced a drink down my throat, but you sure kept a lot of open bottles scattered around the house."

"I like to drink," she said. "Especially wine."

"So do I," he said. "Just not every night."

The front of his shirt was wet again. Damn. Trish watched him clean up, fumbling with the funky clips of the nursing bra. She turned her back to him, part for privacy, part because she didn't want him to see her face. She didn't know whether to laugh or feel sorry for him. She had used her Medical Power of Attorney to get him those breasts, and they were certainly pretty, but like everyone else, she questioned her motive about why she did it.

Who can say? Revenge is a feminine thing, often done in a way that astounds the male mind, especially when carried out with grace and subtlety. She smiled, the smug smile of a clever lawyer who won big time.

There was a distant scream that both sounded and didn't sound like Caroline. She turned towards him again.

"Look, let's stop playing the blame game," said Harry. "We could push each other's buttons all night. Let's channel this energy into figuring a way out of here."

"You never answered my question," she said. "How do we get wonder woman out of your thick head?"

"The last time she came out I was tortured."

"What are you saying?" she asked. "You want live together like a married couple again? Because that would be torture."

"Maybe for you," he said softly. "But not for me. I kind of liked living with you."

He was crying. She softened and gently wiped a tear from the corner of his eye.

"It's only the hormones," she said. "Mine are all screwed up too." He looked away pretending to concentrate on cleaning the pump. The cups were still open on the bra and his breasts hung like ripe watermelons in a mesh hammock. "I see you're all done. I have trouble with those clips. They're cheap nursing bras." She went to the sink and wet a washcloth, then moved back beside him. She slowly wiped his breasts clean. "What I wouldn't do for a good shower," she said. "I'm sick of sponge baths."

He reached out and hugged her as she stood over him. "Thank you," he said.

"For what?" she asked.

"For caring." He squeezed her tighter. Marriage counseling, sermons from the pastor, lectures from their moms, they all seemed like cheap gimmicks compared to the real conversation he was having with her now. Why couldn't this have happened years ago? Why did it take being caged together to get them to talk to each other?

"I often wonder why we never had kids."

She laughed. "We certainly didn't lack for trying." She hugged him back for a moment. "You were a good lover, Harry. Attentive and sweet. You were never rough with me and I appreciated that."

"I loved you Trish," he said.

She winced. "Loved?"

"No," he said. "I love you. We just don't get along. Two different people living an arranged marriage."

"And whose fault is that?" she asked.

"There is no blame," he said. "I thought we said we would stop playing the blame game. It's nobody's fault. Some things are just the way they are."

She pushed him away, just far enough to take his chin and cradle it in her hand. His eyes were still wet and she dried them with the hem of her shirt, laughing again.

"Good to hear you laugh," he said.

"I was thinking how if we had kids, you could be the nursemaid." He laughed and she looked pained. "Fine role model for the kids. Nursing at Daddy's breast." She let go of him and walked towards the wall. "Did you ever have your sperm count done?"

"No," he said. "After we split I didn't see any need to."

She turned. "It was never you, Harry," she said. "It was me."

"What do you mean? You mean you can't have kids?" he asked.

"No, I'm fertile enough," she said. Her own vampire killing vision was blasting her insides. "I lied to you. I used spermicide and drugs to keep from conceiving. I didn't want to get pregnant. My career was more important to me than our marriage. Then, when I found you wearing my clothes I felt vindicated. I was angry and hurt, glad that kids weren't involved. What kind of father would you have made?"

"A good one, I would hope," he said. "It's been my observation that kids pretty much love their parents, no matter who or what they are, as long as they get love in return." He added something he had observed in life. "Sometimes kids love them even when they don't."

"My mother talked me into leaving you," she said. "Tried to get me to go out with other men. If I had a nickel for every time she tried to set me up on another date, well, maybe I'd have fifty cents."

"Fifty cents?"

"I wasn't ever good at dating, even in high school," she said. "I was a cold fish. Boys made fun of me. They called me Westinghouse."

He shook his head. "Westinghouse?"

"It's a brand name of popular refrigerator," she said. "You changed a lot of that. You changed my life."

There was a noise at the door.

"Oh how sweet," said Carlotta. "Lesbian love."

"Who have you come for now?" asked Harry.

Carlotta just smiled, a condescending smirk that said it all.

But in all fairness, the fully loaded hypodermic syringe in her left hand was a definite conversation stopper.

Chapter 44

Fishing Trip

Bernard turned the key and fired up the engines of his thirty eight and a half foot sport fishing boat. They hummed and he felt the gentle tremor of the twin Volvo D13 turbocharged marine diesels as water bubbled out the back of the big boat.

"If those guys aren't here in ten minutes I'm leaving without them," he said. He took a sip of his diet coke and shook his head.

His buddy Tom smiled. "You don't have enough life jackets on board for everyone as it is," he said.

"But I do," said Bernard. "Sometimes I lie about it to keep down the number of people on the boat. If you check under the starboard settee below, you'll find I'm more in compliance for the US Coast Guard. Not that I think you'd rat me out."

"Peugot sound can be cruel. You really should have a survival suit. The temperature in the water can get down below fifty degrees, even in the fall."

"Heard this speech from you before, Tom. Check this cupboard," he said, kicking a door slightly below and left of the steering wheel. "Got three of them."

"I forgot you bought those last time we went out," said Tom.

"It was good advice," said Bernard. "After that green-faced puker we took out with us last time fell overboard I was convinced. If we hadn't turned around and got him back to port he would have died. I never thought that the body temperature could drop that fast."

"I've pulled them unconscious and blue from the waters around here, back when I was a mate on the *Midgett*. It's not a pretty sight."

"What's not a pretty sight," said Red, climbing the short ladder that led to the flying bridge.

Walgamot laughed, looking past her and down at the deck below. "Bill Farbis before ten AM," he said.

Farbis looked up from the single fighting chair mounted center on the rear deck. He held a drink, something red and tomatoey that was probably half alcohol. Tom really didn't want to know.

"Hey, leave him alone," said Red. "He went out drinking last night and had a little too much fun. I gave him one of my hangover remedies."

"Does your recipe include booze?" asked Bernard.

"No, but funny thing, you had everything on board I needed to make it," said Red.

"Looks like you left something out," said Tom. He pointed to the rear deck where Farbis was emptying a flask into the cup.

"What's the matter?" asked Red. "Never heard of Hair of the Dog?"

Bernard turned away. "I really don't care what anybody drinks aboard my boat, as long as they aren't driving."

"Good rule," said Tom.

"Glad the Coast Guard agrees," said Bernard. He scanned the dock looking for Agent Wiggins. "I don't see our other guests," he said. "Maybe we should prepare to shove off. Is Langhelm on board?"

"He's still down below checking email," said Tom. "Seems like he never stops working."

"I know Ron," said Bernard. "He's just clearing his plate. He'll be up and about in a while."

Red looked down at Farbis who looked all too relaxed in the fighting chair on the deck below. "I'll go man the ropes," she said. "Bill may need a little more recovery time." She slid down the ladder and jumped onto the dock, positioning herself next to the cleat that held the forward line.

"I just hope he doesn't get seasick," said Bernard.

"Bill?" said Tom, surprised at the question. "Farbis is an old Navy man. He can put down a quart of whiskey in no time and still have the capacity to do his job. He's a true sailor in the historical sense. Probably would have loved the old British navy where you got a daily ration of rum."

Bernard laughed. He nodded to Red who started to unwrap the line from the cleat on the dock. He scanned the parking lot one more time, then pushed the throttle into forward. The motors hummed and the water churned up behind the boat.

There was a commotion on the other side of the slip. "Hey, hey! What about us?"

Bernard looked down to see Wiggins and three other fellows standing there.

"You weren't thinking of leaving without us?" asked Wiggins.

Bernard checked his watch. "I was," he said. "Told you I was going to shove off at ten, with or without you." Red threw them a line as Bernard tapped the engines into reverse. He gently returned the *Busted Tush* to its slip.

"We got stuck in traffic," said a short, muscular man beside him. His head was as naked as a cue ball, shaved and shiny in the morning light, as if he waxed it for effect.

"This is Jim Renault. I think you met him at our briefing yesterday," said Wiggins. "And the lanky guy next to him is Bud Jones."

Jones smiled and extended a hand. Bernard introduced his crew. "Who's this fourth guy?" he asked.

"This is Sandy 'Bullshit' Hawkins," said Wiggins. "He gave us a ride and is helping us with our gear."

"Bullshit, huh?" said Bernard, offering a hand of friendship. "I've been called worse myself. I won't even ask about that nickname. You coming along with us?"

Hawkins laughed. "I wasn't invited," he said.

"You are now," said Bernard. "Anyone called Bullshit is welcome on my boat."

Wiggins smiled and nodded.

"I brought my stuff just in case," he said. "Let me run back to the car and get it while you get this other gear loaded."

"You need a hand?" asked Red.

"Sure," said Sandy, and they took off together down the dock.

Bernard looked at the remaining stuff, a mess of things that overflowed the overloaded dock cart. How much crap do you need for an afternoon fishing trip? "You can stow whatever you want down below," he said, wondering what kind of landlubbers he had invited. "What's in that cooler?" he asked.

"Sandwich meat, fixings, booze, beer, and lots of ice, for all those lunkers you said we're going to catch," said Wiggins.

Bernard felt the boat rock under the weight of the stuff as the three men wrestled it aboard. "What's in all the sea bags?" he asked, hefting an unusually heavy load. "You got enough here to sink this tub."

"Gear," said Wiggins. "Fishing weights, tackle, change of clothes. Why, Jim here even brought a survival suit."

"I heard people die if they fall overboard," said Renault.

"You got that right," said Bernard. "We were just talking about that. The water is in the mid forties. On a good day you can expect to live about two hours if you fall overboard." He looked as they continue to load stuff, the boat rocking with every transfer. "You can leave your suits and the coolers up here on deck. Try to stow as much of the rest of that stuff below and amidships just to balance things out."

Wiggins came up the ladder to the flying bridge. "I'm curious about the name," he said to Bernard. "*Busted Tush*?"

"*Busted Flush* was already taken," said Bernard. "I painted the name on when I bought her but had to rename her. If you look carefully, you might see the faded *FL* under the *T*."

"Travis McGee?" asked Wiggins.

"You a John D. McDonald fan too?" asked Bernard.

"Only the greatest detective series ever written," said Wiggins. "I was fond of Meyer, McGee's hairy friend. I grew up in Florida. Bought a houseboat after college and lived on it a while."

"What was that like?"

"The boat was old and it rotted out from under me," said Wiggins. "One day I woke up and there was a swarm of termites that came out of a bulkhead. They had a nest down in the bilge. Killed the dream for me. Not long after that I got a job with the FBI Field office in Jacksonville. I rented an apartment and sold the boat, but I still have dreams of living on one again."

"I bought this boat for the same reason," said Bernard. "Roomy. Big enough to live on. Problem is, Government is shutting down that lifestyle. There aren't many places you can dock full time and live aboard. Hell, the city tried a few times to close down Lake Union."

"The Sleepless in Seattle houseboat?" said Wiggins. "That ain't right."

Tom Walgamot broke in. "I see the government side of it, though. Liveaboards impact the water. Most of the Lake Union boats are tied into city power and sewage, so it's minimal impact. The ordinance Matt is referring to was aimed at ones that were not."

"Don't go there, Tom," said Bernard. He explained to Wiggins, "The problem the city has is they can't find a way to tax those people. They live free and loose and it makes the landlubbers jealous. Look at me. I don't need any city services, this boat has everything, including a Coast Guard approved toilet and disposal system, which Tom here would be glad to show you how to operate."

Red came down the dock with Sandy 'Bullshit' Hawkins. They were talking like old friends. They made a good looking duo, Red being a big, blocky smiling redhead and Hawkins a taller version much the same.

"I don't mind you asking, everyone does. They call me that because I deal well with bullshit," he said. They put two more heavy bags on board. The boat again rocked and Bernard raised an eyebrow. "That's it," she said, loosening the lines. The two of them stepped on board and the boat dipped even harder. Bernard estimated that between them they added close to a third of a ton to his cruising weight.

Rita smiled again, her big, happy, glad to be here grin. The twinkle in her eye caught them, and as Bernard revved up the big engines and pulled away, they all started smiling. Like little boys, lured and lulled by the sea, adventure filled their hearts and lit their passions.

"Hope we get a lunker today," said Rita. "I could sure go for some fresh salmon."

Chapter 45

Southern Tied Chicken

"Got a present for you," said Carlotta.

Trish and Harry stared at the syringe in her hand.

Carlotta smiled, a smirk that told them who was in charge here. "You two look quite cozy there all huddled together. I've seen the same thing in a forest fire. Did you know that the animals, prey and predator, all huddle together in a safe spot to wait it out?"

"I don't get the analogy," said Trish. "Unless you've come to join us in this cage."

The smirk disappeared. "Not likely," she said. "This syringe is just in case."

"In case of what?" asked Trish.

"In case you don't do as you're told. Now, get back against the wall."

Harry squeezed Trish's hand, trying to signal something. "Who have you come for this time?" asked Fu.

She laughed. "No one," said Carlotta. "Instead I brought you a present, a new roommate." Carlos stepped into view with a bound and drugged girl. "Now get back, or you'll find out the hard way what's in this syringe."

Trish cowered in the corner, Harry standing between her and Carlotta. She opened the door, brandishing the syringe like it was a hand grenade, a lethal weapon she was ready to use at all costs.

Harry watched how she opened the door. There was an electronic pad, a scanner on the wall outside the bars. Carlotta had raised her arm and presented the tattoo to the scanner which opened the door.

There was no gentle ceremony. Carlos pushed the girl into the small cell. She bumped up against Harry and the door slammed shut before he could act.

"Don't worry," said Carlotta. "She won't be here long."

They disappeared, ghosts against a haunted background. Trish and Harry heard them talking nearby, just out of sight. Their laughter floated like the stale scent of sadness across the barn, emotional cannibalism of the highest caliber. There is a cruelty in the scorn of others that adds to the pain. It reeks of animal planet videos of lions or spiders or fish that prey upon and eat their own species. Bullies thrive in such an environment, shark week heroes that tear the emotional guts out of people. Make no mistake, they'll eat you alive.

There was a noise from across the large room, cries from a distant stall. The laughter and conversation stopped and footsteps quickly moved away.

"Poor girl," said Trish. "I pity whoever made that noise. Carlotta has a loaded syringe and she's looking for a body to dump it in."

"I'm sure she won't spit it down the drain," said Harry. "Just lucky it wasn't you."

"Lucky is not what I feel right now."

The new girl moaned. Trish found herself at her side, helping her just as Charlotte had been there to help her. It seemed to be a ritual. She thought about how Charlotte was gone now, how she may be next. She got a damp cloth and patted the girl's forehead.

She was Asian and beautiful by any standards. She moaned. "That feels so good," she said.

"Where does it hurt?" asked Trish.

"All over," said the girl.

"Didn't they drug you?"

"I rejected it, spit it out. See this powdery white stuff in my bra? I only acted that way for them. Now I'm wishing I'd taken the drugs." She cradled her breasts and rubbed them gently, wincing as her fingers ran over two needle holes. She could feel something rough and subcutaneous, wondered if this is what a lump of cancer felt like during a breast self exam. What had that weird doctor done to her? The life dropped out of her eyes and Trish wiped her cheek and patted the back of the new girl's head.

"You have a beautiful accent," said Trish. "I'm having trouble placing it."

"Throws everyone off," she said. "I speak five languages, including high mandarin, but I grew up in the south."

"When you speak it's like a melody," said Trish.

"Everyone in Seattle thinks that," she said. "Guess you don't hear it often."

"We're pretty bland here," said Trish. "Anything out of the ordinary is exotic."

"How can you say that?" she said. "Seattle is *so* exotic. The space needle, music, culture, I love it here. I want to move here."

"Where do you live?"

"Down in Georgia where I spent most of my life. That's where I picked up this accent. My husband was a Ranger out of Fort Benning. He went out on deployment one time and didn't come back. All the Army could tell me was he got lost. They made me move out of base housing, so I kind of got stuck in Columbus Georgia."

"Where the hell are we?" she asked.

Harry had been studying the cage while listening to the conversation. He tried to reach through the bars and get at the scanner. He thought he could break it open and jimmy the wires, but it was out of reach. When he thought about it, there was nothing in the room strong enough to pry it off the wall. He concluded again that the only possible way out was through the door. They would have to bum rush the next poor sucker that opened it. He could easily take out one, maybe two people if he got lucky. Carlotta and her syringe were a close call but he had to try.

I would sacrifice myself for Trish, he thought. *If I was sure she would get away.* He figured with another girl in the cage now, they stood a better chance. Three against two. Odds were definitely in their favor. Not considering syringes and such.

The new girl continued to complain. "And this god dammed thing too," she said, reaching up to feel the tag in her ear. "This hurt more than when I get my navel pierced."

"Don't I know it," said Harry.

"What do you mean?" asked the girl.

Harry turned and raised his smock and showed her the hole in his navel. "They took my barbell. I'll have to get a new one after we get out of here."

"I'm all for that," said Trish. "Getting out of here, I mean. Nix on the belly piercing."

"I'm in for both," said the new girl. "New barbells and getting out of here. My name is Mei Dao Jackson. Please call me Mei."

"Mei," repeated Trish.

Mei looked at her new cellmates. "You two know each other?"

"What makes you ask?" said Trish.

"I heard you talking when they brought me here. You two yak like an old married couple." Mei got to her feet, studied her prison. "How you figure on getting out of here?"

"We rush the next person who comes in here," said Fu.

"That would last about two seconds," said Mei. "You been hit by one of those Tasers they carry?"

"No."

"Like a Star Trek phaser on stun," she said. "You're out for hours."

"Did they hit you with one?" asked Trish.

"No," said Mei. "One of their own men. They pushed him in the corner and laughed about it. Said he'd have a real hangover when he woke up."

"They're a real fun bunch," said Fu.

"Are you hungry?" asked Mei.

"Hungry?" asked Trish.

"I am. If we weren't locked in here I'd cook us up some chicken with all the fixings."

They both looked at her.

"What? I have a great recipe for southern Thai chicken."

"Southern Thai chicken?" asked Fu. "I'd like to get that recipe."

"Southern fried chicken too," she said. "But Southern Thai sounds good. Breaded with green sauce."

Harry liked this girl. She was full of optimism. No hopelessness here. And she was making plans about what she was going to do when she got out of here.

"I don't think we'd get far rushing them," said Mei. "They got all kinds of shit, needles, clubs, guns. I don't know about you but I don't want to wear that weird bondage stuff they have. I don't like to play horsie." She rubbed her breasts. "What'd they do? These things hurt like shit."

"Stick around a while, you'll find out," said Trish.

"I think we could rush them," said Harry.

"That's not gonna work," said Mei. "You'll just get yourself killed."

Trish cringed. "We have to find a better way."

"I could do it," said Harry. "I have combat training."

Mei laughed. "And I'm a ninja ballerina."

"True," said Trish. "My husband…"

"Husband?" asked Mei. "You two some kind of gay couple?" She quickly added, "Not that I have a problem with that. Just curious."

They were quiet, looking at each other. Mei studied their faces. Somehow he felt like he could trust this girl, hell, he had to trust her. They were co-conspirators. Harry slowly raised his smock and showed her his breasts. "Nice set," she said, raising her own. "Mine are fake too."

He pulled up his skirt. Mei saw the lump and snickered, then stopped, chastening herself. "Sorry," she said, trying hard not to laugh. "It's okay. I have a cousin who likes to borrow my clothes when he comes for a visit." She sneered. "Little shit never brings them back," she said angrily. She walked up to Harry and patted him on the shoulder. "It's okay," she struggled for a moment. "I don't care if you're a bene-boy. What do you call yourself? What's your girlie name?"

"Fu," he said. "Fu Chan."

"Fu Chan? Sounds familiar Where have I heard that name?"

"I'm a detective," said Harry. Recently solved the Sooka case. I also do skip traces, evidence collection, surveillance, basically anything the police won't do."

"Grerat, you're hired," said Mei. "Get me out of here. I'll pay you when the job is done." She studied him closely. "Fu Chan, you say?

"You've heard of me?" asked Harry.

"It was in the papers, all over the news." She looked at his breasts. "Some madman put exploding breast implants in you," she said. "Hey, why can't we use those and blow our way out?"

Harry laughed. "They're gone. Doctors took out the exploding ones and put in these."

"Too bad," said Mei. "Thought I was on to something. I'm all about finding a way out of here."

Harry explained everything he'd learned by studying their prison. Mei observed for herself and concluded that he was right. The bum rush was the only logical answer. "If you're Fu Chan, then we won't have a problem," she said. "You some kind of super woman martial arts belly dancer."

Harry laughed again. "It doesn't work that way. If you heard the story then you must know that Dr. Couture forced me to be Fu Chan. He dressed me in an outfit and put those exploding breasts in me." His voice cracked and there was an involuntary shutter. He began to sweat and a cold chill ran up his back. His breasts tingled and felt strange. Harry looked off for a moment and he was back in Couture's torture chamber. He thought he had put those memories aside, stacked them safely behind the Jersey barricades in his mind, but here they were. Images of a madman who chained him to a treadmill and made him walk in tight high heels. It was absurd, but he was there, tortured until meek, helpless Harry gave way to the strength and defiance of Fu Chan, his disowned feminine self. She was the one who saved Red from the mad doctor.

"We've been talking about this problem," said Trish. She hit Harry up the side of his head with the flat of her hand. "We can't seem to get superwoman out of his think head."

Mei looked in his ear.

"She's in there all right," said Trish. "You got any ideas?"

Mei thought a minute. "You ever try hypnosis?" she asked. "My therapist brought out all kind of junk inside me."

"Of course," said Trish. "Why didn't we think of that? I took a seminar on hypnosis once. I found it useful on more than a few occasions when I had clients that blocked the truth. It's led me to evidence that would have otherwise remained hidden."

"Are you suggesting that you hypnotize me?" asked Harry.

"Why not?" asked Trish. "Don't you think it would work?"

Harry was skeptical. "Don't you have to trust the hypnotist?"

"You saying you don't trust me?" asked Trish.

Harry tilted his head and narrowed his eyes. "What have we been talking about the last few days? Our relationship is a mess."

Trish grabbed his hands and looked into his eyes. "All I need is your trust," she said. "You *do* trust me, don't you Harry?"

"I trust the ninja ballerina more," he said, looking at Mei. "What's wrong with the bum rush plan?"

"We need every advantage we can get," said Trish. "Fu Chan would up the odds even more."

"Thanks for the vote of confidence." But Harry knew she was right. There was something unrestricted and free about Fu Chan. She thought outside the box. She rescued Rita and saved Harry when he was at his worst. She saved them when Harry couldn't.

He looked around the cage again, seeing the same old things. Fu Chan might see things differently. And what was there to fear? He was Fu Chan already, even if he did keep her in a lockbox somewhere inside.

Then there was another truth. He did trust Trish, despite their past. He loved her. How can you not trust someone you love?

Hypnosis? She could make me cluck like a chicken on command.

"You have to trust me," said Trish.

"Like I did when I gave you Durable Power of Attorney?" asked Harry. He looked at Mei. "She's the reason I have these." He shook his breasts and winced. "Ah, that's sore."

"She did good job. They're nice breasts," said Mei.

Harry looked into their eyes, hopeful, pleading, wanting more than ever to escape. He could make that happen. And all he had to do was trust his ex-wife.

Wife, he reminded himself, not ex. The papers weren't final yet.

He was outnumbered. Two to one. Yep, their eyes said it all. His police officer gut was telling him to go with the flow, and when it came down to it, he trusted both these women. With his life.

And the biggest reason to go through with it. He had come here to rescue Trish. So far that wasn't happening. Where was all the momentum he had? He had charged after her with the strength and commitment of the round table, only to fall into the same trap.

"Okay," he said. "Just explain it to me a little more. How do we go about this?"

Chapter 46

Heavy Equipment

Bernard was in his element, away from the office, away from problems, away from it all. The sound of water lapping against the hull of the deep V boat was soothing. The breeze blew into his face as he steered towards open water. Tom had set the outriggers and he was waiting to hear someone yell "Fish On." On the back deck, Wiggins was sitting in the fighting chair flanked by Bud Jones, a lanky looking scarecrow standing beside Jim Renault, who was built like an oblong blockhouse. The three of them were trying to have a conversation as they shouted over the thrum of the twin Volvo engines.

The scenery rolled on in a kaleidoscope of mountains, sea, and sun. Puget Sound swelled beneath the boat and Bernard was lulled like any sailor once romanced by the sea. Birds of every type flew overhead, gulls and huge raptors hunting for prey. Bill Farbis had finally perked up, no thanks to Red's hangover remedy, and he had stretched out on the front of the boat with Ron Langhelm pointing out occasional pods of dolphin, whales, and other sea life.

Red was below with Bullshit Hawkins. Rita told him all she knew about the tattoos, shared her notebook with him, even drew one on her arm with a sharpie so he could get a feel for them. They hit it off, bonding over a discussion of fighting techniques. They were comparing notes on lethal Thai boxing moves.

At one point, Hawkins opened one of his heavy bags to get something out of it. Red noticed it was packed with stuff. She saw weapons and scuba gear, rounds of ammunition and body armor. He quickly pulled out what he was looking for and shut the bag.

"Got a present for you," he said, handing her a short club. There was a heavy ball on one end and she hefted it in her hands. "It's called a mace."

By the size of her smile you'd think he'd given her Miss America's scepter.

He gently reached for her hand and tapped a small release on the shaft. The club snapped and instantly tripled in size. She squealed in delight, so loud Bernard heard it on the bridge. Before he could react he heard Tom yell, "Fish on!"

The outrigger pole bent and the line started to sing as it played out. Wiggins froze, the reel spinning between his legs. Renault and Jones backed away like it was going to detonate. Red stuck her head out from below to see what all the commotion was. She heard Bernard shouting as he throttled back the engines. Wiggins stood up, abandoning the fighting chair as he joined Renault and Jones in a lively jig across the deck.

Bernard shook his head. "Landlubbers."

Rita calmly came up the ladder and sat in the fighting chair. The three men continued to dance like a crowd of women in a mouse infested kitchen. She grabbed the rod and took control. Ten minutes later they were looking at a trophy sized salmon that would be the envy of any Salish gathering. Red was beaming, telling the boys how much she liked the smell of fresh fish.

Bernard went below to get a knife. As he came down the ladder there was Hawkins with his crap spread out everywhere. The floor and the settee were cluttered with his stuff. Bernard shook his head and said, "Pass me a filet knife from that drawer by the sink."

Hawkins twisted around, set a cleaning rag down on the table. As he reached for the knife, Bernard got a close look at the stuff that was cluttering the cabin. There was a weapon lying on the table next to the cleaning rag. There were body armor and scuba gear, a spear gun next to a strange electronic device resting on top of what looked like C-4 plastic explosives. Hell, he didn't have to ask for a knife, there was a collection spread out on the table that rivaled the selection at Lenny's Capitol Hill Pawn Shop. It dawned on Bernard all at once that he was staring at an anarchist's dream kit. At first he tried to put it all in context of a fishing trip, like why the hell this guy would need all this stuff for a day at sea, but then something deeper nagged at him. "What the hell is this?" he said, demanding an explanation.

Hawkins turned and saw him starting at the table. "Oh," he said, not sure of what Bernard meant. "That's my 10 millimeter Glock. Just cleaning it. Go ahead and pick it up and have a look, there's no clip in it."

"No," he said, a little irritated now. "I mean, what is this!" He opened his arms, his eyes taking in the room full of stuff. The only time he'd ever seen this much armament in one place was after it was confiscated in an operation involving a meth gang. "What the hell is all this?"

"I brought it along in case we needed it," said Hawkins.

"Fishing?" said Bernard, still trying to place it in the context of reality.

"Yeah!" said Hawkins. "You'll be glad I did from what I saw."

"What do you mean?"

"Well, Wiggings said we were going *fishing*," he said the word with emphasis, "With that in mind, I thought it was good idea to pack extra gear." He rustled through a pile on the floor next to him and held up a vest. "See? Here's an extra set of body armor in case you want to wear it."

Bernard scrunched his face up. "Body armor, what the fudge would I need that for? Killer whales?"

Wiggins stuck his head in from the deck. "Anything the matter Lieutenant."

Bernard looked up at Wiggins. The Agent's coat was lying open and Matt clearly saw a weapon strapped to his side. From the looks of his ankle he was packing something there as well, maybe a knife or a small caliber sure shot. "Just what the hell is going on here Wiggins?" asked Bernard.

"I was about to ask you the same thing. Lieutenant," fired Wiggins. "All this fishing is good cover but we were wondering when we were going to get down to business."

"What?" Bernard came up on deck. The mystery was lost on everyone but him. He squared off in front of Wiggins and began shouting.

Wiggins tried to calm him down. "Lieutenant Bernard, please."

"On this boat I'm Captain Bernard, and don't you forget it. This is my boat and I say what goes on here."

"Of course," said Wiggins, his voice becoming somber and serious, respect dripping from it like oil from a well-kept machine. The others around him seemed to snap to attention.

Bernard turned away. Tom looked at him from the flying bridge. He did a good job of stifling a smile, trying to fill his face with innocence. It only aggravated Bernard's police instincts. His nose twitched like a detective and his brain tingled.

He looked them all over again. Bullshit Hawkins stared at him from below. Langhelm and Farbis came astern to see what the noise was.

"Did you know about this?" he spat, anger rolling off his tongue like thunder.

Farbis looked caught. Langhelm just smiled like an alter boy. Wiggins made an attempt at a rescue. "Who do you think provided all the logistical maps?" he said.

Bernard started to drop his jaw before Jim Renault interrupted. "Don't worry, Lieutenant," he said, quickly catching his mistake. "I mean Captain. All the support was charged to the Federal Task Force account. It wasn't charged to your SPD budget."

"That ain't the point," said Bernard. He took a deep breath. He suddenly felt like a kid who decided to have a party while his parents were out of town. He invited a few friends who invited more friends and now this party was out of control.

Wiggins continued to backpaddle. "Maybe this is all a big misunderstanding. When I was in your office the other day and you said you were going *fishing,* well, naturally taken in context…"

Bernard looked at Tom. "Is that how you figured it too?"

Tom looked serious. "Jesus, Matt. I don't understand you. You pelt me all week with questions, inquiries about this boat the *Dare Me*, questions about movements, associations, catch logs. Then you have me pester poor Bill here, on his day off mind you, wanting to know more." Bill nodded in support, another choir boy face looking all innocent and guilty. "Hell you even got excited when I told you Bill had a GPS tracking unit put on the boat as a condition of licensure."

Langhelm held up a small hand held while Farbis pointed to it. "It's all in here. I thought that's why we were headed up towards the San Juans."

Bernard's head began to spin. Yep. A high school kid at an out of control drinking party, with guns too. He looked over at the Feds, then at Bullshit Hawkins armed to the teeth. He shook his head, finally looking at Rita.

"I thought we were *fishing*. If it's any consolation, I didn't know," she said. "At least not until he told me," she added, her chin jutting towards Hawkins.

Bernard looked down at the deck for a moment, then over at a cooler the Feds had brought aboard. "There any beer in there?" he asked.

"Ice cold," said Wiggins.

"At least you didn't lie about that," said Bernard. He reached down and opened the cooler and reached in, digging his hand deep in the ice to search for a cold one near the bottom. He hit plastic six inches into it. "Dammit!" he yelled, jerking his hand back.

Wiggins gently reached in and pulled a beer out from the top. "Sorry," he said, offering it up to Bernard.

Hawkins bounded up the ladder like a parakeet and ran to the cooler. With some deft hand movements the top of the cooler popped open revealing an arsenal beneath a shallow tray.

Bernard eyed it like high school contraband. He opened the beer and took a deep draught, then wiped his lips on his sleeve. "I seem to be outnumbered here," he said. "I don't want a mutiny. That would involve keel hauling someone, and it'd be a tough choice." Some smiles appeared, and you could hear a few sighs of relief. Bernard looked over at Langhelm. "You say you have some coordinates? Someplace good for *fishing*?"

Langhelm tapped his screen and an aerial image of the nearby San Juan Islands appeared. There was a red dot that immediately caught Bernard's attention. Ron enlarged the image and passed the hand held to him.

"Hey, I know this place," he said. "It's an old marina. Used to get gas there whenever I motored up to Sucia Island."

"It's not a marina anymore," said Farbis.

"Okay," said Bernard. "We'll check it out. But we're trolling all the way. And if I yell 'Fish On' somebody better jump. Meanwhile, I'm going to enjoy the ride." He took another drink of cold beer, turning to feel the wind in his face, the salt air up his nose, and the sun warming his skin. It dazzled as it reflected across the waves. Bernard was in his element. He slowly went up the ladder to the bridge where the Captain's chair, his throne at sea, awaited him.

They stood around like landlubbers for a minute, until Red began to reset the hook after bedding her prize winning salmon. "I like fishing," she said, her smile as contagious as always. She tossed the rig overboard and looked up at Bernard who was also laughing. She had never seen him laugh like that, but the smile looked good on him.

Chapter 47

Harry's Demons

Harry drifted in a sea of warmth, deep in a state of hypnosis. He heard Trish talking calmly to him, giving him suggestions, but he wasn't really aware of what was being said. Oh, some part of him was, it was all being taken in and written into memory someplace. Nothing to worry about. He took a breath and went deeper… deeper…

Her words echoed off his inner walls. Laughable. His high strung ex-wife wanting him to be Fu Chan.

Wife, he reminded himself. Not ex.

His mind began to empty and he wandered through the corridors of his madness. The last time he had been imprisoned, Fu Chan came to his rescue. She was clever, more cunning than he was, a larger than life woman who rivaled any super hero. Where was she now?

He drifted and he was a kid again, dressed in a pleated skirt and vest, practicing his favorite ninja cheerleader moves. Binky was late as usual, but Harry was having fun with his latest pretend game. Fu Chan flew gracefully across the playground, executing cartwheels and kicks, bending down on one knee for an occasional "Go team!" cheer before springing up into a flying crane, a move she practiced as part of her arsenal of fighting secrets.

Imaginary foes fell at her feet as she struck down bad guy after bad guy with every twist. But evil has a way of sometimes getting the upper hand, and Fu Chan was not unknown to the local population of thugs.

In the middle of a perfect cartwheel Fu felt her foot give way underneath. Before she could recover here were greedy hands on her. Suddenly she was upside down, her head beating against the ground as she was dragged to a nearby cluster of woods. Her shoulders took the brunt of the rocks but an occasional one got through to her head. The blood rushing about her and the confusion made it hard to see where they were taking her, but it wasn't long before she found herself locked in an animal cage, surrounded by laughter and sarcasm.

"Sissy boy!"

"Want to be my girlfriend? I like cheerleaders."

"Here's something to cheer about, baby!"

There were promises. If you do this or maybe that, we'll let you out of the cage. Like some juvenile game of truth or dare, they goaded Fu into finding the limits of what you would do for freedom. In the end it was a game of trust, and Fu quickly realized the bullies had no intention of letting her go, and she refused all of their requests.

When she wouldn't eat the cat food, they threw it at her and rubbed it in her clothes.

They urinated on her, one after the other. Thank god none of them were constipated. They kicked the cage, threatened her with knives, jabbed at her with sticks, and poked at the barriers of her deeper self.

The indignities played on, too disgusting to repeat. These stories are gruesome and revolting, and it is enough that Harry revisited them now, triggered by the bars and the confines of his current prison, set loose as he drifted in hypnosis. There was pain in Fu Chan's past. It was her pain, not Harry's.

"Where are you now?" he asked. The question was answered almost immediately. It bounced back at him from his disowned self.

"I'm here," she whispered. Fu Chan, disowned and lost inside Harry. "You are my jailer this time. You may be in prison, but where am I? Locked inside a prison inside of you. You can't kill me and you can't escape me. You only make me stronger."

Harry remembered. It was how he, no how she, how Fu Chan, had outwitted the bullies. When they urinated on her she cringed, but she did not show it. Instead she repeated affirmations to herself, something she had once read. *This will only make me stronger*, she thought. *Show the animals no fear. These dogs may be marking their territory, but they don't own me.*

When they rubbed cat food on her she thanked them. *I may be in this cage for some time, and I may need that food, but I will not eat it for your pleasure.*

When they jabbed her with sticks, she felt alive. She closed her eyes and tried to anticipate what they would do next, extending her powers of intuition. *You give me the opportunity to test myself against all odds. I will show you that Fu Chan is just as good at waiting as she is at fighting.*

After a while they tired of her. In a phrase, she was no fun anymore. The bullies moved on, their scathing comments less bothersome to her than the flies that were attracted to the cat food.

Binky figured it out. When she wasn't at the rendezvous point he knew that today's detective game would be Find Fu Chan. She was all alone when he found her, but when he unlocked the cage, Harry was back in control and freaking out. They went to Binky's house where Harry cleaned up with a garden hose and borrowed a change of clothes. All he could say over and over was, "Don't tell my Mom. Don't tell my Mom."

Trish's voice droned on. She seemed to be talking to Fu Chan. Harry drifted. Something unsettling in the road ahead. It didn't matter.

But the bump was not in the road, it was inside him. Harry felt the lump, and he wondered if he had remembered the story correctly.

The Halls of Madness were like a Fun House, mirrors and glass in every direction, a maze of confusing alternatives. Harry now saw two versions of the story in his mind, the one he had just replayed, and a vastly different version. In this story, Harry struggled in the cage. He shut his eyes, easily recalling the taste of urine and cat food on his lips. He had eaten things, bugs and mud and... unspeakable things. They promised to let him out, but they didn't say when. He had cried like a little girl and begged them to leave him alone until they did just that. Until Binky rescued him.

Which version is the truth?

Can't they both be true?

Now, Harry, let me out of my prison and let's see if I can figure a way out of yours.

Chapter 48

Skilled Handlers

While Harry was being hypnotized (and inadvertently, Mei),

Oops, didn't want to give that away, but you'll find out anyway, so here goes.

Mei must have trusted Trish a lot because she listened to her words as she hypnotized Harry. Either that or Trish was a better hypnotist than she gave herself credit. So when Trish said to get sleepy, Mei got sleepy. When Trish said she had a deep buried persona, Mei had a deep buried persona. When Trish said that persona had confidence and skill and could help them escape, Mei got pumped. And when Trish said to become that ninja cheerleader (or ninja ballerina, she said them both, they were both stupid in her mind), well, naturally Mei became a ninja ballerina or ninja cheerleader, whatever. Poor girl just filed it all away, trigger words and everything. All the time the real Mei drifting in a nice, refreshing sleep.

They say in order for hypnosis to work, the subject must first be capable of what the hypnotist is demanding. We know Harry had Fu buried inside of him, but what kind of crazy ninja woman was buried inside the mind of Southern Thai cook Mei Dao Jackson? If you know anything about life in the South for a woman, white, Asian, or otherwise, well, you'll figure it out. For the rest of you, bless your heart. Now back to the story.

Carlotta rushed ahead, syringe in hand, her ear tuned to the source of the noise. She had been lax, not enough discipline these days. It had been a while since she used the branding iron. The instruments in her private torture chamber were cold and unused. The iron maidenform, her own inventive version of a wireless bra, was offline and silent in a cabinet.

"Hurry! She's dying." Carlotta could hear the words clearly. The woman had been calling, begging for help. She doubled her steps, moving ahead of Carlos. When she got to the cell the woman was screaming, her arms wrapped around a limp body lying prone on the floor. Her shouts echoed off the steel walls of the dairy, mixing with the sounds of the women in the other stalls.

"Step away from her," demanded Carlotta. She had to act quickly and quell this. Mustn't agitate the other livestock. Carlos arrived, peeking around the corner but staying out of view.

The woman screamed at Carlotta. "You killed her."

"Step away from her forty nine." She called the woman by her number, as she did all the cows in her care. "We'll handle it from here."

"You killed her," screamed forty nine. Shouts could be heard from nearby stalls. The animals were definitely agitated.

"Your last chance," said Carlotta. "Don't make me come in there."

The woman screamed back at her. "Come in here bitch. I dare you."

Carlotta gritted her teeth. She made eye contact with Carlos and gave him a quick nod and a hand gesture. He disappeared.

"Look, now," she said. "I don't know what you think I did, forty nine."

The woman screamed. "I have a name. It's Astra. Use it!"

"Okay, Astra." Carlotta used her calm voice. "Look, I'm putting down this syringe in my hand. I need you to stand up and back away from fifty two."

"She has a name too, bitch. It's Marlene."

"Okay, Astra. I need you to stand up and step away from Marlene."

Astra hugged the prone form, shaking the fallen woman. Marlene's head bobbed like a limp tether ball.

"What's wrong with her?" asked Carlotta.

Astra jumped and lunged for the door, throwing herself against the bars. Her hand reached out, grasping for Carlotta's throat. She twisted, thrusting her other hand through the bars. She managed to grab a hank of Carlotta's hair as she backed away. Carlotta let out a scream.

Carlos was quick, appearing out of nowhere. He had a lasso on the end of a stick, a common tool called a leash. His skills were not exaggerated during his job interview. He had used the tool on horses and cattle before and she was no different. He quickly worked the noose around her neck and tightened the rope. Astra began choking.

Carlotta unlocked the cell and went in. Carlos followed, moving the stick to force Astra into the corner. She struggled against the noose. Carlotta looked down at the prone woman on the floor and stepped over her. She reached in her pocket and removed a small electronic device which she shoved towards Astra.

Astra knew what was next. Carlos watched her eyes bulge. She clawed at the rope around her neck trying to back away, her eyes staring at the device. It made contact, Carlotta thrusting it in her stomach like a knife. There was a crackle followed by a piercing scream. Now there were two limp bodies on the floor.

The barn was full of noise. Carlotta turned her head up and yelled "Quiet, or you'll be next." They were obedient.

She checked Marlene for vitals. "Bitch was right. She's dead."

"I'll get the cart," said Carlos. He started to remove the leash from Astra's head.

"Leave it," said Carlotta. "I'll take care of it."

Carlos obeyed, turned and left.

Carlotta seethed. She stood over Astra, straddling her as she stared down in her face. She pulled her head up by the leash, fumbling with the pole attached to it. She cradled the head with the back of her hand, taking a moment to brush the hair away from her face. "Astra," she whispered. "I think it means morning star, or something like that. I knew an Astra in school."

She gently shifted her hands, wrapping them around the neck. She squeezed, soft at first, a slight pressure as she felt for the correct placement of her thumbs on the esophagus. Then she let loose. "I always hated Astra," she said. "She caused trouble for me, just like you." She squeezed harder, twisting her hands while her thumbs pressed down.

Astra became conscious for a moment, a weak survival instinct. Her body thrashed under Carlotta, her hands reached for her neck struggling to fight her off. The pole attached to the leash clanged against the bars. Her mouth opened, gasping for air. Her tongue tried to force itself out of the mouth but it was held in place as Carlotta continued to squeeze her throat. Astra's eyes became tiny dots inside a milky ball of white, a look of horror staring back at Carlotta as she choked the last bit of life out of her.

The struggle was over. Carlotta tensed, then moaned, a sigh of relief that left her as breathless as a night of satisfying sex. She breathed deep until her breath came regular. Sweat dripped off her face and fell on Astra. She released her grasp but held the head firm as she studied her victim's death mask.

There was a brief moment of satisfaction. A smile curled across her face, then she felt a sinking feeling inside as she slowly lowered Astra's head to the floor. Her knees were weak and she sat down on the chair next to the only table in the room. With a sweep of her arm she pushed the milking apparatus aside and rested her head in her arms. There was a noise and the sound of squeaky wheels coming down the aisle. They stopped in front of the door, the wheels locking into place with a click.

"Are you all right?" asked Carlos.

"Just resting," said Carlotta. She stood up. "Here, I'll help you get them loaded on the cart."

Carlos grabbed Marlene's shoulders and twisted her body around. Carlotta picked up the feet and they dragged her onto the cart. She went back inside the cell and removed the lariat from around Astra's neck. She handed it to Carlos who set it on the cart next to the body. She stood behind Astra's head and pulled her up.

"Her too?" said Carlos.

"She's dead," said Carlotta.

"How?"

"You must have pulled the noose too tight." She grabbed the head from behind and moved it back and forth. It was obvious that it was broken as it fell in an unnatural position.

"I killed her?" said Carlos.

"She was dead when I examined her," said Carlotta. "Now help me get her loaded up." Carlos was hesitant. "Come on. You take the cart to Mandelle and I'll clean up this stall."

Carlos hesitated. The head lay over on its side, resting on Astra's shoulder like a baby being burped, except it was her own head. He looked away for a moment, contemplating what he must have done.

"Oh, don't worry, it was an accident," said Carlotta. "Now help me out and I'll see you get credit for the kill."

They loaded the cart, two bodies limp and pale like overcooked spaghetti. Carlos unlocked the wheels and pushed. Carlotta heard the squeaks fade. There were jeers from some of the cells as he moved past them. Cat calls and threats. He thought about the last time he pushed a cart. The bodies were alive and in cages, pleading for mercy. If not for a small twist of fate, he would have been in one of those cages, gently roasted alive inside a giant pressure cooker.

He had removed the bodies afterwards, the meat flaking like tuna, the skin almost nonexistent. The tripe and innards were rubbery and they came away from the crumbly muscle like jello out of the mold. The bone was fragile, melting together with the other fresh meat, breaking into smaller pieces as he opened the cages and loaded it in totes. The men told him to hurry, that after some exposure the meat got tough and harder to handle. He took it to a large industrial grinder and afterwards to a dumpster sized container outside that stank of dead fish and offal. When he was done, Mr. Morris made a call and a large truck came to take it away. Like a garbage truck, it lifted the container and dumped it inside the belly, mixing it with other agricultural slop.

He looked down at the cart. After mass murder, how can a crime of two bodies be significant

These girls lay quiet, no pleas for mercy, no prayers for his soul.

Prayers.

Charlotte prayed for him. He didn't use a cart with her. He walked her to her death, just like most of the livestock.

He looked down at the cart. "Livestock," he said as he pushed the cart through the stainless steel doors leading out of the dairy. "They have names." He looked down and whispered them. "Astra. Marlene."

Who will pray for me now.

The wheels squeaked against the floor and there was no answer.

Chapter 49

Party Boat

Bernard stood at the helm of the flying bridge and throttled back the big boat. The bow was aimed directly at a small shack at the end of a long, T shaped floating dock. A skiff and a small boat were tied up on inside but the top of the T was empty. A gas pump with a long hose coiled next to it stood on the end, a big sign saying "NO FUEL" on it. A nearby pole displayed another sign, "PRIVATE PROPERTY NO TRESSPASSING". If that wasn't enough, the words were repeated on the side of the shack, large enough to be read a thousand yards away.

Tom Walgamot, Bernard's Coast Guard buddy, sat beside him. He chuckled. "You're coming in pretty fast," he said, his voice on edge with concern. "At this speed you may go over the floating dock."

"Yeah, just watch me. I know how to handle this boat." The throttle gunned again and the twin diesels churned the water around them, bubbling like an expensive hot tub.

"You're the Captain," said Tom. "I just hope you're well insured."

Ron Langhelm laid in his usual position on the front of the boat, completely unalarmed about any impending collision. He was angled back against the windows using them as a lounge chair, his hat pulled low over his head. A cigarette hung from his lips and an empty beer bottle laid beside him. It rolled as the boat lurched, clinking against a cleat as it fell to the starboard side and continued down the scuppers.

On the back deck stood a group of fishermen celebrating a great day at sea. There were four fat salmon hanging from a line rigged across the back of the main cabin. Wiggins, Farbis, Jim Renault, and Bullshit Hawkins posed proudly before them. Big Red was leaning against the back railing, a camera in her hand as she framed a shot of the proud group.

The boat moved with alarming speed. Tom gripped the railing beside him, images of Speed II flashing in his mind, Sandra Bullock watching helplessly as a giant cruise ship tore up the mainland of some Caribbean paradise. "You sure about this, Matt?" he said meekly.

A man came running down the dock waving his arms frantically. Bernard gunned the engines and whatever he was shouting became background noise. "How about lending a hand there forward," he shouted.

Langhelm stood up, taking a moment to adjust his hat. He had sea legs that moved like Dr. Octopus climbing a building, sure and steady all the way. A puff of smoke billowed off his face as he took up position next to the bowline. The engines gunned again and the boat lurched like a cork in a bathtub. The group on the back let out a drunken cry followed by shouts of laughter. Red snapped another picture.

The man running down the dock was closer now. Men emerged from the shack and started waving as the boat rushed towards them, sure now that it would hit the dock. Sealegs Langhelm dug in, wedging himself between the cabin and the railing. He clenched his teeth, biting down until he turned the end of his cigarette into a flattened nub.

There was panic on the dock, jumping up and down, shouts and much waving of hands.

"They look happy to see us," said Tom, waving and smiling back at them.

Bernard smiled and waved too, then throttled back. Twin diesel power quickly demonstrated that Captain Bernard had always been in control. The boat rocked into reverse and he gunned the engines. The crowd on the stern let out another shout and everyone laughed. A beer bottle was raised and fell overboard. Red slipped the camera into her pocket and gripped the rail.

Langhelm was like a coiled spring. He suddenly leaped like an Olympic hurdler, clearing the boat railing with inches to spare. He landed squarely on the dock and wrapped the line twice around the cleat. In one graceful move he stood up, his chest swelling like he'd just been awarded the gold.

The men on the dock surrounded him like a rock star at a concert, their hands waving together as they shouted. The weight of the boat pulled against the line and the floating dock moved underneath them. One of them lost his balance and fell over the other. The third looked down at them as the boat tilted and the dock lurched the other way. They rolled towards him knocking him down and pulling him into the pileup of bodies.

Ron casually tied off the back end of the boat and moved towards the gas pump. He pushed the sign aside and activated the machine. "We're okay," he shouted, picking up the nozzle. "It works."

Two more men came out of the shack, one with a rifle. "You can't dock here," he shouted. "This is private property."

"This is an emergency," said Langhelm. "We need some gas. Just enough to get back to Seattle. The Captain's up there on the flying bridge. He said he's stopped here for gas before. He'll pay you cash and we'll be out of your way in a few minutes."

Bernard smiled and toasted them with a beer. He hit the throttle and the motors growled. A line slipped. The drunks cheered and the fish swayed like pendulums behind them. The bow of the boat twisted, pulling at the rope as it tried to move perpendicular to the dock. The bow pointed menacingly at the two men from the shack, rocking over them like a Chinese dragon at a New Year festival. Langhelm backed away, the nozzle still in his hand. He sidestepped the three stooges as the dock lurched and they rolled closer towards the edge. The man with the gun looked angrily at Bernard.

The boat rocked again, pulling the dock up this time. The crowd on the stern let out a cry. There was a splash and a chorus of laughter. "Man overboard," someone shouted. "Here here," came another shout followed by a toast.

The boat started to drift parallel to the dock again. Red jumped off the back of the boat, the stern line in her hand. Her bulk hit the floating dock adding to the rocking motion. The three stooges tossed like salad in a bowl while the rifleman rocked like a fresh sprung jack in the box. She wrapped the stern line around the nearest cleat. Langhelm was next to her in an instant, playing out the hose as he stuck the nozzle in the open hole of the gas tank.

The rifleman turned to his partner. "Damn drunks."

Bernard cupped his ear and shook his head. "We just need some gas," he yelled.

"We ain't got any gas," yelled the man.

"Sure you do," said Langhelm. "See?" He pulled the nozzle out of the gas tank and squeezed the trigger. A spray of gasoline flew at the men. They backed away. "Sorry," he said. He put the nozzle back in the tank and squeezed the trigger.

Bernard opened his wallet. "We'll pay cash," he said, holding up a wad of bills. His police badge was showing and he saw the men looking at it. "Oh yeah. I'm a Seattle cop, off duty. I've been out fishing today with my friends here."

There were shouts from the back of the boat and a toast of good cheer. Wiggins hopped over the rail and onto the dock as he drunk walked over to the rifleman. "No need for firearms here," he said. He smiled, a beer peace offering in his hand. "I'm Special Agent Wiggins." His other hand gently moved the barrel so it was pointing up and away from everything. The man sneered at him, pulled the gun back and stepped away, but he smiled and kept it pointed up.

He motioned to his partner. The two men looked at each other then took in the scene, the dock rocking, the pileup of stooges struggling for footing, the boatload of drunks, the man pumping gas, stealing their gasoline, and now cops. "Better give control a call," said the rifleman. "This is getting serious." His partner nodded and disappeared into the shack.

About a minute later Bernard looked down toward the end of the dock. An angry mob was assembling, villagers with pitchforks coming to repel the invaders. Red saw them too. She looked up at Bernard who nodded. She unwrapped the line from the cleat and flicked it like a whip. It caught rifleman around the legs. She tugged, dropping him like a rodeo calf. The gun clattered beside him and she secured the line back on the cleat.

Wiggins picked up the rifle. "Don't you know it's a crime to threaten a Federal Officer with a loaded weapon, even if they're off duty?" He set the beer down beside the fallen man. "Fare trade?" he asked. Before the man could answer he jumped back on the boat with the gun.

Partner came out of the shack with his own gun, a high powered hunting rifle that looked like it could bring down a moose. "Leave! Now!" he shouted. He leveled it at Bernard and let off a warning shot.

Bernard watched in horror as a golf ball sized hole complete with spider webs suddenly appeared on his forward windshield. There was a six pack of beer on the deck beside him, half of them empty. He reached down and pulled out a full one. With his left hand he gently pushed Walgamot aside to get a clear view. He tipped his head, nodding as he made eye contact with the man. Partner tilted his head sideways, curious as he lowered the gun. Bernard brought his arm up fast and let loose. The bottle arced through the air until it broke against Partner's head. He went down like a sniper bullet hit him.

Tom looked at Bernard.

"Mariner's baseball camp," said Bernard. "Mom sent me every summer."

There was a splash on the on the far side of the boat near the stern. "Man overboard," shouted Wiggins. A drunken cry followed.

"That's two in the water," said Walgamot, crouching down as he watched the mob coming down the dock. On the shore behind them a panel truck pulled up, the doors bursting open as it came to a halt. They were as good as any SWAT team as they poured out of the back two by two all carrying high powered assault rifles.

"I see them," said Bernard. He grabbed a set of binoculars. "Fourteen if I count right." He scanned the shore and spotted three cars speeding towards them. "Looks like more on the way. Ten, maybe twelve more."

Langhelm spit out his nubbed cigarette and took another out of the pack in his pocket. He stuck it in his mouth but didn't light it. His other hand tensed, squeezing the trigger as if he could make the gas flow quicker into the tank.

Some of the crowd moving down the dock boarded the two small boats that were tied up along the way. Ropes were flung aside as men climbed aboard and pushed them off. The sound of outboard engines firing up drowned out the sound of the clamor moving down the dock.

The three stooges finally stood up and Bernard gunned the engines again. The bow line tightened and pulled against the dock. It rocked under them and they jiggled like puppets. Red picked up a boathook and tapped one on the chest. He fell backwards, his feet moving like a cartoon character as he careened off the dock and into the water. She kicked a second that was lying near the edge and he rolled over the side with a big wet ploop. The third stayed on his feet and squared off against her. Behind him she saw the crowd approaching, the sound of footsteps in cadence with the clank of heavy equipment. Brakes squealed on the shore and a group of thugs assembled, guns drawn and shouting. They quickly followed the SWAT team.

The small boats floated free, the men on board pointing and loading weapons. The engines whined as the captains shoved them into gear and gunned the throttles. There was a loud clunk and some grinding noise followed by two puffs of smoke, a high pitched whine and then silence.

The trundle of footsteps dominated the air again.

"Let's move it people," said Bernard.

On the side away from the dock Bud Jones and Agent Wiggins helped Jim Renaut up the ladder and onto the boat. Wiggins handed him a towel as Jones helped him ditch his underwater gear. "Good job," he said. "You managed to sabotage those engines just in time. You should have heard them whine just before they blew."

"Hawkins little gadgets worked great," said Renalt. "The acid ate right through the impellers and made the props worthless under stress."

"Where is Hawkins?"

"He'll meet us at the rendezvous point," said Jim. "He said he had some bullshit to deal with and we should stay alert. Time to shove off now."

"I'll tell Bernard," said Wiggins.

The last stooge standing faced off against Red, growing confident with the approaching footsteps coming down the dock behind him. Red took a swipe at him with the boathook. He ducked, smiling and wheezing like a pedophile in a day care as he eyed her up. He reached behind his back and pulled a big knife out a sheath somewhere.

"Yeah, I saw Crocodile Dundee, too," she said. "I mean, Crocodile Dundee Two."

He swiped the knife in front of her and she stepped back.

"Time to go," shouted Bernard, Wiggins beside him, gun drawn and aiming at the crowd coming down the dock. "Retreat!"

Langhelm pulled the nozzle out of the gas tank and dropped it on the dock. Gas continued to spill out. He lit his cigarette as he climbed onto the boat.

"Let's go Rita," shouted Bernard. He gunned the engines and the big boat pulled at the dock like a pit bull on a leash.

Stooge lunged at Red. She moved quick, pushing him aside. She caught his knife hand in an armbar and twisted his thumb. The knife fell out of his hand. She twisted again, her leg moving just enough to slide under his legs as she pushed him down. As he hit the dock she picked up the knife. Men seemed to be everywhere at once, close and menacing.

There was a small skiff tied up at the end of the T just past the shack. Bernard seemed to know what she had in mind. She cut the bow line of the *Busted Tush* with the knife. The taught rope had been pulling against the bow of the fishing boat and it snapped. The bitter end flipped back and she ducked. It hit the man behind her like a wet towel in a locker room. He fell back into the crowd behind him. Red signaled Bernard, waving goodbye, and bolted for the skiff.

Langhelm threw his lit cigarette on the dock as the boat backed away. It laid there like a time bomb.

Red rolled into the skiff and cut the line that held it to the dock. A man dove at her, landing in the belly of the skiff and plopping near her. The boat moved away from the dock as another man leaped and fell into the water where it had just been. Red laid in the bow of the skiff on her back, the knife in her hand at her side. The man in the boat got to his feet and lunged at her. She brought the knife up instinctively, aiming at his gut like her father had taught her. He saw it too late, falling forward on the tip as the weight of his body pushed it deep into his intestines. He groaned and she arched her back trying to pull her hand and the knife free. Bullets hit the body and it recoiled on top of her. She arched her chest and pushed him off like a Saturday matinee wrestler shaking off a game match pin. He went limp, the skiff tipping as he slipped over the side and into the icy water. Red pulled away, compensating for the weight and the movement of the boat. There were shots and pock marks in the water beside her. She dropped low below the gunnels, as if the thin fiberglass sides of the skiff offered any protection.

Matt gunned the engines and the big fishing boat sped up as it backed away from the dock. Two men leaped, their arms reaching for any part of it. One fell in the water but the other caught the rail and hung on to it. His feet swung up toward the deck as he fought his way on board. Langhelm ran forward with a fish billy and clubbed at him. A couple of swipes was all it took. He hit the water like a turd in a fishbowl.

Red saw a set of oars beside her in the skiff. She dropped the knife and wrapped one hand around them, studying the oarlocks and planning her next action.

The end of the dock was a mob scene. The angry villagers parted, allowing the swat team to take up position and aim their rifles at Bernard's retreating boat. The Volvos were doing full duty but it wasn't fast enough. Langhelm stared at them, the only figure on the foredeck, an easy target for any of them. The fish billy slipped out of his hand. He saw a small cooler sitting on the deck near the windows. He thought about what a nice day it had been. He had seen whales and seabirds and caught the biggest salmon on board. An empty beer bottle rolled up against his feet and he thought of grabbing a last cold one from the cooler.

There was a fizzle on the dock. A man looked down and spotted a lit cigarette. He noticed that it had a fuse wrapped around it and it had just burned to the point to ignite it. The end fizzled like a fourth of July sparkler. Gas ignited, spreading fire like spilled orange juice. It crept towards the shack where men danced to get away from it. The wall of the shack caught fire and black smoke billowed upward. There were screams and suddenly the SWAT team had other priorities. There was a crowd struggling to escape the flames and the dock became a bottleneck of fleeing men.

The thugs coming down the dock turned and ran back towards their cars. Before they could take ten steps there was an explosion between them and the shore. Sections of the dock flew up, twisting in midair like falling cards in a game of fifty two pickup. Men screamed, weapons discharged and hell was suddenly everywhere.

On board the *Busted Tush* Bernard smiled as he twisted the wheel and pushed the throttle forward into all ahead full. The boat spun around as if it were on a lazy susan and the bow pointed seaward. The dock and the shouts faded behind him, the trapped men now fighting for their lives.

Red felt a damp coldness creep across her leg. She looked down. A hole in the bottom of the skiff was erupting like a miniature geyser. There was a line of holes along the side close to the waterline. She peeked over the railing of the skiff and saw the pandemonium. The powerless boats had their engines up and oars out. Smoke from the fire blew like fog between her and the dock. The coast seemed clear. She set the oars in their locks and meekly took up position in the seat. There was a rag at her feet and she stuffed it in the leaking hole. She could hear the water churning with the thrum of the twin diesel engines as Bernard's boat moved further away. She knew where they would be headed next. She could never get to them before sinking. It wasn't far to row to shore, which seemed her only option.

Suddenly she wanted to scream she was so excited. When she had signed up to be a detective at Harry's agency, he had told her how it was all routine skip traces, surveillance, and stuff the police wouldn't do, but this is more what she imagined. Guns, danger, car chases, fist fights. That stuff over Manny Ballston, that was hard hitting detective work, even if it was a job for Binky. In her mind, she imagined herself a kind of a detective celebrity, like her old heroes Nancy Drew, Trixie Belden, and later Kay Scarpetta. It played through her head like a report you would hear on some Hollywood gossip show:

"Rita Rockwell was recently spotted at the morgue talking to the coroner about gang symbols and tattoos. You remember, she was the one who cracked the Sooka case a few months ago and recovered the valuable charity gown. Big Red, as she's lovingly known to her friends and fans, spent the week doing interrogations for the Seattle police. After reporting her findings to the Federal task force, she took the day off to go fishing. *Cut to scene of Red landing a giant salmon on Bernard's luxury fishing yacht.* Now she's on a mission to find a missing person and stop human trafficking. Tell us Rita, what's it like being a successful detective?"

"Never a day off," she said. "Take today for instance. I would have never guessed I would be rowing away from a gun battle trying to make a beachhead to investigate an evil crime lord's lair."

It went on and on in her head as she rowed. Rita Rockwell, Private Eye, complete with theme music. Who knew what was going to happen next? She felt alive. Her heart was pumping adrenaline for her two favorite things, and there wasn't another lesbian in sight.

Chapter 50

Carlos in the Heart Cave

The wheel squeaked and Carlos leaned forward as he pushed. It felt like he was moving through mud, his feet struggled against gravity and life suddenly seemed difficult. The cart was heavy under the weight of the two bodies, but he struggled more against his inner demons. They were pushing back, trying to keep his conscience at bay, but something was going on inside. He had seen some kind of truth behind the façade he was living. He had been doing things that went against his grain. Men had cheered him on as he put others to death. He knew what he was doing was wrong, he felt it in his heart, but he had done it anyway.

There are some men, dangerous men, who seem to lose all sense of humanity when they are granted the right of sanctioned murder and violence. You can argue that humankind has come a long way since the Crusades, giant strides since Rome, where raping and pillaging could provide a humble soldier with slaves, wealth, and a family. And although many corporations get rich off of war, there are still rules, and civilized governments don't allow such horrid practices. Just ask Lieutenant Calley or the guards at Abu Ghraib or anyone who has been a guest at Gitmo since September eleventh two thousand and one.

Carlos was not these men. He was a quiet man, a man with a family. He once had a future, led a simple life, and laughed despite hardship and poverty. Poverty and hardship were gone, as were his family and his future. His internal dialog was terse, filled with equal portions of guilt and vindictiveness. He was on the path he chose not long ago outside a giant pressure cooker.

He walked under the weight of his own thoughts.

I am an animal handler.

No. Worse, I am an animal myself.

No, I am not the animal. These men are the animals. L'Enfant, Mandelle. Even Carlotta and Kathy. I'm not responsible for what I did. They made me do these things. I was only following orders.

No, they didn't make me, I did them. I had a choice, I remember thinking that I should have chosen death. It would be better to die like a human being than live like an animal. I still have that choice.

And if I choose not to be an animal? At what price? They will kill me if I don't do what they say.

What is my life worth now anyway? I have become the devil's tool. Father Markham would advise me to pray for strength and guidance.

There's that thought again. Pray. It never hurts to pray.

The wheel squeaked. He pushed it into the butcher shop at the end of the corridor. There were two bodies on the tables. Mandelle was hunched over them busy, humming as he deftly cut away with a small pneumatic oscillator saw. He turned, a smile on his face. "Put them in the coolers. Plenty of open spaces."

Carlos did as he was told. Mandelle stopped to help him move the bodies from the carts to the slabs. As they moved her, Astra's head bobbed and looked at Carlos at a weird angle. Inner demons poked at his heart, his soul roasting in a fire he could not quench.

The handset on the wall rang. Mandelle picked up the phone and spoke.

Carlos looked down at the body on the table that Mandelle had been working on. It was Charlotte. She was open, her chest cavity cracked and spread like flower petals. Blood dripped from her neck through a hole into a small bucket under the table. Some of her organs had been removed, stuffed in bio bags that were sealed at her feet.

Who will pray for me now?

Mandelle put the phone down. "I have to go. Che's plane will be arriving within the hour. Clean up in here." He turned his back to Carlos, moving to a small sink where he removed his gloves and washed his hands. He bent over the sink, splashing water on his face before straightening up and running his hands through his hair.

Charlotte's head was turned, looking up at Carlos. "Pray with me," she said.

Hail Mary, full of grace, the Lord is with thee.

Carlos heard the words but he couldn't pray. He tried to form the words but his mouth wouldn't say them. He reached deep into his heart, past a pain he felt there, deep into his soul where the fires of hell were trying to burn away the last of his humanity.

Mandelle turned, his hair spiked. It looked like he had horns. His face was stained red with blood. He reached for a towel and wiped his face.

"Diablo," whispered Carlos. The fire in his soul stopped, frozen by the realization of what he had done recently.

Mandelle put the towel down. "What?"

"What are we doing?"

"Wonders," he said. "We've increased our efficiency. Processed what would have otherwise been waste into salable product. Struggling medical students will appreciate our bargain priced cadavers."

Carlos looked at the table

…*Holy Mary, Mother of God, pray for us sinners, now and at the hour of our death.*

He felt something move inside him. The words seemed to grow from his lips, sprouting like a summer blossom. "Now and at the hour of our death," he repeated, praying with her.

"What did you say?" said Mandelle.

Carlos remembered now. He knew how to pray. The ability came back to him like an amnesiac hearing a phrase that restored his memory.

"Forgive us our trespasses, O Lord." He picked up the pneumatic saw and jabbed it forward. Mandelle backed away. The hose pulled against the wall. The doctor grabbed a scalpel from the table and swung it. It sliced across Carlos' cheek and a line of blood appeared.

Carlos dropped the saw and lunged. He pushed Mandelle back towards the wall up against a table. They struggled, Carlos gripping the knife hand while trying to keep it away.

Lord give me strength, he prayed.

Carlos had labored in the fields, Mandelle indoors. Carlos had the advantage of youth, he was in a better fighting position. His back was not towards the wall. A man of science might point to these obvious facts, but it cannot discredit the power of divine intervention. Carlos was filled with the Holy Spirit, transformed to do battle with Satan himself. He easily overpowered Mandelle.

"What are you doing?" cried the Doctor.

"Do unto others as you would do unto me," said Carlos. He twisted the doctor's arm, the tattoo towards Carlos, the scalpel pointing at Mandelle's throat.

"If you stop now, I won't report you."

"Make ready to slaughter," said Carlos. "Lest they rise and possess the earth, and fill the breadth of the world with tyrants."

Mandelle's eyes widened as the tip of the scalpel pierced his neck.

Carlos stared at the tattoo. "Thee with Satan's mark, thy days are numbered!"

Mandelle went to scream but Carlos pushed hard and twisted. The scalpel went in an inch and stopped. There was a crunching noise and then it slid deeper. Blood splattered against him and ran down the front of his clothes. Carlos shifted his grip, pressed against the scalpel with the palm of his hand. It went deeper until only a small piece of the handle was left sticking out. Blood ran in a river down Mandelle's neck, gushing out from around the scalpel.

Mandelle twitched, his mouth opened in surprise. The butcher became the bacon and Carlos slowly let the lifeless body slip to the floor.

Charlotte smiled at him. He opened the bio bags and dumped the contents into the open cavity in her chest. He cried as he sewed her shut, singing church songs and quoting Bible, as happy in his work as Mandelle was only a short time ago.

"Rest in peace now," he said when he was finished.

She spoke to him.

"Yes, yes," he said. "I know you were close to her. I'll let her go." He hugged the corpse, tears of sorrow and madness dripping on her. "I'm sorry."

He turned. Carlotta was standing at the door. She didn't see Mandelle on the floor behind the tables. There was always too much blood in this room. "Good, I found you. Something is going on and they need all hands at the floating dock. Have you seen Klaus?"

He picked up another scalpel, removed it from the sterile wrapper. *I shall wield my sword in His name.* He held it tightly in his hand. He looked at Carlotta's arm, staring at the tattoo, full of Bible venom. "If anyone worships the beast and its image and receives a mark on his forehead or on his hand, he also will drink the wine of God's wrath."

"Right," she said, agreeing with him. Carlos was rabid, blood dripping down the front of his shirt. This work is grisly and not for everyone. She saw the last assistant break down and she had doubts that Carlos would make it much longer. "Look," she said. "I have other priorities now. I'm going to make a quick search for Mandelle then head to admin. There's a secondary assembly point there. If you see him, tell him we're meeting up there." She glanced around. "You look like you're in the middle of something. Can't leave the place looking like this. Might as well finish up and join us later. I'll tell them you're busy."

"My angel will go before you and bring you hence, and I will wipe them out." He tensed his arm, clenching the scalpel until his hand shook.

"Yes," she said. "Of course." She turned and was gone before he could act.

He relaxed and his hand stopped twitching. He set the scalpel down and spoke to Charlotte. "Yes, my angel, you're right. It's a perfect time for that. I'll go get her and be right back."

He turned to the lifeless body of Klaus Mandelle. "Yes," he said. "I almost forgot, a message for you, in case you didn't hear. There's an all hands meet up. They want you over in admin."

Chapter 51

Shore Leave

There was a bulkhead with a narrow beach exposed by low tide, rocks and pools of ick to stumble over. Red steadied herself with an oar as she got out of the boat. With two feet firmly on land she pushed the boat back out to sea and dashed for the bulkhead. It was lower than her, only a few feet high, and she crouched down as she scanned the area.

The skiff was drifting, soon to be hidden again in bales of smoke that poured from the docks. The fishermen had caused a lot of damage. Langhelm's stunt with the gasoline worked better than expected, maybe too well. If ever there was a distraction this was the king pot pile of them. She could hear the trapped men on the broken section of dock, panicked cries and desperate shouts. She saw a burning body fall off the end and hit the water. Against the backdrop of flames motorboats circled, pumping salt water on the shack and dousing the flat end of the dock in chemical foam.

She lifted her head and peered over the top of the bulkhead. Nearby was a cluster of randomly parked cars. More were arriving. A team of men deployed a firehose down the dock where another group directed it at the flames. A large man in an expensive suit was shouting orders. "We have to get this under control," he yelled. "We don't need a visit from the authorities."

"It's Mr. Che you should be worried about," said a low, squat man beside him.

As the big man turned, Red caught a glimpse of his face. "Jason L'Enfant," she whispered. He turned and looked in her direction as if he'd heard her call his name. She ducked down, her back pressed flat to the wall. The wind shifted and clouds of smoke wafted past her. She held her breath trying to avoid a cough.

The skiff floated away. Had it been a mistake to abandon it? Further out was Bernard's boat, steaming away as fast as it could, becoming a tiny dot in the distance. Maybe they had decided to abort phase two of the plan. There was a lump in her throat and she swallowed several times but it wouldn't go away. She reached in her pocket and felt the mace there, some comfort. She wondered what happened to Bullshit Hawkins and if he had managed to make it back to the boat.

She had to trust that her friends wouldn't leave her. "Okay, Nancy Drew, what would you do?" she asked herself. The answer came back obvious. "Snoop." She peeked over the bulkhead. She saw him again, arrogant, barking out orders, making others jump to the sound of his voice, like he did Caroline. "Jason L'Enfant," she whispered, her jaw locked, her eyes narrowed. She seethed. She thought of Caroline and of the things he had done to her. She had seen the medical records, felt the pain between the pages. He had to be responsible for her disappearance. If anyone knew where she was now, he would.

She slapped a meaty paw in her left hand, smacking it like raw meat. Unlike Nancy Drew, Rita Rockwell had other ways of getting information out of suspects. The time to act was upon her. She glanced around, then with the grace of a championship wrestler, she rolled up over the bulkhead and came to standing, running to the nearest car for cover. She glanced inside. It was empty except for a pile of clothes and some junk scattered on the back seat. There was a cellphone on the dashboard and it started to ring, a distinct ringtone that she couldn't figure. Jason L'Enfant walked over and nervously picked it up.

"Yes," he said. "Everything's under control. The fire will be out shortly." There was a pause, then panic in his voice. "Now? But I thought he wasn't due until much later." Another pause. "I'll be right there." He hung up the phone and turned to the squat man who was listening.

"Che is back. His private plane is due here in half an hour. I have to go to the airport to meet him."

"I will go with you," said the man.

"What about the fire, Mr. Lo? Shouldn't you see to it?"

"It is under control. It would be inefficient to assign more manpower. As I said, I will accompany you to the airfield."

There were more shouts and Jason and the squat man turned towards the disturbance. "Are you sure?" asked Jason. "The presence of management always seems to motivate the workers."

Lights flashed as a truck turned a corner and came towards them. Red looked around for cover, and seeing none, quietly opened the back door and slipped into the car. There was a construction tarp and she pushed herself towards the floorboards as she hid beneath it, swearing at herself for being so big, thankful the back seat was so messy. She settled in, turning her ear like a giant antenna at a remote listening post.

Jason signaled one of his lieutenants who hustled to his side. "Report," he said.

"We've extended two ladders across the broken section of dock and secured them in place. Men are beginning to cross to safety. The fire has is contained at the end of the dock and we expect to have it out in the next five minutes."

"What about the drunk fishermen that caused this?"

"They high tailed it out of here the moment there was trouble," said the lieutenant. "The sight of guns made them run. Should we pursue them?"

"Not now," said L'Enfant. "We have them on our security cameras. Someone must have seen the name of the boat. I'll file a report with the authorities and we'll take them to court for full damages plus the down time to our business." He smiled, a tribute to his own cleverness. "Get this situation handled. Attend to the wounded and get me a damage report. Nobody died, right?"

"Not yet," said the lieutenant. "Three men burned, one in critical condition. The ambulance just arrived and we're getting them prepped for transport. Lots of smoke inhalation, cuts and bruises, but nothing we can't handle."

Mr. Lo smiled. "Corporate training is excellent. Our soldiers can handle any emergency, from bullet wounds to heart failure."

"Yes, Mr. Lo," said the lieutenant. "We can handle anything."

"I leave it to you, then. I have to meet Che," said Jason. "Wrap this up and report to me later tonight." The Lieutenant moved off. L'Enfant nodded to the squat man. "You're right. This is under control. Let's go meet Che."

They got in the car, L'Enfant driving. He dialed a number and spoke, Mr. Lo listening to every word as hard as Red was. He spoke into the phone. "Che is due to arrive within the hour," he said. "Meet me at the airstrip. Bring Mandelle. The Chairman has something for him." There was a pause. "Don't complain. My men are handling an emergency. Just do it, and meet me at the hangar office." He put the phone back on the dashboard.

"How will you explain your problem to the Chairman?" asked Lo.

"It was not my fault. This was caused by trespassers. We'll find them and make them pay for the damages they did."

"I have no doubt. I meant your other problem," he said. "The sudden and hostile death of your ex-wife. It was not corporate sanctioned violence. How will you explain that to the Chairman?"

"I was in charge," he said. "I authorized it." He looked Lo in the eye. "I handled the paperwork as a transfer of resources from the Dairy to the Medical Recovery project." He looked back at the road.

"Yes, you did indeed," said Lo. "Leaving us to dispose of the body by selling it to the cadaver markets."

Jason smiled.

"You forgot one thing," he said. "Your ex-wife was reported missing. The data on her body, her DNA, fingerprints, and dental records, they are all part of the public record. You put us at great risk."

"It's done," said L'Enfant. "We're doing a chop shop number, the parts will be in Europe by the morning, installed in their new owners in time for Monday night football."

"They don't watch football in Europe," said Lo.

"You know I meant soccer," he said. "That's what they call it there."

"Correct," said Lo, with all the emotion of computer program calculating actuarial tables.

"Don't get me off track," said L'Enfant. "I assume you're asking me this because you've seen the paperwork."

"Yes. There were a few details missing," said Lo.

"And you've just heard them," said L'Enfant. "Any more questions? Did you approve the paperwork?"

Lo stared at him, studying L'Enfant like a Persian rug. It was easy to spot the flaws in this one.

"I'll ask again," said L'Enfant. "Did you approve the paperwork? I want this settled before the Chairman gets back."

"I did not," said Lo. Yes, lots of flaws in this carpet. Lo wondered what the Chairman saw in this man. Whatever it was, he should not question it, but there was something about Jason L'Enfant that he did not trust. Still... He cleared his throat. "Why don't you drop me off at the administration building? I'll take care of it while you go on ahead. Anyway, it's probably best that you greet Mr. Che alone." He smiled. "I'm sure you have a lot to tell him."

"As you wish, Mr. Lo." The car screeched to a halt and Lo got out. L'Enfant drove on in peace.

The Corporate airport was further inland on the property. The airstrip had been lengthened to accommodate Mr. Che's choice of private jet. At the end of the pavement was a hangar with offices lining one wall. L'Enfant parked the car and got out.

Red lay perfectly still. She heard his footsteps echo as he stepped onto the concrete and walked through the hanger. She waited a minute and slipped out of the car. It was getting dark, the sun beginning to set behind the mountains, leaving long shadows to compete with street lights for illumination. Red moved to the dark side of the hanger and looked through a window. L'Enfant was across the way in an office talking to someone. The man bowed and left, footsteps in the hanger again.

From the conversation in the car she knew Caroline L'Enfant was dead, that much was certain. Red suppressed a tear, thinking about the children. She wondered if Jason were enough of a monster to assign his own children to the cadaver project. She thought of Caroline's medical records, her pain, her fears for the children. It was clear what Jason could do with his fists, but there was a ruthlessly dark canyon in this man, darker than anything she had imagined.

She had never been one to run from a fight, instead she sought them out. Some of her favorite words were, "Why don't you pick on somebody your own size?" The big red head had a big heart, and she wasn't afraid to throw her weight around in the name of justice.

She crept back in the shadows, watching the crony drive off in Jason's car. No one else was around. They were alone. She walked into the hanger, her right hand balled into a fist, gently beating against her thigh.

Chapter 52

You Don't Mess With a Bitch in a Skin Tight Leather Suit

Carlos appeared at the door. He stood looking into the cell, madness in his eye. "She wants to see you," he said, staring at Trish. "One last time I'm afraid."

She was freaked. He was a mess, blood stains down his front. His eyes had an empty look, like a patient who had just been lobotomized.

Mei and Fu tensed. Carlos raised his arm and passed it in front of the scanner.

The girls were ninja ballerina quick. The door clicked open like the starting gun at the beginning of a race. They bolted out the door. Fu hit him first, ramming his midsection and knocking him off balance. Mei went high, leaping up and spreading her legs, she caught Carlos around the neck as she rode him down backwards to the floor. She was all over him, relentless, punching him in the face like he was a speed bag.

He didn't resist. "Hit me harder," he said. "Harder."

Mei obliged him.

He started to cry. The pain felt right. Justified. He deserved this penance. He needed to suffer for his sins. *If someone slaps you on one cheek, turn to them the other.* He threw his hands out to the side, becoming as limp as a dead fish. *If someone takes your coat, do not withhold your shirt from them.* The Lord was telling him to accept this punishment.

Carlos groaned. The sound of meat tenderizing, brutal and saltless.

Trish rushed out of the cell. "Stop it! Stop!" she yelled.

Carlos lay there crying. "Again," he screamed. "Again. Put me to sword and let thy vengeance take root."

Mei hit him again. His left eye began to swell. She hit again.

"Stop it," yelled Trish. She grabbed her arm. "Can't you see he's not fighting back."

"Carlos rocked his head back and forth. "Hit me. I deserve it. Punish me." He sobbed like a baby.

Trish went to his side. His nose was bleeding and his eye was swollen. Mei and Fu held him down. He had cuts across his face.

"What did you say?" asked Trish. "who did you say wanted to see me?"

"She does."

"Who?" demanded Trish.

"Your friend," he said. "The one who prayed for me."

"Charlotte?" asked Trish.

"Yes. Jason's woman," he said. "L'Enfant. He's finished with her. She asked for you." He looked into her eyes. "I'll take you to her. She asked me to."

Trish looked at Fu. "Let's go."

They got him up, watching him carefully as he led the way around the corner and out of the barn through the big double doors. There was no one around but they remained vigilant, checking every open door, every room. They walked around several corners and down the long corridor past storerooms and offices to the butcher shop at the end of the hall.

Carlos opened the door for Trish and smiled, as if he were the doorman at a Park Avenue apartment house. Inside there was blood everywhere. The floor was a mess and there was a bucket of blood under the table. The smell hit her first. Blood has an earthy smell, coppery, not bad, not sweet, something else. The antonym of the air after a thunderstorm. It was sticky, everywhere. As she looked up she saw Charlotte on the table. Her hand went to her mouth and she gasped air deep into her lungs. She turned and hid her head in Fu's chest.

Mei discovered the dead body of Doctor Mandelle. "Got one down over here, too," she said. Trish pulled away so Fu could have a look. There were wet spots on Fu's blouse, signs that the milkmaid would have to do her duty soon. She grabbed a towel from a nearby table.

Fu breathed deep, unsatisfied, anger at Mandelle. She would have enjoyed putting this villain down. She looked at the tattooed numbers on her breast, then down at the only man who knew their meaning. He had done this to her, injected her breasts with some kind of weird stuff. Made her cry and everything. She rubbed her chin. *Stopped my beard from growing, too, come to think of it. Hmmm…. Can there be a bright side to this?*

"Do you know how he died?" asked Fu.

"A scalpel to his neck, from what I can see," said Mei.

"But who?" asked Fu. They looked at Carlos who shrugged.

"Does it matter?" asked Trish. "He's dead. And so is Charlotte."

"What now?" asked Mei.

"I wouldn't mind a change of clothes," said Fu, fumbling with her wet blouse.

"Next door," said Carlos. "I'll take you there. He spoke to Trish. "I'll come right back. I have things to finish up here." He gently took Charlotte's hands and crossed them over her stomach. He stroked her hair. "Important things."

Trish put a hand on his shoulder.

Carlos took them a short distance down a hall and through a door. There was a large room, as big as a barn, filled with racks and totes. It looked familiar.

"The stuff from Fashion Bargain Depot?" asked Fu.

"The clothing store where I was abducted," said Mei. She looked into a tote. "Hey, this is my stuff."

"Mine too." Fu figured it out quick. Rummaging through a pile of shoes, she found a familiar pair of high heel boots. "This is probably all our stuff," she said. "No wonder they could sell it all at rock bottom prices. They recycled everything."

"Some of it looks new," said Mei. "They probably mix it all together so no one can tell."

Carlos went to a row of open boxes on a table near the wall. He took some makeup and left.

Fu rummaged through the goods. When she turned around, Mei was half dressed. She had found a skin tight leather suit and pulled it on. "I like this," she said. "No one takes shit from a bitch in a leather suit." She struck a ninja pose and Fu could see she was right. Impressive. Mei had a hand full of rejects that she threw at Fu. "I think you'd look plenty good in this stuff."

There were black tights and a black low cut long sleeve shirt. A short skirt and a pile of hard looking silver leather jewelry. They went through totes finding hats and gloves and accessories to die for. It was a ninja cheerleader, ninja ballerina fashion extravaganza.

Trish helped Carlos put makeup on Charlotte, covering the bruises that Jason L'Enfant had given her. They posed her, a funeral home state, and they sewed the body into a canvas bag. There was some closure as they gently pushed it into one of the refrigerated holding slabs. They prayed together and cried together and then Trish tended to Carlos' wounds.

She was finishing up when the girls appeared.

"Okay. What now?" asked Mei.

"We set the others free," said Fu. "And then let down some milk." She looked around nervously. "At least, that's my plan. For now."

They turned to Carlos. "I have restricted access. I can only open one cage a day," he said. "Haven't you noticed, Carlotta has been the one holding all the keys."

"Where is she now?" asked Fu.

"Over at the admin building. There's something big going on. Rumor is Mr. Che is returning from an important meeting overseas."

"Che?"

"Yeah, the Chairman," said Carlos. "They always get excited around him. They worship him, praise him for his corporate efficiency and his brilliant schemes." Carlos' voice cracked. He collapsed into a chair. "He made me do bad things, evil things." He shook, his eyes empty, staring into the fires of hell where his immortal soul was turning to black ash. "He is the devil. These men are demons from hell that do his bidding. He tried to turn me into one, he's still trying to twist me into a demonic shape to suit his whim." His eyes were wet. "He made me kill people. Twenty, maybe thirty." He cried out. "My own cousin. My uncle's son." He bent forward, a terrible weight suddenly upon him. "This farm. These women." The tears came, the sobs sounding like hiccoughs, his voice devoid of any human sound. An animal that has just chewed its leg off to escape a terrible trap. Carlos was that and more. The awful truth he had been ignoring, the lies he had fabricated, the false confidence from his coworkers, it all fell apart. Underneath was raw humanity and the realization that these horrors were his doing. The women were no longer livestock, and they would never be again.

The scalpel was on the edge of the table, within his reach. So easy to grab it and end this. He deserved to die. Peace. Eternal rest. Very inviting.

Trish was observant, but it didn't take Sherlock Holmes to figure out what Carlos had planned. "Don't do it," she said, holding his hand.

His hand shook. "How can you be nice to me, after all I did to you?" he asked.

"Charlotte told me to," she said. "She also told me you were smart. Maybe you can help us with a plan.

Fu was studying the surgical instruments, pneumatic tools of the finest quality. The reciprocating saw was lying on the floor attached to the hose. She picked it up and pulled the trigger. It whirred like an eighteen wheeler trying to start. There was a set of safety goggles in the instrument tray and she put them on. She dragged Mandelle within reach and bent over him. The saw whirred. Blood splattered as the blade bit in, hitting hard bone through the soft flesh. Trish and Carlos moved away. Mei stared in fascination. The pneumatics strained and ragged pieces of meat flew off. When the whirring stopped, Fu held the severed arm of Klaus Mandelle, his gold family ring on the finger, the corporate tattoo on the forearm. There was a cauterizing iron, a big one, and she activated it, pressing the raw end against it. There was a sizzle and the odor of flesh. She pulled the end away and inspected the freshly sealed wound.

"I think I have another way to open the cages," she said. She plopped the arm over her shoulder like it was some kind of fashion accessory. The hand rested over her left breast as if groping it.

"Creepy," said Mei. "But I like it. Where do I get one?"

The arm was like the key to the city. Fu freed the prisoners while Mei organized and assembled them. Many of them recognized the ring on the finger as belonging to the good doctor. Fu was making friends faster than she could count.

The crowd began to spill out from the barn. Their keepers, except for Carlos, all seemed to have disappeared, and no one was complaining. The curious wandered around cautiously, checking out rooms and offices. Temporary nursing areas were set up as it seemed there was constantly a need. Like all packs of women, however, they grew loud and agitated, and only when they saw the room of no exit, the butcher shop, did they become somber and silent. The dead and mutilated body of Doctor Mandelle brought no sympathy.

Finally, when all were released and assembled, Trish addressed the masses.

"It's time to leave this place," she said.

There were cheers and shouts and she tried to calm them, but in the history of frenzied mobs of women, you never saw anything like this. The determination of suffragettes with the anger of the women's rights movement, they were an army mobilized, an army of hormone crazed lactating women.

"We have a plan," yelled Trish. "As far as I can tell, out captors are gone."

"It's the rapture," someone yelled.

"No," said Trish. "There's been an emergency. They're all at someplace called admin."

"Doh," said a voice in back. "Bad people don't rapture. They get left behind."

"This place is an island, how are we going to get away?" someone asked.

Carlos spoke up. "There is a boat nearby and we're going to make a run for it."

"It's going to be dangerous," said Trish. "The boat may be empty, or it may be full of Che's men. We may be in for a struggle."

"Bring 'em on," came a shout.

"Yeah!"

"Anyone who wants to can stay here," said Trish. "I'm not asking anyone to put their life at risk, but I can't guarantee that we'll come back for you."

"I'm in," yelled someone. "I'm not going to wait around for Carlotta to come back."

"We don't have any weapons!" yelled a timid young blond in the front.

"I found a taser in an office," came a shout.

"I have one too," added another, holding it up and making it crackle.

Fu raised her hand and was recognized. "We'll put together an attack squad. Anyone who has any fighting skills is welcome to join us."

"Ninja ballerinas," yelled Mei. "Pointed toe of death!" She did a quick move, a martial arts flying kick that made the girls oooh and aaah.

And, clad in skin tight leather, she looked fine.

"Where do I get some of those clothes?"

"No time for that. On to freedom."

The clamor rose, like the frenzy at a revival, the crowd was worked up.

Carlos felt right again. He had a plan. His friend Ngu had a boat nearby. He would help. All they had to do was get to the docks, and that didn't seem far.

He drew it all out on a paper map for her to see. Some, for whatever reason, elected to stay, and they were not pressed into service or forced to come along. Instead they barricaded themselves in a safe place where they could wait out the storm. After careful discussion General Trish gave the command.

"Let's roll."

Chapter 53

The Red Zone

"Jason L'Enfant?" Red stood in the doorway between the hangar and the small office. She recognized him from photos she had seen in a file the night before at Trish's apartment. A portrait photo doesn't say much, and she was flooded with new information. He was much bigger than she pictured, at least a head or two taller than she was. His hands were huge and beefy. His knuckles stuck out like spikes and his nails were curved and sharp like claws. His feet were cement blocks, easily clad in size fifteen shoes.

"That's me," he said, wondering what this big redheaded woman wanted. She was coming at him in a calm hurry, like a slow, polite shark at a feeding frenzy.

"Very glad to meet you." Red brought her fist up to his chin so fast he didn't have time to react. He went rolling backwards, falling across the desk and landing in a heap behind it. He picked himself up, straightened his coat and tie, and gave her the curt smile of a survivor. "Just what do you want with me sweetheart?" he said, his voice a poisoned apple.

She moved closer, coming behind the desk to confront him.

"Let's talk about this," he said. "I don't like to hit a woman."

"So, you're a liar, too," she said, letting him have another blow to the chin. He reeled backwards and before he could recover she let loose with one more. "Bet you don't like to hit children either." Whap, whap. Quick to the jaw as he staggered backwards.

"If that's the way you want it," he said, his smile becoming curt again as he rubbed his chin. "You asked for this."

He squared off against her and they traded blows. She came at him like a prize fighter and L'Enfant was finding her more than his equal despite their size difference. It was all Queensbury rules until he kicked Red in the crotch. She let it slide until he did it again.

She laughed, but women hurt too when they get kicked in the crotch. "I see you can't fight fair."

L'Enfant didn't know Red was wearing Bullshit Hawkins approved body armor, which included an athletic cup protector. It was the indignity that spurred her retaliation. "Okay," she said, squaring off against him again. "If that's the way you want it."

So much for the rules. She kicked back, a few false starts to throw him off, but then she delivered a perfect foot to his groin. He winced, doubling over. She spun around, her foot sweeping his leg. L'Enfant toppled like pixie sticks.

"Fair is fair," she said. "You kick me in the crotch, I kick you back."

L'Enfant groaned, his hand nursing the pain. No time to hurt, time to act. She had accused him of hitting women and children, wounding his pride and arousing his arrogance. He seethed, becoming a hate factory, a full time crew ready to process pain into anger.

"You'll pay for that," he said. He was quick for a big guy. He rolled to his feet, his old football moves coming into play. He had the grace of a matador as he stood defiant before her. He looked her over seriously, his eyes scanning for muscle beneath her fat. He wondered what her vulnerabilities were. Like most women would it be her face?

He took a swipe at her, the claws coming within millimeters of her cheek. She saw the feral look in his eyes, the lack of control. He was like an animal fighting for survival and for dominance.

The hair on the back of her head rankled and she felt his energy. She had her own survival instincts as well. She had once put down a rabid dog that came at her in Tacoma when she was a teen. She still had to take the rabies shots, but she made sure the dog never hurt anyone again.

Suddenly they were like pit bulls, as if they were raised for the fight, and they came at each other with all the fury of a high stakes game.

He swiped and kicked at her. He bit her on the arm. He eluded her jabs with savage quickness. His cement block feet moved like junkyard pile drivers looking to crush her own. She swore she could see foam dripping from the side of his mouth.

She switched fighting styles, wondering if he knew any oriental techniques. She started with judo, skillful and defensive. She was the center of the wheel and he became the moving flurry around her. She deflected his blows, turning always to lessen the impact of them. From that calm center she observed him striking with random fury. While he expended energy, she conserved it, storing it like an electric dynamo.

She felt him weaken and she switched styles again. This time she was all Thai boxing, jumping high and striking downward, trying to run up his leg and pummel his head. When he tried to back away from her she attacked, crouching and lunging from down low, trying to push his chin up into his brain.

"Is this how you hit Caroline?" she asked. She hit hard, speed bag tough, her fist becoming a rock at the end of an iron beam. "Your wife!" she said. "What kind of marriage oath did you swear?" She hit harder, anger seething, a storm that raged against Jason L'Enfant and everything he stood for. She began to beat him in rhythm with her words. "Is this what you mean by love honor and obey, Buck?"

The name came out of her mouth from the past, adding furor to her spirit. Other names began to pour into her head. She was suddenly fighting for all the beaten, bruised women in her past.

He hit back, by no means a defenseless animal, more like a cornered beast. Despite the protection of the body armor she could feel his blows. The more they tangled the dirtier he fought. He spit in her face, pulled her hair, and tried to scratch her eyes out. In her worst cat fight she had never seen crap like this. Through it all she held her own, but more and more his moves became those of a desperate man.

He scooped up a letter opener and grabbed a piece of art off the credenza. It was deadly art, a long, varnished mahogany board, inlaid with light wood and tinted in a native design. At one end a set of iron figurines were mounted perpendicular to the wood, jagged and metallic with sharp spikes.

Red laughed at it. "A knife? And a stick with a nail? Is that the best you can come up with Jason?"

He hit her with it and the sharp edge beat against her side. An iron figurine bent under the force. She felt a prick through the armor and thought she heard her rib crack. She didn't care. The tight body armor would hold it fast along with the pain.

It throbbed. She felt the blood surge in her head, pounding like bass speakers, amplifying the beat of her heart to mind numbing proportions.

Most people thought she was called Big Red because of her hair, or maybe because she was twice the size of the average woman. History would show she got that name in high school, back when her fuse was shorter than her tolerance for stupidity and injustice. Whenever she got in a fight, she saw red. Like a curtain of flame it would descend on her until the only red left was spewing from her opponent's nose or draining from the open hole of a missing tooth.

The curtain came down to the beat of the pounding in her head. Jason was locked in her crimson death vision. It was time to put the rabid dog down before it hurt anyone else.

She reached into her pocket and felt the short weapon that Hawkins had given her. She hadn't intended on using it. Even for her, it seemed too violent. But the curtain of red had descended. Her rib cried out for vengeance. So did Caroline and her children, Buck's wife Candice, and a slew of others standing with her behind the red curtain. Rita's hand gripped the end of the mace and she extended it as she pulled it out of her pocket.

A quick whack on the back of his hand and the artwork went flying across the room. He raised the knife, a ten inch dagger that could open her up like yesterday's mail.

"Paper cuts?" she asked, mocking him. She swung the mace and he ducked low. He felt the weighty ball fly over his head, the wind from it raking his hair. He crouched lower, thrusting the knife forward and upward. As he came up it sliced into the inside of her forearm. Her grip on the mace loosened. She spun around and kicked him, at the same time switching the mace to her good hand.

Daddy had trained her to be just as good a southpaw as a right handed hitter. She switched her stance and changed her fighting style again, confusing L'Enfant. She kicked, the mace moving sideways into his ribs. She heard the crack and he inhaled a quick gasp of air. The knife came up again, through the curtain of red and into her personal space.

Her right hand was weak and a stream of blood poured from her forearm. Her head began to spin. She knew from her daddy that it was time to get serious. She felt like she was at the center of a Christmas wreath, lights flickering all around her. The knife came towards her again. She moved sideways and she felt a fist hit the side of her neck. The mace slipped from her grasp and her knees buckled under her.

The breath came out of her, a harsh rasp, like a stand-up comic imitating a crowd roar. The lights began to flicker faster. Now on her knees, her head rocked forward. L'Enfant raised the knife overhead, the point aimed down at her shoulder.

Desperate moves. Hail Mary plays. Red could hear the blood pumping in her head like the roar of a crowd. It was time for the quarterback to try one last play and either win or lose this game.

Her toes curled and her legs flexed. She was like a defensive lineman waiting for the snap. It wasn't long, her sanity shattered like a twig in late fall. She pushed forward, head butting him in the crotch as she barreled him over. The knife flew out of his hand. He fell back, toppling onto the desk over the expensive artwork. The spiked ends pierced the flesh easily. The weight of the big man pushed down and they drove deep into his back.

He squealed, his legs kicking like a frog stuck at the end of a gig. He flopped backwards, falling behind the desk until his head hit the wall. A glass picture fell off a nail, cracking down across his forehead. A gash opened, like the sliver of a filet knife on the belly of a fish, his head burst open. Brains oozed out, fat and ripe, juices flowing like a fresh grilled sausage. His mouth hung down and his eyes went cold.

She was mad. There was so much more she wanted to do to him. She didn't want him dead, she wanted him alive and suffering. She wanted him to know what it was like to have a broken leg, busted collarbone, and shattered wrist. She wanted his dental bills to exceed his annual salary. She wanted him to feel pain deep in his organs, wondering if it was something fatal or not. She wasn't quite through fighting.

Chapter 54

Luchessi a la Rosa

A car drove up. She heard the sound of the door slam, heels clicking across the cement floor of the hanger. Red wiped her bloody forearm on Jason's shirt. There was a tape dispenser on the desk, the kind used to seal packages, thick and wide. She taped up her arm and covered the wound.

The footsteps got closer. She stepped over L'Enfant's body, moving out from behind the desk. Cathy stopped, standing in the doorway. From where she stood, she could not see Jason L'Enfant lying limp, sliced opened like a ripe watermelon beside the plush leather chair.

"What are you doing here?" she asked.

"I'm looking for Harry Takanawa," said Red.

"Who?" She recognized the name, but who was Hairy?

"Harry Takanawa?" repeated Red. "Fu Chan?" trying an alias.

"The Takanawa woman has been assigned to the farm," said Cathy. "Didn't Jason tell you? Maybe Hairy is with her. Who are you?"

"Who are you?"

"Why, I'm Cathy Daniels, Head of Human Resources for the Corporation. I thought I knew everyone here, but I've never met you. Did you come in on the plane with Che tonight? I didn't think it arrived yet." She stepped closer, her eyes studying the tattoo or Red's forearm, the fraternal sign of the Corporation. Rita became painfully aware it was drawn on with a sharpie. She covered it with her hand. "No need to be shy," said Cathy, rolling up her sleeve and displaying her own. She stepped closer to Red. "Let me see yours. I'm always interested in the subtle differences between the divisions." She reached for Red's forearm, bringing her own beside it.

Red pulled her arm back, staring at the floor to avoid eye contact. "Nice boots," she said.

"They're Luchessi boots," said Cathy calmly. "Now let me see your forearm."

Red complied. It didn't pass muster and she knew it. One edge was smeared from contact with the water. Cathy bent down for a closer inspection. As she did, Red brought it up forcefully, smashing her forearm into her face.

Cathy jumped back, catlike reflexes that surprised Red. Blood began to trickle from her nose falling on her perfectly pressed white pleated blouse. She wailed, like the loss of an old friend or a cry of agony when everything is ruined. She huffed and planted her feet, giving Red the full shoulder treatment as she pushed them out like pistons. Her head bobbed between them, vibrating like a motor getting ready to rev.

"You'll regret that," she said, wiping the blood off her nose with the sleeve of her blouse. Her eyes were charged with electricity. She moved her hand away from her nose and fresh blood dripped down her front. She twisted, quick from years of training in a Corporate environment that perfected violence, even made it a goal for advancement. She rolled and when she came to standing she had a lamp in her hand. She threw it at Red. "Duck, Fatty," she yelled.

Red dodged right, the upper half of her body moving sideways as the lamp whizzed past her and smashed against the wall.

Cathy scanned the room and spotted the fallen body. With two sidesteps it came into full view. "Jason," she whispered. She looked down at L'Enfant, his body still warm and limp. This woman was an idiot, someone to be dispatched immediately. She clicked her heels together.

"Nice boots," said Red. "Do we go to Kansas now, Dorothy?"

"The name is Cathy," she said. "And these are Luchessi boots." She clicked her heels together again and a knife blade slid out from beneath the toe of her right boot. "I had these custom made for me."

Red looked down. "Pretty cool. I saw this trick in a James Bond movie," she said. She became excited, her memory kicking in now. "Yeah. My Dad loved all those old Bond movies, especially the ones with Sean Connery. Watched them over and over."

Cathy kicked at her and Red jumped back. "I always liked Roger Moore," she said. "He never seemed to get injured, didn't even dirty his hair." She kicked again.

"*From Russia With Love*, right?" said Red. "At the end of the movie, Rosa Klebb tries to kill Bond with these poisoned dagger shoes." She thought some more, her big redheaded brain kicking into overdrive. "That's not poisoned, now, is it?"

"Why don't you come closer and find out?"

That didn't sound friendly. Red saw the sneer and the upturned lip, powers of observation that made her a good detective. Let's see, what did Bond do? Used a chair! She looked around and saw only a heavy office chair, thick legs with wheels on the bottom. It looked like it weighed a ton.

Cathy swiped the boot in front of Red, poison coming within inches of her ankle.

"What the hell," she said. With surprising strength the big redhead picked up the heavy office chair and swung it around like it was a beach ball. Her ribs ached, blood in her forearm pushed against the packing tape. She leveled it at Cathy and pushed her back into the nearest wall. The five pointed star, each with a wheel in casters, pressed against Cathy's chest. She coughed, her foot kicking wildly.

Red reached down. There was a lever in the office chair that adjusted the height. She pressed the lever twice and the chair elongated, pushing Cathy harder against the wall as it lifted Red further away from the deadly knife blade.

"So you want to be Rosa Kleb?" asked Red. "Seemed to me she died at the end of that movie."

The boot flung wildly, Red angled the chair up, the bottom pressed against Cathy's chest. The casters rolled up against the wall and the chair slid upward locking one of the legs against her neck. It was heavy, the wheels against the wall, and it slowly began to roll towards the floor. As the head of human resources slid downward her body angled, drawing her feet closer to Red. She kicked wildly as she continued to slide down the wall, coming closer and closer.

Rita angled back, trying to avoid the deadly blade. As she did, her weight pressed forward against the chair. Cathy gurgled, her foot thrashing like a fish on a hook. Red angled her lower body back while continuing to press forward. Cathy rocked her head and moved from side to side but the chair leg continued to press against her neck. Her color changed becoming first mottled, then red, then blue. Her eyes bulged out, as if they were growing on stalks and trying to extend out. There was anger on her face, then panic, then desperation. The foot kicked and Red pressed on the chair with all her weight.

There was a snap, like the sound of a fire popping. The foot stopped thrashing and went limp. The chair was suddenly heavy and the wheels rolled the rest of the way down the wall, the body of the dead human resource director pressed beneath it.

Red let her fall to the ground, dropping the chair beside her. She was sweating with the effort and her breath was heavy. She walked out into the hangar to confirm that she was the only one around. It was quiet, her own deep breaths echoing in the empty hangar as she struggled to calm herself. She went back into the office and pulled a Nancy Drew, rummaging through papers and looking through file cabinets. She didn't know what was useful but there were flight logs and documents that looked promising.

A plane flew low overhead and the noise startled her. Expensive jet engines whined and the plane banked. The wings dipped and it circled back for a landing.

Jason's car was gone but there was a new one parked in its place, a black SUV with smoked windows and huge mud-slinging wheels. A quick search of Cathy and she had the keys in her hand.

Her mind was racing. What to do? Anything was better than here.

The plane was swooping low. She saw cars approaching in the distance. It wouldn't take them long to find L'Enfant's body.

She dragged Cathy's body out of sight, laying it with Jason's. She set the chair upright and straightened the desk, shut the office door on the way out.

She ran to the car and got in, her stomach pressing up against the wheel. "Little bitch," she said, groaning as she reached down to adjust the seat. She drove off, down the only road leading away from the hangar, ducking slightly as the parade of oncoming vehicles passed her by. Stuff rattled in the back as she sped over the bumps. There was blood on her hands and adrenaline was pouring into her system. Her eyes were wide and alert and her muscles twitched from the workout.

Big Red was in full bloom.

Chapter 55

If I Should Die Before I Lactate

The army of hormone crazed lactating women moved out of the barn and through the streets. Led by General Trish, they had a plan and they were on the move. Marine Corps training had helped them organize into platoons with advanced scouts, a main body, and a supply crew. The belly of the group moved in formation, two by two, built on the buddy system and structured after the best civilian militias. They looked paramilitary in their matching skirts, flip flops, and nursing shirts. Behind the army rolled the supply wagon, a cart containing oatmeal, nursing equipment, and empty milk bottles. The Great Escape was underway.

Carlos spoke to Fu. "You're a detective, I hear," he said. "Seattle Police Department."

"That's right."

"Something you should know. There's a laptop computer in admin. It sets on Mr. Che's desk. It has everything you want to know about this place. Financials, operation plans, logistics, even marketing material. Might even have information about other locations."

"It's all on single laptop? Doesn't make sense."

"This whole place doesn't make sense," said Carlos. "That laptop is special. They bring it out at every meeting like some kind of showpiece. They hook it up to projectors and show us corporate data, slides, and financials."

"Isn't there a server somewhere? How do they back it up?"

"Offshore somewhere. They have some sort of secure cloud service, but we'd never get to it. Every other computer is like a dumb terminal, except that one. The laptop is your best chance at getting everything."

"Then I have to go for it," said Fu. "Where is admin?"

Carlos pointed. "Not far," he said. "Big building towards the center of the compound. Follow the signs to Mr. Che's office. It's always on his desk."

"I'll go with you," said Mei.

"It only takes one ninja to retrieve a laptop," said Fu.

"What if you run into trouble?"

"Then I'll handle it." Fu struck a ninja fighting pose, then relaxed. "Look, you need to stay with the group," she said. "Your priority is to get them to the boat and to safety. We don't know what's waiting there. Carlos says it could be empty, or we could be in for a fight. You have to be there to assess the situation. A ninja like you could make it easy, take out the sentries and disable the alarms before anyone gets hurt."

"Okay," agreed Mei. "You're right. One ninja should do it. I'll go with the group."

"I'm headed out in that direction," said Fu, pointing towards admin. "You go forward and tell Trish the plan. I'll rendezvous with you at the boat afterwards."

"We'll wait for you as long as we can," said Mei.

"Don't wait for me," said Fu. "I plan on making this quick. If I'm not there in time, shove off. If you can, try to leave me a message so I know you've gotten off okay."

Mei nodded. Fu turned and ran at top speed, her black outfit fading into the nearest shadow.

The column was spread out over the length of a football field, moving towards the dark waters where the *Dare Me* sat tied to the wharf. Mei worked her way to the front, encouraging the refugees as she went along.

"How do I become a ninja ballerina?" asked one young girl. She looked about fifteen, too small to be noticed, yet her breasts were huge and swollen, misshapen for a girl her age. Mei could only wonder what Mandelle did to her.

"Is that what you want?" asked Mei. "To become a ninja ballerina?"

"I want to be strong like you," she said. "I don't ever want something like this to happen to me again. I want to learn to fight."

"You believe in yourself," said Mei. "Good!" She sized the girl up. She had the right stuff. She clapped her on the shoulder. "You have just gone through a terrible ordeal, and you are here, a survivor. If that's not a miracle then I don't know what is. Remember what happened here and every day from here on out will be precious to you. Start there, and practice, because you have already begun the journey."

"Let me come with you," she said. "I can help."

The girl had muscle and youthful vigor. Mei examined her again with all the scrutiny of a matron at an expensive boarding school. "What's your name?" asked Mei.

"Holly-olly-okla," she said. "It's native. My friends call me Holly."

"I'm Mei," she said. "Come with me."

Holly smiled, threading through the ranks as she followed Mei toward the front. "Do you like southern cooking?" asked Mei.

Up ahead, Trish spotted headlights coming down the road towards them.

"Out of sight," she said, ordering her troops to get down. They took cover like pros, flattening in the ditch that ran beside the road. The supply team pulled the cart behind some trees and hid it under thick brush.

Mei crept her way towards Trish, Holly close behind. "We could use a car," said Mei. "Maybe we should capture it."

"Good idea," said Carlos. "Let me give it a try." He stood up and walked into the center of the road, raising his hands and signaling it to halt. As the vehicle slowed down, Mei crept out of the shadows and stepped behind it, following it to a stop. Holly watched closely, admiring her stealth and studying her style carefully.

"What is it?" said a woman's voice as the window rolled down.

Carlos nodded to Mei who started to make her move. Her fist came up, aimed at the driver's head. There was a something in the road and Mei stepped on it making a noise. The driver turned and looked. One fist shot blindly out the window. Carlos grunted and fell to the ground. The driver turned, the door opening as she spun out of the car. Her fist was suddenly in Mei's face.

The ninja ballerina was quick. She dodged the fist, spinning like a pinwheel as she retreated out of sight around the back of the SUV.

The redheaded woman was big. "Come on," she said. "I see you behind the car. Come out and show yourself."

Trish stood up. "It's okay Mei," she said from the ditch. "Rita? Is that you?"

Red stared into the dim light. She relaxed. "Who is it?"

"It's Trish," she said. "Harry's ex." It was like a family reunion. Trish signaled her troops. They came out of hiding, along with the supply cart.

"What are you doing here, Rita?"

"Looking for you and Harry," she answered.

"You found us!"

"How about you?" asked Red. "What are you doing here?"

"Long story," said Trish. "Working on a farm."

Rita looked confused. "Where's Harry?" she asked.

"He went to someplace called admin," said Mei.

Trish was surprised and a little irritated. It was just like Harry to disappear when she needed him most. "Why'd he do that?"

"He's going to pick up a computer," said Mei. "He said he'd meet us at the boat afterwards."

Carlos groaned, still doubled over. "It's a valuable computer," he said. "Containing all of Mr. Che's secrets."

"This is Carlos," said Trish, introducing him to Rita. "He's on our side, one of the good guys. Carlos, this is Rita."

"Call me Big Red," said Rita. "Sorry about the sucker punch."

"Thanks. We could use your help. Especially someone with your skills," he said, rubbing his jaw. "My friend is waiting for us at the boat, but there could be trouble. His crewmates aren't the most sociable people and we may need to take the boat forcibly."

"I have a boat nearby, too," said Red. "Matt Bernard brought us here looking for a boat called the *Dare Me*."

"That's the boat," said Carlos. "The *Dare Me*. That's where we're headed. It's big enough to carry us all away."

"Then I'm in," said Red.

Trish suddenly looked at Mei. "Wait. Why didn't you go with Fu?"

"I wanted to but she insisted I didn't. She's a ninja cheerleader," she said matter-of-factly. "She doesn't need any help. Besides, she's just going to get a stupid laptop computer."

"Where is admin?" asked Rita.

"Over across the compound," said Carlos.

"I better get over there," she said.

"I don't know. Carlos is right, Rita. We sure could use your help," said Trish. "You got a car. Once we secure the boat, you can go pick up Harry."

"Looks like you got an army here," said Rita. "What difference will one more make?"

"What? This group of unarmed, nursing women?"

"Unarmed, huh?" Rita stepped around the back of the SUV. She heard something rattling in the back. "Let's see if there's anything useful in here." She popped open the door. There were large, canvas bags and boxes of stuff. Mei pulled a bag out. Holly was standing beside her and she passed her a bag and grabbed one for herself. Red pulled out the boxes, throwing them on the ground behind her in a big pile. There were two more bags and a large square box that was bulky and heavy. She looked down at the rest of the stuff.

"Sneakers, cleats, a trophy?" She picked up a trophy and read. "Cathy Daniels, 1st Place Marksman, Annual Company Picnic." It was huge and ornate and she held it like a club, wondering if the marble base would hold up to consistent whacking. There was scuba gear and, oh, a spear gun."

As she went for it, the spear gun disappeared, jerked out of her reach by an agile hand. When Rita turned around, it looked like a holiday sale on Black Friday. Girls were grabbing stuff everywhere.

"Baseball gear," said Holly, spilling the bag out on the ground.

"Oooh! I want a bat!" said a woman.

"Golf clubs," said Mei.

Four women stepped forward. "We'll take those."

A lady opened a large sack. "There must be a hundred baseballs in here."

"Croquet mallets," came an excited call.

"Duck calls?"

"Here's a pair of shoes for you Holly," said Mei.

Trish stood back. In a matter of minutes they had transformed into a force to be reckoned with. There was a woman swinging a baseball bat, dressed like a catcher complete with face mask and padding. The foursome were opening packs of golf balls, practice swinging and loading their pockets with Titleist ammunition. Not far away, a woman was sizing up a tennis racket before trading it for a hockey stick. One girl had skates on her hands, wondering what damage they would do as she fought with an invisible foe.

They were ready. She pulled her Captains together, Big Red, Mei, and now Holly. The squads were standing by, with codenames like golf, baseball, and soccer mom. The elite taser and archery group, their seal team six, stood at attention, their weapons proudly in hand.

"Ninja ballerina," shouted Mei. "Pointed toe of death!"

Red turned to Trish. "I like this girl. Where's you find her?"

"Okay ladies," said Trish. "Calm down. Now here's the plan."

Chapter 56

Airport Baggage

The sleek corporate jet touched the runway with gentle perfection. Mr. Che would have it no other way. It's what he would expect from a six sigma corporation that hired motivated pilots. It was exactly what happened.

The sun was just below on the horizon and the lights were on in the hangar. The jet taxied to a stop and the crew began the debarkation. The single passenger put down his drink and followed them out of the cabin clutching his only piece of luggage, a small lunchbox sized case.

"Where is everybody?" asked Mr. Che. "Jason was supposed to meet me here." The pilot shook his head and shrugged his shoulders and went back to writing notes on a clipboard. The crew busied themselves servicing the plane and preparing it for storage. Che turned, the sound of expensive shoes echoing across the hanger as he made his way towards the office. The bodies of Jason L'Enfant and Cathy Daniels lay beside each other, hidden behind a desk. Jason was flat on his back, eyes bulging upward, blood pooling at his midsection. Cathy was draped over him, face down, as if they were lovers who had fallen asleep after a heavy session on their hotel bed. One knee was twisted backward, a Luchessi boot resting sideways in the pool of blood.

Mr. Che reached for the door handle to the office. There was a disturbance behind him. A car arrived and parked next to the plane. Mr. Lo got out.

Che turned and walked towards him, the shoes sounding like the ticking of a doomsday clock to Lo.

"Mr. Chairman," he said, bowing low. "So good to see you. Did you have a nice flight?"

"Where is Jason L'Enfant?" asked Mr. Che.

"He's not here?" asked Lo. "Not what I expected. He dropped me at my office only a short time ago. I was supposed to meet him here to prepare for your arrival. Have you checked the hangar office?"

"No one there. What about Mandelle?" He clutched the lunchbox tightly, holding it close like a newborn child across his chest. "He was supposed to be here too."

"Probably detained," said Lo. "We have been very busy since you left."

"Improving efficiencies, eh, Mr. Lo?" said Che, relaxing a bit. He cleared his throat. "And how did L'Enfant do in my absence?"

Lo twisted his neck, a sudden impulse making his muscle twitch. After a moment's pause, he said, "It would be best to let him tell you personally. I would probably leave out important details."

"Yes," said Che. "Good. Drive me to the admin building and then go find him for me. Mandelle, too. I will wait for them both at my office."

Chapter 57

Office Décor

The arm worked as planned. Fu held it up to the scanner and the door clicked open. She entered Che's office, unprepared for what she would find. As she stepped in, lights automatically came on illuminating a large desk at one end, gently backlit sandstone walls behind it. There was a boardroom table to the right and a lavish sitting area to the left. There was an alcove next to the door lined with stainless steel appliances and kitchenware, the envy of any suburban princess. Expensive art adorned the walls with showroom statuary tastefully placed. The furniture looked handmade. She ran her hand across the leather as she approached the desk. It felt like stroking a lover at midnight.

The desk was empty except for a laptop computer, the only one in the compound according to Carlos. It sat on the glass desktop as if floating above the richly tiled floors. Like Trish's phone, that laptop contained everything about the owner, a prize worth reaching for, one last grab at the brass ring before getting off this crazy merry go round. The wall moved behind the desk and she stood perfectly still staring at it. The realization of what she saw was too fantastic to accept. *Ants?*

As far as evil lairs, Che had it going. Like Couture's there were no windows, evil guys like their privacy, I guess. The desk was huge, almost as big as Harry's office. It looked out at the empire, across the long promenade that led to it. Like an indoor park, paths between the board room table and leather couches, the gardens of business. The ant farm dominated the room, running across the ceiling and behind the ornate desk. Fu stared into it, you couldn't help it. Like a television set it was a window into another world, but this one real and now. She watched as a group of ants struggled with some large white flakes of something. As they moved through the tunnels, they stopped to greet each other, their antennae flailing until they moved on. She followed one to the bottom and off to one side where she saw the queen's chamber, a large cavern filled with activity.

A light flashed, something built into the desktop. There was a noise at the other end. Senses went into overtime. The desk was no cover and she was too far from the board room table or the furniture in the sitting area. There was a door nearby, a scanner pad beside it. She grabbed the laptop and made for it, pulling the arm off her shoulder and readying it for display. There was a beep and a click and she slipped through the door like a Fremen in the desert. Not even a sound as it gently closed behind her.

The lights came on. There was a small flight of stairs that turned and opened into a hallway. She climbed the stairs.

The hall of the disloyal was like the entryway to hell. The arms were sad, reaching for something they would never attain. She touched one of the trophies.

Oh my God. Human arms. Not plaster casts. Not mannequin parts. Human arms. On walls, on tables. God knows what that tapestry hanging over there is made of. There's even a head!

She began to process this new information. All the arms had tattoos on them, the same as she had seen in the coroner's office so long ago, the same as the arm she now had draped over her shoulder. Che's own men. She wondered what they had done to meet this fate. She picked one up and examined it, a flat base with a stuffed arm extending upward. It felt strange to the touch, hard yet yielding, like an overripe peach with something soft and rotten beneath the skin. She set the trophy arm down and it fell over on its side. She tried again but it fell down and she left it. There was a door at the other end, the only other exit to the room, a scanner beside it. She held Mandelle's arm up and it clicked, the door opening inward.

She hoped for an exit but it was a dead end, a small room, a single chair placed near a railing. It was well lit, a bright light hung above the center suspended over a pit. She glanced over the railing. About six feet down was a flat sand floor. There was a set of manacles tied to a post with leg irons attached to another post close by. There were bits of bone and skeleton near them. Ants swarmed over them, several trails leading off into tunnels behind the walls and beneath the sand.

The chair was comfortable, heavily padded with thick legs, ornately expensive. Along one wall was a long, thin table, a display case in the center illuminated by track lighting overhead. She set the laptop computer down on the table. There was a book resting under glass, an expensive pen beside it. It was open to some handwritten pages. Fu read:

Ants are very similar to humans. We both have the largest ratio of brain to body mass. We live in complex social structures, cooperative communities that have members willing to sacrifice themselves for the good and survival of all. We are territorial, expanding at times by establishing new colonies far from our homeland. There are wars between the tribes, and we hunt in packs and kill our own. We take slaves and force them into labor of our own bidding.

It is the unobserved similarities that I hunger to know. Do the ants conduct business, cheat each other, gossip, or plot to steal? Do they worship a god, some divine power manifested in an ant like body? Do they have messiahs? Do they have Hitlers? Do they know fear?

There was a noise. She took the severed arm off her shoulder and set it on the table, taking up position behind the door as it opened.

Chapter 58

The New Girl in My Office

Che entered his office and set the lunchbox on the glass top of his ornate desk. He took a deep breath as he surveyed his office. It was the same warmth anyone would feel when they got home after a long journey. Looking down at the box he felt the world was within his reach.

He turned to the ants, his elaborate farm. "My children," he said. "There is a place for you in my new empire. It won't be long now. Have you been busy since I've been gone? Let's see." He walked over to the door that led to his private torture chamber, nothing more than a comfortable chair beside an elaborate ant hill. As he walked down the hall of the disloyal he admired the trophies he had collected. He noticed his latest addition was out of place. The arm of Chinatown Joe was lying on its side.

"How disrespectful," he muttered. He tried to stand it upright but it kept falling. It irritated him, an imperfection in his otherwise perfect, secret world.

"Someone has been in here," he whispered. His inner sanctum had been violated. It felt like a home intrusion.

"Who is in here?" he shouted angrily. "Jason?" he called. "Klaus?" These were the only two men who could possibly be in here. No one else had access.

He went back down the stairs to the keypad below the lock and pressed some buttons. Lights flashed and he read the screen where it displayed the time of entry and name of the most recent scan.

"Klaus," he called. "I know you're in here. Come out. I'm not mad, but you shouldn't be in here." He went back up the stairs. "Klaus?" he called, turning the corner at the top of the stairs. He slowly walked down the hall and past the arms of the disloyal. There was only one other exit, the door at the other end. "I know you're in there. Come out, come out wherever you are." He held his arm out and the scanner read his tattoo. There was a beep and the door popped open. He pushed it in. "I know you're in here, my friend. It's me, Che."

He got halfway through the door when it pushed back against him. His arm was caught in the jam and he screamed as the door bounced back open. A hand gripped his arm and he was pulled, spinning in a circle until he fell over the chair in the middle of the room.

Che lay flat on his back beside the chair. A woman stood over him, dragon fire in her eyes. She spit on him. As his hand came up to wipe it away she kicked him in the side. "Pointed toe of death!" She yelled, kicking him again, the new battle cry of the ninja ballerina. "This one is for Carlos." And again. "This for Mei," an extra hard whop. "And this is from me."

He winced. "Who are you?" Che was surprised, taken aback with her. He smiled as he nursed his wounds, studying this latest challenge. His mind was analyzing, taking in data. She stood there, fashionably clad in black, silver accessories and high heel boots making quite a statement. He admired the perfection in her makeup. She seemed to be frozen, like a statue, standing defiant over him. He chuckled. How presumptuous.

His question hung in the air like too much humidity, making Fu uncomfortable. Deep inside, the question resonated as Che asked it again, this time a little more formal. "Excuse me for the oversight. We haven't been properly introduced. I am Mr. Che, the Chairman and authority here. And who are you?"

"Who am I?"

Harry was there. He wanted to answer, but he was confused. Why was he dressed like this? Black, skin tight outfit, his favorite high heel boots, silver accessories, bracelets like Wonder Woman, and his long hair pulled tight and bound in a ponytail. His breasts tingled; his missing ribs no longer ached. The emptiness was filled with femininity and self-assurance, hips that could do flips.

He felt good dressed like this, so natural, comfortable. He wasn't hunched over hiding under an oversized jacket. These clothes felt good. The old sensations that assaulted him every time he cross dressed were gone. There was no need for guilt, pain, and humiliation. This was his authentic self.

Harry Takanawa drifted inside. He remembered this was just a game, that he was just a kid playing detective. So what if he was a girl detective? He liked it. More than a few of his male friends liked to be women when they played their video games. This was no different.

Something in his head clicked and the confusion was gone. Che's question demanded an answer. He shifted into another fearsomely feminine pose and in his best, larger than life Fu voice announced, "My name is Fu Chan, daughter of the great Charlie Chan. I give you this one opportunity to surrender, Che. Otherwise I will be forced to dispatch you with my ninja skills."

Che laughed. "A girl like you? You are so far beneath me you don't even know."

"I see you're a champion of equality," said Fu.

"There is no equality in this world," he said, rubbing his side. "Any fool can see that. I'm more than your equal."

"So you think," she said with a smile. "Let's find out if that's true."

Fu reared back, but the Chairman was not without his own skills. Fu tried to kick him. He was fast and deadly, a cobra with the strength of a lion. He rolled and deflected her foot again and again. She double-timed, a ninja cheer coming out of her mouth. "Rah, rah, rhee. Kick 'im in the knee."

Ouch!

"Rah, rah, rass. Kick 'im in the other knee."

Che went down, staggering back against the table that held the display case with his manifesto. It tipped over and broke. A leg snapped off. He picked it up, jagged wood with exposed nails at the tip. He started swiping it back and forth in front of her.

She twisted as he came at her, trying to dodge with a dancer's skill. The nail caught on her clothes and ripped away a piece of the midsection. White fabric showed through the black outerwear. Fu's panties were suddenly uncomfortable. Che laughed, seeing what the problem was.

"What's that you have there? Padding, or a penis?" He laughed, mocking her. "When you look in the mirror, do you see a man or a woman?"

"Yes," said Fu.

"It's not a yes or no question," said Che. "Are you a man or a woman?"

"Does it matter?" she said.

"To me," he said. "To most of society. All but your sick little circle of friends."

"I've heard it before, Che. You think anyone who falls into the LGBT category is the same, right? We all sleep with one another and dance and drink at gay night clubs while the human race goes to hell in a hand basket. AIDS is God's vengeance for being gay, right?"

"Keep going," he said.

"We'll pay for our sins in hell, our crimes against marriage and family, our corruption of the film and music industry and the general moral collapse of the free world."

"You see what I'm saying now," said Che. "You are imperfect, a design flaw in the fabric of humanity."

"Your flaw, Che," she said. "It takes imperfection to make us grow," said Fu. "We will never know our flaws if we don't observe them. The mother of all invention is accident and imperfection. Science has learned as much from our failures as it has from our successes."

"What about efficiency?" spat Che. "If our number one goal is to improve as a species…"

"Who's goal?" asked Fu. "Mine? Yours? That's not my number one goal. Besides, the species will improve despite your intervention, but I don't see that happening with you in charge. I've seen how you treat people."

"Now you're being the fool," he said. "The world is more complex than you imagine, controlled by people you'll never see."

"You're talking like Hitler," she said. "The world hates tyrants, or haven't you noticed? History repeats itself. Your days are numbered, Che."

"Listen to me," he said. "We have a lot in common. I myself was born a woman."

"You're a tranny?" asked Fu.

"I hate that word," he said. "I am a man."

"So am I," said Fu. "But unlike you, I'm not afraid of words."

"You say that, but I know you've been hurt by words the past. You're different, and you have the intelligence to know it."

"You flatter me," said Fu.

"What would you say if I offered you a job?"

"I heard about your job offers first hand," she said. "All I have to do is murder and butcher people? No thanks."

Che grew angry. He started swiping at her again with the broken table leg. She looked around for a weapon but there was only the chair and the broken table and…

Fu retreated and picked up the severed arm off the floor. She grabbed it by the wrist wielding it like a club, hitting Che with the charred end. The table leg fell out of his hand. Che assumed a defensive posture, his arms up and circling, a wide stance as he studied his opponent.

"Where did you learn to fight?" he asked.

"Ninja cheerleading school," she said.

He laughed. "That's absurd. There is no such thing."

She spun the arm, holding it in the center, it whirled like a baton. In a deft move she tossed it in the air and it landed on her shoulder. The hand plopped over her breast.

Che saw the ring on the finger and recognized it. "Klaus," he whispered.

"You knew this sick piece of flesh?" asked Fu.

"He was my friend, my doctor," said Che.

"Then this must be yours." Fu threw the arm at him. He ducked. It whizzed past his head and went over the railing behind him. There was a thump as the arm landed gently in the sand. Che looked over the edge.

"How about this?" she said, a sudden jab to the ribs knocking Che back. She didn't wait for him to recover, instead she delivered two swift blows to the head followed by a chop to the throat. Che bounced and twitched like he was in an old pickup truck rolling down a bumpy country road.

His hand came up, a small electronic device in it. It crackled and an arc of electricity shot out.

"Yowch," yelled Fu. There was a black mark on her arm and the room stank of burned flesh. "You talk like a big man but you can't face me without a weapon in your hand. You're a coward and a fraud, Che."

He thrust the device forward again. Zap, discharge and sizzle of electricity.

The pointed toe of death came up, a pirouette of doom pointed at Che's neck.

He saw it coming. His hand moved to deflect it but instead took the brunt of the blow. Her foot hit it dead center on the back, right on the metacarpal. There was a crack and Che winced. His hand went limp and he dropped the weapon.

"Ready to surrender yet, my great, commanding equal?" she taunted.

"Where did you come from?" he asked. "How did you get in here?" He ripped a piece of cloth off the bottom of his shirt. His eyes flinched as he wound it around the damaged hand. It didn't feel broken and there were no bones out of place, but it sure smarted.

Fu relaxed her posture but remained ready. "I was your guest," she said.

"The cottages?" he asked. "Were you here with the Burmese investors?"

She kicked him. "Wrong answer."

"Stop that a minute," he said.

"Why?" she asked.

"Because I asked," he said.

She kicked him again. "I am not your slave. I do what I want."

Che swung back, rage behind his blows, but Fu was every bit his match. She knew how to win a fight. From a center of calm she was in control. She struck with forethought and not emotion.

The same could be said of Che. There was guidance and thought, but rage packed in every punch. He didn't feel the pain in his hand anymore, his will overrode it with the desire to see his opponent crushed in his grasp. Like a dime store villain he started talking crap, diarrhea of the mouth spilling out everything he would do to her. It was an old tactic: try to demoralize your opponent through threats and fear mongering.

"So, you want to be a woman?" he said. "When you are beaten, I'll have your penis for my trophy room."

"You'd make my dreams come true, Che," she said. "But you'll never get the chance." Whap, whap.

"Then I will have your arms removed, just as you did to poor Klaus," he said.

She hit him hard. "Then I better get my use out of them now."

"I'll cut your legs off," he said.

"These?" she popped him one up the side of his head with her foot. "This one too?" She hopped, a ballet dance step that ended with the other foot hitting the opposite side of his head.

He rubbed his ear with his good hand and narrowed his eyes. "You'll spend the rest of your life as a paraplegic in a brothel somewhere in Asia. There are sick men who pay well for that kind of entertainment."

"Don't give me ideas, Che," she said. "I could do the same to you. You're not much of a man, so I figure you don't need that thing between your legs."

"It wouldn't bother me," he said. "I told you, I started this life as a woman. I took destiny in hand and changed all that. Klaus did that for me."

"Your doctor prescribed a sex change for you?" mocked Fu. "He wanted a buddy instead of a bride?"

"We have a plan," he said. "A perfect plan. Don't disrespect Klaus, he was a genius. Like me, he knew life for a woman was limited in Asian cultures. He gave me new options. I have never looked back." He kicked hard, then spun, his fingers reaching for Fu. It caught her. "You, on the other hand."

"What's wrong with me?"

Che just laughed.

"You're a fool, Che," she said. "Women have more influence on society than any man. They are the heart and soul of humanity."

He hit her hard, pushing her backward with his blows. "You're the fool. A weakling of a woman trying to prove she can beat a man in a fair fight."

"That would be true, Che, but you don't fight fair."

"There's only one way this can end. Why not give in now and avoid the pain?"

"I can fight," she said, "And I'm going to win." She delivered a series of Marine Corps blows that made the Chairman reel. "Government trained." A foot sweep followed by a kick to the ribs. "What's the matter Che? Don't like getting beat up by a girl?"

"You're not a girl," he said.

"You just said I was a weakling woman. Did you change your mind?"

He grabbed her upper arm and pulled her forward, twisting, thrusting his leg out to trip her, a judo move called *osoto-gari*. His grip was tight and the next thing she was on her back looking up from the floor at him.

He jumped, a primitive move in an attempt to stomp her. Her eyes widened as the feet came down, a slab of force aimed at her head. She rolled, the feet landing beside her with a thoom. She could feel the floor shake with the impact. She spun around on her back, her feet kicking the long, broken table towards him. He stumbled over it and fell backwards.

They were more than equals, more than evenly matched. The chair became a centerpiece to their combat. They both circled it, alternately trying to use it for cover and as a weapon. Neither let the other succeed. Throughout it all they bantered, Che never admitting that Fu Chan could be his better.

Chapter 59

Attack of the Killer Tomatoes

The black Corporate SUV drove up to the dock and parked facing away from the *Dare Me*. The crew was on high alert. Ralston was on guard duty up in the wheel house. He stroked his gnarly beard, combing god knows what out of it. "What's this?" he said to himself out loud.

The boat rocked slightly and he tried to sense whether it was the gentle action of the waves or if someone had just come aboard. He looked out at the SUV again. There was no activity. It just sat there, dark, quiet and parked.

The Captain came up from below. "What's up?" he asked. "Did someone just come aboard?"

"Don't know," said Ralston.

"Well," said the Captain angrily. "Go check it out."

Ralston grabbed a semi-automatic rifle that was leaning in the corner. He hoisted it on his shoulder and went out the back door. He called down to the SUV. "Who goes there?"

Quiet. Too quiet. He leaned back inside the door to the wheelhouse. "Better get the rest of 'em ready Cap'n. Just in case we have trouble."

The Captain nodded and went below.

Ralston turned around. There was a big redhead standing there. "Hello," she said.

He twitched, like he was going to do something. The rifle started to slip off his shoulder. It made it about half way. A hand came down from above and grabbed it, pulling his right shoulder upward as it got caught in the strap.

"Ahhh," he cried, twisting to one side as his head turned to see what was happening.

Red stepped behind him, clamped an arm around his neck, grabbing the other in a handshake, the knuckle of her thumb pressed into his esophagus. She put her foot in the back of his knee and pressed. The leg collapsed and he fell into her grasp, struggling as she tightened her grip. The choke hold took about five seconds to work. He slumped to the deck falling into a heap. Before he could settle, six women were upon him, guiding him into one of the large canvas bags that once held athletic gear. They taped his hands and mouth and locked the bag shut with a clasp. Then they rolled it towards the center of the boat where it fell into the hold with a soft meaty thud.

The Captain heard the noise and appeared at the door. "What?" he said.

The bagging team took cover. Mei and Red ducked.

There was a barrage of balls like you never saw. They let loose like medieval archers, a dark rain of baseballs, golf balls, tennis balls and even one handball, all falling on the ship like a black rain. They thumped against the hull, the deck, and the Captain's head. He collapsed like an empty sack.

Another crewman stuck his head out. More balls. Whap. Thump. Collapse.

The bagging crew went into action putting the last two canvas bags to good use. Two more soft meaty thuds and the hold was that much fuller.

Trish watched the operation from behind the smoked windows of the SUV. "Time for the mop up crew?" she asked.

"The *Dare Me* had a crew of six, but I think they're down a man," said Carlos. "One of the remaining two has to be my friend. Let me give it a try." He got out of the car and moved close to the boat. "Ngu!" he called.

There was a sound from below deck. Carlos called again.

"It's Brett. Is that you Carlos? I was asleep. What do you want?"

There was another thud. Brett didn't know what hit him, nor that he had just been used by the ninja ballerina team as a training dummy.

"Great work, Holly," said Mei.

"Thanks for the opportunity to prove my skills," said Holly. She was smiling ear to ear.

No bag, but Brett fit nicely inside a long spring locking cupboard in the lower part of the galley. Bound by duct tape, they marked the place so they wouldn't forget to retrieve him later.

The Taser and Archery team, aka Seal Team Six, went to work like pros. They went single file through the door on the back deck, spear gun followed by archer and then two tasers. Red, Carlos, Mei, and Holly brought up the rear making the rest of the column. Like a swat team, the first in line broke at the doorway while the rest followed through. "Clear" she said. Same procedure at the next doorway. One by one they went through the boat until every room had been inspected. As a last procedure, two girls wend down in the nasty engine room.

Carlos returned to the SUV and reported back to Trish. "My friend Gnu is nowhere to be found," he said. "But the ship is ours."

Trish opened the door and stood on the floorboards of the SUV, her body sticking half above the roof. "Load 'em up," she shouted.

The ditch shuddered. There was a victory cry. Backs began to rise out of the ground and the army moved towards the boat. The supply cart came out of hiding, the team rolling it hastily towards the captured fishing vessel.

Trish saw guards along the back deck as she climbed aboard the *Dare Me*. She looked at Red.

"We may need to defend boarders," said Red. "We can't afford to relax our defenses."

"Smart thinking," said Trish. "Get the nursing mothers below where they'll be safe."

"You mean, all of them?" asked Rita.

The teams had been so effective that Trish though if them as foot soldiers and not milkmaids. "Just the ones that need it," she said. "Our next step is to get the boat ready to sail."

"I haven't been able to find my friend Gnu," said Carlos. "I don't know how to operate a boat this size."

"Anyone have any experience with boats?" asked Trish.

"I went canoeing once," came a volunteer.

"Tracy was in the Navy," said someone, raising the hand of the girl next to them.

"I was never on a boat," said Tracy. "All I did was paperwork."

The engine room team emerged from the dark hold. "We need help," said one of them. "We found someone trapped in here."

Carlos had a gut feeling. He ran to the hold and disappeared inside the darkness.

Behind the engine in a pile of grease there was a prone body, bound and gagged. He recognized the shape. "Gnu?" he said.

There was movement and a groan.

"Help me get him out of here," he called.

They lifted him out of the grease and brought him outside into the light. They took him to the Captain's cabin and laid him on the bunk. Gnu was shivering as Holly attended to him, cleaning the grease and the dirt off him. Underneath the grime she found black and blue marks.

"They beat me," he said. "Just a cruel joke. I didn't fit in, didn't want to play cards all the time, didn't want to drink or fight. It didn't matter that I worked hard and really wanted to fish. I was just different." He didn't understand it.

"It's okay," said Carlos. "We're going to be okay. We've taken over the boat. The Captain and crew are tied up in the hold, but we don't know how to operate the boat. We need your help."

Gnu strained against the pain. His left leg was weak and he tried to stand. "Take me to the wheelhouse," he said. "I can have us out of here in twenty minutes."

Chapter 60

Bad Company

Che was at his best, full of himself, certain of his talent. He began to talk and brag, a sign that he considered her an equal. She listened, but never relaxed her stance. She found it curious that he would divulge so much, but she knew he did it with the knowledge that he would ultimately silence her forever.

"What do you think of my Corporation?" he asked.

"Not much," she said. "Why can't you just make cellphones or sell processed food? Why this twisted milk farm? Why deal in cadavers?"

"Profit," he said. "The secret of all marketing is the right product with the right placement at the right price. There is a lot of money in cadavers and mother's milk."

"Why would you need so much money?"

"Why does anybody?" he said. "I'm no different than the robber barons of Wall Street. I run a simple multinational corporation."

"You imprison people, steal, and break the law."

"And you think they don't on Wall Street?"

"What else is your evil corporation into?"

"Oh, you'd be surprised," said Che.

"So, surprise me," she said.

"Money isn't my only pursuit," said Che. "Power is also a goal. My latest little project will make me a true world shaper."

"I think your Corporation is crap," she said.

"Be careful what you say," he said. "Corporations run the world, not governments. They are the handful that rule the masses."

"Consumers vote Corporations in and out of existence every day," she said. "You'll lose in the end, Che."

"What do you mean?"

"Buying something is like voting," she said. "People show support for a corporation by giving them money. It's simple. If you stop giving corporations money, they'll go out of business."

"Corporations still win," said Che. "Like me, they can just sell to other corporations. The profit margins may be lower, but my Corporation takes in millions from other organizations."

"And so the voting continues," said Fu. "Until that organization pays the price for doing business with you."

He laughed. "So naïve. Some of our biggest customers are famous east coast universities. Would you like to see your greatest educational institutions voted out of business?"

"Come on, Che. Who's being naïve now? You know full and well that these institutions wouldn't do business with you if they found out you weren't legit."

"Where else will the get bargain priced cadavers? They are just as concerned as I am when it comes to keeping costs down. And how do you know that for sure?" he asked. "In case you haven't noticed, business ethics are at an all-time low in this country, hell throughout the world. The enemy is no longer at the gate, he's comfortably beside us in the living room gathering data on our tastes, wants, and needs. When the peasants wake up and storm the castle there will be nothing left. In the end, people will exist to service corporations. It's already happening. Humanity has become a slave to consumerism."

"People won't let that happen," she said.

"Believe me, it's happening," said Che. "Labor laws are changing. There are more contractors working now than ever. Companies aren't paying benefits and they cut down further by forcing people to work less than a forty hour week. Many have to take a second job to meet ends, still with no health care, vacation, or sick leave."

"That may be happening in your world, Che, but not mine," said Fu. "Corporations in the Pacific northwest are part of a community. They take responsibility, something you wouldn't know about."

"Really? Who gets the money when the economy goes bad? How many personal bailouts have you seen?"

"We call it unemployment," she said.

"A hand out," he said. "It destroys a person's pride and makes them lazy."

"It helps people in need."

"You're so uninformed," he said. "Here in your own state there is a corporation that received record welfare tax subsidies, even while they slashed worker's benefits. All they had to do was threaten to move to another state. They blackmailed the legislature, and the CEO pocketed a fat check for his smooth business acumen. Meanwhile, the union lost benefits and nobody got a raise that year. And you dare accuse me of being evil? What good have companies done for you?"

There was some scary logic to what Che was spouting. Fu had nothing to say so she hit him, but striking out at something often does not silence the voice. Che continued to lecture, trying to use his twisted arguments to confuse Fu.

"You are a fool. Corporations don't care about you," he said. "Name one company you like."

"The company I keep," she said.

"Governments exist to service corporations. We buy the best politicians we can afford," said Che. "They love us. We can contribute more to their election campaigns than individuals ever could, that's why they court us. Do you ever hear of people getting incentives to relocate?"

"All the time," said Fu. "They call them relocation packages."

"A gift from the corporation," he said.

With nothing to say, she hit him again.

He chuckled. "Communism is no longer something to fear," he said. "It is a philosophy, too. On the other side of the ocean, much of the same is happening, except power is being concentrated in black market corporations that exist outside the law. Do you really think that climbing the corporate ladder, competition, and free market are the answer? Think about the efficient use of resources. Imagine what we could do if we shared a common goal and worked together. A corporation does that, gives people a single vision."

"Like ants beneath your feet? You don't need a corporation to do that, Che. People can make a difference if they put their minds to it. It's called a community."

"I agree," said Che. "Except your society doesn't do that. It purports an every man for himself philosophy. It breeds competition and elitism. He who dies with the most toys wins."

"There are more things to life than money and power," said Fu.

"Every time you open your mouth you prove to me what a fool you are," said Che. "Money and power are only stepping stones."

"You talk as if you plan on taking it with you," said Fu. "You'd be the first. Even the Pharaohs didn't succeed at that."

"They didn't have my brains and my organization," he said. "I will be immortal."

He reared back.

"And you will be dead!"

In a swift move, Che kicked the chair with a roundhouse sending it crashing into the railing. Fu dodged it just as the railing collapsed under the impact of the heavy chair. It broke through and fell the short distance down onto the sand landing next to Mandelle's arm. Ants had been summoned by the scent of rotting flesh. Scouts had found the new resource and claimed it for the community. The arm was covered, hardly recognizable, a living squirming sleeve made totally of ants.

Fu stared at it, the tattoo buried under the writhing mass. Where skin was exposed it was already changing color. Thousands of workers were beginning to break it down and strip it clean with tiny injections of formic acid, grinding mandibles, and the strength to carry it all away at ten times their body weight.

Che laughed. "You're doomed now." He pushed her and she toppled towards the rail. Che leaned forward, pushing harder. She gripped his sleeve, pulling and turning, forcing his back to the rail and reversing their positions. She tried to push him over the side, but then he twisted and suddenly it was her being forced backwards.

Fu searched her memory for ideas, tricks she might use to survive and turn the tide. She remembered a fight Harry had recently where he accidently flipped Manny Ballston over the hood of his Volvo. She stopped struggling, pushed Che away and pulled him back, a move you might see on Dancing with the Stars. She did it again. As he came back this time she spiraled like a ballerina, her hand gripping Che's wrist. She was suddenly the wheel in the center of a carnival ride, leaving Che to become the cart helplessly whiplashing on the outside. She bent over, her feet crossed as if to curtsey.

"Fu Chan fights with style," she said. Che rode helplessly up her back, now a ramp that led directly over the rail. Down he went towards the sand.

She underestimated the strength of the Chairman. He grabbed as he fell, gripping her arm like a parent grips their kid in a tight crowd. He hung there, holding her with the power of vice grips. He put his feet against the wall trying to work his way up, pulling at her arms like they were climbing ropes.

Fu had no choice. He was heavier, stronger. He hung like the back end of a truck accident dangling off a bridge. The rail creaked as he beat against the wall with his feet. Finally it broke and he and Fu tumbled onto the sand below.

Fu got to her feet first, kicked the ant covered arm towards Che.

Che ducked, picked up a handful of sand and threw it at her. He stumbled towards the chair, trying to use it like a ladder to climb out of the pit. He leaped, his hands extending towards the floor above. Fu ran after him. He kicked back, using her as a stepping stone, he coiled his feet then pushed off her back as he stepped on her shoulders. It wasn't far to the floor above, maybe six feet off the sand, but he was there. He stood up, owning the high ground, kicking Fu back every time she tried to breach the hole in the rail.

The ants were becoming a nuisance. Dots appeared over her body. She felt the tiny sting of acid, the bite of skin tearing teeth. Ants were no stranger to the idea that you could eat an entire elephant one bite at a time. They were angry, beginning to swarm over her, inspecting her with ant like curiosity. Would she make good food for the queen? Can we use the hair for bedding? Will her moist insides feed the children?

"And the many will devour the one," said Che. "Just like your corporate voting. Eat well my children."

Fu leaped for the edge but it was no use. Che had the advantage, and the ants were on his side. "Sayonara bitch," he yelled. "I wish I could watch, but I have to go. Once I shut this door it will remain locked, even from the inside. Without the tattoo to scan, you'll never get out." He laughed. "You don't happen to have Jason L'Enfant's arm handy, do you?" He chuckled. "Well… As I said, sayonara."

Fu jumped, the sand offering little to press against. Che stepped back, grabbed the laptop off the floor and turned. Fu watched him scan his arm and step through the door. As it slammed shut she fell back into the sand.

The ants were suddenly at a picnic.

Chapter 61

This Ain't No Picnic

Fu danced across the sand, shaking ants off her body. The door clicked shut above. She reached down and grabbed the arm and shook it. Ants scattered everywhere. She brushed off the tattoo and it was intact. She threw it onto the floor above and climbed up herself. In three steps she was at the door with the arm. She held it to the scanner. No beep. Ants were all over it. She took the arm back to the pit and brushed them off, clearing it as best as possible. Back to the scanner. No beep. No ants but no beep and no click. She threw the arm down and kicked at the door. It was thick, stainless steel or something like it. It didn't budge.

An ant bit her on the ankle. She looked down. They were all over the floor.

She hit the scanner pad, Nothing happened. She tried to rip it off the wall. It wouldn't budge.

Another ant bite. Soon they would be everywhere, more and more bites until they chewed and pulled the skin off her. Then madness would follow, insanity as she would be eaten alive.

Fu composed herself, took a deep breath. For some reason she thought of Mrs. Lee, an old country witch who had once told her about breath control and the harmony of nature. If you are one with nature, then you have nothing to fear, for what animal would harm itself? To become one with the ants. Yes.

She took another breath and sat calmly on the floor. In her mind she extended a field of protection around her body, an aura that told the ants that they didn't need to be there.

Another breath. *Fu Chan knows no fear.* An ant crawled across her arm and she stared at it. "We are so similar. We have much in common," she said, gently as if talking to a child or a beloved pet. She remembered Che's manifesto. "We both teach our young and raise them up to be good members of society. We build complex homes and workplaces, use tools and farm animals. We communicate with each other."

The ant stopped, wiggled its antennae, twisted its thorax and moved on.

Fu took another deep breath and shut her eyes. Complex homes and workplaces. Her mind was drifting. She felt the ant crawl across her arm and onto the floor. It didn't bite her. It didn't want to.

Another deep breath. More drift. Complex homes. Yes! The ants had a maze of tunnels. They led to Che's office to a wall of glass behind a desk.

There was a spark, and suddenly she was seeing the architecture in her mind. The stairs, the turn, the hallway of arms, all leading to this room. She looked down in the pit and spoke to the ants. "We are both resilient. We survive disasters and wars with other tribes, the loss of our young to predators and accidents. I need your help, no, your understanding. What I do now I do for my survival."

She picked the arm up off the floor and threw it down in the sand to the far side of the pit. The table was next. She stood it up and pushed it through the hole in the railing where it fell to the sand, leaning against the chair. She reached for the book, Che's manifesto. She ripped the insides out leaving an empty hardcover. The broken leg of the table was nearby. She took that too, climbing through the hole and down onto the sand. The ants were curious, they swarmed all over her. There was no recognition, no oneness. They began to bite.

She used the book like a shovel, opening it like a V to dig a hole in the sand as best as possible. "I'm going to go through here," she said to the ants. "Far from the queen. I know she's deep down, on the far side of the room."

The ants were everywhere, stinging, not hearing her words. Where were her chemical messages, her antennae, the things they understand and know?

She dug, frantically. A lot of the sand fell back into the hole as she dug. Suddenly there was a barrier, a wall of glass, she could see through it. She was above and behind Che. He was on the phone. The laptop was on his desk next to his lunchbox.

She continued to dig. Che was animated, his arms waving. He was shouting, she could hear his muffled shouts through the glass wall. She wondered how thick the wall was, what it was made of. It felt like glass, but that could be deceiving.

Dig!

The ants swarmed. No understanding. She was standing on their barracks, digging up their dormitories, their food storage chambers. A contingent was already busy moving the queen even though she was in no immediate danger.

They bit Fu and treated her like any other enemy. More and more ants began to assemble. It was an all-out war.

She had a v shaped hole. She got on top of the table, pushing it like a battering ram. The sand made it difficult but she positioned it in the hole and pushed it down hard. It hit the wall and the glass cracked. Che twisted, surprised. The phone dropped out of his hand.

Fu pulled the table back, rammed it against the glass again. A small hole formed. Sand fell through it like an hourglass.

Che was horrified. He reached for the fallen phone.

Fu got the table leg and stuck it through the hole. She flattened it against the glass, using it like a lever. The glass cracked, the hole widened. More sand fell through. The panes heaved at odd angles like broken pavement. It creaked and tinkled.

Che spoke frantically in the phone. He reached for the laptop and the lunchbox.

The table came down against the glass again. It shattered, sand rushing forward like water from a broken dam. It poured over Che's desk. He squirmed, struggling away from it as it fanned out like a lava flow. His foot caught on something and he twisted and fell. Sand covered the laptop and the lunchbox burying it out of his reach. Fu Chan came tumbling out of the hole like a body caught in an avalanche. She hit his arm. He grabbed her, pulling himself free of the sand. As he stood, he pushed her down into the pouring sand. It pooled at her feet. She lost her balance and fell forward face down.

He stepped on her head as he stood up and shook himself off. He moved back to where he thought the laptop may have been and began digging in the sand.

Fu was trapped, the lava flow continuing to pour on top of her. She turned, Che just within reach. She grabbed the back of his head by the hair.

He yelled.

She reached his arm with her other hand and latched on the way he did to her. Che turned and beat her with his free hand. The cloth he had used to wrap it was bloody and it was coming off. He winced with every blow as he continued to pummel her.

The door opened at the far end of the room and a small squat man entered. Lo called to Che. "Now, Mr. Chaiman. We must leave now."

Che wiggled free. Sand covered the area where he had been digging. It continued to pour through the hole in the glass, piling up around the girl. More and more she was getting trapped under the sand. He stood up and kicked her in the head and she swooned.

"Now," yelled Lo. "The window of opportunity is closing."

Che looked down and spit. "I am more than your equal," he said. He ran off to join Lo.

"Where is the prototype?" asked Lo.

"Lost," said Che. "Pershing can prepare another one for us. I'll have a new list of test subjects anyway. We will also need to modify our operations. I'm afraid our laptop may also be at risk."

"Perhaps the ants will do what we couldn't," said Lo.

"The sand will also do its job," he said. They reached the other side of the room. Che opened the door, knowing again that when he sealed it, it could not be opened by anyone without the proper identification. The girl was trapped in the sand, unconscious, the ants all around her. For all her effort, she had only succeeded in making her tomb larger.

"Come, Mr. Lo. We always knew we would abandon this facility, but I did not expect it so soon. It's not efficient. We could have leveraged it more."

"Yes, Mr. Chairman. We will rebuild," he said. "Like the ants, we survive. We are resilient."

Che clapped him on the back. "You learn well, Lo. Come, it's time for us to leave."

Chapter 62

Don't Miss the Boat!

Red checked her watch. Twenty minutes and no Harry. "Do you think he needs our help?"

"I'm worried, too," said Trish. "Let's give him a few more minutes. Besides, we have to finish loading."

The boat was idling, the big diesel engines growling beneath the deck like caged lions. Gnu was at the wheel, ready to shove off. Girls manned the lines and stood watch, prepared for anything. There were guards on Gnu's captured crewmembers, nothing left to chance. The rest did what milkmaids did best, ready to take over when their sisters in full time needed relief.

A small crew was loading supplies. Three totes were already on deck, two more on the dock, and the last being brought over by a forklift. Holly dropped the tote exactly where it needed to be. Carlos called from the controls of the crane. "You're a pretty good forklift driver, Holly. I'll work with you anytime."

"Don't leave me out," yelled Mei. She jumped up on the tote and rigged it to a hook dangling from the crane. Then she moved into a *developpe*, a ballet step that opened her thigh as she drew her leg towards the knee. She finished it with a perfect *sout de chat*, leaping off the top of the tote and landing with the grace of the best prima ballerina at the Met. There was a curtsey followed as a series of *entrechats*, those pretty little flutter kicks, as her feet carried her like hummingbird wings off toward stage left.

"Hurry up with that booty, girls," someone yelled. "We set sail for Seattle tonight.

The totes were full of merchandise from the Fashion Bargain Warehouse. Pirate girls had definitely taken over the ship, a nursing bra flew from the mast. All hands were preparing for a party as soon as the boat set sail and the crew was appropriately attired.

There was a commotion. A corporate SUV sped towards the wharf at high speed. There was a cluster of shipping containers that cluttered the dock near the *Dare Me*, the big kind that are loaded off boats and then attached to tractor trailers for final delivery to their destinations. They were lined up perpendicular to the water, the doors facing inland. The SUV screeched to a halt near them. All attention turned towards it.

The doors flung open and two men got out. They hurried to the nearest container and fumbled with the padlock.

Trish saw him through a set of binoculars. "Che," she whispered.

"Che!" said Gnu. "He's the one responsible."

"Get him!" yelled Trish, pointing at the men. The girls sprang into action. A squad poured down the gangplank. Mei appeared from offstage, running towards the containers. Holly was quickly beside her. Red bounded out of the wheelhouse and leaped over the railing, ahead of them all.

Che struggled with the lock, trying the combination again. A spear from a spear gun chunked next to him, sticking out of the side of the trailer. Another followed. Two arrows were suddenly hit on the other side. A baseball struck him in the side.

The army descended on them. They were waving bats and mallets and hockey sticks. It was an angry mob with one intent.

"Better hurry," said Mr. Lo.

"Haste makes waste," said Mr. Che. His hand jerked and the lock was open. He pulled the chain off and they stepped inside, closing the door behind them.

The squad reached the back of the trailer, some spilling down the side towards the water, beginning to surround the container. Red pulled the door open.

There was a blast of hot air, like a tornado wind. She flattened and the girls held back. A taser fell out of someone's hand and clattered across the ground. The smell of jet fuel was heavy in the air.

The front end of the trailer ripped open, exploding like a firecracker. Something fast shot out of it at cannon speed. It flew through the air, a heavy black thing with fire roaring out of its tail. It hit the water with a giant splash sending spray everywhere, so wide that some of the crew on the *Dare Me* were doused.

There was a whine and a roar as the turbine engine kicked into full speed. The black boat was invisible and gone so quickly that no one had time to register what had happened.

Chapter 63

Huh?

"Ahoy the *Busted Tush*. *Busted Tush*, come in please. Captain Bernard, are you there?"

The voice sounded hollow over the radio but he recognized it immediately. Bernard reached for the microphone and pressed the button. "Rita? Is that you?"

There was relief in her voice. "Thank God!" Then she started to babble, Big Red style, all excited and happy, spilling out details of what happened.

Bernard pressed the button repeatedly trying to interrupt her. All he wanted to know was where he could pick her up.

Walgamot was suddenly beside him. "Matt, something coming up fast on us two points off the starboard bow."

Bernard looked out the window. He could see something fast and blurry moving, a fireball rolling across the water. "What the hell is that?"

It shot by them coming close enough to spray Langelm, who was stretched out on a lawn chair on the back deck. It even woke up Bill Farbis who was passed out in the fighting chair.

Rita continued to squawk over the radio. Bernard thought he heard her say she was aboard the *Dare Me* and needed help. He went down below.

It looked like a miniature command center. Wiggins and Renault had laptops and cell phones, charts and paper everywhere. Wiggins was on a satellite phone. He held his hand up signaling Bernard to wait. He spoke a few terse words and hung up the phone.

Bernard started to speak but there was a roar overhead and a crack. It sounded like the Blue Angels just did a fly by. He ducked nervously as if they were coming through the cabin and were going to hit him.

It finally quieted down enough to talk to Wiggins. "I heard from Rita, Big Red," he said. "She's aboard the *Dare Me* and needs our help. We've been motoring in circles for some time out here. When are we going back for some mop up?"

"Already done," said Wiggins. "Set course for the *Dare Me.* Meanwhile I'll notify Hawkins and tell him to rendezvous with us there."

"Already done?" asked Bernard, surprised. "What do you mean, already done?"

"Like all emergencies, the fire department responded. Had a little trouble getting in the place, but once they did it opened the door. Police joined them and they managed to bring things under control and shut down the dock crew. Pretty much rounded up the whole gang in that one location. Hawkins trapped the rest in a meeting room. He heard on their comm system that they were assembling at someplace called admin. There was an auditorium there and while they were in there yapping he sealed them in."

"Sealed them in?" said Bernard. "Is that a pun?"

"Yes, but I didn't mean it," he said. He looked puzzled, then laughed.

"What's he up to now?"

"Donno, but I can find out pretty easy. We got Federal teams moving in now. One is securing their private airport even as we speak. They found some bodies there and it's looking to be a full bore crime scene."

Bernard whistled. "Pretty slick."

"Nice day fishing," said Wiggins.

Bernard went back up to the bridge. It had been a long day, and the night was beginning to look longer. The moon was up, reflecting off the water, and the sea breeze was gently blowing through his hair. Tom was at the wheel. "Take her back to the island," he said. "We're going to check out the *Dare Me.*"

"Isn't that what we came for in the first place?" asked Tom.

"We came to go fishing," said Bernard.

"Okay," said Tom. "Fish, we got. Let's go see if we can catch a trawler."

Bernard shook his head. Yeah, it was his boat. "I'm going forward to lay down for a while, Tom," he said.

"Too much excitement old man?"

Bernard shot him a look.

"I mean, aye, aye, Captain."

Bernard smiled. "Wake me up when we get there." As he sauntered off he made a mental note, muttering to himself. "I'm going to be a little more careful about who I invite fishing."

Chapter 64

Time to Kill

Fu woke, dizzy in the sand. The office was quiet. For a moment it was like being in a glass jar, the world looked all strange and curved at the edges. Then she felt the ant bites. There were no apologies. Their world was in chaos and she was their enemy.

She shook herself. Twisting and struggling until she freed one hand. She started madly digging with it, moving sand and ants like a boring machine. There was something beside her, a lunchbox. She opened it. There was a tray and she turned the contents over inside the box and pushed it away. She used the tray like a dredge bucket, moving dirt in massive amounts.

The laptop appeared. She pulled it free and moved it aside, continuing to dig her way out. Rolling, twisting, clawing, digging for her life, oblivious to anything but survival. They were stinging, formic acid burning her skin. Mandibles crunched, breaking off tiny pieces of her. Her mind became a cloud, trying to shut off the pain, the itching, the skin crawling agony. Swatting does no good, she told herself, not while you're still trapped and partially buried. It's just a waste of energy. Brushing seems to work better, but what's more important, comfort or survival?

She blew them away from her mouth with puffs of breath, careful not to breathe them in on the intake. She shook her head, unable to jiggle them free from her ears and her neck. She could see them crawling across her cheeks. She shut her eyes at times, protecting them from the deadly acid as she continued to blindly dig.

It didn't matter. They were all over her, just as she had seen on Mandelle's arm not so long ago. Maybe not as bad, but it felt like it. What she could not see was projected in her mind with horrid imagination.

How long did she have before she passed out?

Dig!

There was a catharsis, a sudden feeling of euphoria that somehow killed the pain. Her knee moved and now a leg was free. She tried to stand, sand and ants falling off her body like water from a shower. She shook, fighting, digging, pulling her other knee free.

Her focus had paid off. She was loose, trying to shake her body free of sand and ants. She looked down, grabbed the laptop and the lunchbox and ran for the kitchen. Water! The universal solvent will wash it all away, counteract and dilute the acid. She set the stuff down on the counter, noticing a bathroom adjacent to the kitchen.

Ants and sand fell around her as she ran. There was a shower in the bathroom and once again she admired Che's lair. She found a hank of his hair caught under her nails, surprised it was still there. She pulled it out, admiring the size of it as she set it in the soap dish. Fresh towels and a long rinse and she was free of formic acid and the grit of sand in every fold. She had started with a cold shower, trying to wash away what she could before opening up her pores with hot steamy water. There was a closet full of Che's suits but also casual clothes. She found some sweat pants, a t-shirt and a hoodie that worked nicely. There was even a shoe valet which she used to clean her boots.

She checked the door. Just as Che had announced, no id, no exit. She went to the refrigerator, not surprised to find it was well stocked. Something more substantial than oatmeal, she gathered up a plate and ate heartily, looking towards the door as if someone would come through it any minute.

She checked all the cabinets. There was breast pump kit, thank god, a nice one in an expensive travelling case with extra bottles and pads.

She spread herself with lotion from the medicine chest in the bathroom. It relieved some of the pain and itching. There was some petroleum jelly that she used to create a barrier across the floor of the office, marking her territory close to the ant mound at the other end of the room. The ants would not cross this line. When she was finished she stood there thinking for a while, staring into the colony and all the activity.

Where have they taken the queen? How much is left of Mandelle's arm? How long was I really trapped? Seemed like an eternity. Could it have been me reduced to ant food? My body torn into so many pieces that they would never find me. How many other victims met their fate here?

She went back to her end of the room. The door remained silent. How long before somebody came?

Bored, she cleaned and examined her booty. The lunchbox was interesting, and she emptied it on the table and studied the contents. It looked like a junior chemistry set. There was a pamphlet with instructions. "I have time to kill. Might as well do a little light reading."

After a short read she laughed. She went into the bathroom and got the hank of hair from the soap dish and returned to the sofa where she had the kit spread out on a low table. She smiled, picking up a vial, thinking of Mr. Che, his arrogance and his demeanor.

"My equal," she said, inserting the hair into the vial.

Chapter 65

Now This is a Party Boat!

A car pulled up to the dock. The door opened and all weapons on board pointed towards it.

"It's okay girls," said Rita. "Bullshit Hawkins, where you been?"

"Got a girl in the car that's been asking for you," he said. The passenger door opened and out stepped Fu Chan. She had a laptop in one hand a lunchbox in the other. Mei spotted her and ran to her side. "Sister, you don't know how bad you look in sweat pants. Not to mention, you're a little wet up top."

Fu reached back into the car and grabbed the expensive breast pump in the discreet carrying case that she took from Che's office. "Got it covered," she said.

A contingent of pirates swarmed down the gangplank. Red waved hello to Harry, a meek smile on her face as the tide of women swept Fu away. The *Dare Me* had been secured, the battle won. Music was playing through the speakers, the ship's stores had been looted, and celebration was the order of the day.

Red had radioed Bernard and he was on his way. The girls had nothing left to do but wait and party. They had tried to give the big lesbian a makeover earlier, but now that their hero Fu was here...

"I think they found their victim," said Red.

"It was my suggestion," said Trish. "After all, Fu Chan is the one who set them free."

"Yeah, about that," said Red. "Did I hear you say she used a severed arm?"

"Hold that story," said Hawkins. "I'd like to hear it too." He got serious as spoke to Red. "I hate to break up your party but I have few instructions from command," he said.

Red had almost forgotten that she was a part of some kind of weird multi-jurisdictional task force or something. But, that was all sort of unofficial. Really, she had been along for the ride, just wanting to go fishing. She had done all that and more. She thought of L'Enfant, of justice, and of Charlotte and the kids. A tear formed in her eye. She wasn't used to crying. Girls just want to have fun.

She felt in her pocket and took out the mace. "This came in real handy." she said.

"Then you better keep it," said Hawkins.

She started to protest but he insisted. "I have more at home," he said. "Now, we still have work to do. The *Busted Tush* is about ten minutes out. We need to abandon the *Dare Me* and get out of here before the red tape arrives."

"I'll pass the word and have all hands ready," she said. "There's sixty or seventy women here. Will we all fit on his boat?"

"Just make sure everyone has a life jacket," he said. "We don't have much time. If you could prepare a manifest, a list of the passenger's names and country of origin, I think we can board and get out of here quickly. I'd like to see Seattle at sunrise."

Hawkins got his wish. Matt's boat powered into the harbor looking like a playboy yacht. Tom didn't bitch about the lack of survival suits, but he did insist they raid the *Dare Me* for enough life jackets for everyone. There were women hanging over the rails in every direction. Thanks to liquor and Fashion Bargain Warehouse, they were very happy women.

Langhelm had a girl on his lap, sharing the lawn chair with him. She was insisting that he call in sick today, whispering something in his ear that made his eyes light up. Farbis was making another toast. He was drinking something made with mothers milk, vodka and Kahlua, swearing he would never drink anything else but this.

Down below was another story. Wiggins and Renault tried hard to get their paperwork done. Suddenly there were mounds of it with calls coming in every ten minutes over the satellite phones. Renault was talking now, begging forgiveness for stepping on somebody's turf. He was promising somebody that he would give them credit and include them as contributing positively to the operation.

Wiggins gave him the thumbs up. It was fine with him if nobody ever heard of the *Busted Tush*, Captain Bernard, or him for that matter. He had managed to clear the list of women with his agency, but there were a few caught in the red tape. It was being handled. Like a good spook, he was slowly erasing his presence. As far as he was concerned, he spent a quiet Sunday fishing, and he had the salmon to prove it.

Bernard was enjoying the privilege of being Captain. He was in the wheelhouse surrounded by beauty, telling tall tales of his adventures on the Seattle Police Force. What man could ask for more?

Even Fu was contented. Her hair had been done and as leader of the revolt the crew had seen that she looked extra good. Not an ant bite was showing thanks to quality makeup and careful application, as one of the girls kept stressing, but she sold makeup for a living. When he looked twice, even Bernard couldn't believe it was Harry. He didn't know it really wasn't Harry, it was Fu. Harry was there all right, somewhere deep inside where he was a child again, not a worry in the world, pretending to be Fu Chan, the greatest detective ever.

Chapter 66

Trish

"I love you and all that Harry but I deserve more, don't you think so?" Trish had been giving Harry this lecture all the way to her apartment. It was a continuation of the debate they had been having while in lockup at Mr. Che's Boarding School for Wayward Milkmaids. "Besides, we're just not compatible."

"You do deserve more than me, Trish." *Why do I feel so inadequate,* he thought. *Last night I felt fine.*

"You deserve better, too Harry", said Trish, touching his cheek for a minute. It was hard to think of Fu Chan as her ex, but Harry was buried somewhere under all those Fashion Bargain Depot clothes. "Once you figure out what you want I'm sure it will come easy."

What do I want, he asked himself. *Why do I feel so confused now?*

Trish went on yakking. Harry began filing these thoughts away for later. "People make you feel bad," said Trish. "Why?"

"I'm something people would rather not see," he said.

"I don't know," she said. "With your nipples in a cup, you pass pretty well for a woman. Isn't that what you always wanted?"

"I don't know what I want right now," said Harry. "You were good for me, Trish. Our moms were right. We were a good fit."

Maybe we could work it out. If there's anything I learned in the last week or two it's that there's a way out of every cage.

"I'm thinking of altering my legal practice," said Trish, the subject changing again. "I'd like to try immigration law. I think I've had enough of divorce. Or maybe criminal. Remember when we first got married? I wanted to be a criminal lawyer. Gotta be safer than divorce lawyer."

There was tension outside her apartment when she slipped the key into the door lock. She half expected Harry to kiss her goodnight or something. She turned with her eyes closed, ready for it, but when she opened them, Fu Chan was lost in thought.

The moment was lost to her. She turned away from him. "I never really was bi-curious," she said, turning the key and opening the door.

"What?"

"Oh, come on inside for a moment," she said.

Trish opened a bottle and filled two glasses of wine. "I haven't had a drink in weeks," she said. She raised her glass and waited. Harry just stared at the full glass.

"I forgot you didn't drink." She giggled. "It's okay. I won't let it go to waste." She toasted her apartment, downing her glass in a single gulp. "Ain't it great to be home?"

She was suddenly aware that Harry was staring at her. Was it Harry or Fu, she didn't know. Her relationship with Harry had always been... confusing. Probably it would always be. "Thanks for coming after me," she said. "I didn't ask you to but you did anyway."

"Jan asked me to," he said. He sounded like Harry now, back in control, slowly waking up to the fact that he had been made over and high heeled like he had been away on some mega drag queen vacation.

"Oh," said Trish. "I'll have to thank her." She turned and went to the counter. She opened a drawer in the kitchen and took out a checkbook and opened it up. "Well, let me give you some money anyway," she said.

He reached over and put his hand on hers, covering it and the checkbook. "You don't owe me anything."

"Expenses," she said. "Your outfit was ruined. Let me buy you another one."

"No need to," he said.

"Something from my closet, maybe?" she said. "I know you like that casual dress, the tunic with the pretty brown pattern." She moved her hand to his arm.

It was the dress she caught him in, the one that ended his marriage. Awkward. "Thank you anyway," he said. "I think I've outgrown it. Besides," he did a runway turn, "I got my new duds from Fashion Bargain Depot."

She laughed. "So you do."

He turned to leave, the awkwardness returning. "Well, I'd better get going."

"Wait," she said. "You never told me."

"Told you what?"

"How I looked in that outfit," she said. "The one I was wearing when I was abducted. I sent you a picture. Did I look good in that outfit?"

"Good." He smiled. "Better than good. Great. I don't think you need me as a fashion consultant anymore."

She drew closer. "Maybe I need you for something else."

"Like what?" he asked.

She wrapped her arms around him. "I'll think of something."

"Trish, if there's anything I learned from you, it's to be honest. If I stay here any longer, I won't be able to be honest. Not with myself, not with you, not with anyone."

"Then why did you accompany me home? You live in Capitol Hill, close to the docks."

"I don't know," he said. "Maybe I just wanted to see you safely home. Maybe I just needed closure."

"Closure?" she asked. "For what?"

"I don't know," he said.

She squeezed him gently, pulling him close to her chest. The front of his blouse was suddenly wet.

They both laughed, drawing back from each other. "Need a change of clothes now?"

"I'll be fine," he said. "It's not that bad."

"How about a ride home?"

"Bernard gave me cab fare," he said. "Besides, you've been drinking, remember?"

"Take my car then," she offered. "Bring it back in the morning."

"What, and pay for parking in Capitol Hill?" he said. "You know me. I'll take the 550 express bus and be home in less time than it takes to call a cab."

She gave in. Nothing was going to keep him here. She touched his cheek. "Thanks again, Harry."

"I'll always love you," he said. "You're my wife."

"I am your ex-wife. Remember?"

"Yeah." He nodded and turned, opened the door to the hallway.

"One more thing," she said, a mischievous grin on her face. "Antwerp!"

Harry looked confused, then closed the door gently. "Goodbye," he whispered.

Trish locked the door behind him and poured another glass of wine. Her cat jumped up on the counter crying for attention. She stifled a sniffle, petting its soft fur. "How about you. Do you need me, honey?"

Chapter 67

Sue

It was early evening when he got home. The elevator was always broken in the Binkley Arms, and Harry lived on the top floor. He walked up the flights of stairs, the high heel boots pinching his feet. Pain can be good for you. It reminds you that you're alive.

She was there when he opened the door to the apartment, as if she'd been standing just inside waiting. She hugged him immediately.

"Harry," said Sue. "Oh, I missed you so much."

"I'm okay," said Harry. "And call me Fu."

She cocked her head to one side and studied him like a deep water probe. "Okay, Fu," she said. "I was so worried. Rita called me. I got word you were coming home, that something weird had happened to you again." She squeezed him hard, and his chest felt wet. He laughed, an insane welcome home, thank-God-it's-over laugh that almost melted into a cry. She let him go, moved back to get a good look at him. "You look hot. I like that outfit. Where you been? The spa?"

He laughed some more, dropped the breast pump bag on the table. He felt like a veteran coming home from war. He sat down and took off his boots. "I fought another villain wearing these boots," he said. "I'm going to start calling them my combat boots."

Sue put them aside. "I bet you look good kicking ass in those shoes, too. At least you didn't break the heel this time." She kissed him again, passionately, and she rubbed his tender feet. She continued up his legs eventually stroking his arms. Makeup came off in her hand and she noticed the blotches underneath. She was suddenly aware that he had bite marks all over him. "What's this?" She examined him more, lifting his blouse to reveal cuts, bruises and more bite marks. "You're a mess," she said. "Let's get you undressed and cleaned up."

He didn't argue. "Okay."

She ran the bathwater while he removed his clothes and makeup. The girls had worked hard to make Fu beautiful, but the ants were merciless.

His face was mottled and littered with red bite marks. There were even some on his eyelids. They itched, just like the ones over the rest of his body. He could still feel them squirming in his ears and in his nose, laying over his skin like a blanket of pain.

"What's in the bag?" she asked.

He laughed. "Soon enough," he said.

Curiosity got the best of her. "A breast pump? Honey you plan on us having a baby?"

"Why?" he asked, reaching for her. "Would you like to try?"

She wrapped herself around him. "Always with you," she said. "I think we'd make extra good babies. Your smarts with my organization."

"A bunch of Little Fu's running around?" he asked.

"Boys, girls, and everything in between," she said. "They'd all be welcome." As she guided him towards the bath, she saw his back. "What are all these marks?" she asked.

"Ant bites," he said.

"Want me to call mama?" she asked. "I have some calamine lotion but she may have something better."

"Not tonight," said Harry, settling into the bath. "I need rest. I need you. It's time to let loose with your fierce nursing skills."

"Already there," she said. She had it all: ointment, lotion, hot towels. As she cleaned and treated him, Harry caught her up, told her everything we know, the whole adventure. No sense re-hashing it. It was enough that Harry had to go through it again.

"What happened to your belly jewel?" she asked, running her finger around the empty hole, satisfied she had gotten all the sand out.

"They took it," he said. "I have another in my top drawer."

"The bling with the big dangling jewel?" she asked. He never wore that.

"A dancer gave it to me," he said. "She was a nice, kind girl and she wanted me to have it. It's supposed to be a real diamond."

Sue grunted. "If it is, it's worth five thousand."

Harry started crying.

"What's the matter?" she asked.

"Nothing," he said, sniffling. "It's just," the tears started again, "I'm nursing and my hormones are all screwed up."

He took the breast pump kit out and showed it to her. He was too embarrassed to use it in front of her just yet, but he knew sooner or later he would need it. If she was shocked or laughing or even remotely repulsed she never showed it. But there was love and concern and patient listening in heaping amounts.

"I'm glad you came back to me," she said.

"The whole time I was with Trish I felt uncomfortable. I can't say that it was her fault, she just has that effect on me. When I'm with her I feel inadequate, useless, confused, a thousand emotions except the one I should feel."

"And what's that?"

"How I feel when I'm with you."

He looked deep into her eyes, seeing her soul. She was Eve in the Garden of Eden, pure and sinless, where nothing was forbidden and everything was possible. Life is a series of moments, and he knew this was one he wanted to cherish. He breathed deep, a sigh of relief, and he fell into her arms.

She cradled him like a baby. "I'm here for you," she said, rocking back and forth. She held his head, kissed him, and otherwise let loose with her fierce nursing, comforting him, ready to give his battered mind and body time and whatever else it may need to heal.

Chapter 68

Secret Meeting

It was towards the end of the week. Bernard walked into the bar, a noisy place at happy hour. He had received a mysterious invitation to meet someone at Pike's Market, here at one of the largest brew pubs in the area. He couldn't tell who sent him the message, he just knew he didn't like these kind of games. This place was huge, and it probably wouldn't be long before he spotted someone he knew.

He started searching, scanning the bar as he moved from room to room and then to another level. A hand reached out and grabbed him and he was suddenly pulled through a door. "Shhh," he heard someone say.

"Wiggins, is that you?" he asked.

The FBI Agent smiled.

"Why all the cloak and dagger?" asked Bernard. "Where the hell are we? What happened to the bar?"

""You're in a secret room," he said. "Underground Seattle. Turn the lights up, Jim."

Renault responded and the room sprang to life. It was a party and the room was filled with his crew. Red was there and Bud Jones. Tom Walgamot winked and raised a mug of beer from across the room. Bill Farbis lowered his sunglasses showing off his bloodshot eyes. There were cheers and raised glasses and rounds of "For he's a jolly good fellow."

"We just wanted to thank you proper for the fishing trip," said Wiggins.

"You could have thanked me by fixing the bullet holes," said Bernard.

Wiggins pulled him aside and whispered. "You haven't been by your boat recently. Already done," he said. He produced some papers from his coat pocket. "By the way, you need to sign these."

"What's this?" Bernard hesitated. He didn't like signing anything.

"It's an authorization for incidental labor not from force accounts," said Wiggins.

"Meaning what? Speak English."

"The Federal Task Force is disbanding. Che's moved on. We tracked his speedboat as far as Canada but lost him somewhere up the chain. They'll be a few of us left behind but most are heading back to D.C. You might see a few new faces cycle in and out. They may come by and ask you a few questions but this case has gone cold for us. We were successful, gathered a lot of intelligence, but it's time to move on. It all has to be processed, so we're taking it back to the big Federal crime lab at Quantico."

"What's all that got to do with me signing this piece of paper?"

"Some of these people, these Government people, they get a seat at the table because of what they bring. I just want you to know that not all Government workers are dead wood. You may get that impression. I know our meetings can be tough. Whatever we do, though, it works. Now sign the damn paper. Don't worry, it comes from special appropriations and the Mayor's office pays their share. There's always a lot of incidental labor in these big field ops." He winked and Bernard smiled.

Matt signed the papers and chuckled. "Bullet holes fixed and the Mayor's office pays thirty percent? That doesn't sound right, but if you say so, I'm in."

Wiggins stuffed the papers away. "Thanks for the day fishing Bernard. I had a great time"

"We got lucky," said Matt. "I'm just sorry the big one got away." They shook hands.

Wiggins went over to Rita and thanked her for the fish. "I don't know whether I'm going to mount it or eat it but I'm taking it back to D.C with me."

"Eat it," she said. "It's delicious. Expensive fish."

"There's one more thing," he said. "I need your statement. The details of what you did between the time you left the *Busted Tush* and the time you rendezvoused with us is kind of blurry."

She was all nervous.

"Oh, don't worry," he said. "We were just wondering if, in your travels that night, you knew anything about the events at the airport."

Her lips were tight, her jaw stressed with muscle. She suddenly felt like she was talking to the FBI. The wheels were turning and Wiggins was staring at her. When they stopped turning she slowly shook her head no.

"I didn't think so," said Wiggins calmly.

There was a pregnant pause before Red spoke. "Yeah," she said meekly. "What exactly happened?"

"Nearest we can tell there was a scuffle between the Second in Command and the Head of Human Resources," he said. "They managed to kill each other. Looks like he strangled her, but not before she managed to stab him with a poisoned knife."

"Wow," she said. For some reason her stomach wouldn't stop fluttering. "So why do you need some kind of statement about that from me?"

"I told CSI that you couldn't have made your way from the docks to the airport in a rowboat. Hell, we're glad you were able to make it to the *Dare Me* and support the operation there. But they want a statement just the same." He produced some paper from his pocket. "I took the liberty."

She took the papers and scanned them. Something about her getting separated from her fishing party, drifting ashore in the middle of some kind of weird Government operation. When she recognized members of a Federal Task Force operating in the area, she volunteered to help process evidence and witnesses on the scene. There was an attached voucher for her time, which Wiggins also said she needed to sign, after which again, the papers disappeared out of sight.

"Guess that closes the boot on it," she said. She caught her mistake. "The *book*. I meant to say book. I guess that closes the book on the case."

Wiggins patted her shoulder, and using his calm voice said, "Yes, it does." He raised a glass. "Where's Langhelm today? I don't see him here."

"Why, you got something for him to sign?" murmured Red.

Walgamot smiled. "I heard from Langhelm. Some powdery dust fell up at Crystal Mountain. He's snowboarding. I suspect that pretty young thing that was draped on his arm is with him. I heard he called in sick all week."

"Was he really drunk when he started that fire?" asked Red.

"If only we had the security video," he said. "We may never know."

"Was the laptop any use?"

"We don't know yet," said Wiggins. "But we did find Che's manifesto on ants. Fascinating. We passed it on to the BAU. There's a young PhD there who's interested in reading it."

"The Behavioral Analysis Unit?" she said excitedly. "There is a real Criminal Minds? With a real Spencer?"

Wiggins nodded. "Where do you think Hollywood writers get their ideas? Art imitates life."

"What happened to Sandy?" asked Red.

"Who?" asked Wiggins.

"Hawkins?" Wiggins looked blank. "Bullshit Hawkins? The other guy on the boat with us? Lanky guy? But built like a wrestler."

"Hawkins? I don't know any Hawkins," said Wiggins. "Never heard of him. Guess he was never here."

"What kind of bullshit is that?" mumbled Rita.

"Exactly!"

As glasses emptied beer seemed to appear from nowhere. There was food and Bernard was sure they had a secret door that led to the kitchen. What the hell, he loved a party as much as the next man, and this group had proven itself good company.

He saw Harry sitting off to the side. He was no longer hiding his breasts, at least he wasn't trying to. They were a part of him, just as much as Fu Chan. There was a beer in front of him. Bernard knew it was for appearances. He didn't have to explain anything about AA or about not really wanting a drink, and it kept people from offering him something he consistently refused. There were times when not drinking made him appear rude and anti-social and this was his way of dealing with it. He took a drink of water from a nearby glass. He was still processing everything that happened to him.

Matt sat down opposite him. The noise around them seemed to dim. "How's my old friend, the best detective I ever had?"

"Not so good Matt. My breasts ache and there's no sign that they will dry up any time soon."

Matt could only listen. He felt awkward with no point of reference for anything Harry was going through.

Harry continued. "I'm lactating regularly, producing record amounts of milk."

Bernard just listened, which is what good friends do in times like these. He had talked a lot of young detectives through trauma and combat fatigue and everything ugly that they had to process. It went with the job, but the stuff Harry had been through, first Couture and now this. How do you process this? But curiosity got the best of him, and he hungered for details. "You fought him," he said. "Got buried in some kind of giant ant mound. What was that like? Scary, I imagine."

"Not as scary as what Che was saying," said Harry. "He kept spouting logic about corporations, about how his wasn't any different than legit ones on Wall Street."

"Criminals always justify their behavior," said Matt. "I've heard it all. Twisted logic."

"Except this was making sense. He was talking about how corporations rule the world, how they unite people in purposes, provide a single vision. They are powerful. By and large, they can achieve more than any one single individual. They even survive across lifetimes."

"Look, Harry, I don't know what Che told you, but take it with a grain of salt. His corporation was evil, and so was his purpose. From what I read in reports, his vision was warped and he exploited people, made them do horrible things, commit murder and butcher dead bodies. Then he laughed as they fell into the muck with the dregs of humanity. He set himself above them but he was no better. Sick little shit with a room full of stuffed arms, his corporate retirement program. Don't worry about him. FBI has tons of info. They'll track him down and put a stop to his twisted world. It's only a matter of time."

"Only a matter of time," said Harry. He smiled, thinking about who might find him first, the mighty FBI or a tiny nanovirus with an insatiable taste for Che's DNA. "Thanks Matt. I'm always encouraged after talking with you."

"What else can I do?" asked Bernard. "I can get you a doctor. Someone who can plug the faucets."

"I'm not so sure I want that," said Harry. "Sue sells the milk on the internet. She hopes I never dry up. She says it won't be long before we're caught up on bills and can afford a big luxury vacation."

He looked out into space. "A vacation," he said. "Wouldn't that be nice?"

"What would you do?" asked Bernard. "Where would you go?"

"I don't know." Harry continued to stare out into space. A sense of peace fell over him for the moment. He had no worries, a little money, and the love of a good woman. It was the first time in a long time that he could remember having all the bills paid. Binky was totally off his back. What more could he ask for?

Maybe a little less weirdness.

Chapter 69

I Only Dream In Black, Not White

Carlos Pinal woke in a sweat. His sheets were damp and wet, his mind sieged with haunted dreams. He tried to wipe the darkness away from his eyes.

He reached for the light on his nightstand, knocking over a glass of water. It spilled, then rolled off the table where it shattered on the floor. He turned the light on. There was a picture of his cousin, the face looking at him with smiling eyes.

He had placed it there to remind him, but he found he needed no reminders of the past, or of what he had done.

"How can you smile when so many bad things had happened? Come to America. Find jobs. Make lots of money." He pushed the picture off the nightstand where it fell and shattered beside the glass.

"What do you know," he said. "You're dead." He put his hands around his head, beginning to sob. He pushed against his skull, hoping the pressure would change something inside. He struck at it with an open palm but nothing changed.

He doubled over in bed, crying like a mother for her dead, lost child.

"I have walked through hell with the devil," he screamed, the sobs soon overwhelming his speech.

What is the price of survival?

The devil will have his due one day. You must live for now, Carlos.

"I am tired of living. And when I die, my soul will be his for eternity where I will burn in hell forever."

He buried his face in the sheets, dampness like a stain on his body.

He heard Charlotte's voice, an angel by his side, and he slowly stopped crying, righting himself before he began.

"Our Father who art in Heaven…"

THE END

Thanks for reading. Hope you enjoyed DIAL M FOR MILKMAID

Also by Julie Ann Carver, available on AMAZON.COM

:

CASE OF THE MISSING DICK: The first book in the Fu Chan Mystery Series. Richard Sooka, noted designer and star of Designer Derby, has turned up missing and so is his charity gown, slated for auction beginning at three hundred thousand dollars. Dick's absence puts a halt to the show, and while Hollywood and the fashion industry wait anxiously for his return, a reward is offered to whoever finds the valuable charity gown.

All Harry and Big Red want to do is get enough for a sex change operation and a breast reduction. But Harry has money woes and a landlord that is a part time loan shark. With the pressure on to pay the rent, Harry and Red decide to find the dress and claim the reward. Before they can get going, pieces of Richard Sooka begin turning up all over town. As Harry uncovers the killer, can he be sure that he won't be the next victim?

A fun read with interesting characters. Brutally descriptive, a murder mystery not for the feint at heart, you'll laugh then shiver as you navigate through this total train wreck. Don't miss *Case of the Missing Dick* on your reading list.

 Julie Ann Carver lives and writes in Washington State. She is as imaginary as the characters in this book, but here's a photo anyway. She likes to hang out, watch Lifetime movies, Criminal Minds, and fashion reality shows. The way her mind works is God's own mystery.

COMING IN LATE 2014

The next adventure in the Fu Chan mystery series:

THE CRYPT OF MORGAGNI